Praise for
THE TOUCH

"Intriguing . . . stinging, mournful, pointed writing of consistently high quality . . . a provocative book sure to attract attention. The cumulative effect is profound and frighteningly possible."—*Publishers Weekly* (starred review)

"*The Touch* will take you to a terrifying and disturbing tomorrow and make you feel like you live there."—David Brin

D E P R I V E R S

Steven-Elliot Altman

2003
50TH
ANNIVERSARY

OCT 1 4 2004

ACE BOOKS, NEW YORK

An Ace Book
Published by The Berkley Publishing Group
A division of Penguin Group (USA) Inc.
375 Hudson Street
New York, New York 10014

PRINTING HISTORY
Berkley trade paperback edition / December 2003

Library of Congress Cataloging-in-Publication Data

Altman, Steven-Elliot.
    Deprivers / Steven-Elliot Altman.— Berkley trade paperback ed.
        p. cm.
    "An Ace Book"—T.p. verso.
    ISBN 0-441-01093-8 (pbk.)
    1. Communicable diseases—Transmission—Fiction.   I. Title.

PS3601.L855D47   2003
813'.6—dc22

                                                    2003065072

PRINTED IN THE UNITED STATES OF AMERICA

10   9   8   7   6   5   4   3   2   1

For every individual who has ever suffered
societal alienation, of any sort,
due to afflictions beyond their own control.

Special thanks
to Hillery Borton, Susan Allison, and Patrick Merla
for their kindness and editing prowess
to Doug Stewart and Ed Wintle
for agenting above and beyond
to David Brin, Ginge Brien, Joe Miller,
and Allan Hausknecht
for their priceless medical and scientific consultation
to Hugh Margesson for offering his Lakota wisdom
to Mindy Yale and Dawn Emery Thorne
for their faith and consultation
and for all you Deprivers out there,
you know who you are.

Part One

UNDERGROUND

1

SOMEHOW she knew that I'd killed a man earlier that morning. His name was Osbourne, and I'd waited for him for just under an hour. I bore him no ill will. After all, I was there to kill him. Maybe he'd sensed it? Maybe he'd stopped off to enjoy a final cup of coffee or taken the longer path through Central Park, the one that ran by the duck pond? Who knows? Wouldn't affect my paycheck. He came in and was startled pale to see me sitting there, enjoying a glass of wine on his veranda. One of the dustier bottles from his collection, quite a charming wine, effervescent, a cherry pick.

I motioned to him with a waggle of my finger. He hesitated at first, then came striding over and slapped his briefcase down on the table in front of me.

"Who are you, and what do you mean breaking in here like this?"

I swished the wine in the crystal and took a sip, gave him a wink. "The name's Luxley," I told him, "and you have a fine taste in wines. May I pour you a glass?"

"No," he said, shaking his jowled face in confusion. "Why are you here? What do you want?"

I slowly rose, offering my right hand. "I've come to make your acquaintance, Mr. Osbourne . . . and to discuss a business proposition from a mutual friend."

Reluctantly, he shook my hand—rightly so, but his options were, after all, limited. It was a firm contact. He sat down and allowed me to pour him a drink.

"Now then," he began, regaining the sense of authority that his position and profession provided. "Which *friend* and what business proposition?"

"Prescott. I believe you were supposed to make a phone call to a certain judge. You know the one?"

He nodded, with some additional color draining from his face. "Oh yes, our Mr. Prescott. Very impatient man. Worked for him long, have you?"

I checked my watch. "Actually, today's my first day. Most likely my only day. You never made that call, Mr. Osbourne, and Mr. Prescott is *very* disappointed."

"Well, a small oversight really," he said. "Nothing that can't be fixed."

I sipped the wine and considered his view of the Chrysler Building. "I'm not sure Mr. Prescott sees things quite that way."

Osbourne laughed, a weak attempt at bravado. "Don't be fooled by whatever he told you. We've had these sorts of differences before."

A bit of a risk, I realized, but I rose from my chair and placed my back to him. I felt the crisp spring air on my face and looked down at the city. Down at the tiny people scuttling about on their errands far below us. "It's sad, isn't it?" I began. "So many people out there. Everyone searching for something they can't find. Everyone making and breaking so many promises. Cheating wives. Abusive parents. Battering husbands. Hostile takeovers. Rapes, robberies, homicides. Bad Broadway adaptations. Politicians taking bribes and breaking promises."

I glanced down at my watch and saw that it was time. "Not everything *can* be fixed, Mr. Osbourne. Do you know what you need in this world of unfixable fixes?"

"No. Enlighten me, won't you, Mr. Luxley," he said.

I turned back to him, put the wineglass on the table, and leaned against the rail. "You need to have a special trick. Something that puts you ahead of the game. Goes without saying that your advantage calls for giving up something valuable, but . . . Lots of people live their lives in this city who rarely ever touch another human being. It's a solitary life, but it pays well."

"Call Prescott! I'll make restitution!"

"Sorry," I shrugged. "I'm afraid he's unreachable." I removed a small case from my coat pocket and laid it on the table.

"I have his private number right here!" he demanded. His movement was sluggish. It confused him considerably.

"Really? Maybe we *should* call then," I said. "Go ahead, Mr. Osbourne. Reach for your gun."

Osbourne panicked. He tried to move his hand and discovered he could not. He struggled against the paralysis in vain. I knew that by this point, only his eyes were capable of movement. They darted furiously.

"You can't, can you? No, the time for that is . . ." I checked my watch for accuracy. "Three minutes past."

I watched a bead of sweat roll down his face. "So there you have my special trick. Never shake hands with strangers, Mr. Osbourne. You never know what you'll catch. And as to restitution . . ."

I unzipped the case and brought out the syringe. Ironic that air is one of the key ingredients of life—yet a single bubble of it in the bloodstream ends it.

"Don't move," I said, inserting the needle. "I don't want to hurt you."

2

I don't have an alarm system in my apartment. I've always considered my special trick to be enough to get me through any situation. Nobody knows where I live anyway. Cops poking blind? Not likely. Clients? All satisfied customers. Friends? None to speak of.

I opened my door, and there she was, sitting on the couch smoking a cigarette; blonde, teenager, body posture relaxed and nonthreatening. I laughed out loud. I thought about running, but all I had to do was get close enough to touch her, right? I took my coat off, hung it up, took off my gloves, stowed them away in the coat, all beneath her watchful eyes.

I came up around the couch within arm's length and saw her stiffen as she rose. I offered my hand: "Robert Luxley. To whom do I have the pleasure?"

"As *if* I would touch you," she said and took a drag off her cigarette, flicking ashes on my Persian rug.

Fascinating. A thousand responses flickered through my brain. *She knows. She knows about my special trick. How the hell can she possibly know?* And yes, she was in range. I could easily have reached out quickly to touch her, and that would be that. But I was intrigued, like never before. *Son of a bitch, she actually knows.*

"Darling . . ." I said. This was a bad choice of words. Suddenly she produced a .38 caliber pistol, and forced the barrel into my mouth.

"Not darling," she whispered. "Cut the bullshit and tell me who you work for."

Screw her. I went for her bare stomach. She anticipated my swipe and cocked the hammer as she moved out of reach. Her lips contorted. "Don't you ever try to touch me, mister. I will blow your brains right outta the back of your skull!"

I dropped my hand slow and steady. I wanted to apologize, but it was futile, what with the gun in my mouth.

"I know what you are," she said and then let the hammer slide back, inching the gun from my face and stepping back. She kept it aimed, of course.

What I am? I smiled at the prospect of an answer. "Would you like something to drink? I could really use one right about now, myself."

"Yes. Water, please," she said.

I thought the *please* was rather odd after a break-and-entry and the forced intimacy of the pistol, but I poured two glasses as she stood over me. Handing her the glass of her choice, I sighed. "Well, then, would you mind explaining exactly what you seem to think I am?"

She seemed puzzled, judging from the furrow of her brow. "Don't jerk me, mister!" she said as she aimed at a most sensitive part of my anatomy.

"Hang on!" I yelled. "I'm not *jerking* you. You broke into my place, and you have the gun, which I've been beautiful about, by the way—I just want to know how you know about my trick?"

"You really don't know, do you? You don't know what you are? You can't sense what I am?"

Questions, more questions. Keep her talking.

"No, I don't . . . I've been doing it since I was fourteen years old. Are you a relative of someone that . . . ?"

"Oh, I'm a relative of yours, all right," she said as she started laughing. "I'm the same genetic stuff, but you—" Her laughter overtook her. "Oh, God, you're too pathetic. You really don't know. I can see it on your face."

I smiled along with her. What else could I do? She knew things, things I needed to know and would pay good money to learn. She evidently sensed this as well because she slipped the gun back into the front of her jeans, flopped down on my couch, and put her boots up on my crystal coffee table.

I sipped my water. "So, how do you know about my trick?"

She licked her lips. "It's *your* trick, huh?"

"How did you find me?"

"I saw you on the street. I've been watching you, *duh.* You're unmissable, but you wouldn't know that either, Mister *Un*touchable, *Un*touched."

She held all the cards, so I dropped my poker face. "What if I touch you?"

At that, she smiled. "What if *I* touch you?"

That thought astonished me. I sat down on the divan across from her. She was telling me that she didn't just *know* what I was, she was implying that she *was* the same. *I'll be a son of a bitch.*

"You do it too?"

She nodded, lit up again. "Hate to break it to you, but a lot of people can do what we can do."

"So, if we touch each other, we're both paralyzed?"

She grinned. "A paralyzer, huh? Rule Number One: Never tell what you can do."

"Oh," I replied. "There's something else that you do to people when you touch them?" I played calm, but I wanted to scream. This girl had the answers I'd searched for aimlessly for sixteen long years.

She shook her head. "My questions first, Robbie."

I just nodded. She had me, and we both knew it.

"How long do Normals stay zapped when you touch them?"

Normals? "Fifteen minutes or so," I replied. "And you?"

She rolled her eyes. "If they come out of it—if you don't do something nasty, I mean—are they like, still healthy after?"

I didn't want to think about the answer to that one. I'd touched this girl I knew in college ungloved once by accident and had spent half an hour praying to God that she'd be okay. She'd seemed all right, I think she was all right. She didn't seem psychologically screwed up or anything. "Yes," I replied. "They're always healthy afterward, as far as I know."

"Does it always happen with you, or only when your heart starts beating really fast?" she asked.

That did it, no more doubts, this is the real deal on my couch. "It only happens when I am either excited or stressed. But I never trust it. Always gloves. Believe it or not, I go far out of my way to avoid touching Normals, when it's not . . . necessary."

She sank a bit at that, and her eyes were far away for a moment.

"It always happens with you, doesn't it?" I asked softly.

She looked back to me, tears starting in her eyes, and

she nodded. She almost touched me there—emotionally I mean—but I'm not one to pass on an advantage.

"You could at least tell me your name, couldn't you?"

A drop rolled down the curve of her cheek as she opened her mouth. "Cassandra," she told me. "My name is Cassandra."

"Tell me, please, Cassandra. I *need* to know. What are we that we can't touch them?"

She wiped at her face with the back of her thin-fingered hand and said, "We're Deprivers, Robert. They call us Deprivers."

Yes! That is the perfect name. Deprivers. That is exactly what we are!

I asked her if she might not care for a glass of cognac. She accepted. I dosed her second glass with phenobarbital and within twenty minutes she was out on the couch.

I stood over her, considering for a few minutes. If I touched her, her touch would affect me also, but how? Certainly I would be able to kill her—strangle her or use any number of weapons I own, but at what cost? Stalemate.

I delicately removed her wallet from the back pocket of her jeans, careful of her bare midriff. I found a notepad and scrawled down useful-looking bits of information. I slid her wallet back into her jeans and then tucked her in with my softest blanket.

It took another shot to put me out.

3

THE next morning I awoke with a hangover and found Cassandra still passed out on the couch.

I made us coffee, orange juice, eggs Benedict, and toast before waking her, all the time thinking, *My life has changed now; nothing will be the same again.* I was about to tap her, then thought better of it.

"Cassandra, Cassandra, wake up. I've made us some breakfast. Cassandra."

She startled awake and was over the side of the couch in a blink, eyes wild.

"Don't touch me!"

"I won't! Calm down."

"I dreamt that you deprived me, and I was never gonna wake up again."

"I had the same dream. Well, both still intact, eh?"

"Looks like it."

I gestured to the table I'd set. "Hungry?"

"Yeah."

We sat down and ate together.

"How many people . . . like us?" I asked.

"Deprivers," she replied harshly. "It's not the word that'll kill you, Robert. You are way too uptight. I've known about two dozen or so. Most on bad terms. Good eggs, just the way I like 'em."

"Thanks. What terms are we on, provided I can forget the gun in my mouth?"

"You're not dead or deprived, are you?"

"No. And neither are you."

"I've noticed."

"Mind telling me why you're here? Are you the Depriver Welcome Wagon?"

She lowered her eyes to her plate and spoke into it. "I tagged you on the street, and I thought you might be working for someone. I thought you were hunting me."

A Depriver working for who? A government agency? Hunted? Why?

"I started following you," she continued, "and I made some calls. Nobody in our network knew who you were and I—sort of *need* some people for this *thing*."

Network? This thing?

"I watched you go into that building on the Upper East Side and—about an hour later—I saw cops bring a man out with a sheet over his head."

I had no response to that.

"Don't worry," she said. "I didn't turn you in. That's the last thing I would do."

I nodded.

"Then I saw you help that woman who fell down in the street over on Lexington, and I was waiting to see if you'd deprive her for kicks—you didn't, so I thought you might be okay."

My mind slid backward, and I realized what she'd witnessed. A woman who'd slipped on a manhole cover in the middle of traffic. I'd helped her up, more for the contact than anything else. "Seems like my good deed paid off," I said.

"I needed to find out who you were."

"So you broke into the apartment with?"

"American Express."

"Of course." I nodded. "Don't leave home without it."

"And I went through the suitcases in your closet."

At that, I paused. Those cases contained all the tools of my trade. "So I assume I should drop all pretense that I'm an insurance salesman."

She laughed. "I'm not afraid of you, Mr. Luxley. You're a pussycat compared to most Deprivers I know."

I smiled. "I emptied the cartridges from your gun," I said, raising a forkful of egg.

She smiled back. "Did you now?"

"Yes, I did. Pass the juice, please."

She checked her load, and exhaled. She passed the juice. "Do I get them back?"

"If you're a good girl and eat all of your breakfast, I'll consider it. Ever think of entering the cleaning business? I think you'd excel."

"No," she snapped. "I don't kill people. I'll deprive in self-defense, but I've never killed anybody!" She was either telling the truth or a much better liar than me.

"I might need to, though, soon," she said, lowering her eyes again. "How much do you charge?"

"You can't afford me."

"Not with cash, but with information. You're a sitting duck to any of us with sight."

"Deprivers who can't touch me any more than I can touch them?"

"Wrong," she said. "By those with much nastier touches than you, who don't mind a fifteen-minute out while the others turn you off. Or by sighted Normals who want you either with them or dead."

Sighted Normals? "Well, nobody's hassled me before. I'm not bothering them."

"You just don't get it, Robbie. You're either allies with other Deprivers, or you're a threat, period. There's no room for neutrality in this shit. You're alive because you're a hermit. If you'd worked in a grocery store, blind like this, you'd be dead and forgotten by now."

I got up and pushed two more slices into the toaster. "Make me an offer. I'm listening." What was I doing, forming a contract with a seventeen-year-old girl? Armed and dangerous, but a child nonetheless.

She left the table, grabbed her cigarettes from the living room, and came back lit. I hate smoke while I'm eating, but decided to suffer it. She dragged incessantly as she spoke.

"I'll get you sighted and offer you safe haven with friends, and in return you help me rescue someone. The rescue could include some killing, but it's not mandatory or anything."

The toast popped up, startling her as I'd expected.

"Who would we be rescuing and who *might* we be killing?"

Long, hard drag. "My brother, Nicholas. You see, there's a whole group of Deprivers banded together under this man Deveraux. He's plugged in just about everywhere. His people contacted me and my brother, and we said no. They didn't like no, and we had to jam. I've lost contact with Nicky, and I know they have him. I need to get him back."

I let it sink in for a bit. *Maybe she lies, maybe not?* Either way, more bad news was probably headed my way. And could she really offer me some sort of extra sight? She did, after all, find me with relative ease. Depriver sight started to sound more and more like an imperative.

"What kinds of things could these other Deprivers do to me?"

"Depends on the Depriver. Hearing, taste, touch, smell, sight, balance, paralysis—anything that can get screwed up in your nervous system."

Breathtaking. "What is it that your brother Nicholas does?"

She tensed at that, but she sensed that it was time to either put up or shut up. "I'll tell you as a token of good faith. He's a blinder—full visual impairment. He's a shy kid. Has to be. You don't get your sight back in fifteen minutes, or fifteen years. He's permanent."

"No wonder they want him."

"But he freaks at the idea of touching anyone." She gave me a cold stare. "Like I do. But I will, if you cross me or join them, I swear it, Robbie. I swear!"

"Relax," I said. "I'm a loner. We just do this one job and I get this sight of yours. Then I'm going back to business all the wiser, and you go your own way. I won't be signing up with anyone. Just relax. Now, how come you're not blind? He must have touched you a million times growing up."

She crushed out her cigarette in the remains of her eggs, thoroughly turning my stomach. "Nicky can't affect me, and I can't affect him. We give each other headaches some-times. It's just like that with us."

Just then the telephone rang.

We let it ring three times, neither of us moving. To not answer might mean losing a client. To answer meant losing ground with Cassandra. I had to make the choice as a mat-ter of potential gain versus perceived loss.

"How do we proceed?" I asked her. *Ring-ring, ring-ring!* She warmed.

"I have to take care of some things before I can take you to get sighted. Meet me at the head of the Astor Place subway station in three hours. No weapons. And I'll take back my cartridges."

"In the coffee can over the oven," I said.

The phone stopped ringing. I sat buttering my toast as she waved good-bye, feeling more vulnerable than I had ever felt before.

4

I shaved, showered, and checked for messages. No new clients. Good. Missing an assignment would be unfortunate.

I dressed and put together a few bare essentials. Glass knife, handy for unforeseen metal detectors and close-range disagreements, into my coat-sleeve sheath. Pocket telephone scrambler, rearview glasses, and microbinoculars.

The only New York address in Cassandra's wallet had been a business card from a bookstore in the East Village called Seven Rays of Light; specializing in books on both esoterica and the occult. I like to use my time constructively, and it seemed like going down there was a good start.

I grabbed a cup of coffee from the deli on the corner and cabbed it downtown.

A wind chime announced my arrival, and a kitten scurried out of my way as I walked into Seven Rays of Light. It was a warm yet spooky little place and the proprietor, a thin man of about forty, graying sideburns and sharp features, glanced over the book he was reading and gave me a welcoming smile. The place looked empty. I'd almost expected Cassandra to be standing there accusingly as I came in. I shuffled around the stacks for a bit. I looked through the *D* section and was not surprised to come up empty-handed. Lots of books on chakras, mantras, Tibetan philosophy, the art of war, books on astrology, tarot, whatever. No *Complete Idiot's Guide to Deprivers*.

I felt someone move quietly behind me, and I smelled a distasteful, pungent smoke. It was the owner, come to check on me, looking very philosophical with a pipe in his left hand. His right hand was inside the pocket of his sweater, so I slipped my right hand into the pocket of my jacket.

He said, "Looking for anything in particular?"

I smiled and said, "Actually, I'm looking for information on the supernatural."

He nodded knowingly. "ESP, extraterrestrial, occult?"

I said, "Well, maybe more along the lines of biological afflictions."

He paused for a moment, then said, "Come with me. I think you might be interested in some of my private stock that I keep in the back." He turned and I followed him down to a small office, fingering the leading edge of my knife as we went. Once inside, I noted the walls were lined with ancient-looking books, no doubt filled with generations of mythology. He closed the door behind us.

His tone changed. "You're new around here, huh?"

I shook my head. "No, I've lived in New York for twenty-two years."

"Don't get out much, I see."

"I get out plenty."

"Uh-huh. Who sent you here?"

Come on baby, lucky seven. "Cassandra," I said with a warm smile.

The briefest flicker of approval passed over his face. "Cassandra, huh?"

"Yes sir. Said you'd help me out *for sure*."

"Hmmm," he offered and puffed at his pipe. "How do I know you're not one of Deveraux's people?"

"I guess you don't," I replied. "How do I know you're not?"

He thought for a moment, then looked curiously around as if somehow we could possibly be observed. He said one word: "Amsterdam." He said it with a certain presence, and I countered with equal poise when I replied, "Okay, I trust you." At this, he removed his hand from his sweater, and I did the same.

"Pardon me for not shaking hands," he said.

"No problem," I replied. "Pardon me for not wearing gloves."

"What is it you do?" he asked, one eyebrow arched. "I'll need to know to get you the right literature."

"I understand," I said. "I'm a blinder. What do you do?"

He chuckled. "I just work in a bookstore. You people are a fascinating lot. Can't say I envy any of you. Let me see what I've got for blinders."

The wind chimes sounded, and he said, "Wait here."

I poked around some books on witchcraft and waited. I worried that he might call Cassandra, or someone else who might order him to get back in there and kill that guy! I cursed myself for not bringing a gun. Then I heard the man cry out. I popped my knife and opened the door to the office from arm's length, then darted out quickly and used a row of books for cover.

He didn't see me, but I saw him. A solid-framed, dark-skinned man with dreadlocks who rose quickly and made a fast exit.

The proprietor was down on the ground. I cased the store quickly to make sure we were alone, and then I moved slowly toward him. He wasn't looking so hot, curled into a painful-looking fetal position, but I didn't see any blood.

I bolted the shop door, pulled the shade, and took a closer look. His eyes were vacant, and his breathing was panicked. I had no idea if he was deprived, or if so, what he was deprived of. He seemed predominantly disoriented. I watched him in a detached way as I thought about my next move. Then he started banging his head against the back of his desk, producing an awful metallic thud with each blow.

I picked up the phone and dialed 911. "Yes, hello. This is anonymous calling. I'm at a bookstore called Seven Rays of Light. The owner is having some sort of seizure. Send an ambulance. You'll find him back behind his desk. Thank you. Bye." And I hung up. That may or may not make points for me someplace, I thought. He was making with the head-banging a little louder now, and I couldn't take it.

I did the only other thing I could think of. I did it for him as much as me. I rubbed at my hands and felt my heart start to race. *Better not be a Depriver,* I thought, reaching down to touch his cheek. I knew he'd be down in a couple of minutes, and that it would probably stay with him until the ambulance got there. Maybe it would save him from bashing his own brains out. I unbolted the front door and quickly blended in with the crowd as I departed, wary that there could be eyes on me now. I left as empty-handed as I'd been when I'd arrived.

5

STILL an hour early, I put the bookstore out of mind, and was uptown scoping out Astor Place. Cross streets merging, continuous car and foot traffic, bookstore, drugstore, coffee and bagel stand, ice cream cart, subway entrance—and a large metal sculpture of a precariously poised cube in the center of it all. People milled about on their way to work, pigeons fought for their scraps, and kids dodged around the sculpture on their skateboards.

I sat on a bench with my back to the subway, rearview-scanning and munching my sesame bagel with a schmear. *I was a Depriver waiting for another Depriver, who is being pursued by still more Deprivers as she enlists my Depriver ability in the hopes of rescuing her Depriver brother. Outstanding.*

I caught a glimpse of yellow hair bobbing up in the distance and brought the binoculars up to my face. Cassandra, running this way, dodging in and out of the crowd. Running makes me nervous. She would be in range within moments. I made a quick decision and went with it.

Reaching from behind the wall of the subway entrance, I grabbed her by the arm and pulled her out of view.

"You're being chased?"

She nodded frantically, an ungloved hand on my coat, catching her breath. "Dark suit. Sunglasses. Not a Depriver."

Suddenly there he was, between the vendors—about six feet, medium build, dark gloves. No gun yet, but I anticipated one soon. He was no more than five feet away, and I was about to pop my knife.

Instead, Cassandra shoved me backward and dove for him. He wasn't any more ready for it than I was. She slapped him barehanded across the neck and rolled behind the ice cream cart, tripping one of the pigeon feeders as she went.

Dark Suit never flinched. He pulled a Smith & Wesson from his underarm holster, aimed the gun, and motioned for me to rise. I did so with my hands in clear sight. Pandemonium broke out all around us. I heard shouts, screams, and running feet, but saw only one thing: the barrel of the gun. I'm dead. Game over. Good-bye.

And then Dark Suit took a step backward, shook his head, and fired off three rounds—the first about ten feet over my head, the second at the concrete in front of me, and the third into the chest of the ice cream man. I was baffled, but I was alive.

He tripped over his own feet, fell flat on his back, and fired his remaining rounds straight up into the air, as if he were aiming at the sun or something. I moved quickly to him, kicked the gun from his hand, and took his wallet. I wanted to kill him for pointing a gun at me.

Then I felt Cassandra pulling at my elbow as she yelled, "Let's go, there are more where he came from!"

We ran three blocks or so, then flagged down a cab.

"Drive!" she yelled, and off we sped.

A few lights later I was breathing better. I tried to get a handle on what had happened. Death and I had rarely been so close, save for that time in Vegas years ago when this common thug picked the wrong guy to shake down. Dark Suit was a professional, at point-blank range, and he'd just . . . *missed.*

I looked at Cassandra; she was scanning as we drove.

"You touched him, right?"

"Shut up," she snapped; then, to the cabbie, "Let us out here."

She threw the guy a fiver, and we went down into another subway entrance.

"Where are we going?" I whispered as she bought us two tokens.

"Port Authority," she replied.

I sat next to her on the train, reading a banner for Colgate in Spanish and trying to piece together what had happened. She touched him, and there was maybe a thirty-second reaction time. It wasn't his sight that went. Maybe a physical spasm on the trigger. No, it was his aim that was off, and his balance.

"Causing a loss of one's sense of direction?" I asked like the third-place contestant on *Jeopardy*. "Is that it?"

She looked away and nodded.

"Not very aggressive."

"No, but it saved your ass," she snapped.

"True," I had to admit. *Losing your sense of direction, hmm? No driving, no sports, no shooting, no a lot of things. No fun.* "How long does it last?"

She was silent.

"What, Rule Number Two? Don't tell your duration?"

She raised an eyebrow and looked right through me. "Eternity, babe. It lasts for all eternity."

We pulled into Port Authority and headed upstairs to the buses. Cassandra took money from me to buy our tickets and a pack of cigarettes, and I bought myself a soda and a candy bar. We found our bus and took seats in the back.

"Okay," I said. "Care to start filling me in on this Deveraux character and how he nabbed your brother?"

She was staring out at the traffic as we entered the Lincoln Tunnel. "Yeah," she said. "Deveraux's setting himself up to be this sort of Godfather type. He finds lost Deprivers and takes them in. Only Nicky and I weren't lost. We've lived with this since we were kids, and we have our own group. When Deveraux contacted us, Nicky thought we could be like ambassadors or something."

"To bring your two groups together?"

"Right," she said. "So we agreed to meet up with him. We made it a public place, a nightclub. We didn't actually meet him, it was one of his goons—this really creepy Rastafarian guy. Over drinks he started spewing a lot of lunatic bullshit about the government. Didn't take us long to realize that he was talking acts of terrorism. When we turned him down, got up to leave, the fucker grabbed me—*touched* me. There were lots of his men there, but Nicholas and I are pretty hard to hold, and we busted out. They chased our car down with Nicky shooting at them from the window. Then basically my head got wiped and I ran us into a ditch."

"Because you were deprived by the Rastafarian?" I asked, remembering the incident at the bookstore.

"Yeah," she nodded. "I forgot who I was even. I woke up days later on this old man's couch and God knows how I got there. The old guy was deprived though, so I know he touched me. Soon as I got my head together, I headed back up here."

"You came back to gather reinforcements, huh?"

"Something like that," she said.

I remembered that I had Dark Suit's wallet, and I brought it out. "Care to see who you just deprived?" I asked, flipping the leather case open to reveal a silver badge and an identity card. One glimpse and she turned white and looked out the window.

Now, I considered myself familiar with all government agencies; it's basically a *must* in my profession, but this one was new to me. The identity card had the guy's photo and thumbprint, the rest was all symbols and bar codes. The badge was in the shape of an owl clutching a snake in its talons. Pretty impressive.

"What agency is this?" I asked her.

"The Ministry," she answered with notable distress in her voice. "They're global. They answer to no one. They want to take us apart and find out what makes us tick. They—" she stopped short. "Just pray they never get their hands on you."

I took another look at the owl before I pocketed the wallet. *Just what I need—another invisible enemy who has some way of spotting me. Marvelous.*

Soon after, we ramped on to the New Jersey Turnpike and Cassandra fell asleep on my shoulder. I was very careful not to touch her exposed skin. She wasn't a bad kid, I decided. I wondered if touching her hair would be dangerous.

6

SHE awoke when we stopped in Freehold, New Jersey, around dusk. We got off, and I looked around at a whole lot of nothing. She stretched and yawned and said, "Still a bit of a hike yet."

"What, no cabs?"

"Nope." She lit a cigarette, and we began walking.

"Mind if I ask you again where we're going?"

"Safe house," she said, absentmindedly pulling the tabs on her sweatshirt. "Where we can all gather in peace."

"Like an underground railroad?"

"Yeah. Hold up a sec." She moved her hand toward my shoulder, and I pulled away.

"Just need to lean on you to take off my boots. Please, my feet are killing me." I let her lean on me. "Scare easy?" she asked.

She stuffed her socks inside, slung the boots over her shoulder, and continued walking barefoot alongside me in the grass. "Thanks," she said.

"So, you're going to do something to me that will give me the sight, correct?" I asked.

"That's incorrect, Robbie," she said. "I won't be the one who does it to you, someone else will."

We walked in silence for another mile or so, then turned down a dirt road by a stream in a dark, wooded area. I dislike wooded areas. I'm a city dweller. I avoid jobs that send me off to either deserts or forests. They're always trouble. *How the hell does one acquire Depriver sight?* I was not letting anyone touch me.

We came to a large clearing where a two-story house with a landscaped garden came into view. Smoke was coming out of the chimney. "Someone's home," I said.

"Let's hope it's someone who can help," she said.

She had a little spring in her step as she reached the porch and produced a key from beneath a potted plant. "Best behavior, Rob," she instructed, "these people are like my family."

We went in quietly. She led me into the den, where a dark-haired woman, late thirties, sat cross-legged in an armchair with a book in her lap. She was the sort of woman you realize is positively striking, but not until your second glance.

"Terry," Cassandra said as she ran across the room to carefully embrace her.

"Terry, this is Robert, Robert, Terry." I crossed to them, nodded and smiled.

"News on Nicholas?" Terry asked, removing her glasses. *She should get contact lenses,* I thought. *Captivating eyes.*

"No, but Deveraux and the Ministry are both all over me," Cassandra sighed.

I looked around the place, avoiding their intimacies. There was a nice fire in the grate, lots of books piled about, photographs on the walls. I noticed a telephone and considered using the scrambler to check my answering machine, then decided there was little point. I was less than available at the moment anyway.

Terry's question, "And what sort of Depriver have we here?" brought me back.

"He's a paralyzer," Cassandra said without hesitation, then to me, "No secrets here, Robbie."

"Fine." I said after a pause, "What sort of Depriver are you?"

Terry smiled, raised an eyebrow. "No sort at all. I see that you're blind."

"That's why we're here," Cassandra added. "Who's around? Geraldo, maybe?"

"Nope," Terry said. "Sparrow's here."

"Oh, Sparrow will do just fine, we're not in a hurry. Where is he?"

"He just went upstairs."

I noticed, on the mantel, a silver-framed picture of Cassandra holding hands with a young man who strongly resembled her. They were standing by the shoreline, and she was pointing toward the distance, at a lighthouse. I got the impression that this "safe house" belonged to her family.

"We'll talk tomorrow, Terry. Is my room empty?"

We said our good nights, and Cassandra led me upstairs. She knocked on a bedroom door, and a young male voice said, "Come on in."

The room was almost empty, save for a hammock with an Indian kid in it. American Indian. Looked about sixteen or so, long black hair and high cheekbones. The boy rose, eyes wide, and took Cassandra in his arms with great care. "Cassie," he said. "I'm so sorry about Nicholas."

He was good-looking, with a soft voice and a solid build. I liked him right off.

"I've missed you," she said. "We'll get him back. This is Robert, he's a paralyzer, fifteen minutes, no bad news. Can you sight him?"

"Yeah, sure," the kid said.

"Sorry," she said then. "Robert, this is Sparrow. He's a Lakota. Do whatever he says. Sorry I can't stay up to watch. I'm beat. Crash wherever you find an open bed. Okay, Rob? Good night."

She swished out of the room and left me standing awkwardly with the Indian kid.

"So," I said, crossing my arms and trying to sound calm, "how does one acquire this vision?"

Sparrow pulled his hair off of his face. "Well, all you have to do to see is get yourself deprived. Then, it's a gift from the spirit world."

Spirit world. Great. I had no intention of letting him touch me, and I'd have slit him wide open if he'd taken a step closer. He sensed my tension and moved instead toward the room's single window and raised it. A brisk, cool breeze came through. He dropped two pillows off the hammock onto the floor and invited me to sit. Cautiously, I did. He sat across from me, within arm's length. I was fingering the knife in its sheath against my forearm.

"Do you get high, Rob?" he asked, producing a joint and then lighting it. "Maybe some dope would loosen you up for this."

"No, thanks," I said. "Listen, Sparrow, there is no way you are touching me."

He took a drag and then offered again, shrugging his shoulders as I declined. "Hey man, no big deal, but I'm really one of your safest bets if you want to see. Cassie seems to think you need it. I'd trust her if I were you."

Kid, if you were me, you wouldn't trust anybody, ever. "What would I be deprived of?"

"Hearing. Audio. You'd be clinically deaf. I'm good for first-timers. Most people can handle not hearing for a while."

"Duration?"

"Six to eight hours. It varies with me. Never had a permanent impairment or anything like that."

"And then I get this sight of yours, right?"

He nodded with a stoned smile. "You'll see. Trust me."

Deafness, eh? That leaves me still able to defend myself. "It's kind of hard for me to imagine real deafness," I said.

"Is it?" he chuckled. "Ever been in a sensory deprivation tank? We've got one downstairs. It's great for relaxing, getting in touch with yourself. Cassie calls it my casket. She's a claustro, won't go near it."

Note to self: Cassandra is claustrophobic.

"All right, let me have a drag off that," I said. He passed it, smiling. I could tell he was already under the influence. The smoke was sweet and stung the back of my throat. I coughed a few times, then took another drag.

"How about this?" he began. "I'll touch you, and you can touch me. Will that make you feel more comfortable? I've never been paralyzed, and I like to try them all."

Waitaminute, wasn't that supposed to happen anyway? "Sparrow, wouldn't you automatically be deprived by touching me?"

"Maybe, maybe not, certainly not a full dose. When I'm sending, I'm really closed off to receiving. Everyone's different. Fifteen minutes of stillness doesn't sound so bad. What say you, Rob?"

This is what you came for, right? "All right," I said with a long exhale, "let's do it. I need a minute to get myself ready."

He nodded, and I started heating myself up, concentrating on my hands, a warm ball of energy in my hands, my heartbeat pushing the energy into my hands, hot hands.

Sparrow moved closer to me and looked into my eyes. His were an odd grayish color with yellow flecks. He would have to touch me first, of course. Suddenly I felt a burning flash run up my spine and then another. He'd touched me on the forehead. Another flash, this one much cooler, then several more, each progressively colder, until they were actually chills. A loud explosion followed, and my ears began to pound. It was as if a vacuum cleaner had been switched on inside my head. I felt my face go numb; my fingers, toes, and back prickled. Blue sparkles danced in front of my eyes, and I felt nauseous. The vacuum kept sucking at my ears. I couldn't reach my hands up to touch them. Then, like a drain plug being pulled from a full sink, it was over. Was this how my targets felt when I touched them?

Sparrow's lips were moving slowly, but he wasn't speaking; or rather, I could no longer hear him. The room was dead silent. The only sound I was conscious of was my own rapid heartbeat.

I tried to read his lips. *"Feel okay?"* he mouthed. I nodded. Then he said, *"Touch,"* indicating my hand and his forehead.

I reached my hand slowly toward him, glad that it was back under my control, and touched his brow.

"Three minutes," I told him, not hearing my own voice. *Weird.* I got up and walked to the window, feeling the breeze hit my face. I looked at the woods, the sky, an airplane flying soundless high above.

I turned back to Sparrow and saw him frozen, cross-legged, midsmile, high as a kite. He didn't seem aware of me at all—off exploring, I guess. I didn't know what to do with myself now that I was deprived. I snapped my fingers near my ears and heard nothing. I left the room and went downstairs. No creaks beneath my feet. I passed a clock. No ticks, no tocks. I went into the empty den and looked at the dwindling fire. No snap, no crackle, no pop. I picked up the telephone. No dial tone. I laughed, not hearing myself laugh. I accidentally knocked a picture off the wall, the glass shattering into tiny shards without sound.

I unlocked the front door and went outside. The wind was so strong I stumbled every few steps. There are tiny audible gusts that act as warning signals to the ear that I was missing, Sparrow would later explain. I was feeling more than a little paranoid, and blamed some of this on the marijuana. I moved around the perimeter of the house, stepping on pine cones that did not crunch under leaves that refused to rustle. I half enjoyed all this, but thought, *This better all be temporary, or I am screwed.*

It began to drizzle, and I could really smell the pine trees. Then it began to pour. I was drenched before I made it to the porch. I looked out. Clouds completely obscured the moon. Lightning flashed repeatedly to the north without accompanying thunder. I watched for a time and became somewhat aware of the way that thunder is anticipated. How it reverberates. How it feels. It was my favorite part of the experience.

Sparrow was no longer in his room when I went back inside the house. Not surprising—I was reasonably sure he'd be up and about by now. At the end of the hall I found Cassandra, sleeping fitfully. *What's going on in that pretty little head?* Hauntings, I guessed. Like my own. What kind of childhood would it be in a family with two Depriver children?

I came up to her bed and stood directly over her—and that's when I saw it, the faint blue sheen to her skin. It sent hackles up the back of my neck. I wasn't sure if the blue glow was what I was supposed to be seeing, or if it was real, or if it was just a temporary side effect of deprivation. Whatever it was, it was damned unsettling. I considered waking her to demand an answer.

Then I remembered that Sparrow's things were set up in the basement, and so I went slowly, soundlessly, down the pitch-dark stairwell to find him. His deprivation tank, or casket, as Cassandra called it, was indeed coffin-sized and equipped with a polarized glass viewing window. Looking in, I saw him there, naked, dark-goggled, arms outstretched, floating at ease. He looked so vulnerable like that. *Could I ever let my guard down to such degree?* I wondered. *No, probably not.* Still, Sparrow's experimental nature pointed out what we each shared in common: that we both enjoyed using our touch and were excited by it. I watched him float for a while, distressed to confirm that his body did indeed cast the same blue glow as Cassandra's. Then I fumbled my way back upstairs and found a bed.

7

CASSANDRA was standing over me when I awoke, her mouth moving silently. And then, ". . . et up, Robbie." I could hear her again! *Hallelujah!*

Her skin, what I could see of it, anyway, still cast the blue glow, even in full daylight.

"You okay? Deprivation worn off?"

I nodded, rising, pulling on my shirt.

"Can you see now?"

I nodded again.

"Good. Come downstairs for breakfast."

She left, and I finished getting dressed. My ears were a bit numb but worked fine. I went downstairs, each creaking step a joy, and found the three of them sitting on the back porch. Sparrow still held the glow as well, though more subdued, a pale bluish outline. I wanted desperately to count it as a trick of the sun, but it was terribly clear to me, by contrast, that Terry wasn't radiating. I blinked, I squinted, but still the alarming glow on both Cassandra and Sparrow persisted.

It was then that I looked down at my own hands and stopped dead. Faint, but I was marked as well. *This is not good!* I thought. They laughed at me, standing there like an idiot, staring down at myself.

"Like a halo," Sparrow said.

"Or a warning signal," Terry said. "Depriver blue."

More like a homing beacon, I realized. *A serious threat to my life and my livelihood!*

"Morning, all," I said, sitting down at the table. "Blue's never been one of my better colors."

We ate breakfast, and I submerged my discomfort for later review. I listened quietly, seeming disinterested, as they spoke of other Deprivers who'd had dangerous encounters with both the Ministry and this man Deveraux. All the while, Terry took notes in a leather-bound ledger. Afterward, Cassandra and Sparrow brought the dishes inside, leaving Terry to me.

"So," I asked, "what's your part in all this?"

She pushed her glasses up into her dark braids, revealing those eyes again, and smiled. "I'm documenting it. Cataloguing here and there. Helping those of you I can to deal with your special needs."

Special needs, hmm. I poured us both another cup of coffee. "I can't fathom how a beautiful young woman like yourself managed to get involved in such a hazardous mess."

" 'What's a pretty girl like you doing in a place like this,' huh?" she said, embarrassed, staring down into her cup. "I just sort of fell in with this crowd."

"You found someone worth falling for?" I asked.

"No, I didn't get involved for *that,*" she said, cheeks reddening. "I'm a psychologist. Cassandra's family brought me to the twins when they were children, and we all became close."

"You're sighted, so you've been deprived."

"Yes," she said cautiously.

"Obviously not by either Cassandra or Nicholas."

"Obviously," she said.

"So who deprived you?" I asked.

Her hand trembled, barely perceptibly, as she sipped her coffee. "That's a very intimate question, Mr. Luxley."

"Only if you were intimate with that person," I said.

"Let's just say I have no regrets regarding the relationship."

"Would it be too forward of me to ask what you were deprived of?"

"I'm still deprived," she said. "It's just more subtle than you might expect. If you stick around long enough, you might figure it out. But enough about me. How old were you when you realized you were different?"

"I was nearly fifteen," I said, and she reached for her ledger.

"Mind telling me about it?"

"No, I don't mind at all. I'd be honored to be part of your research."

"Really," she said, pleased. "I'd have thought you'd be more reluctant."

"Nah, I'm the first one to lend a hand to anything research oriented, as long as it's confidential. You can take down my address and phone number, if you'll promise me you're the only one I'll hear from."

She ate that right up and flipped to the back of her book, jotting down my name in an address section. I dictated a few bits of misinformation while looking over her shoulder at her myriad other private listings.

She fired the next question before looking up. "Would you say your affliction negatively affects your career opportunities?"

"No, quite the opposite," I said, smiling. "Does yours?"

She sighed. "No, quite the opposite, Mr. Luxley, but you seem very reluctant to allow me to practice mine."

"Okay, I'll let *you* play doctor," I said.

"Okay, so tell me where it hurts?"

"Come again?"

"What part of your lifestyle would you say is the most impaired by your condition?"

"I wasn't aware of any impairment."

"Right," she replied. "Everything is just fine. Plenty of friends, social interaction, job satisfaction, lots of romantic possibilities . . ."

"Well, to be honest with you, Terry, I'm *entirely* satisfied with my current situation and prospects."

She settled back in her chair, a dubious look on her face. "Well, Mr. Luxley, I guess I'll have to consider you one of the lucky few. Most Deprivers tend to use their condition to self-isolate themselves from all possible relationships. But your willingness to join our little family clearly suggests that this is not one of your issues. I'm quite impressed with your ability to adapt."

"And I'm equally impressed by your astuteness," I told her. "Hey, you don't have a tape recorder, do you?"

"Why yes, I do, Mr. Luxley," she said, excited. "It's upstairs."

"How about you bring it down and I'll give you the story of my life?"

"Great, I'll go get it right now."

"Great," I said as she walked off. Then I picked up the ledger and scanned the addresses for a listing I highly suspected would be there. I replaced the book and went into the house.

"Cassandra, I'm going out for a short walk, okay? Will you please tell Terry that I'll be right back?"

"Fine," Cassandra said, after a pause, "but don't go too far. We've got to start planning our next move."

As soon as I was out of earshot and visual range I pulled my cell phone, jacked in the scrambler, and dialed. A secretary answered, refusing to put me through at first. "Tell him I'm from Amsterdam," I said. "He'll take my call."

Moments later a man answered, gruff sounding, all business, the kind of decisive voice I like to hear.

"Mr. Deveraux," I began, with a grin I could not contain. "I've got a proposition for you that's so juicy it's glowing blue. Would you be interested? Great."

8

NICHOLAS awoke on a cot in an unfamiliar room to find his hands encased in steel gloves, and a red-haired girl staring at him through a three-foot-square glass portal. He felt pain in at least a dozen parts of his body, especially his forehead, and dimly recalled a car accident. Inspection of his forearm revealed that he'd had blood samples taken within the past forty-eight hours. He got up slowly and took in his accommodations. A desk, with drawers his encased hands could barely open, and a door bolted from the outside. His hands were sweaty and itched beneath the gloves, but he found no way to remove them. Whoever had put them on knew exactly what he was.

"Hey," the girl called, her voice dulled by the glass. "Are you okay?"

He raised his hands in response.

"My name's Claudette," she said, placing one of her own encased hands against the glass.

He looked her over. "You're not a Depriver," he said.

"That's what I keep telling them," she replied. "They disagree. I keep testing positive. They say it means I'm about to leave dormancy or something."

He nodded, unconvinced. "Who are *they?*"

She shrugged. "All I know is the lab guy is called Ames. Some head guy's name is Deveraux. And some Rastafarian guy kidnapped me and threw me in the trunk of his car."

Deveraux. That brought back a lot. "Do you know where we are?"

She shook her head. "Not exactly. But I'm pretty sure it's someplace in Florida."

"Have you seen other people here? Other Deprivers?"

"Yeah, sometimes they take me outside, there's lots of people. But I can't tell who is or isn't."

"How about a blonde-haired girl. About my height, pretty thin?"

"You mean Cassandra?" she asked.

"She's here?" he asked, coming so close to the portal his face nearly pressed the glass.

Claudette backed away. "Umh . . . she was here. I didn't actually speak to her, but I saw her the day they brought you both in. Then they took her out of the lab, and I haven't seen her since. You're her brother, Nicholas, right?"

"When did you last see her?"

"Two days ago," she said.

Nicholas leaned his head against the glass. *How long have I been knocked out?* He remembered the car fishtailing across the road, slamming against the embankment.

"But she was okay, right?"

"She was pretty banged up. Limped a bit. Seemed mostly worried about you. She's very pretty."

He looked back to the girl, peering through the glass, trying to see the room she was in. "Are they trying to cure us? Enlist us? What?"

She shrugged her thin shoulders. "I don't know."

There was a long pause. "What sense do you deprive?" she asked finally.

"I'm sorry," Nicholas said, "that's none of your business."

His door was unlocked and a pudgy-faced man, in the midstages of balding, appeared in the entrance looking perturbed. His lab coat reached nearly to his ankles, and his knuckles were white against the clipboard he held. "Nicholas, my name is Dr. Ames. I see you're feeling better. Will you come with me now, please?"

"Bye," Claudette said, as Nicholas left the room.

As they walked the sterile corridors, Nicholas looked for potential escape routes, noting the overhead air vents. If he could get the damned gauntlets off his hands, or even just one hand, and then pull a garbage can over . . .

"I wouldn't consider trying to deprive me," the doctor said, "we're being monitored at all times here, and you'd be gassed immediately."

Nicholas shrugged as he walked. "Believe me, Doctor, I have no intention of depriving you or anyone else."

The doctor led him through a stainless steel corridor, and Nicholas said, "I haven't seen any windows. Are we underground?"

Stopping Nicholas abruptly before a large door, the doctor replied, "Save it."

They entered Deveraux's office, and a brusque, authoritarian voice called, "Come in, come in, gentlemen."

Nicholas was taken aback. He'd expected an aged kingpin type in a striped suit, smoking a Cuban cigar. Instead, he saw a gaunt, austere man wearing khakis and a short-sleeved

alligator shirt. The graying sideburns put him in his late forties or early fifties.

Sitting on the desk next to Deveraux was a man Nicholas
had seen before. The Rastafarian who'd contacted them at
the nightclub. His long dreads reached nearly to his waist.
He dangled his sandals and smirked.

"Nicholas, please sit down," Deveraux requested, indicating a leather chair before the desk. Nicholas sat, and the doctor stood behind him. He looked around the room. There
were bookshelves lined with leather-bound volumes, two
television monitors, a computer, a chess table, and an over-
sized picture window that made him realize his senses had
already been deceived—they were at least two stories above
ground.

"This is Roody, whom you've already met."

"The asshole who deprived my sister," Nicholas said.

"Hey man, just followin' orders. My touch is temporary."

Nicholas stood, knocking his chair over, and the big,
dark-skinned man rose to meet him, clearly interposing
himself between the boy and Deveraux. "You made her crash
the damned car!" Nicholas said. "How temporary would it
have been if we'd died?"

"I'm payin' the price, little man. She depped me
permanent!"

They stared each other down, Roody flexing his hands;
feeling sparks on his fingertips.

"You gonna touch me?" Nicholas whispered. "You want
to swap with me too? Go ahead."

"Nicholas." Deveraux spoke calmly, and pointedly.
"Wouldn't it be nice to see your sister again? Unharmed?"

Nicholas reined in his anger and sat back down.

Deveraux shook his head. "We're getting off on the
wrong foot here, Nicholas. . . ."

"Where's my sister?"

"We'll discuss your reunion after you've heard my proposal." Deveraux paused for acquiescence. "We're on the same side, Nicholas, like it or not. We're Deprivers, and the political climate out there is slowly building against us. I know things your people in Amsterdam don't know. I know there are machinations already set in motion that will end in a Mandatory Registration Act. . . ."

Nicholas did not flinch, but he did not object either.

"Soon after Deprivers syndrome is revealed, and the public accepts it, certain accidents will be transformed by the media into threatening incidents. The man on the street will be terrorized by the idea that his neighbor's kid might blind his whole family. It'll make the AIDS scare seem like a carnival ride. Mass hysteria fueled by the dissemination of misinformation through the CDC and the National Institutes of Health will justify this Mandatory Registration Act. Months later, we'll be dealing with the Glove Act. Then, any Depriver who removes his gloves in public will be subject to automatic arrest and imprisonment."

Nicholas looked down at the steel casings around his hands.

"And I'm not talking about our current prison system. I'm talking about *specialized* facilities—terror chambers— facilities that are already being designed and funded, mind you, by individuals wielding world influence. And it won't stop there, Nicholas—you're a bright boy, you can see where this will end, can't you? Full quarantine. Then isolation camps for all known carriers. You think that's a stretch under this administration? I understand it sounds unlikely—not here, in America, but God help us, it's already started. I've set up my organization to try to stop this insanity. I have to provide countermeasures against impossible odds. Sometimes these measures are extreme. It's the old, 'Would you go back in time and kill Hitler?' dilemma. Well, this time around we know who the Hitlers are."

Nicholas shook his head in bewilderment as Deveraux continued.

"This is a matter of self-preservation, and you will side with us, sooner or later. They'll see to it that you do. We can stop this from becoming a race war, Nicholas, but to do that, we're going to have to strike preemptively."

Nicholas's mind was caught in the crossfire of perceived evils, and Deveraux knew it. He'd been through this with countless others. The boy was frightened, unsure, at the tipping point.

"I need to think," he whispered.

"Of course," Deveraux replied.

"Now bring me to Cassandra."

"I'm sorry, Nicholas, but I'm reluctant to bring you together with your sister until each of you has made certain choices. Take some time to think, and then we'll talk again."

"Where the hell is she?"

"Safe," he said. "Doctor, will you please escort Nicholas back to his room. Roody, will you ask Karla to copy some of the transcripts we've intercepted for Nicholas?"

"Right away," Roody said. "Hang tough, kid."

As the doctor led Nicholas back through the door, Deveraux called out, "There's a method to my madness, Nicholas, and you'll see it, eventually."

9

NICHOLAS sat on his cot with the world on his shoulders. *A Mandatory Registration Act? A Glove Act?* These were not new concepts. These fears were discussed often in his circles. What troubled him was the thought that they were already in motion. He believed that much from Deveraux's propaganda. He wanted desperately to talk it all over with Cassandra.

The redhead was peeking at him again. "How old are you, Nicholas?" she asked.

"Seventeen," he replied, "in a few days . . . or maybe a few days ago. You?"

"Sixteen."

"You look older."

"Yeah, well, all these tests, and being locked in here. I'm not feeling my best."

"Yeah," Nicholas said. "This must be really screwed up for you. I've been on the move since I was a kid because of what I am. Every time I turn a corner, I expect the rocks to come sailing. You're just a Normal. I feel for you."

"Tell me about it. My mom must be bugging out. They made me write a note to her that explained why I had to run away—I had to say I was pregnant. They starved me for three days until I wrote it."

"That's their way of interceding before an investigation gets started on you. Still, I don't see how anybody could know you're going to turn Depriver. There's never been a valid test."

"Something about electrolytes, they said. A secretion on the skin."

If what she was saying was true, Deveraux's research was leaps and bounds ahead of anyone else's. "And how exactly did they find you?" Nicholas asked.

"I went to a clinic for a pregnancy test. I was really relieved when it came back negative, but I guess that wasn't all they were testing for."

"That's criminal," Nicholas said.

"Jesus—tell me about it."

"Hey, kid," came Roody's deep Jamaican voice from behind the door. "Here's some reading material. Enjoy."

A file slid under the door. Nicholas clumsily picked it up and brought it to the desk. "Have you read this stuff?" he asked.

"Yeah, they made me read it all," Claudette said, rolling her eyes. "In short, the public at large is still in the dark but won't be for long, and lots of government dudes know exactly what's going on and have this fascist itch. This whole thing scares me shitless."

Nicholas began reading through stolen police files, documents marked Interpol, FBI, and Homeland Security, transcriptions of wiretapped conversations, and a volley of memos between notable politicians. One name was highlighted on several occasions, some governor named Tyrsdale.

By the time Nicholas was through reading his first batch of files, he'd come to two conclusions: there were rough times ahead for anyone labeled a Depriver, and Governor Tyrsdale was a dangerous man, fanning the flames.

"So what do you think?" Claudette asked through her portal.

"I think things are going to get bad, maybe not tomorrow, but eventually. They're projecting ridiculous Dep-to-Normal ratios, like one to a hundred in less than five years. And then they're using those inflated numbers to predict deprivations at an epidemic level. It's insane. Tyrsdale's insane."

"And Deveraux?"

"I don't trust him either, look what he's doing to us. Our hands are bound. We're locked in our rooms. He won't let me see my sister."

"Yeah, he's a prick," she said. "But some of the other Deprivers here think he's right. You're one of them—so you must sorta sympathize, right?"

Nicholas shook his head. "I don't know."

"I want these things off me." Claudette demanded, knocking her gauntlet against the glass. "I gotta get these fucking things off of me!" She banged the hand that was out of sight, and the sound rang through the walls.

"Hey," he said. "I'm sorry."

Nicholas pored through dozens of folders containing photographs, memos, and classified documents. Although there was evidence enough that the world was on the verge of discovery, which was terrifying news in and of itself, there appeared to be far greater threats on the immediate horizon. For one, a coven of government officials who were gearing up to run a study on the military potential of SDS, playing a close second to a pharmaceutical company who saw the syndrome as a billion-dollar industry they could exploit. Drug company disclosure to the general public would be one of the very worst-case scenarios, he decided, since they've always put the darkest spin on things to generate demand for whatever they're selling. He read on, absorbing as much as possible, hopeful that he'd be able to regurgitate the majority of this information to his own people were he to manage an escape.

"Do you think there could really be concentration camps in this country?" Claudette asked through the portal.

Nicholas thought about it a moment. "If no one knew," he replied.

"What if—" She was holding back tears; he could see it. "What about if nobody cared? What if people were so scared of us, they allowed it—pretended it wasn't happening?"

Nicholas got up off the bed and went to her, the thin portal between them seeming nearly invisible. "They're not even sure you're one of us," he said.

She let the tears roll. "They're sure," she said. "Whether it's true or not. Wanna see something?" Her lip quivered.

He nodded, already afraid of what she would show him.

Claudette turned her back to him and lifted her shirt, slowly revealing her skin. As he watched, part of him thrilled unexpectedly in the curve of her hips, the small of her back— and then he saw the wound, the dark stitches, the inflamed flesh between two vertebrae of her spine. He'd reviewed enough research to know what they'd been checking for. He looked away quickly, and she dropped her shirt.

"Does it look very ugly?" she asked.

"No," he told her. "Nothing about you is ugly."

"Thank you," she said, turning back. "I don't think I can take much more of this."

The more he thought about it, the more he worried for the girl. Logically, the next step for the bastards would be to

take samples from her pituitary, which would require inva-
sive surgery, or worse—they might even fork out one of her
ovaries.

"Do you know anything about medicine, Nicholas?" she
asked him.

"Yes," he said, "I do. My father was a doctor. A surgeon.
I've taught myself a lot about the body, the senses, I—"

"I know this is a messed-up thing to ask, but I need to
know . . . I need to know how to end it. Not that I'm ready
or anything? Just if I had to?"

Nicholas closed his eyes, "Claudette, I don't—"

He looked at her again, and her stare pierced him.

"If I had to," she repeated.

"Yes," Nicholas whispered, "I can tell you what to do,
but you have to promise me . . . promise that you'll wait as
long as you can. I just need a little time."

"Okay," she said, "I promise."

"So, you've read the bulk of the surveillance," Deveraux
said. "Any thoughts?"

"I'm concerned," Nicholas answered, his voice small.
"But I'm not convinced. I still can't accept your methods. I
won't be sent out to deprive people."

Deveraux nodded. "I understand, but I'm hoping you'll
come around, son. We need solidarity. I was like you once,
you know. And someday, you'll be like me."

"Okay, enough of this we're-on-the-same-side crap,"
Nicholas replied in frustration. "I'm your prisoner, not
your friend. I've listened to you—now I see my sister."

"Cassandra is doing well, I'm happy to report. Her injuries
from the accident are nearly healed. Eventually, she'll be
required to make the same choices that you will make."

"You'll never persuade her," Nicholas said. "Even if you were to threaten to kill me."

"You may be right, Nicholas. She's as strong-willed and intelligent as you are. Still, you'll both be on my side eventually."

"And what if we both ultimately decide against joining you? Won't you kill us—two of your own kind?" Nicholas asked. "Of course you will. Isn't that how terrorism works?"

"Do you play chess, Nicholas?"

"Yes," he replied.

"Well then, you know that the best moves are multi-purpose. Never a sacrifice without a benefit." The boy nodded, and the man continued. "I'm guessing you're familiar with a global bureau of investigation called the Ministry?"

Nicholas was shaken by the mention of the agency. They were above the law and held to their own morality. Their agents had been responsible for the deaths of people close to him. He'd run from them on many occasions—and in fact, had feared he was their prisoner, not Deveraux's, when he first awoke here. "I know them," he said.

"I figured you would," he said. "They've officially formed a branch to handle us now, and they're holding several of my key people."

"So you'd be willing to trade us," Nicholas said.

"Yes, they'd be quite interested in the two of you."

Nicholas was sick of trying to gauge how much of Deveraux's tale was actually bullshit. "What the hell happened in your life to make you like this?" he asked, exasperated.

Deveraux sighed. "I'll tell you, son. It was a lifetime of having this bigoted world kick the shit out of me. Never mind the usual isolation that each of us knows too well. The self-torture. The itch that can never be scratched. I was taken prisoner once by the Ministry. I was tortured—experimented on in ways I won't relate, because they would sicken you."

"Like what you're doing to Claudette?" Nicholas asked.

Deveraux shook his head. "Much, much worse, Nicholas. And I deeply regret what's being done to her. But our need to know and understand our own condition far outweighs the suffering of one girl. It's wrong, I do realize that. And I must seem a monster to you—but it is for a greater good— it *is* necessary."

"What else will you do to her?"

"Continue our tests," Deveraux said. "Pineals. Pituitary. Marrow. Reproductive capacity. Brain tissue. I'm sorry if this is upsetting you."

"It's inhuman—she's not a lab animal!"

"I know, but the fact that we can test her so extensively here, both before and after her transition, allows us a unique opportunity. One we cannot dismiss."

"You can't even be sure she's going to turn Depriver."

"Dr. Ames has developed an accurate epidermal exam. I'll be happy to share the technology with your European friends once we've reached an agreement. As for Claudette, if you can think of some greater value that outweighs our testing, or maximizes it, I'll certainly entertain your suggestions."

10

THE next morning, looking through the portal, Nicholas watched Claudette sleeping. The door to her room opened, and Dr. Ames, in surgical gear, came in with a female attendant. Claudette's eyes fluttered open, and Nicholas could see that she was beyond struggling this time. She let out a small moan and looked at him. "Please," she whispered.

As the attendant took her elbow and helped her up, something broke within Nicholas. "No!" he shouted. He began to pound at the portal with his encased hands in a frenzy. "No! No! No!"

Much to the terror of both the attendant and Dr. Ames, the portal suddenly shattered, sending glass shards in all directions. Ames hit a button by the door, and an alarm began to sound. Nicholas dragged his chair to the portal, stepped up on it, and squirmed through the broken opening, ignoring the upturned shards of glass as his weight brought him over and down. He hit the floor in the other room hard, his encased hands doing little to ease his fall, but he was quickly up on his feet. Ames stepped back, and Nicholas moved toward his attendant, who shrieked as he grabbed her roughly by the shoulder, twisting her body in front of him like a shield and locking his arm around her neck.

"Nicholas please! Don't hurt her! Stay calm!" Ames pleaded.

"No more tests on her," he yelled. "Bring me to Deveraux!"

"Right, have it your way," the doctor stuttered.

Claudette's face was ashen, and she sat back down on the bed. Nicholas released the woman, and she immediately ran from the room. Nicholas knelt by the girl. "I'll be right back," he said. "No one will hurt you. Your door will stay open, and you're gonna be okay."

The door buzzed, and Nicholas pushed Ames out of his way as he entered the office and slammed the door behind him.

Deveraux sat, relaxed, unimpressed. "What can I do for you, Nicholas?" he asked.

Nicholas stepped up to the desk and pounded his metallic fists down so hard they damaged the wood. "You want to talk," Nicholas yelled. "You take these fucking things off my hands first!"

Deveraux pulled open a drawer, removed a silver key, and placed it in Nicholas's encased hand. With his teeth, Nicholas picked it up and managed to unlock the gauntlets from his sweat-soaked hands. He let them fall to the ground. He stretched his fingers, balling them in and out of fists. Then he pocketed the key.

"Talk," Deveraux said.

"What does it take to let Claudette and Cassandra go?"

"Deal time, eh?" he said. "I hadn't realized you were that concerned with Claudette as well. Tell me, if I were to let her go—where exactly do you think she'd be safe?"

"Anyplace is better than here," Nicholas said.

"Nicholas, can I show you something? Will you take a walk with me down to the lab?"

Nicholas approached the taller man. "I could blind you right now."

"You'll have other opportunities, I'm sure," Deveraux said calmly. "Come take a look first."

The two walked out of the office. "You do realize," Deveraux said as they passed through a hall lined with guarded doors, "that I could have all three of you erased at any moment?"

"You do realize that I don't really give a shit at this point," Nicholas said. "Wouldn't further your cause anyway."

"True," Deveraux said, as they reached the end of the hall, a doorway with a digital security keypad. "I like you more and more each day," he added, swiping his key card and unlocking the door.

They stepped into a small, sterile room lit by harsh fluorescent bulbs. The room had two occupants, an elderly Asian woman in a lab coat and a late twenty-something Depriver with curly brown hair, sunken eyes, and a bit of a beer belly. The Depriver sat at a table with his right hand taped and wired up to a strange-looking machine. A small meter was *clicking* and *beeping* in a language of its own.

"Nicholas, this is Dr. Tsuen-Yahn, and she's working today with one of our newest recruits. Doctor, Mitchell, this is Nicholas."

The doctor smiled and gave a quick bow.

The lines on Mitchell's face suggested a harsh life and a matching attitude that made Nicholas instantly wary. "We had to rescue Mitchell here, at great expense, from a federal penitentiary," Deveraux said.

"A pleasure," Nicholas said.

"Same here," Mitchell replied.

"Doctor, please explain to Nicholas what you're working on with Mitchell," Deveraux said.

"Surely," she said. "Mitchell's deprivation, like yours, causes blindness. When he first came to us, we observed that it took around six minutes for his deprivation to set in. Using biofeedback, we've been able to offer him a great deal of control over how and when he deprives."

"I can offset my deprivation for up to forty minutes now," Mitchell said with a wink. "Lots of getaway time."

Nicholas did not want to think about how they were gauging Mitchell's delayed deprivation. He hoped it was by electronic means. Still, he had to admit to himself that the results, if true, were impressive. His own network had no such technology.

"We're helping our people here," Deveraux said. "Our research will give them chances that the National Institutes of Health and their pharmaceutical companies never will. Not if people like Tyrsdale get their way."

Again, Nicholas felt confused, unsure where he stood. He let Deveraux lead him back out into the hall.

"One mission," Deveraux said. "You stay with us. You train with us. You go on one mission—with no fatalities, I swear. After that, you're free to choose. In return, you keep that key. Go to Claudette—I'll suspend her testing. I consider you worth that chance."

"And Cassandra?"

"Not yet, Nicholas. Not yet. She's my trump card with you, of course."

Defiance coursed through the boy's veins. He wanted to blind the man. For the very first time in his life—he *wanted* to do it. "If you hurt her in any way, I think you know what I'll do."

"Yes Nicholas, I know. . . . Why don't you go and see how Claudette is doing."

Nicholas turned and walked back down the hall, regaining control over his thoughts and emotions more and more with each step farther away from Deveraux.

He found Claudette sitting alone where he'd left her and carefully unlocked her gauntlets. She flexed her delicate hands and brought them against her face.

"You've done so much for me," she whispered. "Please tell me what I can do for you."

"FROM now on you five will be collectively referred to as Delta Team," Deveraux announced as he paced back and forth before the group.

Nicholas had been briefly introduced to the two new men, and was of course already acquainted with Mitchell and Claudette. Removing the gauntlets had given the girl a good dose of her vitality back. She was unaware of the bargain that Nicholas had made to save her from further experimentation. And for Nicholas, she agreed to participate in Deveraux's training sessions.

Deveraux continued with, "Gavin here is your team leader," nodding toward the tall, lithe man with the blue eyes. "That means he will receive my instructions directly through Roody when you are in the field."

"Where is my good friend, Roody?" Nicholas asked.

"On assignment," Deveraux replied. "Don't worry, he should be returning this evening. But let us continue. Gavin is a scrambler. His duration is variable." Gavin flinched as Deveraux revealed his deprivation.

Next came a man of obvious Arabic descent. "Ahmet has, up until now, been employed by the Iraqi government as a spotter. He's an audio Depriver. Victims are rendered clinically deaf as well as incapable of speech. His duration is less than one hour."

Deveraux moved on to Mitchell, the Depriver that Nicholas had seen in the lab. Nicholas had met other Deprivers in the past like this one, those who obviously enjoyed depriving Normals without cause. He feared and loathed him. "This is Mitchell; he's a blinder. His causation time is variable. His duration is permanent."

"Next we have Nicholas," Deveraux said, "who has not yet decided to make our cause his own. He is also a blinder, and his duration is also permanent. Let's help him make the right decision."

Then Deveraux got to Claudette. He reached up and touched her covered shoulder in a tender way that sent a strange shiver of jealousy through Nicholas. "And this is Claudette, who is also undecided. Her deprivation is still latent. Her duration unknown. We look forward to her awakening and hope for an aggressive touch."

Introductions made, Deveraux left Delta Team to their evening meal period, allowing them to converse freely. Nicholas learned that Gavin had spent four years in apprenticeship with a professional assassin. Ahmet had led a normal life until age thirty-four, marrying into a wealthy family and raising three children—children who'd been murdered by the government that had employed him. He was more than happy to offer his services to Deveraux, who'd promised to assist him in gaining retribution.

Mitchell didn't say much, except for the comment, "Why team two blinders together? Seems a waste to me."

To which Gavin, assuming his leadership mantle, answered, "It's an aggressive, permanently damaging deprivation. I wish we had three of you."

Claudette was undoubtedly the center of attention; her youthfulness and charming demeanor guaranteed her to be the subject of many sleepless nights. "What do you hope your deprivation will be?" each of them had asked at least once during the course of the meal.

After dinner, Delta Team sat in a small projection room viewing footage of actual missions. They watched as three Deprivers entered a hospital, dressed as laundry personnel, using false identification. They were obviously making a game of it as they recorded their movements on a small, hand-held digital camera. One of them followed his target, a doctor who'd begun putting two and two together, out to his car. One touch on the target's neck, followed by an apology, and his part was over. Then the team quietly removed the doctor's files from his office and evacuated, mission accomplished.

"Could you earn your money any easier than that?" Mitchell remarked.

The team then listened to recordings of several wire-tapped conversations, with one that Nicholas found particularly jarring, "This is Jerry Tyrsdale. Yes, Mr. Director, I understand your concern. I've got one of them in custody as we speak. Oh, he'll talk all right. I'll have the location of that safe house by tomorrow if I have to start pulling fingernails."

Nicholas thought about his own safe house back in New Jersey. He pictured his friends sitting at home in front of the fireplace, Terry, Sparrow, Geraldo, maybe Felicia—not suspecting they could be in danger. He wondered if the Depriver in custody was someone he knew. He looked over at Claudette, sitting next to him in the near dark, feet on chair, chin on knees, as she listened, horrified. He wanted to hold her—to shield her from what she was seeing and hearing.

After the briefing, the group was allowed some free time. Since both Nicholas and Claudette had become agreeable, they'd been moved to their own rooms in the barracks along with the other recruits. Nicholas surveyed the twelve-foot walls that surrounded the compound, and the guards with their automatic machine guns. *Is Cassandra on the grounds someplace, or is she being held elsewhere?*

"I'm scared of what the world will be like for us after the laws are passed, aren't you?" Claudette asked, as they sat alone in her room.

"Don't worry, I promise I'll protect you. I have friends . . ."

"Pacifists," she shot back. "Deprivers who won't fight back. We're going to be hunted down, Nicholas. Are you blind and deaf? And what if my deprivation turns out to be something weak like—taste sensitivity or smell degradation? What if my touch only causes mild headaches? Then Deveraux won't even keep me. I'll end up getting my fingernails yanked out for not giving away my friends!"

"No," Nicholas whispered. "Don't wish for a harsh deprivation. You don't understand what you're saying. You won't ever be able to touch anyone. Never kiss anyone. Never be safe. Trust me."

"I do trust you, Nicholas. But what should we do?"

Nicholas lowered his head. "I'm not sure yet, but I promise I'm going to get you out of here."

"We'll escape you mean—you're trying to find a way out?"

"No, just you. I can't leave."

"Because they have your sister," she said.

"Yes."

"But if you help me escape, they might kill you. . . ."

"No," Nicholas said, wishing he could reach out and touch her. "Deveraux realizes that my sister and I are valuable. He'd be a fool to kill either of us, and he knows it."

11

"LISTEN up, Delta Team," Roody called out in the cafeteria. "We're sending you out on a test mission late this afternoon that will be conducted off premises. This is our way of deducing your capabilities and determining your allegiance to the cause. Your performance and effectiveness will be evaluated." He stepped purposefully in front of Nicholas and Claudette and asked, "If there be any conscientious objectors unwilling to take this test, speak up."

Test mission? Nicholas wanted very badly to object—this was not in the plan. Still, it was a chance to get outside the compound. A chance to get Claudette free of them. He knew he had no choice, and he held his tongue.

Roody continued, "You touch no one except the target listed in your envelope. You got that, Mitchell? You do not open your envelope until instructed. You will regroup at the appointed time, and lateness will not be tolerated. Go to your lockers and get dressed."

Nicholas was outfitted in ripped jeans and a varsity

letterman's jacket from someplace called Hillside High School. Claudette was also in jeans, with high-top sneakers and a tank top. Ahmet was instructed to shave his beard and was dressed as an auxiliary policeman. Mitchell was put in scrubs and a doctor's coat. Gavin was dressed as a paramedic. Roody handed out envelopes to each of them and led them down to a garage where an ambulance sat waiting. Guards with side arms snapped to attention as they passed.

Roody pulled Nicholas aside, just before he got into the van and whispered, "Remember, we still have your sister."

Gavin drove the ambulance out of the garage. *Of course, Roody can't drive—he's deprived,* Nicholas thought. He smirked, looking out through the glass at the sky and the wild palms. *Miami,* he decided, *this is without a doubt Miami.*

At the first red light, Roody handed out the envelopes. "Not until I tell you," he instructed. "And when you finish, you meet me at the south gate of the hospital."

A few blocks later, he had Gavin turn on the sirens and punch the gas.

NICHOLAS and Claudette were dropped off three blocks before the South Broward Medical Center, and Roody told him to open his envelope. Then the ambulance sped on. "It says we're to sign in at the hospital as guests of Mr. Jason Skulnick, our grandpa. Then go to his room."

As they walked toward the hospital, Claudette said, "We could just split, you know."

"No, we can't." Nicholas answered. "They're watching us."

"Where?"

"There," Nicholas nodded toward the street. "Grey Sedan. Guys with sunglasses."

"Deveraux's people?"

"I don't know. Maybe yes, maybe no."

"What do we do?"

"Stay with the plan. Watch for an opportunity . . . and trust me."

"I trust you," she said. They entered the hospital, half solemn, half goofing around, and signed the register with scribbles. They were given visitor passes by a sour receptionist. In the elevator, Claudette said, "I'm scared to run alone with those men out there, Nicholas."

Nicholas nodded but kept his eyes to the floor.

They got to the right room and closed the door behind them. Two unconscious patients lay there. One male, presumably Mr. Skulnick, the other female.

Claudette tore open her envelope. "It says that you're to deprive Mr. Skulnick—and that I'm to wake the woman, touch her, and observe the results. We have three minutes, and then we have to leave the room and head to the rendezvous."

"Three minutes?" Nicholas said. "It takes at least two before my deprivation even sets in."

"Jesus, Nicholas, I'm scared. Hurry!"

Nicholas went to the man's bedside. He'd abhorred his curse since childhood, even as others had seen it as a gift. To him, use of it was tolerable only as self-defense—and even then he felt nothing but sorrow. He'd only deprived four people in his entire life. But this was different, right? This was for Cassie and Claudette. This was essential. He stood by the bedside, within easy range, willing his hand to move. To touch. To blind. To deprive.

As he hesitated, Claudette picked up the man's chart and read, "Skulnick. Age: sixty-one. Status: Post—cardiac arrest with end-stage AIDS. Prognosis: Medically futile," her voice was choked with compassion when she added, "Nicholas, he's dying anyway."

Yeah, but does that make it all right? Nicholas thought. *God forgive me!* He reached out and brushed his bare fingertips against the man's sagging face. "I did it," he whispered.

As he turned back, he saw Claudette standing over the woman and went to her side. The woman was also in declining health, her breathing shallow, hair almost entirely gone. "She's terminal too. I checked," Claudette said.

"You don't have to touch her," Nicholas whispered. "We'll say nothing happened."

"No, I should find out. It will never be as safe as this. Deveraux was kind to assign these poor people to us, don't you see? He needed to test us, but he's being merciful. To them and us. I *want* to do it."

Nicholas did not really understand, but he knew she was harmless. "Okay," he responded. "Wake her. Hurry up."

Claudette shook the elderly woman and she opened her eyes.

"Yes," she said, confused by her surroundings.

Claudette touched the woman's hair, and then let her fingers brush a bare patch on her scalp. Nicholas saw no change in either of them. Claudette asked the woman, "Can you see me?"

The woman nodded.

"Hear me?" A second nod. "Can you move?" The woman feebly raised one hand, nearly disconnecting a tube.

"It's time," Nicholas called, carefully touching her shoulder.

They turned and left the room, moving from corridor to corridor until they came to the stairwell. Nicholas pushed through the doorway and took a sudden blow to the back of his head.

His world went black.

12

WHEN Nicholas came to, there was a dark-suited man standing at the top of the stairs, holding Claudette at gunpoint.

"Yes, I have the girl," the man said to the air. "Confirm if she lives or dies."

"Who are you?" Claudette asked.

"The Ministry, Deprivers Branch," the man replied. "That means you have no rights whatsoever. If you so much as wiggle a finger, I'll put a bullet in your head."

Nicholas knew this man could kill them both without repercussions—there could be no bargaining, and he'd need to move fast.

"Confirmed," the man replied through his earset. Claudette took a quick step backward, and the man cocked the hammer of his gun just as Nicholas lunged off the floor. . . .

The gun went off, the bullet missing its mark as Nicholas rammed into the man at stomach level and they both went tumbling back down the stairs. As they hit the bottom, the Ministry man was unconscious, and Nicholas was dazed and bleeding from the nose. The boy untangled himself and slowly got to his feet.

Claudette ran down the stairs and pulled him into her arms. "You saved my life," she said.

Nicholas's reflexes instantly kicked in. *What is she doing?* "Don't touch me!" he said, but it was already too late as she slid her hands and arms around his neck and brought her mouth to his. It was the sweetest, most terrifying contact he had ever known.

As they parted, a shiver passed through Nicholas that left him trembling. She had less than two minutes left of sight, and there was nothing he could do. "I'm sorry," he said softly.

"I'm not," she said. She took his hand and pulled him down the corridor and into a supply closet. "There are probably more like him around." They stood there in front of one another, ignoring their orders, staring into each other's eyes—as he waited for it to happen. . . .

And it didn't. Two minutes passed. Three. Four. And still the girl could see. His touch was not depriving her. He shook his head, "I don't understand—how can you still . . ."

Suddenly, the girl began to radiate before his eyes. *Now,* he thought, *she's turning right in front of me!*

She just smiled. "Something they did to me in the lab, maybe? I don't know. I just somehow *knew* that I could touch you. I always knew."

He pulled back to look at her aura—and what he saw amazed him. She *was* glowing—but not blue. She was giv-ing off a crimson red. *What the hell does a red aura mean?* Nicholas was stunned. "It just—it makes no sense. You're glowing red."

"Red?" she asked, looking down at her own hands, "but I thought Deprivers glowed blue?"

"No, I mean—yes, we do. This is something I've never seen or heard of."

"Here, there's blood on you," she said, reaching up to wipe his face. He jerked back to avoid further contact, and she dropped her hand. "Okay fine, so what do we do now? We're already overdue."

"I have to go back—I need to make Deveraux release Cassie. But you could get out, I'll—"

"No way," she replied. "I won't leave you."

"Then we go back with them—but say nothing," he made her promise.

"YOU each did exceptionally well, I understand," Deveraux said, as the team sat through debriefing in his office late that evening. "I will ask that you keep the details of your test to yourselves. That said, I officially instate Delta Team as active." Deveraux looked first to Nicholas, then to Claudette. Neither moved. The boy was deep in thought, watching her red glow from across the room, struggling with the impossible idea that she'd touched him. It was obvious, from the lack of reaction, that none of the others could see it on her. Like a typical Dep aura, it must not be visible until after contact. What if she were immune to SDS? She could be the key to ending the entire crisis.

And, if the Ministry had gotten that close, Deveraux's security was failing. He had to get all three of them out of there as quickly as possible. "Things have escalated," Deveraux continued, "I'm afraid we've reached critical mass—our existence is about to be revealed to the general public."

Nicholas's internal debate halted at that. He attempted to mask his concern as he looked to Claudette and saw she was trembling.

"By the government?" Mitchell asked.

"Yes," Deveraux replied, holding up a sheet of paper pinched between his fingers. "But more specifically by the Centers for Disease Control. What I'm holding here is a draft of a Nationwide Hospital Alert requesting notification of any instances of patients suffering blindness, deafness, or other sensory deprivation, of unknown etiology, over the past five years."

"Somebody's putting the pieces together," Gavin said.

Deveraux nodded. "Yes, the CDC's director for human quarantine, a man named Richard Slater. He's being systematically led down the path of discovery by Tyrsdale's people. This document was faxed to Governor Tyrsdale's office less than an hour ago. It seems that Director Slater has been tapped to be the man who discovers Deprivers syndrome."

"What happens if the alert goes out?" Ahmet asked.

Deveraux considered a moment, then offered, "More than likely it'll be followed by enough corroborating evidence to warrant a full public health alert. That should be enough to send the general public into a panic, enough to provide the government with the excuse they'll need to justify a quarantine."

"Does the CDC have a Depriver in captivity?" Nicholas asked. "Any hard evidence?"

"Up until today," Deveraux replied, "they had only a few deprived patients, no Deprivers."

"Up until today?" Nicholas asked, growing more tense by the moment.

Deveraux directed their attention toward his wall monitor as he picked up the remote control. "This is footage of a criminal trial that's currently under way in New York. It's revolving around a fifty-five-year-old man by the name of Duncan Cameron who allegedly blinded a teenager with some sort of concealed weapon. This was recorded around four-thirty this afternoon. Watch."

Deveraux pressed a button and a digital clip started, depicting a very crowded courtroom. The angle of the tape seemed to be from someone standing in the back of the room, from about hip level. Deveraux continued. "This man, Cameron, is obviously one of us. He's claiming self-defense, that he merely struck back. The young man and his friends were apparently trying to mug him."

"The victim becomes the accused," Gavin said. "That's fucked up."

"Kid deserved what he got," Mitchell added.

"Yes, I agree," Deveraux said. "Unfortunately, there were witnesses who have come forward to testify that there was no weapon involved. This morning some hotshot prosecutor—we're not sure if he's working for the intelligence community—proved that the blinding was a direct result of Cameron's touch, in front of the entire courtroom. That's Cameron there."

Cameron was a thin, feeble, gray-haired man who suddenly leapt up from his chair at the defense table, raising his gloved hands in frustration. "I'm innocent! I did not intend for this to happen!" he told the judge at the top of his lungs. "You don't understand—"

"Control the defendant," the judge ordered, and Nicholas knew what was coming when the two court officers stepped forward and one of them placed his hand directly on Cameron's exposed skin.

"Oh, my God! I can't see. I can't see!" The officer crumpled to the floor in front of the jury box, hands pushed hard into his eyes. Several people in the courtroom rose in distress and blocked Cameron from view.

Deveraux stopped the tape. "That courtroom was filled

with reporters. You can bet that this incident will eventually hit the national news. Now we have to consider this event, coupled with the stepping up of action by the CDC, as an uncontrollable leak."

"But do you really think that people will believe it?" Ahmet asked.

Deveraux pondered. "That depends who comes forward first and explains it. If it's Tyrsdale's people putting the slant on things . . . Well, you fill in the blanks."

"Will we intercede?" Gavin asked.

"We'll be determining our involvement during the course of the evening. Your team may or may not be involved, but I suggest you all get a good night's rest. That's all, Delta Team, you're dismissed. Nicholas, stay a moment."

As she left the office with the others, Claudette gave Nicholas a nervous glance.

"I'm sure you realize that all of us, your people as well as mine, are now in grave danger," Deveraux said when they were alone.

Nicholas was momentarily taken aback by the man's attempt at sincerity, until he asked, "This Duncan Cameron, do you know him?"

Nicholas shook his head.

"He's not part of your underground?"

"I can't know every Depriver we've contacted, can I?" Nicholas replied. He needed to push it, to gain something, to strengthen his position. "On the other hand, this whole situation could have been orchestrated by our network. Here with you—I have no way of knowing."

THAT night, as the others slept, Claudette slipped out of her room and went to Nicholas. The red glow cast off her exposed skin like burning ember. She went to touch him with her bare hands, and he pulled back. "It's okay, you can touch me," she whispered. "Please."

"Claudette, we can't be sure it's safe—I can't risk taking your sight forever just for this moment, I—"

"*Shhhh,*" she whispered. "It's okay, it'll be all right—"

"I want to believe that, but we don't know what will happen."

"No one ever does," she whispered. "I just know I want to be as close to you as I can. It can't be any more dangerous than when we kissed, can it?"

"I guess not—"

"And if it's all some fluke, if it doesn't last, think of what we'll have missed. I don't want that kind of regret, Nicholas. I want you."

Nicholas had run out of arguments and restraint and allowed her to kiss him. He slid his hands along her waist, then up her back, and she winced as he accidentally brushed her incision. "I'm sorry," he whispered, suddenly stopping.

"It's all right," she said, encouraging him with her hands upon his as he kissed her more deeply. Then she shifted her body against him just so, her hair brushing over his face, and felt him truly take hold of her.

In the early hours of the morning they lay nestled together in exhaustion.

"Has it been very long since you've been touched?" she asked.

"Yes," he said. "Although Cassandra and I can touch."

"Really," she said. "Is it because you're twins?"

He nodded, then asked, "How did you know we were twins?"

"Everyone knows. Deveraux told us that you two were famous for being the only Depriver twins."

"I think I just figured out something," he said after a pause.

"What?" she asked.

"Why Deveraux needs me. It's the only possible reason he's giving us this freedom. Maybe the only reason we're alive."

"Why? Why does he need you?" she asked.

"Because I'm his only link to our underground. He doesn't have enough people to carry out his plans once the shit hits the fan. He thinks the game's lost without us."

"But what if Cassandra shows him how to reach them?"

"Cassandra doesn't know how to reach them. I'm the contact for our group. And it's not just about reaching them—it's about convincing them."

"Do you think you could really do that, Nicholas? Convince them?"

"Maybe," he said. "But why would I?"

"Because we're all in the same danger, aren't we?" she said. "Aren't you at all scared about what happens when the world finds out?"

"No," he said. "I'm full of hope. And your immunity could change everything. We need to get out of here. I need to talk to Cassie about all of this."

"Forget about your sister," Claudette whispered back. "This is about you and me now. Nicholas, look at me." He looked into her tear-streaked, frightened face. "I think I love you," she said, "and you're the only person I can trust."

"I think I love you, too, Claudette," he told her. "And if you really trust me, you'll hang on a little while longer—we're gonna get out of here—all of us."

Aт first light, Deveraux had Nicholas brought to his office. The man looked near exhaustion—had obviously not slept.

"I'm sending Delta Team into active service today, son, and I'd like both you and Claudette to participate."

"Yeah, well, I'd like to go sit on the beach with my sister and suck back some Long Island iced teas," Nicholas said.

"Go along on this one," Deveraux said, "and the three of you walk the minute you touch down. All I'll ask is that you leave with an open mind."

"Do you really expect me to believe that you'll let us leave?" he asked.

"Yes," Deveraux said. "I give you my word. This mission is of the utmost importance."

"You have other teams, don't you?" Nicholas said, fishing for confirmation. "I don't see why we're important."

"I have other operations happening simultaneously, son."

"Just level with me," Nicholas said. "What do you want?"

"The underground, of course," Deveraux replied. "The same thing I needed when I first contacted you. Without solidarity, we're all as good as dead. Trust me. Give me access to them, and all of the technology I've developed is theirs. We *are* on the same side, Nicholas. You just haven't accepted it yet."

There was something strangely obligatory about Deveraux's insistence, Nicholas thought, as he watched the man's aura softly pulsing. *Something almost compulsory . . .* For a moment, the boy felt faint, then he leaned on the back of the chair and asked, "How do you plan to proceed?"

"We think it's necessary to let the CDC disseminate the information, but it has to come without Tyrsdale's direct influence over the initial policies," he said.

"Which means?"

"Which means I have to mobilize all of my people to neutralize Tyrsdale's puppets as quickly as possible."

Nicholas stood there, considering, when a buzzer sounded.

Deveraux went to his desk and punched the intercom. "Yes, Roody?"

"Alpha Team is just in, or what's left of it. There's been an accident. It's bad."

"I'll be right down," Deveraux said. "Choose your loyalties with care, Nicholas. When I return, I'll expect an answer."

Nicholas sat down at Deveraux's desk and rubbed his temples. *How will this change things? Will Deveraux really free us if I go along just this once? Will he really share his research? Was keeping him from the underground truly in their own best interest?*

Then the intercom sounded again, distracting him at the moment of decision.

"Mr. Deveraux, there's a very persistent man on line one. He said to tell you he's from Amsterdam."

Amsterdam? Someone was using their password to contact Deveraux. *Someone he knew, perhaps?* He lifted the phone to his ear, and making sure he was unobserved, pressed the button that read LINE-1 and in the deepest voice he could muster, he said, "Yes?"

"Mr. Deveraux, I've got a proposition for you that's so juicy it's glowing blue. Would you be interested?" the man on the phone asked.

"Yes," Nicholas replied.

"Great," the man answered. "I have some people here I think you'd like to meet who are attempting to hire my services against you to recover a boy named Nicholas."

Nicholas's heart raced. "I'm aware of the situation. Who have you got there?"

"The sister and two friends, one normal, one blue."

"I'm listening," Nicholas said, barely able to contain himself as the man gave his terms and particulars, including an address that Nicholas had no need to take down. At the conclusion, he said, "The pleasure is mine, Mr. Luxley. Wait where you are, and no harm comes to them, understand? I look forward to meeting with you, personally. Good-bye." He cradled the phone and sat back down.

A few moments later, Deveraux reentered the office and asked, "Have you made your decision, son?"

"Yes sir, I have."

13

THE plan was simple. A three-hand touch, leaving the target scrambled and out of commission. The director of the CDC's Division for Human Quarantine, Richard Slater, was now a marked man.

Gavin handed out the envelopes to each of the team members sitting with him in the demilitarized Blackhawk helicopter. "We should be in Atlanta in less than five minutes," he said, his voice competing with the constant drone of the blades. All five were dressed in casual attire and standard CDC lab coats with photo IDs clipped to their collars.

Shoving the envelope into his back pocket, Nicholas counted his blessings that Roody and Deveraux were not along for the ride. Clearly, this mission was not the highest priority on the day's agenda. Mitchell had overheard that Deveraux's Alpha Team had fucked up royally in Moscow, and now dozens of people were dead or deprived as a result.

Nicholas had one focus now that he knew Cassie was safe, or relatively safe—to escape with Claudette.

As soon as the helicopter touched down, the team moved to a waiting limousine. Nicholas stretched out and listened in a detached way as the others bantered. Gavin and Mitchell were in it for the money, he decided. Still, Mitchell's sick streak was becoming more and more apparent. He told a story about blinding a woman in a subway once, just for kicks. Ahmet was here for vengeance's sake and out of desperation; he honestly had no place else to go.

The car pulled down Clifton Road and passed through the first security gate. "Things are very 'laxed here," Gavin explained. "They're not expecting the seeds of a pandemic."

Or an assassination attempt, Nicholas thought.

The car stopped. "Ahmet, Nicholas, you get out here. Enter the building there. Find an office marked 8A. It will be unlocked. Once secure, tear your envelopes."

Damn, Nicholas thought, *they're separating us!*

He got out of the car with Ahmet, and they walked casually away.

"Where will the others be going in?" Nicholas asked.

"Over on Executive Drive," he said. "The communications center."

As they entered the building, they continued their conversation and barely acknowledged the presence of the Marine who was standing guard, rifle slung, as they passed.

"See, that's how you do that," Ahmet whispered. "Confident is invisible."

Three corridors later, they arrived at the office marked 8A, Director Slater's office, and found it unlocked. It was tidy, with an absence of personal items, save for a single photo in a mahogany frame on the desk. Slater with his wife and three children. Two girls and a boy. Ahmet turned the picture frame facedown on the desk and tore his envelope.

CLAUDETTE had her ID checked three times before she was admitted to the communications tower. According to her instructions she was to remove a file from a particular cabinet and then deliver it to a separate office within the same building. She went to the file cabinet, returning a smile to a man at a nearby desk, and then pulled open the drawer.

GAVIN was standing in a men's room in the west wing of the Executive Building trying to adjust the collar of a Marine uniform. The door was locked from the inside. The Marine he'd just stripped was sitting huddled on a toilet in the first stall, drool dribbling out of his mouth and a glazed look in his eyes. Gavin finally got the clasp hooked when he heard a loud pounding begin. The Marine, smacking his head against the wall in delirium. Gavin grabbed hold of the stall supports with both hands and kicked the guard into unconsciousness. He tore his second envelope, read the instructions, and laughed to himself. He slid the Marine's side arm into the holster, shouldered his rifle, and locked the men's room behind him.

MITCHELL entered the small amphitheater and took a seat in the back—just one more white coat attending the closed session of the division heads. He nodded in false recognition to a few participants. A rough head count came to about sixty. Mitchell felt nothing but disdain for these scientists and policy makers. Wealthy men who'd gone to the best schools and led privileged lives. The fact that each of them was a Normal, able to touch and be touched, would have been enough to make him loathe them all. Now, these balding idiots thought they were going to decide the fate of Mitchell and every single Depriver out there. Mitchell was the bomb in the building, waiting to go off.

NICHOLAS and Ahmet were instructed to wait in the office. Director Slater would either return there before the closed session began on his own initiative or be summoned just prior to his speech by an emergency phone call.

"Did you ever consider that taking out Slater could actually hurt our cause?" Nicholas asked.

"No, to hell with all the Normals. This is war."

"Yeah," Nicholas said, reaching a decision. "I suppose it is." He reached out quickly, and a shower of blue sparks flew as he touched Ahmet's hand. Ahmet jerked away reflexively, overwhelmed by confusion, and knew it was already too late. He looked up at Nicholas with murder in his eyes.

"You've deprived us both, you son of a bitch!" Ahmet cried, taking a pointed letter opener off the desk.

Nicholas lost his balance, stepping backward as his ears popped; and his throat swelled. All sound was lost to him. Deaf, for less than an hour, he knew—*But man, it came on fast!* He held up his hands with the intention of pleading, but no more than a gurgle escaped his lips. Deaf and mute, he realized. *Two minutes, dear God, I need two minutes!*

Ahmet rushed him, caught hold of his shoulder, and jabbed the opener toward Nicholas's head. Nicholas kicked Ahmet hard in the groin and twisted away. He moved behind the desk and reached up to touch his face—his hand came back bloody. Ahmet came around the desk, and Nicholas scrambled to keep it between them, sending a chair sprawling backward and seeing it crash soundlessly into the wall.

Ahmet started hurling things at him from the desk. Nicholas dodged several trays but was struck hard in the stomach with a paperweight. It knocked the wind out of him. Ahmet jumped on top of the desk and flew down, landing them both hard on the floor. Nicholas almost blacked out. Ahmet got his hands on Nicholas's throat and began to squeeze. Nicholas got a knee up against Ahmet's chest and with every ounce of his strength he managed to force himself free. Suddenly, finally, Ahmet's world suddenly went dark.

Nicholas rolled out of harm's way and got to his feet. Ahmet got sightlessly up and tried to listen for Nicholas, craning from side to side in desperation. That's when Nicholas closed in and hit him with the chair.

MITCHELL sat agitated in the audience, listening to the associate director of minority health going on about the dangers of a vaccine-resistant tuberculosis outbreak in Tierra del Fuego, and its potential for reaching the U.S.

He looked over at Director Slater's smug face patiently waiting his turn to reveal the existence of Sensory Deprivation Syndrome—and he secretly hoped that Deveraux's plan would get botched. If the plan worked, Slater would leave the meeting, and brat boy would get to deprive him. If something went wrong, however, the director would become Mitchell's target. And Mitchell had been authorized to blind every bastard in this building to get to Slater.

Claudette found what she was looking for, a file contain-
ing backup copies of every incoming fax for the month of
August. She scanned the dates and pulled one out. A com-
muniqué from a CDC lab in Nebraska, where doctors had
extensively tested nearly four dozen patients, all of them
suffering from blindness or deafness of unknown etiology.
A fax that was not received by its intended recipient,
Director Orwell, of the Office for Genomics and Disease
Prevention. Instead, it had been intentionally misrouted to
Slater at the Division of Quarantine.

She read the last line of the report: "These unexplained
symptoms are not communicable." She closed the report
and walked out of the communications department with it
under her arm.

NICHOLAS adjusted Ahmet's binding and gag and
then locked him in Slater's closet. He went to the private
bathroom and washed the blood off his face and hands.
The cut was not too deep and had pretty much stopped
bleeding.

GAVIN stepped up to the guard post down the corridor
from Slater's office and tapped the guard on the shoulder.
"You're late," the Marine said, perturbed.

"Bathroom troubles," Gavin shrugged.

The Marine slung his weapon, gave a weak salute, and
turned his post over to Gavin.

CLAUDETTE stepped into Director Orwell's office and
handed the file to the man's secretary. "This is classified, for

Director Orwell's attention only," was all that she said before turning and leaving the room.

MITCHELL sat on the edge of his seat, watching Slater shuffle his papers together. The speaker at the podium made his closing remarks. Slater pushed back his chair, coughed into his fist, and prepared to rise. Mitchell mirrored him. This was it. Something had gone wrong. Slater was his. . . .

And then Slater reached for his phone, turned away from the table, and began speaking. *Damn,* Mitchell thought to himself.

NICHOLAS stood, ear to the door for a time, and then eventually gave up. He stuck his fingers in his ears and gave them a firm toggle. Nothing. He hoped the deprivation would subside before Slater arrived. Without the ability to hear or speak, he was going to have a hard time warning the man. He settled on writing the director a note. He sat at the desk and wrote: "Dear Director Slater, you're in grave danger and should leave immediately! A quarantine on SDS carriers is not necessary. I can provide information that—"

The door opened without warning, and Slater stepped inside, stopping short when he saw Nicholas. "Who are you?" he asked. "And how the hell did you get in to my office?"

Nicholas tried to speak to Slater, his mouth contorting, producing only a gurgle. He held the note out. Slater stepped forward to take it, asking, "What's the matter, can't you speak?"

Nicholas shook his head, having never felt more frustrated in his life.

Slater took the paper and read it. "You're an SDS carrier?"

Nicholas nodded.

"Why are you here?"

Nicholas took the paper back carefully and started to write, just as Slater's door opened and a Marine sentry entered, gun drawn. "Sir," Gavin said, stepping close to Slater. "We have reason to believe there are intruders in this building."

Nicholas went for Gavin just as he palmed Slater across the face with an accompaniment of sparks. Slater fell backward, clutching his head. Gavin tried to struggle away from Nicholas, defensively lashing out at his hands with the barrel of the gun. Nicholas swung wild and connected with Gavin's face. He made two-finger contact. It was enough.

Nicholas fell to his knees, instantly feeling Gavin's deprivation. The room spun, buckled, and twisted. He couldn't hear. He couldn't think. His world was utterly scrambled.

"You fuck!" Gavin yelled. He kicked Nicholas hard in the stomach, sent him sprawling, and brought up the gun.

Claudette's voice boomed, "No, Gavin! Put the gun down. You fire that in here, and we'll all end up in custody!"

Gavin turned to see her standing by Mitchell's side. "He deprived me! I'm gonna go fucking blind—*forever!*"

She walked up to Gavin, grabbed him hard by the wrist, and took the gun. "I don't care if he pulled your beating heart out of your chest. I know you had orders to kill him. Now get to the car. You've still got time before it kicks in. Go—or I'll leave you here. Go now!"

Gavin obeyed despite himself and left the room running.

"Any dissent from you, Mitchell?"

"No, ma'am," he said.

"Good. Check the closet," she ordered.

Mitchell went to Slater's closet and carefully helped Ahmet out. "He's a mess," Mitchell said.

"He's still useful," Claudette said, helping Nicholas to his feet and slinging his arm around her shoulder. "Come on, baby," she whispered. Nicholas was too delirious to understand what was happening. He wanted to push away from her, to protest the fact that she was touching him in front of the others, but he still had no voice.

Claudette called back to Mitchell, "Wait until I'm out of the room. Deprive Slater and then take Ahmet to the car."

"Yes, ma'am," Mitchell said.

She helped Nicholas into the corridor, and soon he was walking again on his own. None of this made any sense to him. It seemed as if she was giving out orders, and the others were following them without question. . . .

He pulled her to a stop and raised his head to meet her eyes.

She moved in close and kissed him, stroking his face, her red aura vibrating. Suddenly, Ahmet's deprivation subsided, and he realized that an alarm was sounding throughout the building.

"I won't let them hurt you, I promise," she whispered. "Come on now, we've got to get back to the car!"

Nicholas shook his head, fighting to shake off the remaining deprivation. "No, we've got to escape now, on our own, Claudette! We can't let Deveraux find out the truth about you. My God, he'll use you as a bargaining tool—claim you as the key to a cure. You have no idea how important you are—"

"Believe me, Nicholas, I do know," she said, taking his arm and leading him toward the exit. "And as for my bastard of a father, he's well aware of what I can do."

THE boy awoke on a bed in a motel room in a truck stop in Atlanta, Georgia. He could hear, but sounds were weak, distorted. He could think, but his thoughts were all mixed up, and it was hard to concentrate. Someone had slipped a pair of thin, black gloves on his hands. He sat up on the bed and leaned against the wall, trying to get his bearings.

The last things he remembered were hazy. Claudette helping him into the front seat of the limousine. Gavin and Ahmet, both blind by his hand, screaming threats from the rear of the car. Mitchell laughing. Bits of tense telephone conversations. Claudette leaving him for a time, and Gavin's deprivation slipping back and stripping the world away.

He discovered a handwritten note in his back pocket.

My dear Nicholas,

I leave you here as a token of good faith between your people and mine. I sincerely hope your deprivation wears off. If you're reading this yourself, it did. Nicholas, I do think I love you, but my first loyalty is to my father's cause. Not just because he's my father but because the atrocities I've seen with my own eyes have convinced me he's right. You saved my life back at the hospital, that was real, and that's something I can never repay and will never forget. You did that out of love. How could I not love you back? Letting you go is the very least that I can do. Please forgive my deceptions. We played you from the start— but these are desperate times. And never doubt that what we shared was real. Someday, if the world turns upside down and Deprivers really are hunted and herded into camps, we will welcome you back to our ranks. All of you. Until then, you keep trying to keep other Deprivers safe. I'll miss you terribly. Just thinking about your idealism and your gentle soul makes me want to cry. You touched me, in so many ways, and I swear I will never forget you.

Love, Claudette

*PS: We lied to you when we said we had Cassandra. We
don't. I hope you find her.*

Nicholas folded the note back into his pocket, took a
deep breath, and stood up on shaky legs. He needed to get
home fast. He feared he would find his life drastically
changed by the time he got back to it.

14

I think I was the only one who actually liked Robert Luxley. I mean, Cassandra liked to make jokes with him, but you could always hear a note of contempt in her words when they spoke. She put him on my path when she asked me to sight him. Our mutual exchange of deprivations left us just shy of blood brothers as far as I was concerned.

Terry was fascinated by him, mostly for love of the twisted adolescence that he, like most of us, had spent. But there was something else going on there. You could feel it.

"Careful, Sparrow," she whispered when we were alone. "Keep in mind what he does for a living."

I guess I liked him because he was true to his form. Like the rattlesnake that I felt was his totem in the spirit world, I figured he could eventually turn and bite, but I enjoyed him while I could—his dry humor, his wild tales, his rich tastes—all the while listening with an open ear for his rattle.

I think he liked me too at least he'd said that he did more than once. And we shared the common view that our

Depriver abilities were benefits, not prison terms. Most Deprivers had the phrase "Don't touch me" ingrained in them so deeply that it had achieved reflex status. Not so for Robert, or for me; we welcomed any opportunity to make physical contact. My people call what we can do "gifts," but my friends don't share that view. I have to cut them some slack though, since the duration of my deprivation is only a few hours, and most people can handle deafness for a few hours just fine. And Rob's duration is only fifteen minutes or so. If he doesn't kill you while you're paralyzed, you come out just fine. Most Deprivers screw you up for a lot longer. So in relation to our own little world of untouchables, Robert and I are both practically Normals.

We had just sat down—Cassandra, Terry, Robert, and me—to the Chinese food we'd ordered in. Robert said something like, "After dinner let's review our equipment list," to which everyone agreed. The equipment list was everything Robert felt we'd need when we went to rescue Nicholas.

From our own surveillance sources, we were pretty sure that Nicholas was being held in a maximum-security facility in Dade County, Florida. It was never really a question of how we would find him really—just how we would get past the bad guys to get him out alive. That's why Cassie felt we needed Robert. This was his type of game, his profession, and his touch was perfect. He was gifted not only in planning for quiet, nonconfrontational episodes, but also in using his intuition for improvisation. I watched as thoughts rolled around in his head. I watched his eyes. His cleverness would be to our advantage. Of course, we knew we ran a high risk of being captured ourselves. In all reality, Deveraux would probably have welcomed our attempt as an opportunity to snare us all. But we had no choice but to try, or be lost in the trying.

We were discussing when we should leave. Cassandra thought we should fly down first thing in the morning. It was then that Robert proposed a new point of attack. "What if," he began, "I contacted Deveraux openly, gave my credentials. Set up a meeting?"

"Posed as a recruit, you mean?" Theresa asked.

"Yes," he said.

We paused at that, and I saw Cassandra looked doubtful.

"I think I could get in there easily under that pretense, then find Nicholas," he added.

Needless to say, it was a bit of a shock when Nicholas kicked in the back door.

He rushed to the table, overturning it and sending all the food to the floor. He pulled Robert from his chair and slammed him hard up against the nearest wall. "Who the fuck do you think you are!" Nicholas shouted, "To come here and jeopardize the life of my family!"

We all stood dumbfounded as Robert stayed silent, a look of desperation in his eyes. I knew that look. Robert was fighting his reflex to reach out and touch Nicholas, fearful of the reverse damage it might cause. Nicholas seemed to recognize it too. He slid the index finger of his gloved left hand into his mouth, bit the tip, and pulled his hand free in one quick motion. He held his bare hand, fingers splayed, only centimeters from Robert's face and yelled, "Give me a reason not to blind you forever, you son of a bitch!"

"Nicky!" Cassandra said, confused but in control, from across the room. She had left the table and returned, holding her dad's .38 with both hands. "What's going on? Tell us before you deprive him. Please, Nicky!"

Nicholas pulled his hand back, but only an inch or so. Theresa had backed herself into a corner, as far away from the scuffle as possible. I still had not moved from my chair, although I'd been pretty much covered with noodles and peanut sauce when the table had flown. Nicholas slammed Robert against the wall again with his gloved hand and dropped him back into his seat.

"Tell them what you did, *Mr. Luxley,*" he said.

Robert cleared his throat. "I called Deveraux," he said, "and I named my price for delivering all of you to him."

I cursed myself for not having heard the rattle.

Cassandra bit her lip and scowled, cocked the hammer back on the gun. Terry's voice cracked as she said, "You stole the number from my phone book, didn't you?"

"But guess who answered the phone?" Nicholas asked.

"It was you. It was your voice," Robert said.

"Correct," Nicholas said. "And now you pay with your sight."

Robert rubbed the back of his head and came back with a brush of blood on his fingertips. "I thought you told me your brother was a shy, gentle person who abhorred deprivation," he said to Cassandra.

"Shut the fuck up," she said. "Your contributions, as well as your commentary—are no longer required." Then to her brother, "Nicky, how did you—?"

"I'll explain it all later," he said. "We've got a lot to do. Not just because of *him.*"

Then Nicholas forced his hand into each of Robert's pockets in turn, removing and reviewing all contents. "Is this the phone you called on?" Nicholas asked, displaying the sleek chrome-plated device. Robert nodded affirmative, and Nicholas cracked it in half against the arm of his chair.

That's when I asked, "Nicholas, are we safe here?"

He looked at me warmly. "Yeah, Sparrow. For the moment, we're still safe here. How are you?"

"Well, besides being covered with food, I'm quite okay, thanks," I said. "Welcome home."

Nicholas stepped to Cassandra and grabbed her up in his arms. She must have kissed him ten times. They're lucky, those two. They've always known it was safe to touch each other. I admit that it always made me a little bit jealous.

I kept an eye on Robert. He just sat there, frozen, looking defeated, but I already knew him better—he was considering his next move. "I think we should put him in the tank," I said. "Until we decide what to do with him."

Robert offered no resistance. Nicholas and I took him downstairs to the basement at gunpoint, made him strip, and turned on the tank. I showed him how to enter the hatch properly and assured him that he would float.

"Use your time in there constructively," I said, just before I closed the lid. "Eventually, everyone needs friends. Maybe you should choose yours sooner, instead of later."

Robert nodded, and I locked him into the sense dep tank.

For the rest of the evening, Nicholas held Cassandra's hand and told us all about his time with Deveraux. He explained the hard-line position Deveraux and his people had taken and admitted that some of Deveraux's politics were beyond argument. He told us about his mission, and the specialties of the other Deprivers he'd worked with. I got the feeling that he skipped a few details when he talked about Deveraux's daughter, Claudette. He told us about the Mandatory Registration Act, and we cringed collectively at the government's plan for the use of gloves to be mandated by law. He confirmed that the future we dreaded, the time when the whole world would wake up and know we exist, had arrived.

As soon as we were up to date, we decided that Nicholas

needed to contact the underground. The news that the CDC was about to leak misleading information regarding our condition, under the direction of someone as obviously fascist as Governor Tyrsdale, was something every Depriver needed to know.

So Nicholas made the call and spoke with a man named Gerrit. Cassandra must have smoked at least half a pack of cigarettes while they talked. After a tense twenty minutes, Nicholas hung up and turned back to us with, "It's started. Pack your bags. First thing tomorrow, we're flying to Amsterdam."

15

CONSCIOUS dreaming, that's what it starts to feel like after several hours. Your body is fully relaxed, and your mind is fully alert. At first you're just floating there, afraid you'll sink, but then you realize the water is too buoyant, and you understand, and finally you let go. It's too dark to see even your own hands. There is no sound, save that of your own breath, which eventually calms and fades and becomes indistinguishable. As the water temperature builds to match your body heat, there comes a time where you no longer recognize the parameters of your own form. You ask yourself, *Where are my legs? Is that the wall of the tank? Have I changed my position?* After several hours, you're detached far enough from your senses that real exploration is possible. I always think of floating as an opportunity to shrug off the world and take control of my future—and I hoped Robert would come out with some newfound awareness. He had nothing in there but himself all night, down in that dark, soothing water, where even passing time itself gets lost.

The house seemed at peace as I got out of my hammock and touched the wooden floor. I pulled on my shirt, tied my hair back with a bandanna, and went to Nicholas's room. He was already up. "Morning, Sparrow," he said, "Sleep well?"

"Like a cat," I told him. "Nice to sleep in your own bed?"

"Beats the shit out of the room they kept me in," he said. "But I kinda miss the girl next door."

"Deveraux's daughter?"

"Claudette," he said, half-smiling. "I'll tell you all about her sometime. What do you think we should do with Luxley? He must be a prune by now."

"I think he deserves to know what's happening; it's going to affect him as much as any of us. But I'll leave it up to you."

Nicholas picked up his father's gun. "I guess I can't take this with us on the plane, huh?"

"Guess not."

"All right," Nicholas said. "I'll go have a talk with him. He can join Deveraux if he wants, I'll give him directions. I don't suppose he'd try to hurt any of us, now that he knows there's nothing in it for him."

Nicholas put the gun in the nightstand drawer.

When Nicholas and Robert came upstairs a while later, Robert had toweled off and dressed. It was clear that some agreement had already passed between them.

"Good morning all," Luxley said, with some of the pleasant snobbishness back in his voice.

Terry pushed her glasses up on her head. "Good morning. Sleep well?"

"Yes," he said, skirting a potential confrontation. He could tell she was still miffed about his earlier deception. "I've never felt so refreshed in my life. After a pause he said, "Look, I know that none of you trust me at this point, and who could blame you? I also realize now that we're all in the same boat. In all reality, I may hire on with Mr. Deveraux—he's buying what I sell—but Nicholas has convinced me that this is not the immediate issue. I'm quite concerned about the world finding out about what I do. So, I'd like to come with you, if you'll allow it. I have nothing to gain from doing any of you harm. And Nicholas has kindly promised to have me deprived of every sense imaginable if I so much as walk when he says run. I sincerely hope you'll have me."

"Who the hell taught you to talk like that?" Cassandra asked.

"Parochial school," Robert said.

"Grab some couch," Nicholas directed. "We need to put it to a vote."

While Robert sat alone in the living room watching television, the rest of us stepped outside on the porch. "What do you think?" Nicholas asked.

"I think we should give him a second chance," I said. "It's not like half the Deprivers we've brought in weren't hostile and dangerous to begin with."

Terry shrugged. "I have to agree. If we start picking out who's worthy and who isn't, we're no better than our worst fears of government intervention."

"Are you two bleeding hearts brain-dead?" Cassandra asked. "I mean, dick head in there was about to sell us out. I think we should triple dip him and leave him in front of the police station."

We all turned to Nicholas for the deciding vote. He was our group's leader, after all. "Sometimes it's better to have the bad guy on your team," he said after a time. "Don't you prefer keeping an eye on him to wondering what else he's getting into? Besides, it's not like Cassie and I can't overpower him, right?"

Cassandra controlled herself out of adoration for Nicholas, but I could tell that she wanted to object. "You brought him in for a reason, Cassie," he said. "He's muscle in a pinch." When she didn't respond, he added, "C'mon, I've got some good ideas for getting use out of him. We'll keep him on a short leash, okay?"

It was then that Robert poked his head outside and said, "I think you all need to see this."

We followed him back inside, and Nicholas took one look at the screen and said, "Shit, it's gone public."

It was on the news, the latest of those breaking bulletins we'd grown so used to. That famous newscaster, what's-his-name, announced, "Scientific controversy regarding the mysterious blinding of a court officer . . ." The video clip behind him depicted a very crowded courtroom. "The accused is a fifty-five-year-old man named Duncan Cameron, who is standing trial in a New York City court for allegedly blinding a younger man with a concealed weapon, earlier this week," the newscaster said. "Now watch closely, as we review this exclusive footage, shot within the courthouse, this past Monday afternoon."

Cameron was a thin, gray-haired man, struggling impotently while three court officers held his arms. His hands were gloved. "I'm innocent! I did not intend for this to happen!" he screamed up at the judge.

"Control the defendant," the judge ordered.

Then one of the officers placed his bare right hand directly upon Cameron's mouth in an attempt to silence him. "Oh, my God! I can't see. I can't see!" The officer crumpled to the floor in front of the jury box, hands clutched to his face.

Theresa caught her breath. Nicholas looked pensive; he'd seen it before. Robert was thinking a mile a minute. I heard Cassandra whisper, "Shit," beneath her breath. I was just completely dumbstruck.

The newscaster's final commentary: "The question on everyone's mind, from those who were there when the shocking event occurred, to those who are watching from home, being: How could a single touch, from a bare hand, cause a person to go blind?"

There was a dramatic pause for reflection before a new clip came up, the latest commotion from the Middle East. Nicholas muted the sound with the remote.

"Okay, now this feels real," Theresa said. "I think I need a drink."

"Where are my cigarettes?" Cassandra demanded.

"Hey, it's not like they're gonna figure this out all at once, right?" I said. "I mean, we know because we *know*. If the CDC gets involved, they could blame it on anything, really. It could be okay."

"You have to take me with you," Robert said finally. "I promise, I'm at your command."

Nicholas turned to Cassandra. "Fine," she said with a scowl, then stormed off to find her cigarettes.

Nicholas delivered his list of restrictions to Robert, who humbly agreed on each point. He grinned and concluded with, "Oh, and I forgot to mention—you'll be bankrolling our little adventure."

"First-class!" Cassandra yelled back from outside.

A brief pause from Robert, then, "Of course, least I could do."

Four hours later the five of us were seated in first-class on a nonstop KLM flight from Newark to Amsterdam. Robert and Terry sat together, and I sat alone in the row ahead of them, hoping for a hot girl to sit next to me. Cassandra and Nicholas were seated across the aisle, hand in hand. I sighed when I saw an old man with a cane go for the seat next to mine. Fortunately, he was conked out by the time we took off. It was my first time leaving America, and as I watched the coastline disappear I was filled with awe. I knew that when we returned, if we returned, things would be different. *We* would be different. The world would know about Deprivers, and the dominoes would start to tumble. People might shun us, hunt us, throw stones in the streets; lock us away, who knew?

Theresa continued interviewing Robert. She always looked so intense while she was counseling. She's got a gift for helping people. I know—she'd done a lot of good for me.

"Tell me about that girl you were seeing in college. What happened when you accidentally deprived her?" she asked. One of the things that Nicholas had demanded from Robert was that he make it up to each of us somehow. Answering Terry's questions and becoming a part of her research was how he would begin for her, a chore he now seemed more than willing to take on.

"She was paralyzed, of course," Robert replied. "Shocked. Confused. She urinated next to me on the couch in her dorm room and was quite embarrassed. I told her everything would be all right. . . ."

"You told her that you were responsible?" Terry asked.

"No," he shook his head. "I didn't."

"You let her believe her paralysis was brought on by natural causes?"

Robert nodded. He seemed very emotionally detached from his memory, which at first seemed bad to me, but I later decided it was actually a good thing. The past is dead. He rubbed his eyes. "I wasn't sure myself at that point, exactly how I'd developed my *special trick,* or what it meant. I was young. I was reasonably sure she'd come out of it. I blamed it on whatever we were drinking. I calmed her as best I could. I imagine she never drank again, which is probably not such a bad thing, eh?"

"You don't know? When was the last time you saw her?"

"About five minutes after the deprivation wore off and she could move again," he replied, "just before I left her dormitory."

A sad story yes, but a typical one, I thought. How many Deprivers could recount almost identical tales of their first intimate encounters, or their second, or their final one with a husband or wife or girlfriend who decided that love and friendship took a backseat to sound or taste or vision? Life for us could be so messed up. When it came to personal relationships, Depriver syndrome may as well have been leprosy. I was lucky. I'd had a few girlfriends who'd stuck around for a few months apiece. My deprivation was short-term enough that I could talk a Normal girl, or a Depriver girl with a short burn, into bed once in awhile. Few Deprivers could say as much.

Cassandra had confessed her virginity to me one drunken evening, along with a very detailed list of what she *would* do when she found someone who could accept the impairment she caused. Nicholas had been untouched as well, though I suspect something intimate might have happened with Claudette. As long-term Deprivers, their touch was much too damaging to risk. And they were both glowing since infancy. Add up all the pain and suffering they'd survived together, and you've got a tragic couple. A quiet remark in certain circles was that both of them should overcome society's conventions and take full solace in each other. Weird as it sounds, who could blame them if they did?

"Okay," I heard Robert say. "It's your turn now."

"My turn?" Terry asked.

"Yes, isn't that how it works? I just told you something personal. Now *you* should ante up."

I didn't have to look back through the seats to know Terry was blushing, it was obvious in her voice, and so out of character for her when she said, "You show me yours, I show you mine?"

"Something like that," Robert said.

"Umh, that's not how therapy generally works," she said.

"Hey," Robert said, "we've got six more hours to kill. Tell me something about you. Something personal. Let's have a little doctor-patient transference."

She actually giggled then, and I thought, oh man, this could be good.

"What would you like to know?" she asked.

"Let's go back to how you got involved in this. I'm truly interested."

"All right. It's actually sort of interesting to tell the story to someone who knows the truth about the people involved—I'm so used to hiding the details from other doctors."

"That's quite understandable, Ms. Godfrey, please begin and don't hold back."

I had to laugh at Robert's vain attempt at humor. He was playing the good doctor in more ways than one.

"I was working as a therapist in the D.C. area," she said,

"counseling children, most of them living in foster homes or halfway houses, many of them abused, physically or sexually. Children teetering on the verge of emotional collapse." Then she stopped for a moment. Robert must have looked upset. "I'm sorry, is this too troubling a story? I guess it's not a subject for anecdotal conversation."

"No, no," Robert said, placing a gloved hand on hers. "Please, go on."

"Okay, well, I had a really good track record of breaking through the barriers that children build, especially in cases where one or both parents had died. I wrote several published articles on the subject and one result was a rather strange invitation from a reclusive industrialist named Arthur Wilkes."

"Nicholas and Cassandra's father?" Robert asked.

"No, their uncle, who had recently become their legal guardian, following the death of both their parents. Parenting was not exactly his strong point," she said. "And as you can imagine, these ten-year-olds had some pretty hefty trust and abandonment issues. I'll never forget the first time I saw them. A little blonde-haired girl in jeans and a pink blouse, hanging upside down off a jungle gym, and her twin brother, dressed in combat fatigues, demanding she be careful."

Robert nodded. "How did the parents die, if I may ask?"

"It was a terrible car accident," she said. "Both dead on impact. The children were both injured."

"You're saying they were actually *in the car* when the parents died?"

"Yes," she said. "Cassandra doesn't remember the accident, but Nicholas has conscious memory of everything that happened. He saw them die. With the amount of guilt he was already carrying around regarding his mother's condition, I think you get a pretty good picture of—"

"What condition?" Robert asked.

When Terry hesitated, I closed my eyes, recalling my own images of the once lively and beautiful Mrs. Wilkes.

"For some reason I thought you knew," Theresa said after a pause, "that their mother went blind during childbirth."

"No, I didn't," Robert said. "But I guess that explains a lot about Nicholas. He must have been devastated."

"They both were, though Cassandra dealt with it much better at first. Talking through her odd issues of self-isolation, her fears of adult persecution, already sarcastic as hell. She sculpted back then, brought her frustrations out through the clay—she's quite good you know. Nicky, on the other hand, was a very angry young man when I arrived on their doorstep. Slamming doors and demanding I leave. And for the first few days I was of course confounded by their mysterious repeated demands that I not touch either of them, ever. Even at that age, Nicholas had amassed more medical knowledge, from his father's library, than I had, and he assured me I would never be able to fully comprehend their problems, much less solve them. To be honest, I thought I was in over my head."

"Rough case you stumbled into for sure. But something made you stay. Somehow you discovered what you were really dealing with, right?"

"Of course," Theresa said. "I was too stubborn to leave, and I relentlessly dug at them both for the truth. And learning what I did, and the way it touched my life, meant I signed on for the duration."

"That still doesn't tell me what sense—" Robert stopped talking when I turned and glared at him over the seat back. He dropped it down to a whisper, "What sense you were deprived of and by whom?"

Theresa leaned in close to whisper back, "That's still none of your business, Mr. Luxley."

16

THE plane touched down at Schiphol Airport, and we were the first ones off in an attempt to avoid the crowding and groping of the other passengers. A sandy-haired man with gray gloves was standing at the gate. Tall, like almost seven feet, no kidding, with ruddy cheeks, a broad smile, and a glowing complexion. Gerrit, of course. We made introductions all around and, as promised, gave an alias for Robert. For this trip he was Corbert Huxley. We grabbed our bags and loaded into a van that was parked outside in the handicapped section, motor running.

"Everything is being arranged," Gerrit told us. "And I booked you adjoining suites at the Hotel Van Blau. They'll be under the credit card number you provided, Corbert."

From the window, as we drove, I saw acres of green farmland, slowly giving way to patches of cityscape. In the distance, windmills turned slowly. Amsterdam, the most liberal city in the world. Everywhere bricks and steeples and canals and people riding bicycles. Coolsville.

"How much attention is the Duncan Cameron case getting here?" Nicholas asked.

"It's getting worldwide coverage," Geritt told us, "but no one has stepped forward with any explanation—not yet."

We arrived at the Hotel Van Blau and took our bags in. Robert signed one of those names that was his, but certainly not his own, on the registry, and we went up to antique-filled rooms. The guys in one and the girls in the other, with an adjoining door between them. Gerrit told us that because of Nicholas's call, there were more Deprivers gathering in the coming days than had ever assembled anywhere. Conferences regarding press strategy had already begun—but we'd have the night to get adjusted. He recommended a restaurant a few blocks away, gave us maps and a guidebook, and left, telling us he would phone in the morning.

I sat on the bed with the guidebook, and Nicholas stood looking out at the magnificent view of the city, skylined with churches and ancient monoliths.

"It says there are over three thousand cafés in Amsterdam," I read aloud.

"I could use a cup of coffee," Nicholas replied.

"It says that a coffeehouse is a place to drink coffee, but not to be confused with a coffeeshop which is actually a place to purchase tolerated soft drugs like marijuana and hashish. Oh man, all right! Hey Cassie, pot is really legal here!" I called.

"Duh," Cassandra said, coming out of the bathroom toweling her face. "That's what the Dutch are known for—their tolerance. Prostitution and euthanasia are legal here too." She lit a cigarette and offered me one. I think everyone had one, though Nicholas and Terry don't really smoke, and Robert hates them.

A little later the jet lag caught up with Terry, and it showed on her face. Robert seemed overly concerned. "Maybe you should go lie down," he said.

"We'll bring you back some food," Nicholas told her. "C'mon Robert, dinner's on you."

"That's fine," Robert said, pulling out his money clip and passing us a wad of Euros. "But I think I'd like to stick around too, if Terry doesn't mind the company."

"No," Terry said, "I mean, no I don't mind."

The three of us stepped into the warm evening scuttle of Amsterdam foot traffic. The rhythm of the city was very different from that of New York—you could feel it immediately. We walked around giddy, stopping to stare in shop windows, cooing at buildings with stained glass, and forever sidestepping trolley cars and stoned tourists. Cassandra stepped into the street and barely avoided a collision with an ancient woman and two children, all riding on one bicycle. The woman cursed something in Dutch and Cassie yelled, "Sorry!"

We found the restaurant, on the edge of a canal, right where Gerrit said it would be. We had steaks on Robert. Coffee afterward was served in these tiny shot glasses, which our waiter explained was the norm throughout Europe. The beer was stronger here too, he warned.

"Do we keep going?" Cassandra asked, dragging a cigarette and putting her legs across my lap.

"To avoid the worst effects of jet lag, it's best to force yourself to stay awake until you are in phase with the time zone," I told her. "We should try to stay up a few more hours, at least until ten."

We passed several coffee*shops* and I longed to go in and sample their wares. We passed head shops and sex shops and street performers juggling fire. It seemed like every

building had a staircase that led down through some dark
passage to a secluded bar or disco. But we finally selected
one, a place called *Daan Weg,* and paid an entrance fee of
about fifty cents apiece.

The place was crowded, all young people, less than a
quarter of them over eighteen, I'd guess—my kind of
crowd. The music was house, and the beer was Grolsh. We
split up for a while, though Nicholas insisted that none of
us leave alone. I went out on the dance floor, half-drunk off
a single beer. A girl who was the epitome of Dutch—tall,
blonde hair with bangs, ruby cheeks, and broad hips—but
who actually turned out to be Swedish, started dancing
with me. I think she was tripping on ecstasy. I had to
maneuver to keep her from touching my bare hands. She
was fascinated with my hair.

"I've been told that all American Indians have huge
lils," she said. "And like to do it five times per day." She
winked one blue, bloodshot eye for emphasis. Man, I liked
Amsterdam already.

"I started that rumor," I told her. "Hey, what's good to
do here in town?"

"It's all good," she replied, and then danced back into
the crowd.

17

ROBERT sat on the edge of the bed, clinking the ice in his glass. "Go ahead, tell me about it. Tell me what was done to you."

Theresa let her head fall back against the chair. "You make it sound as if he committed a crime," she said.

"Maybe *he* did," Robert said. "As a criminal, I find myself particularly well suited to judge. What's his name?"

She slipped her shoes off, then stretched. The plane ride truly had taken a lot out of her. "Arthur Wilkes," she said. "And I don't see why I owe you this story."

"Because you cheated me before," Robert said. "You gave me a load of watered-down bullshit, and completely glossed over the ending. Arthur Wilkes? Come on, I know you can't share this with the others. But tell me."

"All right," she said after a pause. "But first I want a drink."

Robert dropped the cubes in glasses, then poured the scotch twice. "Shoot," he said, placing one down on the table beside her.

"I was going through a strange time in my life, but I was unaware how vulnerable I was. My career was going well, I was published, respected, quite successful. But I was lonely, my father was dying. I had no real evidence my intervention was helping any of the children I counseled. I was lost but hadn't admitted it to myself.

"So, on a whim, I responded to this strange request to fly up to Jersey and help this troubled man and these two unusual, orphaned children, at the request of a former professor from my university. I was offered a great deal of money, but that's not why I went."

Robert nodded. "You needed a change," he said. "Some adventure."

"And I got one," she said. "First-class airfare, a great house, expense account, chauffeured limousine rides to Manhattan each day to deliver my reports."

"To their Uncle Arthur?"

"Yes."

"He didn't live with the children?"

"As I said earlier, he was not the fatherly type. He just made sure they had money and stayed out of sight."

Robert sipped his drink. "What was he like? Describe him."

"Arthur Wilkes was a very put together, powerful man— about forty-five back then. The first time I met him, after hours at his company, he had his shoes off, necktie slung over his shoulder, five o'clock shadow, and his hair was sticking straight up. I remember I had the strangest urge to comb it back down for him."

"You were attracted to him," Robert said.

"At the time," she said.

"You didn't think he seemed unusual?" he asked.

"Other than the fact he wore leather driving gloves

when we shook hands, no, not then. I guess from his absence in the children's lives I had envisioned him a beast. But quite the contrary, I found him rather charming at first."

"And what did you report to him?"

"The psychological condition of his niece and nephew. That I found them exceptional with an accompaniment of unusual problems. Not the least of which was their adult-like cynicism, their refusal to be touched or to play with other children, and their unlikely fascination and expertise with firearms."

Robert grimaced at the description of the children, how little they'd apparently changed. He took another sip and leaned back on his elbows. "I take it he was not surprised by anything you told him."

"Of course not, he knew exactly what they were," Theresa said.

"Because he was also one of us?"

"Yes," she said. "Though I didn't understand these things yet."

"When did he first touch you?" Robert asked.

She squirmed a bit; he was probing too deep too fast. "On that first meeting, now that I think of it," she said. "He thanked me for agreeing to work with the children, that he could see I truly cared for them, and then he kissed my cheek. It wasn't until later that evening, when I was checking in on Cassandra, that I began to feel strange."

"Strange how?"

"Well," she began, "It felt sort of like . . . being very much awake. But awake in a different way. It's hard to explain," she said, turning and smiling. He could tell that the drink was beginning to affect her; she had dropped her defense.

"Please do try," Robert said.

"Okay, I'm trying. I really am. By the time I got back to the house, I'd developed the worst migraine ever. Walking upstairs, I experienced my first round of vertigo."

Robert nodded.

"So I went to check on Nicky, and his door was locked. When I went to Cassandra's bedroom, and observed her sleeping, guess what I saw?"

"A blue prismatic halo?"

"Yes, which I of course chalked up to my hypoglycemia. As I stood there in her doorway, the pain subsided, leaving me relieved but confused."

"Why confused?"

"Because I was feeling all of these intense, foreign emotions. I felt intensely scared, trapped, and claustrophobic. I had a rush of suicidal thoughts. I experienced a terrible loneliness that was stronger than I had ever experienced. Then I managed to shake it off and went to bed. It's amazing how the human mind can so easily dismiss the incredible."

"It was somehow part of your deprivation," Robert said.

"Yes," she said. "But it wasn't quite revealed yet; you see, it required a stronger dose to take full effect."

"A stronger *dose?*" Robert asked.

"Um . . . yes," she said. "You've got to understand, from that point on, all the things that I felt were tremendously heightened emotional experiences. Which led to the Nicholas incident."

"You said that you couldn't get through to him at first."

"Right. He was suppressing his anger to a destructive level. He refused to let me in. He would curse, scream, smash things. The only reason he allowed me to stay was for Cassie. In sessions, he'd reveal *her* problems to me, but he refused to unburden himself. So I changed my strategy to getting each twin to talk about the other, and it became pretty clear that even if they were holding back some grave secret, they understood the root of each other's problems."

"In my profession we call that playing both sides against the middle," Robert said.

Theresa nodded. "And right in the middle I was," she said. "It was during an outburst between them, when Nicholas had insisted I pack my bags, and Cassandra had begged him to let me stay. . . . I tried to intervene, and Nicholas got right up in my face and started shouting that I didn't really care about them, that I'd be gone when I got what I wanted, that I had no idea what the hell I was talking about or how to deal with it!

"So why don't you just *fucking tell me!*" Theresa called out, momentarily caught up in her own narrative. She'd had enough to drink, Robert decided.

Theresa reclined her head against the chair and sighed. "It wasn't my rage, it was his rage, you see?"

"I think so, but—"

A key in the door cut him off. Nicholas and the others were coming back.

"Boy-o-boy is this place cool," Sparrow said, rushing into the room. "You guys don't know how much fun you missed."

18

GERRIT'S wake-up call came much too early for a Sunday morning. I woke up with a hangover, still in yesterday's clothes. Nicholas was the first out of the shower, and Theresa poked her head in through the door that connected our suites to announce that room service was on its way up with coffee. Gerrit was sending a van for us. Cassandra keyed her way in while I was changing my clothes, looking as pert and awake as ever. "You won't believe this," she said, waving her cigarette. "They're friggin' everywhere."

"Who is?" Terry asked.

"Look out the window," she said, crossing to the curtains. We followed her and she pulled the drape lines, revealing the eight o'clock street traffic two floors below us. People were glowing. A lot of people. A gloved couple holding hands. A woman riding a bike. Two more on bikes. A guy on a motorcycle, his aura flashing out from his helmet like a headlight. Some Dep walking his dog.

"I counted seven Deprivers just now," Terry said.

"This place is Depriver central," Cassie said. "Gerrit told me we're all housed in the same district. The guy I bought my cigarettes from was a Dep, and sighted too. He smiled at me like we were both in the same friggin' fraternity."

"We're sure not invisible here," Robert said. "And that is not cool."

"Unbelievable," Nicholas said. "Who knew there could be so many?"

"Poor lonely bastards," Cassie offered as an afterthought, closing the curtains. "C'mon, move your asses. We've got a party to go to, and Nicky's guest of honor."

The same gray van was waiting curbside when we stumbled out of the hotel, but Gerrit wasn't driving. The gloved young woman who met us, twenty-something, with short, bleached hair, a nose ring, and dimples the size of dimes, introduced herself as Astrid.

"I'm Sparrow," I said. "This is Nicholas, Cassandra, Terry, and Corbert."

"My pleasure to meet you," she said.

"Does everybody here speak English?" Cassie asked her.

"Yah, just about," Astrid said. "We have to learn it in school from grade five. Are you ready to go?" Then she hesitated, noting Terry's lack of color. "*Umh,* I'm not sure she can come."

That shocked us all. It was the first case of reverse discrimination I'd ever seen.

"Terry's been helping people through this from the very beginning," Nicholas said, "and she goes where we go."

"Okay," Astrid said, "but I need to check." She went into the van and called someone on a cellular phone. She spoke for a moment or two and then, "It's okay, sorry about that." Relieved, we all piled into the car, and Astrid peeled out, maneuvering in and around the bicycles like a race car driver. "You're the first Dep-friendly Normal I've ever met," Astrid told Terry, "are you sighted?"

"Yes," Terry said.

Astrid peeked back at her in the rearview mirror. "You can see me?"

"Blue as the sky."

"Wow, *leuk!*"

"What is *leuk?*" I asked Astrid. "I keep hearing people say that word."

"*Leuk* is like, *umh,* cool—I like it. And I like that you Americans have Dep-friendly people who can see. It gives me hope in my heart."

"Where are you taking us?" Nicholas asked.

"We're going to our temporary processing center in a place called Diemen. It's about twenty minutes by car. We're assigning jobs for tomorrow and gathering contact information, trying to improve the network."

"Where will the press conference be held?" Nicholas asked.

"That's still up for discussion," she replied. "And won't be officially revealed until a few hours before it begins. Some feel it should be in The Hague, the legal seat of Holland and the World Tribunal. You know it? Others are pushing for somewhere that's highly recognized here in central Amsterdam."

We arrived at the ugliest warehouse ever imagined at the end of a dirt road in a very industrial section of Amsterdam. No charm there. We went in, passed two armed guards with automatic machine guns that were clipped with ammunition belts, the first I'd ever seen up close. I looked back at Robert and saw that he was impressed too.

The warehouse was chock-full of Deprivers. I mean, among the two hundred or so glowing faces I saw there, not one Normal could be found but Terry. Crazy.

Astrid led us to a row of tables. "You need to give your name and any contact information you want recorded at that first table. Choose whatever level of privacy you like, but remember we're the good guys. If you don't know how to set up fictitious E-mail accounts or nontraceable addresses, we'll show you. Nicholas, however, is requested for a meeting that's scheduled to begin as soon as I can get him upstairs."

Astrid led Nicholas away, and we stood around gaping. None of us had ever seen so many Deprivers. It was awe inspiring. In an instant I felt truly part of a greater community. We went to sign in. Terry's index card was marked non-Depriver in black marker and Robert's card read Corbert Huxley.

At the second table, I expected they would ask me that extremely personal question, "Which sense do you deprive?" but was surprised to be asked only for my "normal duration period."

"Six to eight hours," I told the man behind the table.

"Side effects?"

"None," I replied.

"Well then," he smiled. "You're one of the lucky ones, aren't you. Are you willing to help us sight the blind?"

"Yeah, sure," I said. "I often do just that."

"Then go to table five, please. *Bedankt.*"

Robert showed up at table five a few moments behind me. "That guy almost fell out of his chair when I told him my duration was only fifteen minutes," he said.

"You didn't happen to mention your profession, did you?" I asked.

"Uh, no."

"Good choice."

We both got assigned to "sight-provider" status and

were given vibro-pagers. "If your pager goes off," the woman behind the desk told us, "proceed to room sixteen, just up those stairs."

Cassandra and Terry found us a few moments later. "They're setting me up with my own office," Terry said. "I'm the new staff psychologist."

"Hang out a shingle," I said.

"And you?" Robert asked Cassandra.

"Floating assignment," Cass replied. "And they gave me a cell phone."

"*Leuk,*" I said.

"They said I had clearance to go upstairs and listen to the meeting."

"Can we come too?" I asked. Cassandra bit her lip, looked at Robert with a slight arch to her eyebrow, and then at Terry.

"How about I sneak just you in there, Sparrow. And give Robert and Terry some more time to talk."

We all agreed, and Cassandra and I headed upstairs. "You still don't trust him," I said.

"No. *Why?* Do you?"

I shrugged.

"Well don't, for all our sakes."

"Okay, okay," I said.

We came into the conference room and took seats in the back. Nicholas was at the point in his story where his Delta Team was arriving at the CDC in Atlanta, and he had his listeners on the edge of their seats.

"The idea was to silence Director Slater before he could reveal our existence to the rest of the CDC," Nicholas explained.

"But why?" asked a gray-haired woman at the far end of the table. "If Deveraux knew that our existence had already been compromised through Duncan Cameron, what good did it do to remove one director?"

"Something to do with how he would paint us," Nicholas said. "Deveraux never really trusted me, so the details he provided were sketchy."

"Director Slater, head of the CDC's Division of Human Quarantine, was one of Governor Tyrsdale's puppets," Gerrit offered, "and I'm sorry to inform everyone that our latest surveillance confirms that the CDC does indeed have Cameron in their custody. Living among Normals as we do, sooner or later, some Depriver was going to be discovered. But information is a whirling top—until someone stops it. From what Nicholas has told us, we know that Tyrsdale will reveal us in the harshest possible light. We can only speculate as to whether he orchestrated the Duncan Cameron incident. We believe his motives are either purely racist or at best, protectionist. He could have had Director Slater inform the heads of the CDC that Deprivers syndrome itself is contagious, or that all instances of deprivation are irreversible. He could have initiated a state of emergency or quarantine. I can't fault Deveraux for prompting his organization to delay the possibility of such false allegations."

Nicholas completed the tale that our group knew well but failed to mention Claudette, which I thought was odd. When he finished, he had a faraway look in his eyes. He left the table and came to sit by Cassandra and me, momentarily drawing more attention to us than I would have preferred.

Gerrit spoke again. "Thank you, Nicholas. Your ordeal may offer us a good enough head start to control a great deal of potential damage and better the quality of life for every Depriver."

Cassandra put her arm across her brother's shoulder as

the room gave a brief round of applause. The clapping trailed off, and Gerrit continued. "We've been racing to fill in one of the holes in the reconnaissance that Nicholas provided. May I direct your attention to the view screen."

A projection came up before us from what I guessed was a portable laptop. Pretty cool. It was a 3-D map of Russia, and we moved in closer and closer to the star in the center. "As Nicholas mentioned, rumor had it that one of Deveraux's field operations had gone sour in Russia." Demographics that I really didn't follow flashed across the screen, probably Dep-to-Normal ratios and stuff. "Moscow. One of the highest Depriver populations. We've learned that the Russian army formed a special operations division, strictly enlisting Deprivers, as early as five years ago."

A gasp ran through the room.

"They were way ahead of us, it seems," Gerrit offered. "Many things remain unclear, but we do know that the man pictured here, a colonel named Vladimir Postov, uncovered the existence of the division. Postov set his own division against the Dep division, which began a complex internal struggle. Somehow, Deveraux got his hands in there, and sent a team, we believe, to eliminate Postov. Our information leads us to believe that every Depriver involved—and several held highly visible government positions—was identified and shot. We fear a similar situation to the one we now face, one of uncontainable disclosure, may also be developing in Russia."

A quiet chill settled over the room. "Ladies and gentlemen. We know from past experience that the first raw scientific explanation the public hears is the one it will take to bed. It has to come from us. So with this in mind, I turn the floor over to Dr. Hauske. Doctor?"

I'd heard about this man, Hauske, from Nicholas. Like

Terry, he was a doctor that had stumbled upon our condition and opted for Dep-friendly status rather than blowing our cover. Now he was supposedly conducting research into a cure. He looked about forty, or so, with tufts of unkempt hair and those little round glasses. He wore a corduroy jacket with a mismatched tie and an antiseptic look on his face. He took the spotlight and began to speak in earnest, as if his time was a fast-burning fuse. "Good morning. My name is Dr. Warren Hauske. I'm a neurovirologist, a surgeon, and as I'm sure most of you can see, not a Depriver. I'm happy to be here and quite honored to represent you to the scientific community at large. At present, I have three major concerns regarding possible miscommunication to the general public. They are: falsehoods regarding the affliction's communicability and a potential call for quarantine, exaggerated projections of the Depriver to non-Depriver ratio, and legislation that regulates medical practice on both the Deprivers and the deprived."

He paused to take a sip of water, then fumbled with his notes. "I propose a live demonstration, which I will open up to discussion in just a few moments. . . ."

The pager in my pocket suddenly began to vibrate. I turned to Cassandra and whispered, "They're calling me. I've gotta go. Let me know everything that gets said, okay?"

19

I asked someone in the corridor to point me to room sixteen, and I got right over there. The door was open. Two people sat casually across from one another in an otherwise empty room. One was a blonde woman with a pensive look on her face and no aura. The other, a partially balding man in his mid-forties, had a tainted flush to his cheeks. Their conversation stopped when I walked in.

"Sparrow, is it? You don't happen to speak Dutch, do you?" the woman asked, pulling up a third chair for me.

"No, sorry, not a word," I said, taking the seat she offered.

"That's okay," she said, forcing a smile. "I'll translate for Mr. Kootstra. His English is very poor." The man eyed me suspiciously, to the point that I became uncomfortable.

"What happened to Corbert?" she asked.

"Corbert?"

"Your friend?"

"Oh yes. Corbert. Why?"

She screwed up her face. Her lipstick was way too red for her complexion. "We paged him several times, and he did not respond. He's listed his duration as fifteen minutes."

"It's true," I said. "I've tried it."

"He was my first choice," she said.

"Yeah, well, I'm here. What's Mr. Kootstra's deprivation?"

"Coordination," she answered, watching my face for a reaction.

That's new, I thought. "Never tried that one," I told her. "What's his duration?"

They spoke fast, heated Dutch for a moment, Kootstra nodding all the while. "A week to ten days," she finally answered.

Damn, I thought, *that's a lot to ask.* "How uncoordinated would I be?"

More Dutch. "He says you'll be able to walk fine, but you'll be a poor dancer. Driving is out. And don't bet any of your Euros on a game of darts. Hold on." They spoke some more. "He asks if you play any musical instruments?"

I shook my head.

"Sparrow, I know this is a burden, but Mr. Kootstra happens to be a high-born Dutch national. Your cooperation would be very, very much appreciated, by many, many people."

I weighed the possibilities. *Not permanent. Not too damaging. Got nothing else to do. I did volunteer for this.* "Okay," I said, then looked her straight in the eyes, "but I'm going to have to touch you first."

That changed the tone of the conversation considerably. "Excuse me?" she said. Kootstra seemed amused at her loss of composure.

"I've got a lot of experience with sighting people," I said, "and I know how my own deprivation works. If I

touch Mr. Kootstra, he's deaf for eight hours and I'm . . .
discombobulated for a week to ten days. But, if I touch you
first, you'll drain me out. You'll take my full charge. Then,
when I touch him, like a weak battery, it will considerably
shorten both our Deprivation times. In fact, I may be able
to block out his effects entirely."

The lipstick formed a perfect 0 but produced no sound.
"Your cooperation would be very, very much appreciated,
by many people," I said.

She frowned. She paced. She acquiesced. And then she
explained to Mr. Kootstra what was going to happen. He
chuckled. I suggested she make any telephone calls or
travel arrangements necessary for the rest of her day, before
we proceeded. She had a few somewhat heated telephone
conversations in Dutch on her cell phone. Then she was
ready.

The three of us sat there, a little circle full of nervous
anticipation. "Anything further you'd like to say to each
other before we get going?" I asked. A few words went
back and forth.

"Okay," I said. "I've been told that you'll experience
some intense cold flashes after I touch you. And then your
ears will suddenly pop. It's gonna happen pretty quick.
Enjoy it. It can be really nice. Just watch for cars and bikes,
if you go out on the street."

She relayed my instructions, and then I reached out and
let my hand hover atop hers. She closed her eyes, and I
could see her breathing was uneasy. I touched her hand. I
saw the blue sparks arc like an electric current from my fingers to her freckled skin. "Eight hours and you'll be fine,"
were the last things she heard me say.

She shook a few times. I turned to Mr. Kootstra, who had
paled considerably. I smiled at him. I reached out my hand.

He nervously extended his own in response. Contact. Our currents crossed, and the stream of electricity shot through me. We stopped touching. He rubbed at his hands, then reached up to touch his ears in wonderment. It's always a very intimate and unusual moment—when a Depriver receives his first deprivation. He smiled. He'd been waiting for this for a long time.

A tingling sensation made its way through the various stations of my body. Fingers, hands, arms, chest, head, and then straight down through my legs to my toes, like some magic dust being sprinkled all over me. I hadn't shut him out entirely. I'd been deprived as well. I realized that I'd forgotten to ask him how long it would take before his deprivation took full effect. I'd know soon enough. I got up from my chair and excused myself. I wanted to find Terry or Robert or Cassie before whatever happened, happened.

20

ALONE with Terry again, this time as if by design, Robert asked, "How do you feel about your new digs, Staff Psychologist?"

"Not Park Avenue, but no skid row either," she said, looking around the small office. Chair, couch, desk, the bare necessities. "I am just relieved to have my own space. There is so much going on out there," she said.

"I know, too many people around makes me edgy," Robert said, "Mind if I camp out? I'd like to hear the rest of your story."

"I hadn't meant to be so explicit with you last night. I have a right to tell you about my own life, but I stepped over the line, I think, with details about the family. I hope you will respect their privacy and keep these things to yourself," she said.

"Of course I will, but you have to talk to someone, Terry. These things happened to you too and I'd like to hear about them, as a friend."

"Okay," she said after a pause. Her mind wandered back. "After my shouting match with Nicholas, I felt like I had to get some distance from him, so I went to my room and showered. It sounds strange, but I felt like his anger was all over me."

"How was it part of your deprivation?"

"Well, it's funny that you mentioned doctor-patient transference when we were on the plane, because that's pretty much what was happening. I didn't understand yet, but when I got out of the shower, my cell phone rang. It was Arthur. He sounded desperate, angry. He said he was on his way over to see me, and he'd be there within the next ten minutes. When I hung up, I panicked."

"You panicked, why?" Robert asked.

"For some reason . . . with all the secrecy and the strangeness I'd witnessed in the children, and the state I was in, I was sure he was coming to kill me."

"To kill you?"

"Yes, I was honestly scared for my life. So much so, in fact, that I went downstairs, loaded their father's gun, and put it in my purse. I almost called 911, but I stopped myself, it seemed so irrational."

"And what happened when he arrived?"

"He looked awful, exhausted, extremely paranoid. He asked me to get into his car with him, and we drove a little ways down a dirt road. I had my hand on the gun in my bag when he killed the headlights and parked."

"And then . . ." Robert asked.

"Like I said, I thought he was about to kill me, maybe for finding out some horrendous family secret, who knows why. So I asked him, 'Why?' and he was confused, and made me tell him why I was so upset. When I confessed my fears, he laughed."

"He laughed?"

"Yes, then he apologized."

"Because he realized that your paranoia was his paranoia," Robert said.

Terry looked over at Robert, a faraway sadness in her eyes. "That's almost exactly what *he* said to me, that night," she said. "Just before he explained how this was all indirectly his fault. He said he needed to hold off for a moment on the explanation while I updated him on my progress with the children. As I told him about my difficulties with Nicholas, I kept my hand on the gun.

" 'Listen,' he said. 'This is going to sound alarming, but those children are in grave danger, as am I.' Then he told me their problem. Everything he knew regarding Deprivers syndrome. How he was a first-generation carrier, and they were the second. That they were unique in several ways, and that people from both the government and the pharmaceutical industries were literally hunting them. Of course, I was stunned, and when he explained it was transferred by touch, I recalled that he'd kissed me."

"On purpose," Robert said.

"Yes," she said, looking down. "And I called him on that, and he admitted he was trying to force my involvement and that it was selfish, but there was another, more subtle reason, regarding my deprivation. . . ."

"What?" Robert asked.

"I've spent a great deal of time researching my condition. Want to hear my hypothesis?"

"Please," Robert said.

"While Nicholas affects the occipital lobe, causing blindness, and both you and Cassandra affect the cerebellum, his touch affected my orientation cluster, a segment of the parietal lobe. It's the cluster that regulates our sense of self."

"I don't understand," Robert said.

"Like when a yogi goes into meditation, describing a feeling of selflessness, a oneness with all things. What he's really doing, and this has been EKG charted, is shutting down the part of the brain—"

"That senses self."

"Exactly. My affliction centers there. My deprivation temporarily prevented my brain's ability to distinguish between self and not-self. If you were wired up to an FMRI scan, and experienced anger, we could map it as it registers in your brain. Under my deprivation, I simply witness anger in another, and my orientation association cluster fails to note the separation. My hippocampus cuts the charge to the cluster, as well as the thalamus. The thalamus is what regulates the process of turning outside sensation to emotion. So quite simply, when I encounter someone else's emotion—"

"You can't distinguish it from your own."

"So what he did in effect, was open me up. He broke down my protective barriers."

"Leaving you with an open emotional wound, so to speak?"

"I guess you could look at it that way," she said. "Anyhow, just like you, I was able to use my problem to great effect in my profession. It allowed me to help my patients in ways I could never imagine."

"Because you could truly empathize."

"Yes, that's exactly it. So now you understand how easily I can get hurt."

Robert stared at her for a moment. "You mentioned a second dose. He obviously touched you again."

"Yes," she said, averting her eyes. "We had sex in the backseat of his car. Is that what you wanted to hear? We made love, and it opened me up, and it stripped away the rest of my barriers. I've never regretted it for a moment."

Robert sat back in his chair.

"He's dead now, you know," she said.

"I'm sorry, Terry, I didn't mean to push so hard, I'm just very curious about you. There aren't too many people out there who want to help the vulnerable—none like you."

2 1

OUT in the hallway, just after the sighting, the first hit ran through me, subtle but unmistakable. I took a step, and my foot hit the floor too hard, jolting the bones in my leg. I took another step and was more careful. My navigation skills were still intact, I was pretty sure, differentiating the effects from those that Cassandra produced.

As if in response, I brought my legs into step, how can I say this—wrongly, and ended up flat on my stomach. It hurt my pride more than my nose. I felt hands on my back and heard a feminine voice say, "Are you all right?"

It was, to my delight and embarrassment, Astrid, the girl with the cute accent and the big dimples who had driven us here. "Come on, let me help you up."

"Thanks," I said, indicating it was all right to touch me.

"Did someone deprive you, Sparrow? Or are you just naturally clumsy?"

The grin on her face made me blush. "Deprived," I said. "I just sighted someone."

"*Leuk*. Good for you!" She smiled. "Are you hungry? I was just going out to get something to eat."

I tried to pull my hair back, almost poking myself in the eye. "*Umh*—yeah, I'm hungry. Sure."

"Then it's a lunch date. C'mon," she said, offering her elbow.

I took it, not so much for support, but for the contact. I have to admit that I wasn't quite as helpless as I'd acted while she led me from the building to the parking lot. I even let her help me into the van.

We headed onto the freeway, and she said, "I'm taking you to my place, is that all right? Or do you prefer to eat in a restaurant?"

"Your place sounds nice," I told her. *What is happening here?* I thought. She dialed her cell phone as she maneuvered in and out of the traffic.

"Hallo," she chimed. "Is this Cassandra? Astrid here. I've kidnapped your young friend. Didn't want you to worry. Yes. Would you like to speak to him?"

She handed me the phone. Cassandra asked if everything was fine with me, and I explained that I had been voluntarily deprived, but it was nothing. She said I should meet her back at the hotel afterward, as the meetings were over and our team had been assigned several tasks.

I gave Astrid back her phone, and she slid it into a charger. "I like your gloves," I told her.

"Thanks," she said.

Her apartment was small but homey, a mess of clothing and paper, and posters of American musicians. "Sit on the couch," she told me. "I am going to make the lunch. Any foods you don't like?"

"Asparagus," was all I could think of. She left me alone in the living room. I sat looking at CDs, all of her mismatched antique cabinets, and a discarded purple brassiere that particularly drew my attention. A few minutes later she came in and handed me tea and put some cheese and crackers on the table. "I really like your hair, you know?" she told me. "You look like a rock star."

"I do?"

"Yes. Do you have any tattoos?"

"*Umh*—yeah, I do. Hold on." And I pulled my shirt up and showed her my *D* mark, across my right shoulder blade.

"Wow—*leuk,*" she cried. "I want one. Right on my arm. Here!"

I dropped my shirt back down. "People will know what it stands for now," I told her. "Maybe you should hold off."

She laughed. "I never hold off. Fuck them if they don't like it."

"Cassandra has one on her chest."

"Does she now?" She smiled. She went back to the kitchen. "It's ready," she called after ten minutes or so. "I hope you will like it very much!"

She returned with a steaming black pot and two dishes and forks. We sat on the floor at the coffee table. "What is it?" I asked, as she dished out what looked to me like green mashed potatoes.

"It's very Dutch," she explained. "It's called *stamppot.* Potatoes with sausage and spinach and many herbs. *Eet smakelijk.* That means, 'Good eating.' "

In the least graceful display imaginable I reached for the fork and missed—sending my dish crashing to the floor. She was over to me in a second, and luckily the majority of the food was saved. "My goodness," she said, "you act so natural. I forget you are deprived."

"No, I'm sorry. I'm so clumsy, I . . ."

Her face was inches from my own, so close that my words caught in my throat. "Don't be sorry," she whispered.

"Okay," I replied soundlessly.

She placed one gloved hand on my leg. Then she reached down, picked up my fork, and scooped some food from the dish. She held it just away from my face, and I opened my mouth for her.

"What's your deprivation?" I asked between forkfuls, as she fed us both.

"You don't want to know," she replied sheepishly.

"But I—"

"Shhh," she said. Then she stood up and walked into her bedroom. Moments later, some music, I think it was early Pearl Jam, filtered into the room from hidden speakers. When she came back, she had two pairs of thin, transparent gloves in her hands and a coy look on her face.

"I want to touch you," she said. "Do you want to touch me?"

"Very much." I pushed the table away, and she sat down in front of me. She handed me a pair of the gloves, and I pulled them on. I'd never seen anything like them. She stripped off her leather gloves and pulled on the other set.

Then she very gently put her hands on my shoulders, and staring me in the eyes with a bristling intensity, brought her hands down along my chest. I put my hands on the knees of her jeans. She ran her hands through my hair, and for a moment I thought she was going to cry. Then she took her hands off me and pulled off her sweatshirt, revealing a black bra, which she quickly unhooked from the front and tossed to the floor. She reached down and took my hands and placed them on her soft breasts.

I was hypnotized by her, and I tried to match her level of forwardness. I massaged her softly, then a bit more roughly, thumbing her nipples erect. She moaned and whispered something in Dutch. She had a hungry look to her eyes now, and she tugged at my shirt, which I helped her remove. "I want you to touch me however you please," she said. I desperately wanted to kiss her soft, pink mouth.

Our gloved hands were all over each other, and soon she was down in my jeans. "Lie back," she said, and she propped me on my side and came to lie next to me. "Careful not to touch my skin," she whispered, unzipping her jeans and then squirming out of them. In a controlled burst of desperate tugging and rubbing, we brought each other to near-simultaneous climax, moaning aloud and exalting in the sheer joy of release.

When it was done, we lay apart, breathing furiously. "I wanted to do that from the moment I first saw you," she whispered. "Thank you."

2 2

ASTRID and I were slightly uncomfortable during the ride back to the Hotel Van Blau, but she still managed a genuine smile when I let myself haphazardly out of the door. "I guess tomorrow's the big day," she said.

"Yeah," I said.

"Be careful," she said. "Not every Depriver in this city shares our enthusiasm."

"I will," I agreed and I waved good-bye. When I got to the rooms, I found Cassandra napping. She woke up and called me over to her bed. I sat down on the floor. She yawned and reached for a cigarette off the nightstand. I grabbed her lighter and lit it for her.

"Thanks," she said, dragging. "Was she nice?"

"Yeah, she was nice."

"Good. And your deprivation?"

"Barely active," I said, "judging by how easily I just lit your cigarette."

"Good." She got out of bed and slipped her jeans on,

then moved to the bureau and started brushing her hair.

"I'm sort of scared, Cassie. Is it really happening tomorrow?"

"Yes. Gerrit has press from all over the world confused, but ready to move on thirty minutes' notice. There've been a few problems, though."

"Like?"

"Like Robert," she said, grinding her cigarette out in the ashtray.

"Why? What—?"

"Dr. Hauske wanted to prepare a demonstration for the press just prior to the live broadcast. The idea was to fill them in a bit, show them a deprivation in progress, then let them see the deprived person come out of it okay. Only Robert has a duration short enough. They asked him, and he refused."

I thought about that for a moment. "Can you blame him?" I asked.

"Yes," Cassandra said. "Yes, I can."

"Do you know where he is?"

"Down in the bar, just off the lobby. That's where I left them. Nicholas is there too, and Terry and Hauske. Nicky's taking me out for dinner. We haven't been alone since this whole thing got started. This could be our last chance for a normal night out."

"Good for you," I said, getting up off the floor. "Grab some normalcy. I'll go talk to Rob."

"Maybe you can get through to him." She smiled as she headed for the bathroom. "See you down there."

I found them talking with Dr. Hauske over vodka martinis. Terry had changed into a low-cut dress, had her hair down, and was wearing lipstick. When she wanted to, she could really look stunning. Robert was wearing new clothes as well. I ordered a Coke and dragged over a stool.

"But if we could indicate some path to a cure," Nicholas said, "it would strengthen our position considerably."

"Would it?" Terry asked. "Would it really? When cancer was first misconstrued as a transmittable virus back in the 1940s, the pharmaceutical companies began churning out antivirals, and they were blinded to every other possibility. It took decades for them to concede that cancer was not a virus, nor contagious. Here's another example of medical shortsightedness. The ulcer. We've always treated the condition as if it was stress-related, the result of psychological fallout. I'm guilty of that diagnosis myself. Now we realize that ninety-five percent of the time they're the result of a simple bacterial infection—easily cleared with antibiotics. And don't get me started on how AIDS was mishandled from the onset. The medical community let us believe it was passed on by saliva or mosquito bites. If we point to a direction on the cure for SDS, we could very well be slamming the door to the actual one."

Hauske seemed impressed by her comments, and I began to wonder if that was her intent. "That's very astute, Theresa," Hauske said. "And though I agree there's a danger involved, I still feel I'll have to explain the mechanics of the affliction to some degree, or certainly it *will* be viewed as contagious to the man on the street."

"Excuse me, Dr. Hauske," Robert cut in, "but what exactly *are* the mechanics of the affliction?"

Poor Rob, I thought. I'd forgotten how new this all was for him. He was still very much in the dark.

"Well, to the best of my understanding," Hauske said, "deprivation is bioelectrical in nature. Each Depriver is carrying an individual charge along his epidermal tissues that I believe has evolved primarily as a defense mechanism."

"Don't say that to the audience, Doc," Nicholas said. "Defense mechanism sounds a lot like 'weapon.' "

"Point taken," Hauske said. "I believe the origin of the genetic deviation is linked to certain man-made contaminants, synthetic hormones and pollutants, specifically radioactive isotopes, that my team is trying to pinpoint. We have several likely suspects. Anyway, that charge is merely a delivery system for a very picky virus with an appetite for the sensory apparatus. Though 'virus' is, by definition, not precisely accurate. In the same way that mad cow disease is not precisely a virus, it's caused by a prion protein, which is itself infectious. A complex molecular substance that forces living matter to copy it. So, think of SDS more as a sliver of malign code that transmits bad information to the synapses in your brain."

Nicholas nodded, as if this were perfectly clear to him. Rob shook his head.

"When a Depriver touches a Normal," the doctor continued, taking Terry's hand, "the charge leaps out from him and enters the bloodstream through the pores of the skin. . . ." He continued to illustrate his point by walking his fingers up Terry's arm. I took note that Robert took note. "The 'virus' skirts up to and through the blood-brain barrier and into the brain. If a Depriver's touch causes blindness; it hijacks enough cells to create prions that affect the optic nerves, and a very particular pathway from the hindbrain to the occipital lobe. If it's deafness, or loss of balance, or even paralysis, we're talking about completely different pathways—ergo, the deprivation must be channeling in through the brain's sensory control center, the switchboard if you will, and that's the thalamus, of course."

"Of course," Rob said.

"Once in the thalamus, the virus can infiltrate the visual, auditory, somesthetic, gustatory, vestibular, or motor pathways directly . . ."

Rob gave Hauske a lost look and Hauske nodded.

"To simplify, the deprived is deprived because a bad message is entering the control center of the brain and damming a very specific junction. A junction that gets either permanently, or temporarily, fused. I made the connection, oddly enough, after eating some bad oysters."

"Come again, Doc?" Robert said.

"Shellfish makes some people sick, or in rare cases, deathly ill, because of toxic secretions that block up specific ion channels. In relation—deprivation's basically an electronically induced, synaptic block."

Rob shook his head. "Dr. Hauske, I'm not sure I exactly understood all that. But how sure are you about all this stuff?"

Hauske sat back against the bar. "It's all theory, Corbert," he said, "until we have a cure in hand. If this particular theory is true, we'll need a countersignal that allows the brain to ignore the charge, or refuse the bad info, to avoid deprivation. Now, if you'll excuse me, I think I ought to get some rest for tomorrow." Hauske kissed Terry on the cheek, then swaggered out of the bar, toward the elevator.

Nicholas rubbed his eyes and said, "That man's first words in front of the camera are going to decide everything." A world hungry for an explanation of how some old guy in New York had suddenly blinded a person with his bare hand was about to be answered by someone who actually knew. Or at least knew best.

"So what's everybody's assignments for tomorrow?" I asked.

"Nicholas is helping Gerrit coordinate. Cassandra is one

of the four escorts who will stay with Hauske," Terry said. "I'm part of the team that's briefing the press. And Robert here, or shall I say Corbert here, has declined his part in a staged deprivation, and has, in my opinion, no further value. See you all in the morning." And with that she turned, picked up her handbag, and left the bar.

"Wow," I said. "She's pretty pissed off."

Robert looked after her. "Yeah," he said.

Cassandra came into the bar, beaming, and linked arms with her brother. "I'm ready for our date," she announced. Nicholas motioned for Robert to take care of the bartender.

"I want you following him every minute from now until this is over," Nicholas whispered in my ear.

"Okay," I said.

As soon as Robert was back within earshot, Nicholas added, "And I want the two of you mobile in the crowd tomorrow, all right? We're not sure what kind of opposition may arise."

Nicholas and Cassie excused themselves and headed out. That left just me and Robert. "One more drink?" he asked.

"Sure," I said. He ordered, and we went to work on a bowl of peanuts. "So where were you today? I got called down to handle a sighting that was supposed to be yours."

He flipped a peanut in the air and caught it in his mouth. Two martinis arrived. I flipped a peanut and missed by a mile. Blamed it on the deprivation.

"Sorry about that," he said. "I was with Terry, and things were going pretty well between us. It wasn't a good time to leave. And then when I finally did, I headed upstairs and ran into that girl who was our driver. She stopped me and started asking me all kinds of questions about our group, with some *special* emphasis on you. Then I went to room sixteen, and I saw you were in the middle of a deprivation. Looked pretty freaky."

I sipped my drink. "It was," I said.

"Who was the man you deprived?"

"Some Dutch muckety-muck."

Robert nodded, then winked. "And then you left with the girl, huh?"

"Yes," I said. "We had lunch together."

"Nice. Gonna take her back to the reservation and introduce her to your folks?"

"Now you're pushing it," I said. "But while we're on the subject of what comes next, any thoughts on what you're gonna do after we rock the world?"

Rob sipped his drink. "Back to work," he said. "A lot more cautious."

"Right back in, huh?" I said, digesting what that meant. "Wow, I gotta say, Rob, it's hard to really imagine your line of work. I mean, it's just, I know I make jokes about it but—"

"It's okay, Sparrow, ask me whatever you want," he said.

"Okay," I said, sitting up and getting down to it. "What do you usually charge?"

"It varies from contract to contract," he explained, "but at my current level I make about two hundred fifty thousand dollars, half up front, half on completion."

"How do you usually do it?"

"First, I make absolutely sure I've got the right man, then I deprive him. Usually I give him the lowdown on what he did wrong and give him a minute to reflect on it, then I inject him with an air bubble, and it's over pretty quickly."

Listening to the way he told it, you'd think it was no more difficult than emptying the trash. "I guess what I really want to know is why you do it. Is there some satisfaction beyond the money that you get out of it?"

"No," he replied. "I learned that I had a curse, and that's what set me apart. So I put that curse to work for me. I provide a service to society, and society affords me a certain lifestyle in return. It's that simple."

I shook my head and sipped my drink. Something was missing from his story. Like something was missing from his life. Like something was missing from all of our lives. But where we found solace in contact with each other, he filled in his missing piece with a job that I just couldn't wrap my head around.

"How about that doctor, huh?" he said. "Seems like if anybody's going to cure us, it's him."

I thought about that. What would it be like, being *cured?* That would change everything. My whole life was centered around my gift, just like Robert's was. My friends, my lifestyle—my path. How could I ever *be* normal?

"What if tomorrow you found out you *were* cured?" I asked him. "What then? Suddenly you're no longer a Depriver. No paralyzing touch. What would your profession become?" That hit home. Terry would have been proud. This might make him reconsider his motives—question whether his Depriver abilities defined him or vice versa. I was proud of the question. "I think you should rethink some of your decisions, Rob," I offered as I sucked at my olive. "You could turn out to be the hero in all this, you know."

He finished his drink without speaking further on the topic, then excused himself, saying that he needed some air. I gave him a minute lead time, then followed.

I light-footed out of the lounge area, and watched him leave the hotel. I went outside and saw him standing in a phone booth with his back toward me. He seemed a bit agitated. It made me a little nervous, but I blamed that on the alcohol. I wanted to approach him, but I needed a reason to be out on the street, so I pulled out a cigarette. As I got closer I heard him say, "Yes, understood. Good-bye."

He hung up the receiver and noticed me in the same moment. "Hey Sparrow," he said.

"Came out for a smoke," I said. "Who was that?"

"My father. It seems my mother is fairly ill."

"Wow," I said, taken aback. I'd never really stopped to consider the fact that Robert would actually have family living somewhere.

"Sorry," I said. "It's not urgent, is it? You won't leave?"

"Not until I'm finished here," he replied. "I'm gonna go for a walk now. Clear my head. That's allowed, right?"

"Um . . . yeah," I said. "Of course."

"Okay then," he said. "See you in a bit."

"Sure," I said, thinking, *I am so not the man for this job.*

Then he walked off and disappeared around a corner. I wasn't sure whether to believe him or not, but I knew Nicky would kill me if I lost him, so again I pursued. I saw him come back into the building by the back stairs. *Just changed his mind?* I wondered. I followed him up the three flights to our floor, relieved that my watchfulness had been unnecessary. I waited by the stairwell for five minutes, so as not to appear conspicuous. When I went back to the room it was empty, the window left open.

"Shit," I said to no one. *Had he come back to get something? A weapon or—*

Then I heard sounds from the next room. Theresa's voice, then Robert's. I moved to the door that separated our suites and pressed my ear against it. They were arguing in low voices, and I could not quite understand what they

were saying. I went down on one knee, and I looked
through the door's ancient keyhole.

They were sitting on the bed, his face inches from hers,
and for a moment I was afraid he was going to touch her.
He said something, and her cheeks reddened. Her chest
rose and fell in quick bursts. Adrenaline kicked into my
bloodstream, and I was seconds away from crashing in on
them when suddenly she tilted her head and kissed him
hard on the mouth. He put his hands on her face.

I turned from the view and put my back against the
door, astounded, embarrassed, relieved. "Grab some normalcy," I whispered. "Good for you."

I smoked about a quarter of a joint, then showered and
got into bed. It was still relatively early, but it felt like one
of the longest days of my life.

23

THE next morning we geared up and cleared out of the hotel. Regardless of what might come, we would not be returning. Corbert Huxley checked us out, and Astrid sat drinking coffee from a thermos in the van by the front door. Cassandra nudged me to sit up front with her, so I did. Astrid wore a pretty pink sweater and a skirt that morning, and she gave me a playful punch on the shoulder. "Today's the day, people," she said. "For better or for the worst, we're coming out!"

"Where is it happening?" Nicholas asked, as we pulled away from the hotel.

"The Leidseplein," Astrid said. "Smack center in the middle of everything. It was officially announced ten minutes ago."

"How will the news travel?" Nicholas asked.

"All the Deprivers who live in the city know to tune in to Radio 538, and there will be some *wachtword* announced to tell them where to go. That won't happen for another hour or so. The press will arrive shortly after. Everything else is prepared. I already brought Dr. Hauske there earlier this morning."

"And Gerrit?"

"I don't know where he is, now. I think today he will keep the lower profile. Keeping an eye on things." Astrid said.

I noticed Robert was curiously silent, seated in the back, staring after the traffic as we drove. We had to park and walk. There's no way to drive directly up to the main square of the Leidseplein, which was probably best for security. We got there, and I saw there was already a stage set up toward the center, just in front of a club called The Bulldog, and there were a few small tents propped up behind it. Tourists already milled about, wondering what was being prepared—I even heard American accents. It was a really nice setting, one of the more recognizable scenes from Holland, sort of like the Dutch version of Times Square. The air was heating up, the pigeons were cooing, it felt like the beginning of a beautiful day.

We went to the main tent and saw a lot of Deprivers we had met the day before. From one table we helped ourselves to cups of coffee and breads with sausages baked into them. They were a bit greasy but tasted pretty good. One of Gerrit's people came and greeted us, and then Cassie and Nicholas had to leave with him. Nicholas gave me a nod, and I gave it right back.

Astrid said, "Terry, you must go to the press tent now. I'll show you," and we all walked over to the second tent.

"Being out in the open like this makes my ears itch," Robert said. Astrid was intrigued enough to ask what he meant.

"He thinks it's not safe," I told her. "He feels we're too exposed here."

"But that's what this is all about," Astrid said. "Full exposure. We're going to tell the whole world who we are!"

Robert took out his sunglasses and put them on. "A little early for those, don't you think?" I asked.

"No," he said. "It's never too early to watch your back."

"You can see behind you with those things?" I asked.

"Yes."

"How many fingers am I holding up?"

"One," he said. "Fuck you too."

"Wow, *leuk*."

"Yeah, loke. I'll let you try them later," Robert said.

We arrived at the press tent and a thickset guard with a no-nonsense tone stepped out and said, "No admittance, unless your name is on my list."

"She's on your list. Theresa Godfrey," Astrid said.

The guard checked his clipboard and found Terry's name. "Identification please," he said. She had to show her passport to be granted admittance. She wished us luck and then offered a weak smile to Robert. The brief glance I had into the tent revealed a camera and a guy with a machine gun. It was more than a little unsettling.

"Now we're all three on crowd watch," Astrid said. "People should be arriving soon. Shall we walk around?" We walked, and she talked and taught us the names of things we passed, pointing out the Schouwberg Building with its beautiful grand balconies, the clocktower, anything she could think of to keep our anxiety level down. We were all too aware that the announcement would change our lives. "So what line of work do you do, back in the States, Corbert?" she asked. I chuckled to myself at that.

"Well, Astrid. I work for a sort of—collection agency."

"Ah, you are *de deurwaarder*," she said. "You are the final bill collector."

"That's exactly right," he said.

"Oh, it's hard to like someone with this kind of job. You must move here to Holland and choose a new job."

"Amen," I said.

"Look," Astrid said, pointing to the main entrance to the square. "The radio broadcast must have happened. They are coming!"

Looking around, more and more glowing faces had entered the square from all sides. "It's really happening," I said. We watched them slowly filing in. Deprivers wearing gloves. Deprivers on bicycles. Deprivers banded together in small cliques. A Depriver in a wheelchair.

It felt strange to be strolling through the crowd while such important preparations were going on within the tents. I felt a bit left out of the action. A feeling that grew when Astrid said, "Here come the press crews!" Three dozen people or so, easily identified by the tripods and cases of equipment they were carrying, made their way past us toward the press tent.

A British crew member with a dark beard and a black cap muttered, "Better not be another damned disc jockey announcing some friggin' album!" And then he dropped the newspaper he had folded under his arm into a waste bin right beside me. Something drew me to the paper, and I lifted it out. It was a British daily, the *Independent,* and I caught my breath at the right-hand substory photograph. It was Kootstra, the Dutch national I'd sighted, looking completely deprived of life.

Astrid and Robert saw the distress in my face and began reading over my shoulder. The headline read: "Dutch National Found Murdered in His Hilversum Apartment." Reading further it said that at first, it had appeared to detectives that Kootstra had suffered cardiac arrest; however, the autopsy had suggested that an air bubble injected into his bloodstream had caused—

"Robert, you fuck!" I said, completely losing my composure, using his real name without caution.

He shook his head. "Sparrow, you've got it wrong!"

"What are you talking about?" Astrid asked. "What has this to do with us?"

I threw the paper into Robert's face, and I took off into the crowd. I could hear his footsteps tracking close behind me. He yelled my name several times, demanding I stop. I was sure he'd betrayed us again, and I needed to warn Nicholas. I dove through the crowd, weaving in and out between Normals and Deprivers, avoiding bare hands as I went, realizing that any collision could bring disaster. I headed away from the main tent, toward the press tent, hoping he would not second-guess my destination. Then I really picked up the speed, and ducked into The Bulldog. A few moments of crouching, my breath on fire in my lungs, and I saw him rush past. I waited a few minutes, then swung out the door and *damn,* I saw him, and he saw me.

I had a good distance on him, and I cut away from the crowd, turned down a deserted alleyway and then turned down another, praying I'd find a way through the streets and back around to the tents. I glanced up at the sign that read *VarnixStraat,* trying to keep my bearings.

Then I stopped short as I saw them. There must have been somewhere between ten or fifteen men in black riot gear. I quickly sidestepped into a brick alcove and tried to catch my breath. I could see that one of them had a shield up that read *Speciale Politie,* and I knew that was not a good thing to be headed our way. I knew in my gut that everything was about to get royally fucked up.

Suddenly the small street erupted in violence and

confusion. Six men came out of nowhere and rushed straight into the line of police. Six Deprivers. It happened so fast that no guns were drawn—but there were batons out and there was contact being made. The street was exploding in cries and curses and flashes of blue sparks. I saw one policeman go down on the ground, and a Depriver get hit hard in the face with a baton. Hopefully by now, Astrid had alerted Cassandra, or Gerrit, or Nicholas that something was wrong. I slid out of my alcove and swung around the next corner to see my worst fears realized.

Robert and a man I'd never seen before. They were arguing. The man was a Depriver, gray-haired and sure of stance. From the description that Nicholas had given, there was no doubt in my mind as to who he must be. Deveraux. Robert had been his mole all along, and I was the fool who had championed him. Robert must have seen me just then, through those damned rearview glasses, because he spun around to face me. For a moment, I was powerless to run. I just stood there, all the energy draining away from my body.

"Sparrow!" he yelled—and I ran. *Brick street, brick street, keep your balance,* over the canal bridge and back to the Leidseplein. I got to the main tent and dashed past the two guards before they could stop me. They rushed in behind me and I stood behind Nicholas, who was holding Cassandra in his arms . . . and they were *kissing?* My entrance made them stop.

"It's okay, he's got clearance," Nicholas shouted to the armed guards.

I saw then that the girl in his arms was not Cassandra. She was taller, leaner, her hair a deep red, and I knew that she must be Claudette. *Of course, if her father is here . . .*

Then it dawned on me; they were touching with bare skin and without fear. I was overwhelmed—speechless.

"One second, Sparrow," Nicholas said, then into a

handheld walkie-talkie, he ordered, "Go with the reporters."

Then there was a man behind me, and I heard the two soldiers crank the bolts on their guns. I turned to see Deveraux. *What the hell is happening?* My thoughts scrambled as he passed me and moved toward Nicholas.

"Easy, Daddy!" Claudette said.

"Welcome to the underground," Nicholas said. "You'll excuse me if I offer you the same hospitality you offered me. Security, take him out of here!"

"Wait a minute, son, I've been protecting this little show of yours from adversaries you didn't even know you had. The Ministry. The Shop. The executive CDC. Do you think I could get just a little respect from you?"

"Please, Nicholas," Claudette said, "hear him out."

"I'm listening," Nicholas said.

"I want you to call it off."

"You've gotta be fucking kidding me," Nicholas said.

"I could make you stop," Deveraux challenged. "Believe me, I could."

"What happened to all that talk about putting the right spin on things?" Nicholas asked. "Or does that just apply to *your* spin on things?" Then he lowered his voice to nearly a whisper, "I know what you want—you want a race war. And you want to control the flow of information, just like they do."

"Everyone in that crowd is being filmed as we speak, Nicholas. Our people will lose their anonymity. They'll no longer be able to—"

"Act as your invisible soldiers? That's fine by me."

Deveraux's face reddened. "Son, if you don't stop this, you're putting every SDS carrier out there in grave jeopardy. Dr. Hauske is going to sound like a madman, and I won't be able to clean up this mess."

"You forget that I've seen how you clean," Nicholas said.

"I assure you that I have nothing but the best intentions for my people—"

"Nicholas," I broke in. "Don't listen to him! I just saw him with Robert—and Rob killed that Dutch national I sighted yesterday. It's in the newspaper!"

"Goddamn it," Nicholas said. "I knew I should've deprived him from the start!"

Deveraux raised his hands and said, "Will you just hold on—"

The gloved security guards grabbed Deveraux's raised wrists and held him back.

"Everybody shut up for a second," Nicholas shouted. Claudette ran across the tent to her father. Nicholas raised the walkie-talkie and changed the dial. "Cassandra?" he called.

"Yeah," came her static-filled reply.

"Robert's turned on us. Can you locate him?"

"Uh—*yeah*. I can," she said. "He's standing right onstage with Terry and Dr. Hauske."

"Shit! Let him go," Nicholas said to the guards as he left the tent. Deveraux and Claudette were on his heels, and I followed, of course.

We got outside and saw that everything was already in motion. There must have been at least six hundred Deprivers in the square, no kidding. A few hundred Normals were milling about, with no idea what they were about to witness. Cameras were rolling at the foot of the stage. And off to the right, I saw that Terry and Robert were standing together.

When Hauske stepped up to the podium and tapped the microphone, all our attention turned to him, and everything else in the world seemed at a standstill.

"Hello, can everyone hear me?" Hauske began. "My name is Dr. Warren Hauske, and I'm a neurovirologist from the PolyGen Institute. My colleagues and I are here today to

talk about a subject that's going to seem a little scary to you
at first, but that need not cause too much alarm." And then
he laughed at his poor choice of phrasing. The laugh
revealed his nervousness, as well as his humanity. In retro-
spect, I think it was very important. Something that could
never have been planned. "Sorry about that," he continued.
"Let me start over. My name is Warren Hauske, and I've
spent the last five years studying a very rare, noncontagious,
nonlethal disease that's called Sensory Deprivation Syndrome, or SDS. What the heck is that, you're asking yourselves? Well, I'm going to tell you all about it, but first I'll
need a volunteer from the press to come up onstage. Terry,
have we selected someone?"

Terry pointed down to the press box. A blonde woman
in a smart gray suit, carrying a microphone with a World-
Net News label, got up onto the stage looking *very* nervous.
I couldn't name her, but I knew that she was famous.

The woman walked on stage to Dr. Hauske and sat in a
chair next to his podium. He whispered something to her,
and she nodded. I had a tremendous amount of respect for
the leap of faith she was about to take, and I was incredibly
grateful. I felt a hand on my shoulder and saw it was Astrid,
come to stand by me. I took her gloved hand in mine.

"What is Corbert doing up there?" she whispered.

"I really have no idea," I said.

Hauske went back to the podium. "Okay, you're all
familiar with our volunteer, I'm sure. Next, I'm going to
bring out one of my patients. He suffers from SDS. You'll
note that he'll be wearing gloves, and there's a reason for
that. Again, let me stress that SDS is *not* contagious. It
can, however, cause certain very specific, *inconvenient* side
effects, most of them temporary. Corbert, would you come
out here, please?"

Robert Luxley walked onstage before the cameras, smiling and waving his gloved hands. "He didn't do it," Nicholas whispered to me. "Deveraux's taking credit. Your Dutch national went and sold us out." Hearing that, I was both relieved and a little ashamed.

I looked for Deveraux, but he was gone. Cassandra came back from ahead of us, and Nicholas introduced her to Claudette. Cassandra was a bit uneasy. She looked at me, and I saw there were tears in her eyes. We all turned back toward Dr. Hauske as his voice boomed out over the crowd.

"Now, Corbert here looks like the average man on the street, I think you'll agree. Believe it or not, he suffers from SDS. What that means specifically to Corbert, is that he's got to be extremely careful who he makes skin-on-skin contact with. Say hello to Elizabeth, Corbert."

Robert leaned over and spoke into the press woman's microphone. "Hi, Elizabeth. I'm Corbert."

"Hi Corbert," she said, with only a trace of nervousness left. The almost talk-show atmosphere was having a calming effect on her.

"Now, if Corbert simply touches Elizabeth without his gloves on, he will give her body a kind of a light shock—but it won't hurt. We're going to demonstrate, so you can see for yourselves. Can you remove your gloves please, Corbert? But don't touch Elizabeth unless she gives you permission first, all right?"

I don't know where Hauske learned his showmanship, but it was definitely the ticket. Robert removed his gloves, and the woman sat smartly, aware of the world's eyes upon her. Hauske continued, "Now, when Elizabeth says it's all right, Corbert is going to touch her and cause Elizabeth to have a temporary deprivation. What that means, in Corbert's particular case, is that Elizabeth is going to experience a slight numbing of her body, working its way from her toes up. For approximately fifteen minutes, that's all, she's not going to be able to budge an inch—a fun sort of temporary paralysis. That's the extent of the deprivation, and there are absolutely no other harmful side effects."

"*Leuk!*" someone yelled from the audience.

"Yes, *leuk* indeed," Hauske said. "Now, does that sound scary to you, Elizabeth? Sitting still for fifteen minutes or so?"

"I think I can handle that," she said, speaking into the mike and smiling.

"All right then," Hauske said. "As our demonstration for the day, Corbert will now deprive Elizabeth. We'll all watch carefully to see how she's doing. Meanwhile, I'm going to tell you a little bit about the amazing science behind all of this. And you keep checking, Corbert, to make sure Elizabeth is comfortable. Then, after fifteen minutes, when we see that Elizabeth is fine, we'll all know there's nothing to worry about. Okay, Corbert, Elizabeth, you tell us when you're ready."

Astrid squeezed my hand and made a sniffling noise that told me she was crying. I had tears in my eyes as well. This was it, and there was no turning back.

"May I touch you?" Robert asked.

The newswoman hesitated a moment, then answered, "Yes, but be careful."

My last thought before the world changed was that now Robert Luxley was certainly out of a job. Then he reached out and touched her.

24

SHE had no idea how many contracts I'd fulfilled, and she didn't care. My career in murder-for-hire was erased with a single touch—and they called me a hero. For all that I'd given up in that instant, and all that I'd gained, and the multitudes of lives that would now change as a result, I'd forsaken my anonymity. I felt lost, not heroic.

I stood alone on the cobblestones of the Leidseplein around four o'clock in the morning, watching the wind whirling bits of trash in circles around me. The square looked so much larger, so much more grand, now that the stage and the tents had been taken down.

There was beer on my breath—we'd all indulged in more than our share. Soon after the broadcast, we began to see evidence that things were changing. Nicholas had spent a few hours alone with Cassandra—then announced to the rest of us that he and Claudette would be leaving together, to undertake some sort of research they refused to divulge. Cassandra appeared strong, but I knew she must be terribly upset. Theresa took her back to the new hotel where Gerrit had posted us. Hauske was already on a flight to Washington. My face was all over the media. The world had changed. My world had changed. And for some reason, I was drawn to this foreign place. The scene of the crime, as it were. The place where I'd been forced to make my choice.

I sensed someone moving slowly up behind me.

"I hope you'll accept my apologies, brother," came Sparrow's soft voice, "for doubting you."

"No apology necessary," I said over my shoulder. "I was even doubting myself through most of it."

"What was it," he asked, "that went through your mind when you made your decision?"

"I was standing in a high-rise in Manhattan, I was sitting with Cassandra as she told me what I was, I was walking deaf in the woods from your deprivation, I was floating senseless in your tank, I was falling in love with Theresa, and I was asking myself who I would be if I woke up one day without this blue aura. Deveraux made me an offer, and I wanted to take it. Damn—you don't know how much I wanted to just take it! It meant that I didn't have to care. I didn't need to justify anything I'd ever done. That man is pure persuasion. For a minute, it was like none of you even existed. I was about to agree to his terms, to kill Hauske and stop the broadcast. Then I saw you through my rearview lenses. I turned and I saw this indescribable look on your face. And then you ran—and the decision just got *made* in me. . . . I told Deveraux I was out of the business."

"You've been to the edge and back, my friend," Sparrow said.

"I'm not so sure I am back," I said after a time, "but I know that the world *has* changed. I'm overwhelmed by the part that I've played in it."

He put his hand on my shoulder and squeezed hard. "You're okay, Rob. And your part isn't over. And there's someone waiting for you now. Don't let her down. Think of the world finding out as a game. We're about to see how well they play."

Part Two

OVEREXPOSED

1

SHADOW of the man he was, unshaven, reeking of alcohol, he stood in the alley and surveyed the entrance to the Tarantula. It was a bone-cold Toronto night, but he didn't even notice the icy wind. His mind was racing and his adrenaline surged each time the door opened, but he would not enter the club yet. He needed confirmation that her majesty would be there first.

He leaned back into his shadowed corner as a young couple approached the club's entrance. They were dressed like today's kids dressed—but even at this distance, he could tell they were afflicted. His Depsight was that acute. His prolonged, variable, and repeated exposure to SDS offered him that one advantage. When the door swung wide for them, he saw two muscular bouncers, each with side arms. They were scanning the two kids visually—not using the machines—at least one of them was also sighted. Neither of the bouncers was a Depriver; that was good.

At about three-thirty, a car pulled up and three of them,

a blonde-haired woman and two men, went into the club. Must be *her,* he realized, as the bouncers stepped aside. He gave them ten minutes, then pulled his gloves on and crossed the street to the entrance. He knocked, and the muscle opened the door, giving him the once-over.

"You're not a Depriver," the big guy said. Those same words had excluded him on countless occasions.

"Dep-friendly," he said, with a soft voice meant to conceal his anger.

"That's much appreciated," the bouncer said, crossing his arms. He took in the smaller man's stature, his ragged appearance, and the alcohol on his breath, and obviously considered him no threat. "But this club is strictly Deprivers only. No exceptions."

"I see," the man said, looking into the club. The second bouncer was not in sight. In a second he had the big guy by the neck with his gloved hand. The larger man swung his beefy fist hard and connected with his attacker's face, expecting to break the hold—but the man only grinned in response. Continuing his throat hold, he pulled the struggling bouncer forward, outside through the door, and pushed him against the bricks. He slid the bouncer's gun from its holster and pocketed it. "Listen," he said calmly. "I can break your neck, but I really have no problem with you. Just stay out of my way."

He jerked the bouncer quickly forward, into a sleeper hold, and held him there until he sagged to his knees. He pushed the door open and entered the club. At a rough count, there had to be at least a hundred of them in there, glowing bodies. Of course, very few were actually touching as they danced and milled about, each of them being as potentially dangerous to each other as they were to Normals. He pushed through them toward a darkened area with tables and booths in the back, scanning for her as he went. Deprivers stepped out of his way as he passed, and he heard a young voice yell, "Normal in the house!"

There she was, set up like the queen of the castle in the last booth, with her entourage—the same two men, and another woman.

She looked up, recognition slowly dawning on her face as he stood at the end of their table. As their eyes met, he saw her astonishment, as she tried to gauge his ability to distinguish reason. Her guests became alarmed, first by the fact that this man was not a Depriver, and then by their host's nervous posture.

"Alex Crowley," she said. "My God, what happened to you? You shouldn't be here."

"But I am here, Cassandra," he said indignantly, "and you'd damned well better talk to me."

Two new bouncers stepped up behind Alex Crowley with guns exposed. Crowley stood, unfazed, staring into Cassandra's face.

"It's okay," Cassandra said. "Tonight we make an exception. Mr. Crowley is our guest." The men holstered their arms and stepped back a few feet. "There's a place we can talk," she told him. To the girl next to her she said, "I'm okay, he's an old friend. I'll be back in a few minutes."

Cassandra, wearing a sheer silver evening gown, seemed to glide as she led him up a concealed flight of stairs, her blonde hair bobbing with each step. She opened the door to a small, plush room that might once have been one of those champagne rooms where people went to actually touch each other. Cassandra sat down on one of the two opposing red velvet couches and immediately lit a cigarette.

"Well, Alex, *interesting* to see you here. To what do I owe the pleasure?"

"Do you have any idea what it's like needing to break in here?" he asked coldly.

"You know the situation out there, Alex. In this city there are no Dep-friendlies. You were in once because you married Julia, but those were different times."

He closed his eyes as painful memories of his wife flashed through his mind.

"You were ostracized—you brought it on yourself—"

"Bullshit," he said.

She took a long drag. "I feel for you, Alex. You're obviously very lost. I want you to know that I have thought about you. Wondered how you were."

He could see the upper edge of the *D* tattoo on her left breast peeking out of her dress, twin to Julia's. Years before, it had been commonplace for every Depriver to take the *D* mark. Usually someplace concealed, depending on how far the individual intended to come out in society. They took the mark as an act of will. Crowley had heard many reasons why. Julia said she'd taken the mark so they'd never be able to do it *to* her.

He looked away. "I drank myself into a detox center back in D.C. I was there for months. Theresa dragged me out."

"Well, bless her heart. She was always the kindest among us. Really Alex, what did you expect? You almost killed Jake at the funeral."

"No one ever deserved almost killing more than he did, and he left me deaf for weeks—I call us even."

"Well, the Depriver community doesn't see it that way. He's one of ours, and you never really were." She regretted her choice of words immediately.

"Is that what you think? Nicholas? Irma?"

"I can't speak for them, Alex. But I'm here, now. Listening." She lit a second cigarette from the first. "I will say that a lot of Deprivers think you're dangerous, Alex. You know too many of us. And you're sighted like no other Normal. People are practically *hunting* us out there since the random screenings began."

Frustrated, he slumped down on the couch beside her. "I know. I wish there was something I could do."

"I know you do," she said. "Julia was lucky to find someone like you." She placed her ungloved hand on his shoulder. "Now tell me, what did you come for? Certainly not to rejoin our little underground."

Alex stood abruptly. "I want the one who killed her, Cassie. I need to find the shooter. I need to know who took her life and ruined mine. I can't rest."

"I'm not sure what I can do for you."

"Deveraux," Crowley said. "If anyone has a name for me, it'll be him."

"I have no contact with—"

"Your brother," Alex said. "Nicholas is with Deveraux's daughter. She can get me to her father."

"Okay," she said after a pause. "I'll try for you. I'd like to see whoever killed her brought in. And God knows, finding her killer wouldn't hurt your image with a lot of us."

"Good," Alex said.

"I'll get on the phone," she said. "Why don't you get yourself cleaned up while I'm at it? Across the hall there's a bedroom with a shower, towels, a razor. You look like hell."

She left, and he went and cleaned up, then collapsed on yet another unfamiliar bed. Seeing Cassandra again was a strange blend of pleasure and pain, stirring vivid memories of the only woman that he'd ever truly loved. The soft, repetitious pounding of the music that seeped up through the floor eventually won out against his overactive mind and took him down to a comalike sleep.

2

PROFESSOR Lorimer winced behind the lectern when Terrance Mullins raised his pudgy hand. "Yes, Terrance, do enlighten us with your opinion on Governor Tyrsdale's new bill. I'm sure the class has no idea what stance you'll take."

Mullins smiled and stood, "I think the Mandatory Registration Act is going to prove too little too late. Even if it passes, the government won't be able to implement it now to any real effect. The infection rates warrant much stronger action."

By the comments that erupted between classmates, it was clear that the lecture hall's occupants had divided opinions. Heads nodded, cheeks reddened, eyes rolled, and a radiant young girl in the last row replied, "That's bullshit. The *infection* rates are nothing more than inflated, *un*proven, *un*regulated government projections!"

Mullins ignored class protocol and turned upon the girl, "Those projection rates are based on over five thousand documented cases of deprivation. Deprivations that could have been prevented if the Mandatory Registration Act had been passed when it was first presented, immediately following the New York State versus Duncan Cameron conviction."

She rose, sending several textbooks to the floor. "What? You've obviously been *deprived* of common sense. What the hell are you talking about—deprivations that could have been avoided? This isn't some airborne virus that the government can just quarantine. And it's not lethal. We're talking about people—"

"Not lethal?" Mullins said. "Try telling that to a pregnant mother who's just been blinded by a Dep and steps in front of a bus." The emphasis he placed on the slang word *Dep* raised the stakes of the argument. It also revealed that for all Mullins's obvious education, he was still incredibly ignorant.

Much to the young woman's credit, she kept her wits about her. "You give so few details concerning motive or circumstance that it suggests an accident to me. These people are *not* responsible for their afflictions. If you're standing in a room with a Depriver, you're not automatically deprived. If that was true, I might agree with emergency measures. But you have to get touched skin-on-skin. Accidents notwithstanding, it's a conscious act to deprive someone, just like pointing a gun and shooting someone. If we follow *your* logic, then we should quarantine anyone with a gun because they might kill."

"Well, Julia," Mullins snapped back, "it just so happens that it's constitutionally provided that we *can* all own guns. Deprivers just happen to *be* guns. Unregistered guns, I might add."

"We are also *granted,* to the best of our government's ability, the right to liberty, equality, and freedom from prejudice. *Some* Deprivers could use their abilities for criminal ends, that's true, but Tyrsdale's ridiculous legislation suggests that *all* Deprivers are criminals by nature of their *non*transmittable attributes."

"I think 'defects' is a more fitting term," Terrance said. "And time will tell if it's transmittable or not. God help us if it is!"

Professor Lorimer, who was trying to get a word in edgewise, was finally afforded an opportunity as the two paused for breath. "Each of you raises key issues in the debate. It's clear that the upcoming legislature should not be taken lightly. Questions regarding the ethics of governmental protection versus the dangers of invoking Big Brother are quite apparent. Now, Mr. Mullins, you stated at the beginning of your argument that you felt the Tyrsdale Act was too little too late. What exactly would you propose to control this crisis?"

There was a gleam in Mullins's eye when he said, "Identify them. Round them up. Put a tracking chip in each of them. Say a prayer. And send them someplace safe."

"*Safe* meaning what? Safe from mobs of paranoid bigots like you?" Julia said. "How about a big red *D* tattooed on their foreheads? Would that suit you?"

A tremor of laughter swept the class as Julia stood and mimed the *D* on her head.

Then a third student, one who had always sat silently off to the rear of the hall, entered the fray. A senior who Professor Lorimer quite liked for his soft demeanor and profoundly acute attention to detail in his case studies. A somewhat handsome, dark-haired young man with ruddy cheeks and a pensive stare. A student who had never before, to the recollection of either the professor or any of his classmates, uttered a single word aloud during the course. He spoke up in a gentle voice, drive and surety behind it. "Professor, may I comment?"

"Yes Alex," Lorimer said, eyebrows raised. "What have you to add?"

Julia sat down. The young man did not rise from his seat, as was customary. He merely fixed his gaze on Terrance Mullins as he spoke. "To complement Julia's plea that we, as representatives of the poorly informed general public, need more information before allowing our elected officials to implement such legislation—legislation that could, after all, affect any one of us tomorrow—I offer for exhibit the fact that what Terrance is suggesting has already been attempted in our recent history. In places like Auschwitz."

The room was completely silent.

"WHO *are* you?" Julia asked, as she followed him out of the building. "And what took you so long?"

He turned and smiled. "Alex Crowley. And you didn't need me. You were doing fine on your own. I just came in and took all the credit."

She caught up to him, but came short of entering his personal space. She was nearly a foot shorter than he was, and she cocked her head to avoid the sun at his back. "Well, I believe in giving credit where it's due. Got another class now, Alex?"

He shook his head. "Just heading home."

"Lunch in the student center?"

"I'd like to, but . . . I'm a little short on funds."

"Come on, then, I'm tall on funds."

Walking along the pathways of Georgetown, Crowley would later recall that he'd wanted to hold her right there. Just abandon caution, reach out, and hold her close to him, run his fingers through her loose strawberry blonde curls.

"I'd cared little for either side of the argument until that day in class," he would write in his journal—an evening ritual of his since a near-death accident in high school—*"I was really only interested in making her notice me. All during that course, I'd been waiting for an opportunity to impress Julia."*

"I'M guessing you're prelaw?" he asked.

"How could you not?" she said. "And you?"

"Decidedly undecided."

"You're kidding me. Aren't you a senior?"

Alex nodded, tilting himself back on two chair legs, lost in her face. "Yeah," he said, "I'm one class away from a bachelor's in criminal justice. One away from a degree in chemistry. Three courses to go in Asian studies and four in applied psyche."

"Any minors?"

"Several. Depends how you line the courses up after determining what I'll eventually major in. Although I'll still have a minor in sign language, no matter how you cut it."

She took a sip of her soda. "Sign language?"

"Yeah." He tilted forward, unconsciously mirroring the way she sat. "An ex-girlfriend, who dumped and destroyed me, said I had intimacy problems—anyway, she had a younger brother who suddenly went deaf and she made me take—are you okay?"

She'd swallowed too quickly and was choking a bit. He reached out for her and she pulled back. "I'm—I'm okay. Just gimme a second." He watched nervously as she brought herself under control. She smiled a pale, embarrassed smile. "Sorry. Wrong pipe. Go on. Your ex-girlfriend's brother . . ."

"You sure you're okay?"

She nodded.

"So, she was really steeped in deaf culture—wanted to start her own television production network for the deaf."

"So, you took a lot of sign language classes."

"Yeah." He looked away, across campus, as the jogging crew passed. "Guess they're useless now."

"You never know." Julia shrugged, and offered a wink. "Your next girlfriend might be deaf."

"Yeah, maybe."

"But she'd never get to hear that beautiful voice of yours." Julia said with an embarrassed laugh.

On the way out of the center they passed two student-run tables. The first was for a blood drive. "Either of you like to give blood today?" an elderly nurse asked.

"No, thanks, I gave already this week," Alex said.

"Perhaps some condoms?" she said, pointing to a large plastic bowl. Julia smiled and scrutinized her tennis shoes.

"No, thank you, ma'am," Alex said.

The next table offered free gloves. The glove tables were growing more and more common around campus. Assorted colors and designs. Some had the Georgetown Hoyas emblem embossed on them.

"I want a pair of gloves," Julia said. She rushed to the table. A heavyset woman wearing small wire-rimmed glasses and wrist-length gloves greeted them.

"I've been curious about these," Julia told the woman. "Can they really prevent deprivation? Are they enough protection?"

"Oh, yes," the woman said.

"I'll take the green ones. Alex, what color would you like?"

"*Umh.* Black, I guess."

The woman gave him a sour look. "No black, sir. Deprivers wear black. How about gray, to match your eyes?"

"Gray is fine."

They both slid on their gloves and tested their fit. "Now we'll be safe," Julia said, winking again. Then, to the woman, "You're sure now that these are enough to prevent any horrible deprivations?"

"Oh, yes," she said again.

"Thank goodness," Julia said, grabbing Alex roughly and grinning. "Now we won't grope each other blind!"

They left the woman gaping as they walked off, hand in hand.

"Do you need a lift anywhere?" Julia asked as they reached her car, an old Mustang.

"I live in the dorms," Alex said. "Thanks, though."

They both hesitated, not wanting to part company.

"So, where are you off to?" Julia asked, resting her gloved hands on top of her car.

Alex looked away and then back. "I have a basketball game tonight."

"Don't tell me you're a jock?"

"No, no," he said, shaking his head. "I'm not on a team or anything. I just play with some friends. You live in town?"

"Yeah, over in Adams Morgan. Me and some girlfriends rent a house."

"That's cool."

"Yeah, I guess. So, do you want to see me again?"

Without thinking he said, "Yeah, of course. I'll see you in class." He regretted the inadvertent dismissal as soon as he said it.

She got in her car and waved as she drove away.

That night, on the basketball court behind the dorms, the silent and unstoppable Alex Crowley revolved around his friends, sinking wild shots left and right. Later, in his journal, he replayed every detail of the day's pseudodate. And he switched his major from undecided to Julia O'Connor.

3

THE next time the class met, student participation was less interactive, which was to Professor Lorimer's liking. Terrance Mullins was absent for most of the period. Alex and Julia exchanged flirtatious looks, and they were side by side in the hall moments after dismissal.

"I couldn't wait to talk to you," Julia said. "How'd your game go?"

"Me either," he said, smiling. "We won."

"Yeah, I'll bet you did." She laughed. "Listen, I just happen to have tickets for The Pixies tribute concert tonight. Would you like to go?"

"Sure," he said.

"You, uh, don't know who The Pixies are, do you?"

He shook his head and laughed a little at himself.

"Come on, then, I'll play them for you in the car."

She was wearing blue jeans, and he noticed how they revealed her curves to their best advantage. He also noticed she was wearing makeup. His only regret: her freckles were slightly diminished. He had shaved before class, trimmed his nails, and tried to do something with his hair.

"So, what kind of music do you listen to, Alex?" Julia asked as they walked into the lot.

"Mostly old rock'n'roll," he said. "You know, Nirvana, Sublime, The Doors, Alice in Chains."

"The classics."

"Exactly."

"Well, I hope you're open-minded if you're gonna ride with me, 'cause I'm telling you, I don't tolerate—Oh my God!"

As they came around the side of a passenger van they saw the words *Dep Lover!* across the hood of her car in black spray paint.

Tears brimmed in Julia's eyes, and a wave of anger rushed over Alex. "Terrance Mullins," he said. "I'm gonna kick that kid's ass when I catch him."

"It could have been anyone," Julia said.

"Come on," he said, "we'll drive over by maintenance and see if they have something to get this off."

"Thanks, Alex, you're really great."

As it turned out, the car cleaned up well. Julia convinced Alex not to report the incident to the student government or the campus police. And Alex enjoyed what he heard of The Pixies.

IT was actually the first concert Alex had ever attended, he confessed on the drive home. He liked it a lot. A cavalcade of senses, he'd called it. "I'd like to make sure you get home safe, Julia. Can I swing by your house with you? I can get back on my own," he said.

"Not yet," she said. "Not tonight. I hope that's okay."

He nodded. He was disappointed, but he did understand.

When she pulled up to his dorm, Alex was poised to lean in for the good-night kiss he'd imagined at least a hundred times. But she patted his shoulder before he could initiate, as though sensing his anticipation and moving purposefully against it. He wondered if he could have possibly misinterpreted her signals. *Is it just friendship she's looking for?*

Two weeks passed, and Julia did not show up for class once. He had no phone number for her, nor, he realized, had she ever taken his. There were no listings for her in the campus directory or from information, or even on the library's Intranet system. Professor Lorimer had not heard from her, and her absences were, as yet, unexcused. Alex grew so concerned that he confronted Terrance Mullins. Terrance admitted to his anti-Depriver sentiment and to his distaste for Julia, after his public embarrassment; however, he adamantly denied having any part in vandalizing her car or any knowledge of her whereabouts. Alex wandered the campus aimlessly. On the basketball courts with his friends, his efforts were halfhearted. *Had she left because of him? Had someone kidnapped her?* None of the questions or their possible answers gave him any peace. After the vandalism to her car, it was difficult for him not to suspect that something bad had happened.

He telephoned every local hospital, hospice, and police precinct, playing the lost relative to strangers and seeming a madman to himself. All the while, two distinct voices spoke out inside his drifting mind. One begged him to see reason and give up on the girl. And really, they had only had two dates. The other voice, which kept hammering away, growing louder with each passing hour, demanded he find her. Something terrible may well have happened.

There came a point when these two voices merged into the shrewd, tempered voice of a man who would never give up, and the hunt began in earnest. He phoned Professor Lorimer and requested a leave of absence for both himself and Julia. Lorimer granted both and wished him luck. Then, with not so much as a photograph to hold out to the strangers he met, he began his own systematic search. Adams Morgan, she'd said once. Julia lived in Adams Morgan.

In crowded bars he singled out regulars and told them what she looked like, delivering the facts with a stoic tongue: "Julia O'Connor. Five foot two. Strawberry blonde. Green eyes. Small chest. Prelaw major who lives in a house with a group of girls. Drives a silver Mustang. Call this number. Thanks for your time."

Five days of nonstop investigating passed, and Alex found no sign of Julia. He searched every bar in Adams Morgan and every bar in Georgetown. He checked every hospital. He searched every off-campus sorority house in the D.C. area. On the sixth day, he went to the registrar's office.

"Please," he asked the woman behind the desk, "I need the contact information for Julia O'Connor."

"Why?"

"Because she's missing."

"Legally missing? This office hasn't been notified of a missing student. What is your relationship to the student, exactly?"

A good question. *Who the hell am I to her, after all?* Alex thought. "I'm her boyfriend," he lied. "And she's been missing for two weeks and five days."

"Is there a police report on file?"

"No."

"You've gone to her dorm? Do her suite mates agree that she's missing? Her resident advisor?"

In frustration, partly because he knew his answers would clearly point out his lack of actual knowledge—lack of actual *relationship* to Julia, he answered, "No. She lives off campus."

"And you've been to her place of residence?" she peered over her glasses at him, a what's-really-going-on-here look on her face.

"I don't actually know where she lives. We've only been dating a short time and—"

"Listen, young man," the woman said, "this girl you like is probably home sick. She's missed a few classes, is under the weather, and doesn't want to answer your calls. I can't give you any personal information unless you're authorized by—"

"Goddammit, are you listening to me!" Alex snapped, in perhaps the loudest outburst of his life. "One of your students is missing. I have combed this entire town looking for her. I am not a hysterical boyfriend. I am a dean's list, trustee scholar, and I demand to speak with your superior. This girl is in danger—"

Suddenly security was gripping Alex's shoulders and tugging him toward the exit. Then, from a doorway behind the main desk, Alex caught site of Professor Lorimer, stepping out of the registrar's office to see what the shouting was about. A calm explanation from Lorimer to the security guards, and Alex was released. A few apologetic words to the woman at the desk and a nod from the registrar himself, and a contact sheet was released to Lorimer. It was a lesson in diplomacy that was not lost on Alex Crowley.

Contact information in hand, the professor led Alex across the quad to his office. The room was lined with law books and the occasional science text. "You got me so worried, I thought I'd better check on her myself," Lorimer said. "It's a good thing I was there when you happened to throw your tantrum."

"I'm sorry. I was frustrated. They acted appropriately, Professor. My own feelings of inadequacy made me explode. You see, Julia and I barely knew each other."

"All the more noble your concern," Lorimer said, offering Alex the contact sheet. "Be my guest." He indicated the phone on the desk by his computer, then stepped toward the door. "But please," he asked as he closed the door, "let me know what you find out. As I say, you've got me quite concerned."

There was something odd about Lorimer, Alex decided, something that the professor seemed to be holding back. He looked at the contact list. No local telephone number. No local address. Only an emergency listing: Felicia O'Connor. Relationship: mother. An address in Connecticut and a telephone number. He lifted the professor's phone, tapped an outside line, and dialed.

As the phone rang, Alex almost hung up. He feared the worst. A family member, perhaps a cousin, would answer and explain in hushed tones how Julia had been found dead. They'd want to know who he was. Nobody, he'd reply. To her I am basically nobody. On the fourth ring a voice said, "Hay-low, O'Connor residence. Cynthia speaking." A stroke of luck. Alex was sure she was a child no older than ten or eleven.

"Hi, Cynthia," Alex said in his friendliest voice. "It's Julia's friend, Alex. Is she there?"

"Nope. She's at college," the girl answered. "Do I know you, Alex?"

Fearing an adult might interfere on her end at any

moment, he resorted to uncharacteristic, bold-faced deception. "Yes, and I can't believe you'd forget me. Do you know her phone number at college, Cynthia? I have some concert tickets that I can't use, and I was going to give them to her. Maybe she'll take you with her?"

"Oh," she said, obviously excited. "You really think she'll take me?"

He hated the lie but saw no other option than to compound it. "Sure, why not. I'll tell her she has to take you, as part of getting the tickets. Do you have the number?"

A pause from her, then, "Yeah, I think it's on the fridge." She dropped the phone on its cord, and Alex heard it knocking like a pendulum as it hung. When he heard a background voice call, "Honey, who's on the phone?" his breath caught and held.

"My friend, Alex, Mom," Cynthia yelled back to his relief. *Give me that number, and we will be friends,* he thought. Cynthia came back, "I got it. How bad do you want it?"

"A lot," Alex said.

"Promise you'll tell her to take me?"

"I swear," Alex said.

She gave him the number, very slowly, one digit at a time, as if she were teasing him.

"Thanks, Cynthia, I owe you," Alex said before he hung up the phone.

He had it. Now, how to handle the next call? A group of girlfriends. She lives in a house with a group of girls. Just call and ask for her. Everything could just be fine. He composed himself, punched the keypad.

"Hello?" came a curt, male voice on the other end.

Alex was thrown off by a man answering. "Yes," he said. "Is Julia there?"

The man paused, then, "There's no one here by that name."

"Um, are you sure? She gave me this number."

Another pause. "Who's calling? Where are you from?"

"I'm sorry, I must have the wrong number," Alex said, then quickly hung up. Very suspicious. He knew that he'd dialed the number correctly. The man on the phone had to have been lying. *Why say no one is there by that name, and then ask who is calling or where they're from?* Something was definitely wrong here. Alex felt it like a nauseous sensation.

He powered on the professor's computer, went on-line to a search engine, selected Reverse Phone Directory and typed in the number. Double-click and bingo—the Adams Morgan address was returned. He reviewed the area in his mind. Days spent searching the neighborhood would finally pay off. He could be there before sunset if he ran fast.

4

TWENTY-ONE minutes later, Alex Crowley was standing across the street from the house where he suspected
Julia was being held captive, a two-story colonial in bad
repair that reminded him of New England. The wrought-
iron gate stood open, as though he were expected. For the
first time in his life, Alex wished he owned a gun. He crept
around through the alley until he spotted a lone window
near the back of the house. As good a place as any, he
decided.

Standing on top of an overturned garbage can, fingers
threatening to slip from a filthy sill, Alex peeked through a
mesh screen into the house. It was, as he had hoped, a boiler
room. Clothing hung on makeshift lines. Sweatshirts with
fraternity logos emblazoned upon them. A brassiere. Some
underwear. No trace of wrongdoing. It didn't occur to Alex
when he jimmied the screen that he was breaking and
entering. The can beneath him gave only a small grunt as
he pulled himself upward through the window. He landed

silently, but he felt the pounding of his heart would alert every occupant of the house to his intrusion. He listened at the boiler room door but could hear nothing. Taking a deep breath, he opened the door. It creaked as he entered a bare hallway and then crept toward the back stairwell. He calmed himself and took the stairs at what he gauged a normal, nonintruder pace. He consciously let each stair creak.

As he reached the top of the stairs, he heard indistinct voices coming from one of the rooms. He inched himself forward, down an unlit corridor, until he was up against the door. He pressed his ear to it and listened. Three voices, one male, two female—maybe one of them Julia's? He wasn't sure. He was surprised to hear laughter.

Then the door began to swing open, and there was no place he could hide. A long-haired, thirtyish-looking man came into the hall and almost walked into Alex. He was startled. "Who the hell are you?" he said, squinting in the shadows.

"I'm here for Julia," Alex said, as if he were merely arriving for a scheduled date.

"Yeah? Who *are* you?"

"Alex."

"Alex, huh? Yeah, I heard her talk about you. But I thought you were history."

"Well, I'm not. She here?"

"No," he said, "but she should be home any minute. You can wait if you want. I'm Jake."

Alex extended his hand, but Jake either failed to notice the gesture or simply ignored it. "Pretty desperate, huh?" he said. "You can sit down."

Alex walked past Jake into the room, where two women sat, one on the couch, the other on the floor, each at least a few years older than Alex. The one on the couch had long,

dark, braided hair and wore torn jeans. The girl on the
floor had a shaved head and was wearing a Dead Kennedys
T-shirt. The room was lit solely by candlelight, and there
was incense burning. The women looked up and seemed to
study Alex for a moment before acknowledging him.

Jake said, "Gretchen, Irma. This is Alex. He's a friend of
Julia's."

"Hi," Alex said.

Gretchen, the woman on the couch, nodded. Irma, the
bald girl, extended her gloved hand, and Alex shook it.
"Julia told you she lived here?" she asked.

Alex nodded. The place seemed peaceful enough, but he
thought that it would be best to keep them talking. "How
do you guys know Julia?" he asked.

By the way they looked to one another, he felt he'd said
something wrong. Then Jake laughed and said, "She and I
used to go out."

"Really?" Alex asked. Irma chuckled.

"Really," Jake said, and pulled a cigarette from behind
his ear. He lit it from a candle in the alcove by Alex. "Care
to take a little test of manhood for her honor?"

Alex hesitated. *Was this some sort of joke?* He felt as if he
had little choice but to play along. "Sure," he said. "What
did you have in mind?"

"How about the old cigarette test?" Jake asked.

That piqued the attention of the two women.

"How's that go?" Alex asked.

"You know," Jake said, "whoever can hold the head of a
cigarette against his hand the longest wins. You up for it?"

Alex was puzzled. He looked to the women, who were
looking to him expectantly. He looked at Jake and saw
the man was serious. He was searching for a polite way to
decline the offer, one that would not leave him looking fearful,

that would not offend, when Jake said, "Me first!" Holding the cigarette in his right hand, he brought the burning tip to his palm. Alex looked on while the ember made contact with the man's flesh—this was no trick. Even if his eyes deceived him, his sense of smell did not.

"Count for us, Irma," Jake said, not so much as a tremor in his voice.

Irma counted slowly, as if it were some big joke. "One, two, three, four . . ."

Jake pulled the cigarette away and slapped his hand down hard on his leg, then brought it up to his face and blew on it. Alex could see the dark burn.

"Your turn," he said, "Irma, count."

"Yeah, yeah," Irma replied in a detached tone that said she'd seen this all before.

Alex willed his arm to rise as he looked into Jake's face and attempted to close off the rest of the world. *Would the pain be too much?* he thought.

Jake took a long drag off the cigarette, flaming up the tip, and blew his smoke into Alex's face. Alex extended his hand, palm open. He gritted his teeth and steeled himself for the burn. *I can take this,* he told himself over and again.

"Alex!" came Julia's voice from the hall—but still he would not turn. In a very real way, he now *wanted* the contact. "Alex," Julia repeated. "Don't do it, Jake!"

At Julia's insistence, Jake popped the cigarette back into his mouth, exactly as he had wished to do the moment he realized Alex's bold determination.

"Heck, kid, you win," Jake said.

Julia placed the bags of groceries she was carrying on the floor as Alex turned to her and lowered his hand.

"What are you doing here?" she asked.

"I came to see you—you just disappeared," he said. Julia

stood fast, unsure how to react. Alex looked to her with longing. He drank in the freckles on her face. He took note that she was wearing the green gloves that she'd gotten that first afternoon with him at the student center.

"I'm glad you did," she said finally.

5

"YOU'RE all Deprivers, then?" Alex repeated, a bit bewildered. "Really? You're serious?"

Julia tugged her tank top down a few inches, revealing a dark blue raised *D* tattoo on her chest. Gretchen and Irma revealed similar marks. Jake pulled his shirt up, revealing a *D* on his shoulder blade.

"It's not mandatory," Jake said. "But a lot of Deps do it to themselves for solidarity."

Alex recalled Julia's grandstanding atop her desk that day in class with her hands to her forehead, and smiled.

"I really liked you, Alex. I just couldn't stay. I was afraid you'd get involved in this mess. And besides, you were already getting that hurt look in your eyes when I left. I could tell you needed to touch and be touched, and I *can't* touch you. If I did, I'd deprive you. And I'm not temporary, like some. I'm permanent."

There were tears in her eyes as she spoke. "What would I be deprived of?" he asked after a pause.

Julia looked at Jake, and Alex followed her gaze. "Pain sensitivity," Jake replied, flexing the hand he had singed. "And the majority of hot and cold sensitivity."

"It's one of the better senses to lose," Gretchen said, lighting a cigarette. "If you're going to lose one, that is."

"So, let me get this straight. Jake's deprived, right?" Alex asked.

Julia nodded.

"Deprived by you?"

Again, she nodded.

"But he's also a Depriver himself."

"Yeah," Jake said. "I'm one of the dreaded untouchables too."

"So, Jake must have deprived you, right? What did he deprive you of?"

"Hearing, but he doesn't have much of a duration."

"That's why you gagged when I told you about my ex-girlfriend," said Alex.

"Yeah—you think you've got intimacy problems."

Alex sighed. "How long were you deaf?"

"Less than a week, a couple of times, I guess. That's how long it usually lasts, right Jake?"

Jake nodded, lit another cigarette. "You might try mine someday, Alex. Being deprived actually has its advantages."

"And you?" Alex asked Irma.

She peeled off her gloves and answered, "I usually don't tell on the first date, but I'm a blinder. Some get it back in a month or so, some not ever. I guess I'm kind of a wild card. I've only ever touched three people since I turned. Think about that. If you get really suicidal courageous, though, Jake and I can Helen Keller you."

"No, thanks," Alex said. "And you, Gretchen?"

"I don't know," she said with a shrug. "These guys found

me last winter when I had just turned. I don't think I've ever deprived anybody. I intend to keep it like that."

"Wait," Alex said, rising to his feet with excitement. "Are you telling me you have a way of knowing who is a Depriver and who isn't?"

"Of course," Jake said. "It's a side effect of being deprived."

"But Gretchen can't?"

"That's right," Irma said. "And neither can I. I've never been deprived either. If I could find a short-termer, someone who could risk my blindness. Someone dying maybe, or already blind, I'd be willing to try it."

"Alex, how did you find me?" Julia asked.

"It wasn't easy," he said.

"That was you on the phone before, right?" Jake asked.

Alex nodded. "At first I thought you were abducted by Terrance Mullins."

"By that idiot? No way."

"Then I got some help from Professor Lorimer."

"That old smell-sucker Dep stalker," Jake said. "I'm not surprised he'd give us away, he's been—"

"Hold on now," Alex said. "Lorimer's a Depriver?"

"Yeah."

"Sheesh," he said. "Then I lied to Cynthia and promised her concert tickets."

"My little sister helped you?" Julia asked.

"Yes, and I promised her you'd take her to see a show. I'm sorry."

Alex turned away from them and faced the window. "This is all so . . ."

"Unnerving?"

"No. So fascinating." Turning back, he looked at Julia. "Take a walk with me. Please?"

"Okay. Let me run down and get a jacket first."

Jake said, "Sorry about the cigarette thing. I guess I was a little jealous. It's not too often we meet Dep-friendly Normals."

"Is that what I am?" Alex asked.

"Yeah, I think so." Jake got up and crushed out his smoke. "If not, we won't be safe around here for much longer."

Alex put his hand against Jake's covered shoulder. "I am, Jake. A Dep-friendly Normal."

Jake nodded. "Good. Come back anytime. Bring beer and pizza." He grabbed up his cigarettes and walked out of the room with a yawn.

"You think you'll be hanging around?" Gretchen asked.

"I guess that'll depend on Julia," he said.

"Come on, Alex, I'm ready!" Julia called up.

"See you later," Irma said as he moved toward the door. "Good luck in whatever you choose to do. I'm not sure which way will be better for you—to get together with her or not, I mean."

"Thanks, I guess," he said, then left her to join Julia.

A few minutes later, Irma walked to the window and pulled back the drapes. There was a near-perfect moon overhead, and just down the street she could make out the silhouettes of Alex and Julia standing side by side. After a short while, they came together.

6

AFTER Julia was gone, Alex felt no connection to anyone or anyplace—she'd been his life, and he'd adopted her cause as his own. Her friends who once welcomed him now shunned him. From the outset of SDS, the world had sided off, like with like, and now he was the odd man out. Companionless, he'd found oblivion in the bottle, and oblivion had helped. So much so that he'd ended up in the detox unit of D.C. General Hospital with his left arm in a cast. Three weeks there, and he rarely spoke to another patient or doctor. What could he tell them really? If he told the doctors or nurses he'd been permanently deprived, much less that he'd been married to one of *them,* they'd have refused to treat him out of ignorance.

One morning he awoke to Dr. Godfrey at his bedside. It had been over a year since he'd last seen her, but her voice was imprinted in his memory.

"Alex," she whispered. "My poor, dear Alex."

She was older now, of course, must be nearly forty. The

same dark-braided hair, the same glasses, the same sensitive eyes. "Theresa Godfrey, my savior."

"Let's get you out of here," she said. "And we'll see what's left to save."

"How did you find me?"

She smiled. "When Gretchen told me you went missing, I began checking the hospitals. I am a doctor, you know."

She took him home—a comfortable split-level in a gated community near Capitol Hill, not far from the safe house in Adams Morgan he'd once shared with Julia and the others. There he was introduced to her infamous husband, the Depriver who'd revealed himself to the world—*the* Robert Luxley. Crowley sat on their couch and marveled at how very normally they appeared to be living. *Surely Luxley would be sought out for registration,* he thought. Before any pleasantries were exchanged, Crowley asked for a matte knife, and Luxley went to find one.

"Pleasure to meet you, Alex," Luxley said as he handed Crowley the knife.

"Not many Deprivers feel that way," Crowley said, extending the blade and going to work on his cast.

"Your wife was one of Terry's patients, wasn't she?"

"You were a professional hit man once, weren't you?"

Luxley sat down on a chair across from Crowley with a glass of wine in his hand, watching Crowley as he methodically sawed away at the plaster. "That was a long time ago," he said, then looked to Theresa. "People change. Other people can change you."

Crowley knew that Luxley was a paralyzer, and tried to imagine the hardships that would cause in an intimate relationship. He thought of Julia, always testing him with pinches and pricks and, *"Can you feel that, Alex?"*

"It's amazing how we've paralleled each other's situations,"

Theresa said, sitting down with a cup of tea. "Both of us becoming Dep-friendly Normals . . ."

Dep-friendly Normal—that's what they'd called him when he'd first met Julia. *A Normal who was permitted to walk freely among those afflicted, during a time when mere Dep association could cause you to mysteriously disappear from society.*

". . . and then both of us marrying into the Depriver community and becoming acquainted with so many of the same people," she said.

"That's right," Luxley said. "You're quite close with the twins and Sparrow."

"Small Depriver world," Crowley said.

"You met them in Amsterdam?" Luxley asked.

"Yes, they were at our wedding. We saw them a lot. When they moved back to America, to hide out on the reservation, I went through the Sundance ceremony with Sparrow's people."

Luxley winced. "That's that painful bit, dragging the bones around by the hooks in the skin on your back?"

"Yes, but it's the psychological bridges you cross that are important. I feel no physical pain." Crowley dug deep with the knife and separated the final piece of plaster, accidentally cutting into his palm and drawing blood. He tore the cast off and placed it on the coffee table.

"Your deprivation, I assume?"

"Yes."

"I'll get a bandage," Theresa said.

"Thanks," Crowley said.

Luxley leaned in close to Crowley as she left the room, and whispered, "Have you figured out who shot your wife?"

Crowley shook his head slowly.

"We'll talk later," Luxley said.

Later that night, after Robert and Theresa went to bed,

Crowley lay awake, half asleep and half lucid on the couch, awaiting Robert and recalling better days. . . .

They were in Amsterdam, and it was just as Julia had always imagined. The city with the highest Depriver population and the most liberal attitude toward it was beautiful with its brick-lined streets, old-world charm, and warm hospitality. It was like he and Julia were falling in love all over again. And the Deprivers they met there were simply good-natured *people*.

"I'd like you to meet my fiancé, Alex," Julia said, introducing Alex during a Deprivers-only party in the red-light district.

"Nice to meet you, Alex," said the blonde-haired Dutch girl. "My name is Astrid. This is my friend, Sparrow. He's American, like you."

Sparrow was an American Indian of some notoriety in Depriver circles, who Julia had often talked about. He was an audio-Depriver, like Jake.

"I've heard a lot about you," Alex said.

"And we've heard about you," Sparrow said. "The first Depriver-Normal marriage."

"No big deal, really," Alex said. "Lots of Deps are married to Normals."

Sparrow smiled. "No Alex, you don't get it. Lots of couples are married and then suddenly one of them turns Dep. Then there's almost certainly a breakup. You guys are getting together out of love, in spite of your differences. You're an inspiration. Glad to meet you."

ROBERT Luxley woke Crowley up off the couch around four A.M. and took him out for a drive. Crowley looked around at the familiar streets and waited patiently for the man to offer up some information.

Luxley seemed different to him now, not the same man he was around Theresa. "What are you going to do about your wife's murder?" he said finally.

Crowley turned to Luxley. "How do you know she was murdered? How do you know it wasn't a random shot fired into the crowd?"

"I know because I turned down the posting myself. I was out of the business," Luxley said.

Too shocked to withdraw, Crowley swallowed the information and asked, "What was the posting? Who was it from? How did it work?"

"The posting," Luxley whispered, "was to kill you both. For a very large sum of money. I don't know who posted it. Most posts are anonymous and nearly impossible to trace. They didn't know us; we didn't know them."

As the revelation began to sink in, Crowley sat comatose in despair. Luxley looked out at the road through his windshield. "I know how you feel. If something ever happened to Terry—"

"You'd hunt down whoever was responsible."

"Yes."

"Even if I wanted to, I have no idea where to start."

"Well, I'm out of those circles now. Just like you're out of ours. But, if you do go ahead with this, I have one other piece of information—and a suggestion."

"I'm listening."

"It was strange," Luxley said, remembering the telephone conversation from long ago, "but I distinctly remember the contact trying to confirm that I was a Depriver."

"As if it were a requirement?"

"Yes."

"And the suggestion?"

"If it was a Depriver they wanted, that suggests many things . . . but you draw your own conclusions. If I was looking for a Dep assassin, I'd go to the man who knows them all."

"Alan Deveraux."

"Yes."

"How do I reach him?"

"I assume he's still somewhere in Miami. Theresa would kill me for suggesting this, I—"

"Tell me," Crowley said. "I need this. It's the only thing I have to keep me going."

"Nicholas Wilkes is with Deveraux's daughter, Claudette. We don't know where they are; they've cut themselves off from the network. But I know where Cassandra is. . . ."

"Know a place we can stop for a drink?" Crowley asked.

7

"ALEX, wake up," Cassandra said, gently shaking him. He opened his eyes and had a moment's difficulty in orienting himself. *This is Toronto,* he thought. *A bed in a room upstairs at Cassandra's place, the Tarantula.* He saw that she had changed into jeans and a gray hooded sweatshirt. "I got you an invitation to Miami with airfare included, but you have to leave now. It's not safe for you to stay here anymore."

Five hours later, Crowley boarded a plane headed for Miami International. Cassandra had reached Nicholas, communications were rapid, and Deveraux was actually interested in meeting. Shaved and showered, he looked a lot more like the Alex Julia had met in college, even with a few new scars and some hollowing to the cheeks and eyes.

With nothing else to occupy his time on the flight, Crowley ordered several of the tiny airline bottles of Baccardi and drifted once more into the pleasure and pain of memory. . . .

The five roommates were sitting around the living room

one night watching television. Julia and Alex snuggled together on the couch. Jake sat chain-smoking, watching them.

A television news break. Governor Tyrsdale, with his ugly gray cowlick, urging the nation to "Please, alert local health officials if you suspect one of your neighbors is a carrier of Sensory Deprivation Syndrome."

"That fucker's gonna get his damned Mandatory Registration Act through eventually," Gretchen said. "And then we're all screwed."

"We can always move to Amsterdam," Jake had replied.

Gretchen's face reddened. "Hey, I grew up here, okay? I pay taxes here!"

Then from Irma, a whisper, the only comment she'd make all night. "Somebody ought to kill that asshole."

"Violence calls to violence," Alex warned.

Gretchen turned on him, disgusted, with, "What a typical *Normal* response!"

Crowley was jarred awake as the plane touched down.

AS soon as he stepped out of the security zone, a dark-suited Dep, wearing leather gloves, hailed him. Crowley put him at about thirty. His eyes were deeply sunken, and he was a good fifteen pounds underweight for his height. "You're Crowley?" the man asked.

Crowley nodded.

"I'm Byron. I'll be escorting you to see Mr. Deveraux. Do you have any baggage?"

"No."

"Are you carrying any weapons?"

"No, I just got off a plane."

"Right," he said. "Well, don't do anything stupid, or you'll be a sack of bones with a slow pulse for the rest of your life, *comprende?* Welcome to Miami."

Byron brought Crowley to a waiting limousine and ushered him into the backseat. "Sorry, Crowley, but for security purposes, I'll need to black out your windows." He pressed a button on his console, and all of the windows in Crowley's section diffused to black. It was less than thirty minutes before Crowley set foot on Deveraux's compound.

Crowley was well aware he was under surveillance as he was led through the main building to Deveraux's office. A knock and a "Come in," and he stood before the man himself—Alan Deveraux, the Depriver Godfather.

Deveraux sat on the edge of his desk with a telephone to his ear. Demanding tone, relaxed posture, even breathing, a man who controlled his own destiny. "Make it happen," he said, as he hung up the phone. He then moved toward Crowley, dismissing Byron with a wave, and extended a gloved hand, which Crowley shook. They exchanged a very firm grip. "The handshake will soon be a forgotten art, Mr. Crowley," Deveraux said. "Mark my words."

"Already is, as far as I've seen," Crowley said.

"Ah yes," Deveraux said, nodding. "I forget. You're a Normal who has, until recently, lived freely among Deprivers. It's the outside world to which I was referring, of course. Poor, blind bastards. They don't know who to touch. It's gonna drive them all to isolation and prejudice, the likes of which this world has never seen. Mark my words."

Crowley was silent.

"Your condition is pain asymbolia, am I correct?"

"Correct," Crowley said.

"So you could break your leg and never feel a thing?"

Crowley looked around at the bookshelves, the view

through the ornate picture window, the stone-carved wall, at least twelve feet high. "I'd feel the irregularity, but not the pain," he said.

"Hot and cold sensitivity?" Deveraux asked.

"None."

"Very interesting. I would love to test your threshold levels."

Crowley looked disinterested. "Maybe another time."

"Of course," Deveraux said. "Well, my friend, I feel I am already somewhat in your debt. You managed to get my daughter to call me, close to impossible these days. I could use a man like you in my operations."

"With no disrespect, sir, my services are not for hire."

"I see. Well, consider that it's one way you might someday return to the fold. I certainly consider you one of us."

This man is trying to play with my loyalties, Crowley thought. *And yet, there is something very persuasive about him.*

Deveraux took a seat at his desk and motioned for Crowley to sit. "Aren't you the least bit curious, how I know so much about you?"

"I'm pretty well-known in Depriver circles."

"*Mmm.* How about the fact your parents died together in a plane crash when you were fifteen?"

Crowley made no comment, and Deveraux continued. "Or that you first met your late wife in a legal interpretation course at Georgetown University, and the instructor's name was Jeffrey Lorimer?"

Crowley maintained a look of calm.

"Or that Theresa Godfrey was your wife's therapist. Or that you and a young Indian we both know were photographed together on a reservation in South Dakota. Or that your drink of choice is Baccardi 151, and you—"

"Okay," Crowley said. "You've impressed me and

aroused my curiosity. Where did you get all this from?"

Deveraux pulled a pair of glasses from his drawer and put them on, then lifted a file off his desk and handed it across to Crowley. "That's your file, son. I can't take credit for compiling it, but I can take credit for stealing it for you. It was compiled by an organization called the Ministry. Familiar with them?"

Crowley thumbed through the pages: his high school transcripts, parents' death certificates, psych evaluations, photographs of him with Julia in Washington, in Amsterdam, in Paris. "No sir. Who are they?"

"Bane of my existence, Alex. They're a law enforcement community. A bureau of investigation that has never been officially sanctioned by a single nation or government, yet granted instant and unchallenged sovereignty over any investigation they lay claim to. FBI, CIA, MI5, Interpol—everybody steps aside when the Ministry steps in. They've been around a long time. Now, lucky us, they've created a special branch to deal with Deprivers, and you've got a file. Feel included again?"

"Maybe more than I'd like to," Crowley said, flipping through the documents. He dropped the file on the desk in frustration.

"Didn't find what you're looking for?" Deveraux asked.

"No, there's no mention of the shooter."

"I noticed. Any idea why your wife was killed? Did she do any intelligence work?" Deveraux's interest appeared to be truly piqued.

"No," Crowley replied. "I would've known. She was very verbal when they were passing the original Deprivers' resolutions and health mandates, but not verbal enough to be killed."

"As far as you know."

Crowley met Deveraux's eyes. "How about as far as *you* know?"

"I have no idea who killed your wife or why she was killed. I'm sorry."

Crowley gritted his teeth. "Do you believe you're capable of finding out?"

"Anything's possible, Alex. Someone out there does know."

"If you were to find out," he asked, "would you tell me?"

At this request, the older man stopped to think. "I'll put in the work, yes. It's certainly for a good cause—that is to say, *our* cause. However, it may take time."

"And your price?"

"Let's not name a price just now, Alex. Let's wait and see just how juicy the purchase turns out to be. Meanwhile, I'd steer clear of the Ministry. You've obviously been flagged. How can I reach you?"

"Don't worry about that," Crowley said. "Give me a number where I can reach you."

"Fair enough," Deveraux said, rising and once again extending his hand. "Sure you won't consider signing on for a time?"

"I'm not an assassin."

"No," Deveraux said. "But you certainly could be. Given the right cause."

"I'll bear that in mind," Crowley said.

"So will I."

Byron returned Crowley to the airport in the same fashion he was brought in. Crowley spent that ride meditating on the interview. He was sure of one thing: Deveraux was holding back.

8

CROWLEY, unsure of his next move, decided against flying back up North right away and went instead to the airport bar. The pretty young bartender said, "Hey handsome, what can I fix you?" He smiled and ordered a cup of coffee with a shot of Bacardi. While she prepared his drink, he watched the basketball game in progress on the television monitor that was mounted over the bar. Saint John's versus Villanova. *It's such a shame,* he thought, seeing the players in all those pads and gloves. *It's just not the same game.* He paid up and took a booth in the back.

He thought back to the funeral. He was standing by her coffin, saying good-bye, nodding at guests—staring down at her, beautiful even in death. He looked back over his shoulder at the many mourners, more than half of them glowing. Cassandra and Sparrow, Gretchen and Irma—he could recognize their light signatures even from the other side of the church with the sight Julia had given him. He reached down to Julia, lying there, and gently undid the first two buttons of her shirt as the priest looked on in distress. With the buttons opened, the *D* tattoo was visible. She would have wanted the world to see it.

Like a missionary in a leper colony, Crowley was witness to their isolation, yet unafflicted, an outsider, even at the funeral of his beloved. He could walk by their sides and be spat on during demonstrations, but the *D* tattoo was forever forbidden to him. Screw both sides, he'd decided—Julia and I loved each other, and that was all that mattered. And then Jake had burst in and screamed, "*You!* You're the reason she's dead!"

"HEY sweetie, can I get you another drink?" the bartender asked Crowley, snapping him back from his favorite method of self-torture.

"Uh, no," Crowley said. "Can you tell me where the men's room is?"

"Sorry," she answered. "We don't have them in here. You have to use one of the airport rest rooms. There's one right outside, by gate three."

Crowley thanked her and left the bar. He found the bathroom and was at the urinal when the man came up behind him, shoved the blade into his lower back, and twisted it. Another man might have gone down, but Crowley reacted violently, slamming his elbow back into the face of his attacker, forcing him to release his grip on the knife as he was propelled backward into a stall. Crowley didn't look back. He just ran. Out of the bathroom and into the terminal, with the knife still halfway inside him. *Who would do this? Where do I go?* Thoughts rushed through him as he raced down the escalator. A traveler saw the knife and the blood that was staining his shirt

and began screaming. Soon, several onlookers were
screaming too. Crowley felt the blade twisting itself
deeper with each move he made. He got through the
revolving door, just barely, using the push rail to keep
upright—then he stumbled and fell to the pavement.

HE woke up in a haze on a king-sized bed, and quietly surveyed the bandages over his wound. He opened one eye to a
slit and took in his surroundings. It appeared that he was in
a hotel room. There was a man in the room with him who
he did not recognize, standing by the window. Deciding
that the bandage meant he was more or less safe, he spoke
up. "Where am I?" he asked.

"South Beach. Penthouse at the Ramada. Pretty sweet,
huh? You should see this view," the man said. He had a
cheery voice that reminded Crowley of a talk show host.

Crowley brought himself slowly into a seated position
against the headboard. The man turned to him and leaned
against the glass in a very relaxed manner. He had a robust
face, with a receding hairline, a thin nose, and sharp eyes.
His tie was slung on a chair along with his coat. "Stick of
gum?" the man asked, unwrapping a stick for himself.

"No thanks," Crowley said.

"There's a glass of water there on the nightstand," he
said as he popped the stick in his mouth and chewed.

Crowley sniffed the water, then sipped it. "Nasty gash,"
the man said. "You've got ten staples in you. But then, you
probably don't feel it, do you?"

"I see that you know who I am," Crowley said. "Do you
mind returning the favor?"

"You can call me Agent Kelsoe, Mr. Crowley," he said
warmly.

"Agent of . . . ?"

"The Ministry, Deprivers Branch."

"I figured as much. Am I your prisoner?"

"Does this look like a prison?"

"So, I could leave right now?"

"Most people couldn't in your condition," he replied, scratching his ear, "but I bet you could."

"How did I get here?"

"Airport security carried you back in and called the FBI. We intercepted the call and took control of the case in light of who you are. Got you stitched up. We keep a sharp look-out on Miami. Lots of Depriver traffic in and out to see your man, Deveraux. This is his biggest recruiting station."

"I know you've got a file on me," Crowley said, testing the waters.

"Yeah, so, we figured you'd know. We know that Dever-aux pilfers our files from time to time. He's got some good tech-heads on his team."

"Why am I of any interest to you? I'm not a Depriver."

Kelsoe crossed his arms and chewed. "You're of interest to us because of your Depsight. Because you're highly intelligent. Because you know their network. Sooner or later we would have approached you to work for us."

"And you've chosen sooner?"

"No, we chose to save your life, Mr. Crowley. Obviously, someone is trying to kill you."

"How do I know it's not you?"

"Guess you don't."

"What happens next?"

"I proposition you."

"Go for it, I'm sure it will be amusing. Hey, how about ordering me up a drink?"

"Nah, not good for you. Thins the blood. The first thing

we'd offer you is a proper detoxification. Ministry agents stay clean and alert."

"Sounds pretty dull."

"It has its ups and downs."

"Let's hear your pitch."

"Okay," Kelsoe began. "Deprivers Branch has been assigned the task of controlling the epidemic both medically and socially. We have the finest people in medicine working on a cure for SDS. As for the social aspect, well, tensions are escalating, especially here in the States. Both sides are getting hot, and Deveraux is fueling the fire. We plan to intercede wherever necessary—by the way, can you tell me if your attacker was a Depriver or not? That might answer a few of your questions for you."

Crowley shook his head. "Didn't take the time to look."

"Shame," Kelsoe said. "But presupposing that it was not us, who else might have been trying to kill you, Mr. Crowley?"

Crowley held up his hands. "Normals, Deprivers, Deveraux's people. Groups I've never even heard of before. Who knows? I'm not well-liked these days. Let a blinder put my lights out, and I'm probably better off."

"There'd be a waste of talent," Kelso remarked with genuine awe. "So, back to the proposition. You'd be trained as an agent. The job requires a great deal of travel. They'd make you a spotter."

Crowley chuckled at that. "Let me guess. . . . I'd tell you who was and who wasn't, so you can register them?"

"No," Kelsoe said. "The U.S. government is interested in registering them. We're more interested in separating the bad apples from the good, if you catch my meaning."

"Sounds idealistic," Crowley smirked, shifting his legs off the side of the bed, much to Kelsoe's surprise. "But I think I'll have to decline. Can you hand me my pants?"

"Too bad, Alex," he said, handing Crowley his clothes. "We'd be offering you a home—and a chance to make a real difference in this thing."

"Why don't you offer me something I need?" Crowley said.

"Such as?"

"Information."

"What would you like to know?"

"Who the fuck killed my wife."

"We don't know that. Who does Deveraux say it was?"

"He hasn't said. He claims he doesn't know either."

"Oh no?" Agent Kelsoe asked. "Well, here's a thought." Kelsoe went to the wall unit and pulled open a door to reveal a television. He turned it on and pressed a button. "This is the security camera in the airport rest room."

Crowley watched his own attack with cold detachment. The man's face was never clearly visible. Kelsoe froze the frame. "Now, I can't see if this man is a Depriver, but I'm willing to bet a month's salary that he is."

"I can't help you there," Crowley said.

"You can't tell?" Kelsoe asked.

"No, not from a tape," Crowley said. "If a Dep aura were visible on tape, then anyone could see it. You can only record visible light, not electromagnetic current."

"Didn't know that."

"Well, now you do," Crowley said. Then, "You telling me he's one of Deveraux's men? That doesn't add up. Why not kill me a few hours earlier? Why such a public place?"

Kelsoe shrugged. "I can't say for sure he's one of Deveraux's people, I'm just trying to help you get to the bottom of things."

"Thanks, much obliged."

Kelsoe pulled a microrecorder from his jacket pocket and

set it on the nightstand. He put on his jacket and pocketed his tie as he said, "Here's a second free tidbit. This is a wire-tapped conversation running from the telephone of one of Deveraux's inactive men, a Rastafarian named Roody Caleph. It came in at 3:45 P.M. yesterday. Listen." He pressed Play.

The first voice on the tape was sluggish, with a deep accent. "Yah, yah . . . I need a favor from ya. You know dat Dep who ran with me dat time in Amsterdam?"

The second voice was a woman's, "Yes, I know the one."

Roody again: "I need to put a finger on him for Dever-aux. Not sure what it's for, but it's a priority."

Kelsoe stopped the tape. "Sounds like Deveraux's look-ing for lost sheep. Care to guess why?"

Crowley was lost in calculating time and motive.

"I don't suppose you'd be interested in telling me where Deveraux's compound is located as a return favor?"

"I was driven there in a car with blacked-out windows," Crowley said. "Not that I trust you."

"Understood," Kelsoe said. "Well, I think you'll be okay on your own. Here's my card in case you need to reach me."

It was Crowley's turn to look surprised. "You're just leaving me here?"

"Yeah," Kelsoe said. "The room's paid up for three days, including room service. Sorry, but you don't have a bar tab. As I said, it's against policy."

Agent Kelsoe opened the door, and before leaving, his final words were, "Choose your loyalties wisely, Mr. Crowley. And keep your head above water. You're worth a lot to us." Then, after a pause, "I'm really sorry about your wife."

"Thanks, Kelsoe," Crowley said.

Crowley lay back on the bed and sighed. He was that much closer. He needed a drink. He picked up the remote control off the nightstand and flipped through channels on the television. A woman with dazzling white teeth displayed the very latest in health-care fashion. "Worried about contracting a sensory deprivation? These new clear Dermaseal gloves are ninety-nine percent secretion resistant, proven by scientists to significantly reduce your risk of infection, and you can even wear your jewelry, like watches or wedding bands, right on top of them. No one will know . . ."

9

ONCE dressed, Crowley pocketed the cassette recorder, removed a wire hanger from the closet, and left the hotel. In the back parking lot, obscured from view, he twisted the hanger and used it to break into a Ford Thunderbird. He hot-wired the car and drove it leisurely off the lot. He took Interstate 95 North to the airport, arriving just before dusk. As soon as he pulled up to the terminal where Deveraux's man had picked him up, he turned the car around and headed for the exit, sounding off turns as he went.

Right turn first. He must have taken U.S. 1 South. After taking the same ride twice, even with the blackened windows, Crowley was able to backtrack easily. *The next turn will also be a right, but not yet, another five minutes or so. Feel it. Remember.* Twenty minutes of driving and then, *Should be a gravel roadway coming up, ah yes . . . the final marker, that twelve-foot stone-carved wall.*

Crowley drove a safe distance away and parked the car.

He sat and waited for the sun to fall completely. He closed his eyes . . . .

THEY were bundled up for winter, standing at the rally in Lafayette Park, Julia's gloved hand in his. Governor Tyrsdale's condemnation of all Deprivers was ringing in everyone's ears. "Registration is the only way to keep our loved ones safe! The only way to insure that our schools are safe for our children! The only way to stop the spread of the contamination before it reaches epidemic levels! Our scientists have concluded that . . ."

The governor's words were cut short as two shots rang out. The crowd panicked instantly, but there was no place to run—the mob was too thick. Suddenly the police were returning fire. Alex turned, and Julia was falling . . . falling into his arms . . .

DARKNESS fell, and Crowley left the car, keeping to the darker parts of the road as he moved. He still felt the tug where the knife had gone into his lower back, but it was a simple enough thing to ignore. He circled the wall around the compound twice, seeking best access. He didn't have the best shoes for climbing, but he scaled the wall easily enough and lay flat on its thin shelf, surveying the grounds. There was a structure that resembled a barracks a few dozen yards from the main building. A single guard at the door, with an automatic rifle, stood smoking a cigarette. Crowley knew there would be more of them inside. He slid quietly along the wall until he caught sight of Deveraux's office window. The light was on. Good, that would save him a great deal of trouble.

He looked up at the moon, a half-crescent, and surveyed the telephone and electric wires connecting the
buildings. He slid silently down off the wall to the road-
side, crossed the street to the first telephone pole, and
began climbing.

At the top of the pole, he grappled the wire, first with
his hands, then with his legs, and began moving slowly
into the compound. It never occurred to Crowley that the
power lines could be deadly, and quite frankly he wouldn't
have cared.

He dropped to the roof, spotted the guard smoking
directly below him, then took hold of the edge of the roof
with his hands and pitched his legs over and down. He
caught the startled guard by the neck with his legs as he
descended to a hanging position. He locked his ankles
together and squeezed tightly with his thighs until he felt
the man lose his air and go slack. He slid his right foot
under the rifle's strap before letting the guard fall; then
pulled himself and the gun back up to the roof.

Minutes later, Deveraux dropped to the floor behind his
desk when shards of glass preceded Crowley as he came
crashing through the picture window. Crowley was up in
seconds, scanning the room, gun poised. Deveraux rose
slowly, taking stock of Crowley. He saw the confident way
the young man gripped the weapon, the blood on his face,
the desperation in his eyes.

"Your life for a name," Crowley said. "And that's non-
negotiable."

Deveraux came slowly around the desk, hands in the
open, his aura radiating. "Alex, what makes you think I
already have a name for you?"

An alarm had started blaring throughout the building.
Lights on Deveraux's phone lit up, and a man's voice on the

intercom asked, "Are you all right, Mr. Deveraux?"

"I don't *think* you have a name. I *know* you know who it was that killed her," Alex said, leveling the gun.

Deveraux took another step forward, speaking calmly. "Who have you been speaking to, Alex? Ministry agents? Did they fill you with their platitudes? Offer you false evidence?"

"A Depriver tried to kill me at the airport," Crowley said.

"A lot of Deprivers want you dead, Alex. I assure you that wasn't my doing. I could have had you taken out here this morning."

Crowley was confused and lowered the gun a few inches. Deveraux's aura continued to pulse. "The Ministry is our enemy, Alex. They'd do anything to learn the names you know. Fool you into thinking they're helping you, by any means. Killing you offers me nothing. Killing me solves nothing for you. It won't bring your wife back."

Deveraux's light almost seemed to engulf Crowley.

"No, you *do* know. You *must* know . . ." said Crowley.

"Put the gun down," Deveraux ordered in an almost hypnotic tone. "You're no killer, Alex—you said so yourself."

Crowley's mind was locked in conflict. His will was being tampered with. His strength was draining away. He sensed it was something that Deveraux was doing to him. *A deprivation? How?* He hadn't made contact. *Deprived from a distance? How is that possible?*

There were voices just outside the door. "Mr. Deveraux, are you all right?" someone yelled.

"I have things under control," Deveraux called back. He looked at Crowley in his weakened stance. "Listen to me, Alex, we're the family you so desperately need. I will help you, but first you must put down that gun!"

The gun was sliding down out of his hands against his will. His fingers refused his command that they raise it back up, that he use it to force Deveraux to reveal what he knew. And then suddenly it was falling . . . out of his hands and down on the floor.

"I think you should sit," Deveraux said, now walking directly toward him.

Have to get out! Crowley knew. His legs felt slack; it was getting hard for him to focus. There was a pounding on the door. Deveraux came within arm's length. *Now, go now!*

Crowley ducked beneath Deveraux's reaching hand, forced his legs into motion, and ran for the window. He dove through, connecting with some of the upturned glass, which scraped at his stomach as he leapt.

He broke his fall as best as he could with his hands and arms as he hit the cement and rolled. He forced himself up, expecting gunfire at any moment, and ran for the wall. He grappled his way up and over.

On the freeway less than ten minutes later, Crowley's head was beginning to clear. *Are they following?* he wondered. His shirt was ripped and bloody. He tore a large strip of the cloth away and used it to place pressure on his stomach, to stop the bleeding where he'd hit the glass. He checked the rearview mirror for the tenth time and saw only blackness. The road was empty. He'd failed. He was no closer to justice. He had no home. He had no friends. He had no place to go.

The brand above his heart was clearly visible in the naked green dashboard light, and he ran his thumb along the raised scar. . . .

A few days after the funeral they'd gone out to the woods, Crowley and Sparrow, and built themselves a campfire. Sparrow had told Crowley that in days of old it was custom for his people to scar themselves upon learning of the death of a loved one. So one would never forget. The tattoo wasn't enough, and it had been denied to him. So he'd designed the mark himself, in welded steel.

The brand lay against the red coals, and Alex removed his shirt.

"Where do you want it?" Sparrow asked, raising it from the fire by its crude handle, the steel glowing amber.

"Above my heart," Crowley directed. "Where else?"

And Sparrow placed it against his skin. . . .

Now Alex Crowley held his hand across the mark as he drove on, aimlessly, into the night.

10

IT wasn't the first time that Alex Crowley had ended up on the young man's doorstep, alone, lost, and wounded. There were no pleasantries exchanged, just a silent welcome and a careful embrace. Once again, a stolen vehicle would need to be disposed of, and once more his bloodied laundry would need to be tended.

"Thank you, Sparrow," were the barely audible words beneath his breath before he hit the couch and lay as still as death. He'd been driving for thirty-seven hours nonstop, his body set to autopilot, powered on by sheer determination. Stations of the underground where his face would be welcome were few and far between these days.

The first time Crowley awoke, several hours later, Sparrow asked, "Are you being followed?" To which Crowley had replied, "No."

The next time, as many hours again, he rose on shaky legs and offered, "Sorry, I think I've gotten blood on your couch. Can I wash up?"

Sparrow prepared an herbal paste in his kitchen, a mixture of goldenseal and blue cohosh, while Crowley showered. "Show me your damage," Sparrow said, and he acquiesced.

"No chicks?" Crowley asked as Sparrow applied the salve to the long cuts along his stomach, "You must be in a slump."

"No." Sparrow sighed. "The ladies are hard to find when you're in hiding. Man, Alex—you're lucky you can't feel this. It's pretty deep."

Salve applied, and bandaged, Crowley pulled on his clothes and moved back to his station on the couch. He drank the tea that Sparrow made, explaining where he'd been and how he'd ended up this way.

"Deveraux's a mad bugger," Sparrow said as Crowley concluded the tale. "And you're telling me he can deprive from a distance?"

"It seemed like it. I'm pretty sure he never made contact."

"That freaks me out," Sparrow said. "And you really need to tell Nicholas about it. He's got a lab set up now, and he's trying to re-create a lot of Deveraux's technology."

"He's still with Claudette?"

"Far as I know," Sparrow said. "So, what's your next move?"

"I don't have one. I can't force him to tell me who killed her. I'm not even sure that he knows."

"And this Ministry agent, Kelsoe, do you think he knows?"

"Who knows, Sparrow? Who cares?"

"I care. A lot of people care. Julia was a beautiful person. So are you."

Crowley closed his eyes. "No. I was beautiful while I was with her. Now I'm just fucked. To be honest, I've been thinking I'd be better off dead."

Sparrow shook his head. "I'd kick you right in the face

for saying that," he said, "if I thought it would do any good. Do I have to get Theresa on the phone, you asshole?"

"No, I won't endanger her. Too many people are looking for me," Crowley said.

"Listen, my friend," the younger man pleaded, "I don't want to blow smoke up your ass, but you're important to a lot of people. You crossed the line to be with Julia, and that meant a great deal to a lot of us. Now she's gone, and that's fucked up, but you're still here. Half that vision is still alive. And I don't think she'd be very pleased to hear you're giving up on her!"

Sparrow's words stung Crowley so deeply that he could muster no response.

"Now, you've come here to me, and I see that as a call for help—or you'd have just gone off and done it already. Your suicide would only give the opposition more ammunition— a cover story in some right-wing magazine that shows the downside of taking up with a Depriver. Is that how you want her name remembered?"

Crowley smiled faintly. "You've really been hanging around with Cassandra too long, Sparrow. You sound just like her."

"I'll take that as a compliment," Sparrow said, grinning. "Besides, there are enough people out there who'd be happy to see you dead. You don't need to do them any favors. And now that you've come here, and involved me, I'm honor bound to offer my help. I'm taking you to the res to see the *Pejuta Wichasa* at first light, and there'll be no argument."

"Fine," Crowley replied. "In the meantime, I need a drink."

Sparrow pulled his mane of hair away from his face and tied it back behind his head with a band. "I think that's the last thing you need. I'll make you some coffee if you want, but I think you should go to meet Swift Hawk with a clear head. Out of respect, ya' know?"

Crowley nodded and then mercifully, sleep took him down.

11

CROWLEY peered up at Mount Thunder Butte as Sparrow drove the jeep past the battered, sun-bleached sign that read: Welcome to the Lakota Nation. Home of the Seven Council Fires. Visitors Must Leave by 6:00 P.M. There was a native at the guard post, leisurely sipping a Coca-Cola, who recognized Sparrow and waved them through. Crowley took note of the Remington double-pump that sat within easy reach by the wall behind him.

They passed a perimeter fence, laced with razor ribbon, and Crowley said, "That must be to keep the horses in, huh?"

Sparrow chuckled as they came upon the first of the trailers and parked. Crowley looked out at the firepits. Some women were stringing clothesline. Two men carried shovels. A half-dozen stray dogs darted and yelped as they circled the jeep. Crowley sighed at the apparent level of poverty, then began counting heads. One in particular caught his eye. "How many of your people are here?" he asked.

"Under a hundred," Sparrow answered.

"How many Deprivers?"

"Less than a handful," he said. "This isn't exactly a hot spot in the underground."

They walked along the cracked earth until they arrived at the lodge. Crowley sniffed the sweet-smelling smoke that escaped from the chimney.

"You don't happen to have any money, do you, Alex? Something to offer Swift Hawk?"

Crowley shook his head in response.

When they entered the lodge, both Crowley and Sparrow removed their shoes out of respect. The stoic medicine man, Walter Swift Hawk, was seated on the floor of the lodge before the fire in a thick sweat, his lean, tanned body an anachronism against the harsh lines of his aged face. His thick silver hair, which hung down to his waist, was pulled back with a leather cord.

They walked to the center of the room, then stood silent, staring into the flames, patiently awaiting the elder to offer them his attention. After a time, he looked up and said, "*Hau Kola.*"

"Swift Hawk, *le maske ataya wacin ksto,*" Sparrow began. "May we sit by your fire?"

The old man motioned with his hand that they should sit, eyes burrowing into Crowley. "Who is this friend you bring, Sparrow?" the man said in a deep tone that seemed almost otherworldly.

"This is Alex Crowley," Sparrow began. "He is my brother in spirit and a friend to the Lakota nation. Chief Running Horse let him take the Sundance initiation two summers ago and named him Feels No Pain. He's been through a lot since then, including the wrongful death of his wife. He's really lost, and I'm hoping you can help him find his way."

Swift Hawk nodded, then turned to Crowley. "Greetings from the Lakota, Alex Feels No Pain. Sparrow seems to
feel you are worthy of guidance—but I am hesitant. I have
the gift of open eyes, and I see there is a dark cloud over you
that may bring further hardship here. Tell me why I should
guide you?"

It took Crowley a few contemplative moments to find his
voice, and then he said, "Sir, you have no reason to guide
me. I have nothing to offer you or your people. I have nothing but the clothes on my back. I know what it is to see
oppression and stand powerless. I am full of rage and have
often surrendered to it. My heart cries out to kill a man
whose name I don't know. I fear that makes me unworthy to
sit by your fire."

Swift Hawk raised his hand, silencing Crowley. "Hold,"
he said, then closed his eyes and slid momentarily into meditation. Crowley exchanged an unsure glance with Sparrow.

Opening his eyes once more, Swift Hawk asked gently,
"Place your hand in the fire, Feels No Pain."

Crowley locked eyes with Swift Hawk and did as
instructed without hesitation, placing his right hand, palm
down, within the fire. The flames licked his fingers,
enveloped his wrist. Sparrow could smell the burnt hair.

"Is your cause an honorable cause?" Swift Hawk questioned.

"I feel it is," Alex Crowley responded, his gaze intensified.

"Will you swear to never intentionally endanger my people?"

"Yes," he replied.

"Then I will guide you," the old man replied. "Take
back your hand."

Crowley inspected his skin, which was partially blackened from the contact, yet undamaged. "Fire is a friend to

you, Alex Feels No Pain," Swift Hawk said. Then to Sparrow he added, "*Hanblecheyapi.* I'll see you tomorrow at sunrise. Leave me now to prepare for him."

"What am I in for?" Crowley questioned as they left the lodge, following their noses toward the main cabin of the encampment, hoping to beg up some breakfast.

"Swift Hawk is taking you to the mountains to cry for a vision."

"Visionquest?"

"Exactly," Sparrow replied. "You'll be up there fasting for a few days, so we've gotta get you fed and well rested before then."

WHEN the rooster crowed the next morning, Crowley and Sparrow were there at the lodge, dressed and ready, as Swift Hawk rode up on horseback, leading a second mount. A light cover of hazy orange dust was visible on the horizon.

Sparrow unlocked the strongbox in the back of his jeep, pulled out a leather pouch, and unstrung it. He removed two pieces of teakwood that Crowley recognized immediately.

"Here, take my pipe, you'll need it later," Sparrow said, handing it over. "Don't screw the two ends together until Swift Hawk tells you to. The bowl represents the female. The stem is the male. We only put them together during sacred ceremonies. Creation, ya know? He'll pinch some herbs in there, but you won't smoke until after. I'll be here when you come back down."

"Thanks, Sparrow, I appreciate you letting me use this."

"Don't mention it, brother," he said.

Crowley put the pipe back in the pouch and strung it

over his shoulder. He took the reins when Swift Hawk
offered them, and mounted the dark spotted horse. Swift
Hawk said nothing as they trod out onto the plain toward
Thunder Butte.

12

THE trail wound round and up through a well-worn path the horses knew well. When they reached the highest plateau, Swift Hawk hitched the horses, and they walked in silence up the slope to the sacred ground. *A seat on the edge of the world,* Crowley thought at first sight. *Least I'll have a nice view.* Crowley looked first to the place where the fire would be made, a scored shelf of stone, then to the ledge, like two cupped hands, jutting out to the horizon. The patch of earth, about four feet square, was where Crowley guessed he was expected to sit and pray.

Swift Hawk led him to the edge, chanting, *"Wakan Tanka, unshimala ye oyate wani wachin cha!"*

Crowley looked down, gauging the drop to be at least a thousand feet.

"Repeat my words," Swift Hawk said, and Crowley did so with a mounting sense of reverence. "O Great Spirit. Be my mind. Be my eyes. Be my ears. Be my heart. Be my soul. So that I may walk with dignity and pride."

Swift Hawk nodded and then instructed Alex to enter the sacred patch of ground and be seated. "*Mitakuye Oyasin*, is your prayer," Swift Hawk said.

My mantra, Crowley thought. "*Mitakuye Oyasin,*" he repeated. "What does it mean?"

"It means that you, me—all things are related," Swift Hawk replied. "It is your petition to the Great Spirit on behalf of all that is."

Crowley nodded that he understood.

"You pray looking East when the sun is down. When the sun is up, you face to the sun."

Swift Hawk offered another prayer in Lakota, instructed Crowley to join the two parts of his pipe, and then left him sitting there on his own.

Confined within a four-by-four perimeter, with dirt and a small clump of sage to be used as his bedding, Crowley realized that sleep would be difficult and uncomfortable— but he had not come there for sleep. He lay the pipe in his lap and faced the sun.

"*Mitakuye Oyasin!*" he said aloud. His stomach made grumbling noises. *Four days,* he considered. *Can I really just sit here for four whole days?*

The first hour was useless, a jumbled mass of wasted mental energy. The second, devoted to taking in the scenery, the expansive view of the red cliffs, the danger of the ledge, barely an arm's length away. He liked the idea of a fatal hazard he could touch at any moment. The third hour he was overcome by doubt that this could do him any real good at all. "Cancel that thought," he whispered under his breath, "or this is gonna be long and boring. *Mitakuye Oyasin!*"

He brought up the pipe and turned it over in his lap and thought of Sparrow, seated in just this position, perhaps many times in his life, doing just what he was doing. He wondered if maybe the visionquest was reserved for the Indians for a reason, if they were not programmed in some way to receive visions in a way that he could not. It had to be merely psychological, he thought. At least Theresa Godfrey would have determined it so. He thought of his first meeting with Theresa—how standoffish and rude he had been to her—and it filled him with shame. He caught himself and examined how his memories could so easily stir his emotions. And then, he thought about Julia. . . .

Julia O'Connor Crowley. Julia in Adams Morgan, kissing him for the first time. Julia in Amsterdam, holding tight against him in the rain as they walked the brick-paved streets. Julia reclining against him in the bath and laughing at something he'd said during their honeymoon in Paris. And Julia falling one last time into his arms as the gunshots rang out across Lafayette Park. Curled into a tight fetal position in the dirt, arm dangling over the precipice, he realized he'd fallen asleep.

On the second day, Crowley awoke and was ravenous. He ran his tongue across his lips and found them chapped to the point of peeling. The bandage on his stomach annoyed him. *"Mitakuye Oyasin!"* The silence of the canyon below was his only response.

By his second sunset, he was acutely dehydrated, nearly delusional. His lips were moving, but they made no sound, silently mouthing his prayer. Swift Hawk stood close by, tending the fire, observing without interfering. Crowley had no awareness at all of his presence.

On the third day, *or was it the fourth?* he wondered, Crowley awoke in his seated position, completely deprived of his time sense, and considered the ledge. No vision had come, and he was despondent. A wave of vertigo suddenly overwhelmed him, and he leaned forward on both hands and vomited, just outside the sacred patch of earth. He wiped the remaining mess away from his mouth and nose and rubbed the sticky liquid off his hand against the dirt. Leaning farther forward, he craned his head out over the edge of the cliff and peered downward.

He hovered there, on shaking arms, considering the drop, then spat a final wad of phlegm . . . and dragged himself back to his seat. *I am not finished yet,* he thought, *there's still a man to kill.*

It began to happen when he raised his head back up. His body shuddered once, then twice, and then his extremities began to spasm.

The piercing shrill of a bird sent a rush of adrenaline down his spine. He looked up, and a tree was standing miraculously there before him. He shook his head in disbelief, for all his senses screamed aloud that there could be no tree. Yet, there it was, planted tight to the ledge in front of him, black roots stretching out of the dirt in all directions, some clearly beneath him, the trunk blocking the sun with a polarized glow that flickered out from behind it. He looked up to the thick limbs stretching skyward, with gray bark slick and damp along the gnarled branches that ringed them and terminated in sharp twigs.

Then the bird shrieked, demanding his attention, and he saw it nested just above him in a dark hollowed recess in the trunk. A gray and spotted owl, fiercely jutting its sharp beak. The eyes were large and luminous, and its talons gripped the wood in a hold that Crowley could almost feel.

An intense sound, like the fluttering of a hundred wings, and Crowley saw there were dozens of other owls stationed along the branches, eyes upon him, threatening to dive at any instant. Again the gray owl shrieked, and Crowley saw now that it had a small animal within its taloned grip, one that he could not identify, that clawed frantically for escape. The owl reached down quickly and tore it in half.

From the corner of his eye, Crowley saw Swift Hawk, off to the distance, staring impassively, arms crossed. He convulsed again and began to shiver violently.

Looking back, the tree was gone, but the owl was in flight, wings outstretched and beating hard. Crowley felt a warm rush of air hit his face and delighted in the power of the movement. He felt drugged, high, drunk—the effects of adrenaline. The owl swooped low above a road that was paved with soft, red clay, and it suddenly twisted and dove. It had seen something it wanted, Crowley realized, and as it touched down in a run, Crowley saw what that something was. A tiny piece of gleaming steel. A key.

Suddenly he felt a hand on his shoulder, a real hand, and realizing his eyes had been closed, he opened them. It was Swift Hawk, a thin smile on his face. *Holy shit,* Crowley thought.

"An owl, was there really an owl just here?" Crowley asked.

"Come with me," Swift Hawk said.

Crowley's legs had fallen asleep, and he wiped several layers of drool from his face as he rose to follow, weakly clutching Sparrow's pipe to his chest. Seated by the fire, his mind clearing, great beads of sweat broke out and rolled against his skin.

Swift Hawk took the pipe from Crowley, filled it, held it up to the four directions, then lit it. He took a great puff, then blew the smoke upward. "Don't inhale," he said. "That would be for you. This smoke is carrying your prayers above you." He passed Crowley the pipe and said, "Feels No Pain, you have sent a voice with your pipe to

Wakan Tanka. This pipe is now sacred, for the whole uni-verse has seen it. You are about to put this pipe in your mouth, so you must tell me nothing but the truth. Smoke and tell. *Hechetu welo!*"

Crowley took a long drag off the pipe and sent the sweet-tasting smoke upward. He then proceeded to detail the things he had seen as the pipe passed back and forth. At the conclusion of the tale, Swift Hawk cried, *"Hi ye!"*

The medicine man closed his eyes and fell into a medita-tive trance, offering his understanding to Crowley. "You will walk among the owls and then you will become like the owl," he began.

Crowley nodded that he felt he understood what this implied.

"Through them you will find the enemy you seek, the source of your pain," Swift Hawk added, "and you will come to know his pain. Then you will face a choice. *Wolakota wa yaka cola!* This means, you take peace without surrender."

Again Crowley nodded.

"Afterward, if you survive, you will continue along the red road to complete the second vision and appease your lost love. The understanding of these things I tell you will come clear as each unfolds. *Hechetu aloe.*"

It was over, and Swift Hawk extinguished the fire. The two men gathered up their belongings in relative silence. They readied the mounts and then began their thoughtful descent with the sun setting along the ridge of the moun-tain behind them.

Sparrow was waiting for them in his jeep at the base of the cliff. "Saw you heading down, thought I'd come pick you up." He nodded to Swift Hawk, and the elder nodded back that this was acceptable.

13

ON the drive back, Sparrow passed Crowley his canteen. "I'm guessing your overdriven ass didn't bother to drink enough water when you needed it."

Crowley accepted the canteen and uncapped it. He pinched at the skin on the back of his hand and noted the lack of elasticity. *Severe dehydration,* he self-diagnosed, taking small sips.

"So, did you have a vision?" Sparrow asked.

Crowley nodded, took more water.

"Right on," Sparrow said. "Anything that made sense?"

"Yeah, I think so," Crowley said, his voice still raspy.

"Care to share?"

Crowley nodded, "Swift Hawk said that I should walk with the owls to find the shooter. And, if I live through that, I can walk the red road and *appease* Julia. I thought the last part was a pretty weird interpretation. I mean, finding the shooter *is* appeasing her."

"Well," Sparrow said, "Visionquest isn't an exact science."

"No, I guess not."

"Do you know what the owls mean, Alex?" Sparrow asked.

"Yeah," Crowley said, "and that's what freaks me out. I'm not sure I can handle walking with them. I'm not sure *you* can handle me walking with them. In fact, I'm not sure I believe any of this. . . ."

Several gunshots rang out from up ahead. "What the—?" Sparrow exclaimed. As they rounded a bend and pulled into the camp, they saw police lights flashing out from just beyond the perimeter fence.

As they got out of the jeep and moved up toward the action, they saw several Lakota men lying flat belly atop the lodge, and still more on the tops of the trailers, rifles aimed out toward the police. Sparrow had a quick exchange in Lakota with one of the men.

"What's going on?" Crowley asked.

"Feds are trying to force their way in," Sparrow said.

"What about the damned Indian Civil Rights Act?" Crowley asked.

Another shot was fired off beyond the gate. "They don't seem too concerned about our civil rights just now," Sparrow said.

The sound of a male voice on a bullhorn called, "Attention! This is Federal Agent Kyle Kittridge. We have permission to enter and search this reservation. This is a federal matter, and I assure you we have jurisdiction."

"Shit," Crowley said, as they moved up to the trailer closest to the fence and he saw that there were over a dozen armed officers readying to rush the gate—and noted a van that had CDC markings. CDC meant they were hunting down Deprivers, not him.

Swift Hawk came riding up, Crowley's mount in tow,

and looked to Crowley for explanation. He knew he had to make a decision quickly regarding his involvement here, and was unsure how much influence he could, or should, wield. Not being Indian and not being a Depriver made him the obvious choice to negotiate. This was not an important stop on the underground, but these people had self-lessly opened their doors to him. The Deprivers were the only ones here in any real jeopardy, as long as no one got shot. He guessed they'd all turn out to be unregistered—as would Sparrow, of course. . . .

Crowley looked up at Swift Hawk and knew this was payback time. He hadn't expected it to come around so quickly. "Give me a chance to try to handle this," he said, and the elder man nodded.

Crowley called out, "Agent Kittridge, my name is Alex Crowley, I'm coming out unarmed! Meet me at the gate!"

"I hope you know what you're doing," Sparrow said.

"You and me both," Crowley said. Then he walked out, arms in plain sight, and moved up to the gate. Kittridge was there to meet him, with five marshals standing off to the side, their rifles aimed groundward. Crowley did a quick assessment of the man. Blond hair, buzz cut, too much testosterone.

"Who the hell are you?" Kittridge demanded.

"My name is Alex Crowley, and I'd like to know what gives you the right to violate United States Code Anno-tated Title 25, Section 2803? You can't enter these grounds unless you have an assigned mediator from the Bureau of Indian Affairs."

"I have members of the CDC prepared to declare this area quarantined under USCA 25, Chapter 5, Section 198, Subsection D, due to suspected SDS contamination. We have reason to believe these people are harboring carriers."

"Unless I'm mistaken," Crowley said, "SDS is not a quarantined condition, and being a carrier is not a crime, federal or otherwise."

Agent Kittridge nodded. "Unless a carrier is endangering lives and acting with reckless abandon. I've got three local kids down at the station who've been deprived and swear the Depriver who touched them lives up here. Not to mention my men have been fired on."

The agent had a strong case, and Crowley knew it. He deliberated and made a gut-level decision. "Can you do me a favor?" Alex said. "I need you to make a call on my behalf."

"Now why should I do that?" Kittridge asked.

"Because they're entitled to legal representation," Crowley answered, moving a hand to his hip pocket. "I'm just reaching for my wallet." Crowley fished out a card and handed it through the mesh of the gate. "Call that number for me, and I'll see that the Lakota put down their guns and open the gate."

Kittridge paused, then took the card. He stepped away and brought his cell phone out. Crowley took a deep breath. He was taking a gamble that required a great deal of delicacy. Kittridge came back moments later and slid the phone through the gate to Crowley. "The man wants to talk to you," he said.

Crowley put the phone to his ear. "Yes, it's me. Yes, I'm interested in coming in to talk, but on my terms, provided you do me a favor and turn these goons around. Well, let's see just how much pull you *do* have."

Crowley handed back the phone to Kittridge, and the agent walked away. Crowley looked out at the CDC team, geared up in their white coveralls, their meters at the ready. He looked toward the trailers and saw Sparrow glaring nervously back at him.

Kittridge stepped back to the gate, clearly pissed. "Mr. Crowley, I'd really like to kick the shit out of you right now, I won't lie. But it seems that I'm to call off this search and offer you a ride to the airport."

"Thank you, Agent Kittridge, I know this must be difficult for you," Crowley said with complete sincerity. "But if it's any consolation, I'm going to have to pay up for that phone call."

14

ALEX Crowley wore a black suit with patent leather shoes
and took the steps two at a time up to the main entrance of
the Los Angeles complex. He stopped for a moment to consider the sigil that was engraved into the stone high above
the archway: an owl with a snake entwined in its taloned
grip. It was twin to the badge in his pocket. It was cause for
serious alarm for anyone to whom he displayed it.

He had to show it to gain entrance at the security checkpoint, where a flaxen-haired receptionist greeted him with
a mannequin smile. Crowley knew that he was being electronically scanned.

They had tested his endurance and found him far above
average, tested his intelligence and found him exceptional,
examined his sensory array and determined him off the
charts in his ability to compensate for his deprivation. His
Depsight was reportedly the keenest on record. His knowledge of the Depriver Network was unparalleled by any
Normal—and he was one of the few operatives who could

visually identify Alan Deveraux. He'd been inspected right down to his DNA base code. He'd displayed his loyalty time and again. Hell, they'd even granted him an audience with the Senate when they debated the Mandatory Registration Act—fat lot of good it had done. Still, his superiors did not trust him.

He made his way to the elevator banks and went up to thirteen to receive his new orders. Agent Kelsoe's secretary of the week, a fair young woman with jet-black hair, cropped short, smiled and buzzed him in.

Kelsoe looked tired, seated at his desk, chewing the edge of a pencil. "Morning, Alex. How did it go last night?" he asked.

"Three Deprivers spotted. Two with pending warrants, taken in. One left overnight with special services," he replied.

"Anything I should know about?" Kelsoe asked, tapping the pencil against the desk.

"The girl I left at special services is left-handed," he said, lowering his collar to reveal three dark scratch marks along his neck.

"Did she deprive you?"

"Yeah, I couldn't taste my coffee this morning," he said. "Seemed like a good enough reason to have her registered and ruin her life."

Kelsoe nodded and sighed. "Listen Alex, she'll be released once she's been tested and processed, as long as she's not dangerous."

"So they say," Crowley replied. "Do I have a new assignment? I want to get back out there."

"I know you do," Kelsoe said, rising from behind his desk, picking up a file, and handing it over to Crowley. "And I know why you do. Maybe he's in here?"

Crowley took the file and said, "Thank you, sir," with cool detachment.

"Stop by the lab," Kelsoe said as Crowley was leaving. "They've got a new booster that supposedly decreases downtime in nonperm deprivations."

"Thanks," Crowley said, closing the door.

Exiting the building, file in hand, he passed three high-school-aged kids who were sporting a sign that read: Deprivers Rights Now! Appeal Mandatory Registration! All three were Normals. One of them, a boy with a nose ring and a shock of blue hair, screamed out to him, "Hey you—Deprivers have rights too!"

Crowley kept going, refusing the pamphlet that one of them held out, observing the homemade *D* tattoo the boy had inscribed on his forearm.

He took a seat on the steps and opened the file to review the photo and notes on his next investigation. It was no one he knew. A man who was suspected of blinding three bank tellers during a robbery. The photo showed him smiling, arms akimbo, standing with his dog at the dog walk in Runyon Canyon. It gave his last reported address in Studio City. *Could he be the one?* Crowley wondered, studying the man's expression.

A Depriver in Pittsburgh, who had not realized his condition and accidentally deprived his fiancée of her entire memory, had not been the one.

A Depriver in Nashville, who'd tortured and killed a police officer through a week of repeated exposure, had not been the one.

A sixteen-year-old girl in Montreal, suspended twice from school for marijuana use, who had permanently deprived her vice principal of his hearing as payback, had not been the one.

A Depriver in Hong Kong, who'd deprived his way up the chain of command of a local Triad, to incite the entire red-light district into a bloody gang war, had not been the one.

A Depriver in Alabama, who'd blinded the entire staff of a local abortion clinic, along with nearly a dozen patients, had not been the one.

An assassin in Morocco, who had posed as a Depriver to incite local terror, who'd severely wounded Crowley with a straight razor, had not been the one.

An AWOL lieutenant of the U.S. Marine Corps, who turned Depriver and lost his mind, killing four soldiers, had not been the one.

A Russian immigrant, refusing to vacate his home after nearly being stoned to death in the street, who deprived a social worker of her balance, had not been the one.

Maybe this next one, Crowley thought. *He's out there, somewhere. And sooner or later, my road will lead to him.*

1 5

I was sitting on a stone bench sucking back some of the finest tequila when she sat down next to me with a sneer on her face. I was captivated. Her brown skin smelled of cocoa leaves and was peeking out perfectly from her elaborate evening gown. The raven swirls down her back matched the tapered gloves that curled at her wrists.

She was the perfect model of my desires. Then she spoke—with, to my chagrin, a thick New Jersey accent. "Ya speak any English, Zorro?"

She eyed my tuxedo as if she knew it was neither rented nor borrowed and arched an eyebrow, waiting.

"Uh . . . yes, I speak English," I said with just enough volume to be intelligible only to her. I was still transfixed.

Unfortunately, she could not be tuned so low. "Well, thank God somebody here does," she said. "I slept through Spanish in high school, and now I'm payin' the price. Got a cigarette?"

I pulled two, lit both, passed her one. "Oooh, thanks,"

she said, sucking in smoke like an asthmatic on an inhaler. "I thought I was gonna friggin' die, ya know?"

I sipped my tequila and thought, *Nice house—no furniture.* These embassy parties always had the best tequila. I thought about getting her drunk and putting the moves on. I was lusting pretty hard, and hey, who else at this penguin party was going to seduce her in English? I pictured it vividly: the tearing of clothes, the hot breath, her fingers raking the skin on my back . . . God, it had been ages since I'd touched a woman for pleasure.

Of course, it was out of the question. I was in Cuba to do a job, and business must come *numero uno.* "Excuse me," I said, rising from the bench in a swift movement. "There's something I must go and do."

The party was reaching its apex. I still had more than a dozen people to deprive.

I went into the *caballeros* and undid my fly. I spotted Martinez relieving himself two receptacles down. Photo four, low priority. He smiled a row of gold teeth at me as he shook himself. After we washed our hands and the attendant provided us with towels, I said, "Señor Martinez, remember me?"

"*Sí, sí,*" he replied, in typical diplomatic fashion, clasping my hand in a vigorous pumping motion. "It's good to see you again. Enjoying yourself?"

"Oh yes, vehemently," I said in English, instantly dulling his interest. "Such a wonderful gathering."

He retreated, smiling and nodding with uncertainty. Blue sparks danced on my fingertips. He had less than two hours.

When I stepped back on to the *terrazza,* I had a feeling something was wrong. I scanned for other Deprivers and found none. Just a lot of people getting drunk in nice clothes.

*   *   *

HE stepped out of the limousine and closed the door so gently that it made no sound. Just another tuxedo exiting a limo, nothing for drunken guests or security to remark on. He spoke so softly, one wondered if it were simply a trick of the wind. "Agent Crowley here, front gate," he said, just loud enough to create the necessary reciprocal vibration in his own eardrums that would carry his voice through his earset.

"Confirmed, Crowley," came the static voice, so loud and distorted he wondered if it were audible to other guests floating nearby on the embassy lawn. "Proceed inside. We have no target. You're our only eyes."

No kidding, he thought as he glided up the path. *What else would I be here for?* As the lawn met green marble tile, a serious-looking man in a red blazer approached. Crowley noticed the subtle movement differential of the man's left arm, which suggested a concealed shoulder holster. He also saw that the two large Latin guards by the front gate had assumed more alert postures. *Good, the security here isn't totally inept.*

"Señor, your invitation, *por favor?*" the man asked, his eyes sweeping Crowley.

Crowley tipped the edge of his jacket in a slow motion and dipped his hand within the pocket to retrieve his credentials. Seeing the badge with the Ministry sigil upon it caused the man to catch his breath.

"I . . . forgive, sir, I had no idea. We are at your service . . . I . . ."

"Please," Crowley asked in his characteristic tone, at once soothing and authoritative, "calm down. I'm just here to take a look around. Go about your business as usual. There's no cause for alarm."

That said, Crowley patted the man on the shoulder and moved toward the gate. The man nodded to the militiamen, and they snapped to attention as Crowley passed. Once Crowley was out of earshot, the man extracted a cell phone from his red jacket and dialed. *"Un Americano agent del Ministry. Sí, uno, sí. No se."* Under his breath he whispered, *"Conyo!"*

One by one, through shoulder taps, gestures, and nods, each of the twenty-six Ministry agents planted throughout the party were alerted that their eyes had arrived. Crowley scooped a handful of macadamia nuts from a dish on a pedestal as he entered the embassy. He popped one into his mouth as he took in the scene. He hated merengue music. A line dance was forming. Potential nausea-inducing situation. There was a Depriver somewhere on the grounds, lurking about this seven-acre complex of buildings and gardens, here to cause damage to officials unknown. Twenty-six agents stood ready to take that Depriver down, patiently waiting for Crowley to point a finger.

SIXTEEN targets, can you believe it? At twenty thousand a head. Could you earn your money any easier than that? Three, maybe four Deprivers alive could pull off something like this. Why am I the lucky one? Why, especially after that fuckup in Amsterdam, am I suddenly *the man?* Why is Deveraux throwing me this grandaddy bone after all this time? My scalp started to itch. A bad sign. Too late to back out now.

All right, it was time to start earning my keep, and Deveraux better pay up. I know where he lives. Time to center yourself and get down to business. I *am* the man. There was Defillipo, special emissary to the chairman of

Commerce. Priority one. No clear access yet. Deveraux insisted, if all else failed, that Defillipo get deprived, or I'd be skunked. Guess I might have to make a leap for him in a pinch.

Ah, Señor Pombo, ambassador to Venezuela, there you are behind the palms. Do stay put a moment, won't you? I made my way over to him, a bit of a swagger in my step to indicate drunkenness. I overheard him introducing his daughter, a *sweeeet* little blonde thing in a slip of a dress, to somebody or other. Then somebody or other saw that I was about to trip and called, "Careful. Watch out!"

I fell right in between them, hard marble tiles rushing up toward my face, when—lo and behold—I was saved by the ambassador, who'd skillfully caught hold of me beneath each arm. Both he and his daughter helped me to regain an upright position, dusting me off for good measure. Poor drunken gringo. The politest of handshakes to them both, I don't know how I could have been so clumsy. Two more targets down, and I didn't even have to touch somebody or other. The *man!*

I took a martini off a floating waitress and licked my lips.

CROWLEY moved through the party like a bloodhound, inspecting each niche as though it were an active snakehole. "My back is to Defillipo at present, anybody scoping him?"

"Negative, Crowley," came the voice of Operations Chief Henson. "Nobody's taken as much as a sidelong look at Defillipo. I think your Depriver—if there is a Depriver crashing this fiesta—must have another target in mind."

Crowley stopped at the bar and motioned to the keep. *"Café, por favor."*

"Café? Como?"

"Negro."

The barkeep poured the coffee with a raised eyebrow and muttered, "Gringo."

"I disagree, Henson," Crowley whispered in ventriloquist mode through his earset, "Deveraux's transmission was quite clear. Deprive Defillipo at all costs."

Crowley took a sip of the black mixture and savored the aroma. He thought, *If God wanted a cup of coffee, this is where he'd come.*

"Yeah," Henson said. "I was there when we intercepted it. I know what it said."

"Then why are you doubting its content?"

A sigh came across the transmission. It was almost comical, thought Crowley, it sounded almost like an air leak. "I doubt its content," Henson said, "because it was broadcast on a cellular line over a public access satellite. It was too easily intercepted. It was meant to distract us from the actual target, if not the actual event."

"Hmmm," Crowley said, sipping his coffee and strolling through the garden. "I see the flaw in your thinking."

"Excuse me."

"For starters, you misinterpret the ease with which the transmission was captured for subterfuge, when in fact, it was obviously quite the opposite. Deveraux did indeed expect the Ministry, or some other agency, to intercept the signal to the would-be Dep-assassin. Not to *mis*direct us, but to *direct* us."

Another sigh. By now, half the agents were more interested in the interplay between Crowley and Henson than the observation of their own posts. "And why would Deveraux wish to point us in the *right* direction?"

Crowley noted two lovers embracing in silhouette near

the water's edge, both of whom appeared to be male, and raised an eyebrow. "For the same reason he would direct us to this gala event in the first place, Agent Henson—he's having us do his job for him. He wants whomever he's contracted to do the job to be taken out of the game."

AGENT Henson pulled his cell phone from his pocket to his ear in one fluid movement. "Henson here," he said. "Yes. Yes, sir. Crowley has been inserted, and we are in seamless contact. . . . Yes. . . . No, he hasn't spotted the infiltrator as yet. . . . How do I know? Maybe his Depsight's not what it used to be. . . . No, sir, this isn't the time for comic relief. . . . Yes, sir, I have seen him pick one out of a crowd before. Yes, sir, he is a pompous ass sometimes, but he's a hundred percent accurate. Sir, what's the action on the Depriver if we make contact? Yes, sir."

As Henson clicked off the phone, he wondered if they weren't about to play into Deveraux's hands exactly as planned.

1 6

I came across two party guests of note engaged in the masculine ritual of arm wrestling. Removing my jacket and nodding to the female spectators, I set my drink on a nearby stone ridge and engaged the victor, a man of no English, in a round. He wrestled me to the table in less than a minute, I'm happy to report, scraping my knuckles painfully as he did so. As he and his cohorts chuckled at my expense, I nodded my acquiescence and beckoned the other mark to have a go at it with me. It took him only slightly longer to best me. Again my poor hand was abused. Oh, well, a small price to pay. After all, I was getting twenty thousand dollars a head—and all it took was a couple of scrapes.

"See you later, *Señor*," the second mark said.

I nodded, retrieving my jacket and drink, thinking, *No, you won't.*

* * *

FOURTEEN targets accounted for, all unaware of their impending doom. I checked my watch. Not good. I had a scant twenty-two minutes before the first one, Agnes Daniels, the senator's wife, became privy to her deprivation and more than likely began screaming her head off. I needed to get to her husband, and then I needed to get to Defillipo.

Daniels was in deep conversation, and Defillipo was nowhere in sight. Spoke too soon. There he was, across the lawn, headed toward . . . Our good emissary to the chair was headed toward the brush and unclasping his fly. An interception was in order.

AGENT Crowley, having been unwittingly detained by Senator Daniels, wanted nothing more than to escape. The senator's anti-Depriver ravings were having an undesirable effect on Crowley's stomach. Deprivers were changing the face of the nation! They were not provided for under the original Constitution, and required a slew of new amendments. Mandatory Registration would never be enough. They were the supreme challenge to our rights and a harsher scourge from God Almighty than AIDS could ever be! Deprivers were indecent. Period.

A lot of clever curse words flipped through Crowley's mind in response to Senator Daniels's bullshit. Crowley wished he could just shut him out, wished he could make him feel the loss of a loved one because of an affliction that was no fault of her own. But these were wasted thoughts. Daniels was too far gone in his fanaticism to see reason. He was too much of a prick. Crowley wished he could deck him. Unfortunately, he was here to protect him.

"Excuse me." Crowley said to the senator and raised his hand. Out by the brush, about a hundred yards away, near the beach, a pale blue glow. A glowing man. *Depriver!* "I've got a target. Down by the beach. Converge on my lead," he said calmly into his earset, and started for the brush.

"Depriver confirmed," Henson's voice came across the airwaves in response, a direct inverse in tone to Crowley's. "Gloves on and safeties off."

TAKING out Defillipo was a piece of cake. I slid up beside him as soon as he got ready to urinate and scruffed the back of his head, causing him to shift off balance and wet the front of his slacks. It was a firm skin-on-skin contact.

"Tag, you're it," I said.

"*Hijo de puta!*" he said.

Just before I slipped back through the brush, I spotted one of the penguins eyeing me. Not to sound too paranoid, but even though he was no Depriver, I got the feeling he knew me for what I was. So I'm fumbling through the brush thinking, *Have I been set up here, or what?*

HALFWAY across the lawn toward the beach, Agent Victor Velez, a swarthy Puerto Rican, was stopped in his tracks by the agonized, ear-piercing scream of Agnes Daniels. "I'm blind! Oh my God, I've been deprived! Help me, Jesus, my eyes!"

Victor turned and bounded back to the senator, now holding his wife amid an array of confused spectators. The shit was hitting the fan.

CROWLEY reached Defillipo first and found him still standing by the bushes with his fly undone. Crowley touched him lightly on the shoulder and said, "Sir, please get yourself together as best as you can, and go with these men. They're here to protect you." Defillipo complied in bewilderment as Crowley immediately realized the impotence of his statement. It was obvious Defillipo no longer needed protection, the deprivation had already been rendered, whatever it might be.

Just then Crowley's earset chimed. "Velez to Crowley, come in, please."

"Crowley here."

"I've got Senator Daniels, sir. His wife has been blinded, sir. He wants to see the Ministry operative in charge."

"Damn," Crowley whispered, then, "That would be Agent Henson, not me. I've still got a Depriver on the loose. Protect the senator. Seal every exit to these grounds. Land, sea, and air. Do it now."

So, I've been spotted. Helicopters are swarming all around the place, and every damned exit is blocked off. These people must be Ministry. I'm fucked. Still, there's got to be some way out. *Ahh,* there we are, Ms. New Jersey. "Oh, darling!"

"Hey," she called back, crossing directly toward my hiding spot. "I wondered where you got off to."

"Come see what I've found," I said, leading her out of sight.

"What a cute little alcove," she said, stepping in. "Such a nice view of the rose garden."

Realizing instantly that she was handing out our coordinates, I reached over and grasped her by the hair, bending her back into a painful position. I saw her earset and then, like the gun I wished I had, I aimed a finger within centimeters of her face. "Bitch," I said, "you flinch—you're blind. *Comprende?*"

She nodded.

"Open your purse," I said, delighted as she winced.

She opened the clasp of her purse, and I saw the grip of her gun.

I got two rounds off at the first man who came around the bend.

AND so it happened that by the time Agent Crowley chased down the Dep-assassin, he had a bullet lodged in his shoulder, and the Depriver had an agent hostage.

Crowley stood his ground, his own gun raised, and spoke softly. "Let's run down your options, shall we? Looking around, I'd say you don't have enough bullets—though you could shoot yourself. Deveraux's obviously sold you out, so even if you could manage to escape, you're screwed. If you surrender, I take you back to a security lab. If you deprive the young lady, I take you there in a box."

Crowley's words washed over him without impact. "It's you," he finally said. "Christ—you're like a fucking ghost!"

"You keep playing around," Crowley said, "and you'll be the ghost, motherfucker." But warning alarms were already sounding off in his head. A knife in his back months ago in Miami. The flash from a sniper rifle at the rally in Lafayette Park . . . *Could it be him?*

"The name's Mitchell, and I've killed you twice already, Crowley! Why won't you stay down?"

Crowley remembered Robert Luxley's words from long ago: *"The posting was to kill you both."* He felt it down deep in his bones—finally, this was the one. This was the man responsible for the shell of the life that he led. "Why,

Mitchell? Why were you sent there to kill us?" he asked.

"Why?" Mitchell echoed, nearly chuckling. "You have to ask? Because that bitch crossed the line with a *Normal,* that's why! You two were a public embarrassment that made most of us sick! I'd have done it for free. There is no such thing as a 'Dep-friendly Normal,' asshole. But you know that now, don't you? Mr. Ministry."

Catch or kill? Crowley's finger whitened on the trigger. His training conflicting with his need for revenge caused him to hesitate a second too long.

In that second, it was decided for him, as Agent Pellegrino dug her heel into Mitchell's shin and twisted away, barely avoiding his grasping hand—and Mitchell began firing first as the two men emptied their clips into one another.

Mitchell went down like a puppet whose strings had been cut. Much to the amazement of the spectators, Crowley remained standing. "Is that all there is to it?" Crowley whispered. "That can't just be all there is to it." He lowered his gun, then let himself sag to his knees.

Two gloved agents brought in a containment stretcher and then ran Mitchell's limp body toward the waiting helicopter on the beach.

A doctor was brought to where Crowley sat slumped on the ground.

"*Es un Deprivadore?*" the moleish doctor asked, afraid to make physical contact with Crowley.

"*No doctore, no es un Deprivadore.*"

Once assured, the doctor and Agent Velez helped strip off Crowley's bloodied jacket, tie, and shirt, revealing the raised *D* brand on his chest. The doctor backed off again.

"I'm not a Depriver," Crowley said, suddenly grasping the doctor's wrist. He pulled the man closer and forced his opened hand against the largest of his wounds—the one that went clear through, just to the left of his heart. "I'm deprived. I'm no danger to you."

Crowley's cell phone began ringing. "Would you get that from my pocket?" Crowley asked Velez. He held the phone up to the downed agent's ear.

"Merry Christmas, Alex," said the voice on the other end. "Hope you got what you wanted."

"Deveraux," Crowley replied. "I didn't get you anything."

"Not to worry, I'm a patient man," Deveraux said. "You'll think of something. My door is always open for you, you know. Or for anyone you feel is in need of my protection."

"Judging by this dead body I have here, I'd say your commitment to protection is rather inconsistent," Crowley said. "I'm still trying to *help* Deprivers. Not set them up. But thanks, I'll keep that in mind."

Deveraux laughed, "Hasn't anyone told you, Alex? There is no such thing as a Dep-friendly Normal anymore," and he cut the connection.

Yeah, Crowley thought, *someone did tell me . . . asshole.*

17

THE cat rubbed her head affectionately against Agent Crowley's leg, and he reached down and gave her a stroke. He'd found her, abused and abandoned, in the alley behind his apartment complex. She was Abyssinian, an expensive breed—a former house cat unable to fend for herself, as evidenced by the near-starved state in which Crowley had discovered her. The apartment itself, top floor in a five-story, was not his own. Neither was the bed, nor any of the other sparse furnishings. The whole building was Ministry allocated, one of many like buildings in Century City, where agents were housed while awaiting deployment.

The cat meowed as Crowley got up from the table and poured her a bowl of milk. He set it down and watched as her small pink tongue went to work. Who would take care of her when they sent him in? It was one more thing to consider during the final few hours of freedom he had left. The mission that lay ahead was getting under Alex's skin. It wasn't just the idea of incarceration, though that was a considerable factor. It had more to do with his internal struggle of allegiance. The man he was being sent to protect was accused of murder, convicted of manslaughter. And once again, he found himself at odds with Ministry policy. Any way you sliced this mission, there would be considerable reverberations for Deprivers.

Crowley sat on the edge of the couch, flipped on the television, and found some basketball. The Lakers at home against the Knicks. Watching the players dodge in and out to avoid collision in their full skinsuits left him longing for the good old days. The cat ran up to the screen and pawed at the volley of movement. *She wants to play ball.* Crowley laughed to himself.

He picked up the dossier on Lansing and scanned the man's charmed political career with revulsion. Lansing had been appointed to Governor Tyrsdale's task force after the Duncan Cameron conviction but before the first anti-Depriver riots. That's when so many of them were recruited, young right-wing political guns, just when the misguided fear of epidemic could have been controlled and government could actually have made a difference—and then did, for the worse. Lansing had drafted several of the original Deprivers' rights revocations, including the Mandatory Glove Act. *That fascist bastard deserves what he gets,* Crowley thought.

The cat curled up on Crowley's lap. Alex took great pleasure in the fact that he could make full contact with the animal, and it never spent a moment worrying that it might go blind or deaf at his touch. He could understand why so many Deprivers kept pets. They fell asleep together, mingled in reciprocal affection.

Agent Crowley was awakened a short time later by a knock at the door, two Ministry operatives who had come to take him away to prison.

* * *

CROWLEY looked up from his cuffed hands, out through the van window, at the sign above the fence: Welcome to Salinas Valley State Prison. And, underneath: Hope You Have a Rehabilitative Stay. Alternating strands of barbed wire and razor ribbon lined the fences. Guards with rifles walked stoically along the towers and rooftops.

As the gates closed behind the van, the inmate sitting beside Crowley said, "Home again, home again."

He found it difficult getting off the bus in his leg irons, but managed. He and the eleven other inmates were herded into the processing center. Once inside, their hand and leg irons were removed. The prisoners were then led into a small gray room and told to strip. The concrete was cold against their feet. When Crowley removed his undershirt, revealing the *D* branded over his heart, the other inmates took notice. A heavyset prisoner with a long, grizzled beard started the trouble.

"Hey, we got us a friggin' Dep in the cell here!" he said, stepping up within arm's length of Alex Crowley.

"What are you gonna do, touch me?" Crowley asked calmly.

A guard stepped into the room and pushed the other inmate back with his baton. "Don't be stupid," the guard said, "he ain't no Depriver. He's been screened."

"Yeah," the prisoner said, "so why you got a mark like that?"

"None of your business, shit-for-brains," Crowley replied.

"We'll see about that. . . ."

The guard cracked his baton against the wall. "That's enough from the two of you. Unless either of you boys wanna spend your first night in solitary confinement? I didn't think so. Move on."

The next room was a cavity search, followed by decontamination and a shower, all part of a slow, methodical process to strip away a man's pride. Next, clothing was issued, loose-fitting jeans and blue cotton shirts—and Crowley's name was replaced with the number 845099. Crowley was then given a small pamphlet of prison rules and regulations and led through a maze of corridors and catwalks to his cell.

"This is your new room. I hope you like it."

Crowley gave the cell a once-over. Toilet. Bunk bed. Graffiti-covered, windowless walls.

"You got a cell mate named Briggs. Big black bastard. You ain't from the South, are you? He's down in the cafeteria. Drop your stuff on the lower bunk, and I'll take you down."

The guard led Crowley through the complex and into the cafeteria. He pointed out several men. "Those boys are your unit. Go where they go when they go. That black boy at the table is Briggs. You get your meal right over there."

Crowley took a tray and was served his meal: chipped beef, toast, and mixed vegetables. He took a cup of coffee and headed to where Briggs was seated. Briggs saw him coming and stared him down. Clean-shaven, muscular, he had torn the sleeves from his shirt to reveal his massive biceps. Small, round-framed spectacles seemed an anachronism on his strong face.

A lot of eyes were on Crowley as he stepped up to the table, all from disapproving faces. Crowley stood in front of Briggs.

"Briggs?" he asked.

Briggs nodded. "I guess you must be 845099," he said, reading the numbers from Crowley's shirt. "Have a seat."

Crowley set his tray down and sat in a folding chair, routinely scanning the room. Red bandannas. Blue bandannas. No blue auras. "I'm told you'll show me the ropes," he said to Briggs.

"Yeah, yeah," Briggs said. "What are you in for, 845099?"

"Alex, please."

"What are you in for, Alex?"

"Espionage," Crowley replied. "So they say."

Several heads nodded around the table. There were a few smiles. "Against who?" a prisoner asked.

"You name it," Crowley said.

"Well, I was in money laundry, they say. Joey there was a stick-up man, they say, and that white boy there killed three cops during a smuggling gig, they say."

Crowley made mental notes as Briggs ran down the list of the alleged crimes of those gathered.

"Hey!" came a gruff voice with an accompanying hand on Crowley's shoulder. Crowley remembered the voice. "Hey, you damned Dep!"

Crowley stood and turned as the inmate with the grizzly beard hauled off and punched him in the jaw. Crowley rolled his head with the punch, then straightened, unfazed. Briggs was visibly impressed. "I understand you've got a problem with Deprivers," Crowley said. "I'm not one of them."

"I say you're a Dep-lover. I don't like your kind least as much as them sense-fuckers. Plague as bad as niggers!"

At that, the entire table stood up. So Grizzlybeard smiled, realizing he was about to get the living shit kicked out of him, flipped Crowley the bird, and withdrew. They all sat back down.

"You take a punch pretty well, Alex," Briggs said.

"Didn't feel a thing."

After lunch, Crowley and Briggs took a walk together along the perimeter fence. "You really a Dep sympathizer?" Briggs asked.

"Why," Crowley said, "you gonna hit me too?"

"Nah, nah," Briggs said, rubbing sweat from his neck, "I'm all for the minority. Deps ain't treated that much different than the black man. Everybody sees them as a little less than human. Nobody willing to look us in the eye and decide which is good and which is bad. There was a kid in my neighborhood who went Dep on us. I liked him before then. Didn't see why I should suddenly change my mind, you know."

"What happened to him?" Crowley asked.

"Stoned to death by his own hood."

"You were there?"

Briggs showed the dome of his head proudly. Crowley noted a deep scar.

"I had the unfortunate pleasure of being beside him when it started."

"Wrong place at the wrong time."

"You got that right." They walked over to the water pump and both took a drink. "Assholes like that bigot who hit you are commonplace around here. You should watch what you say."

"Yeah, it's kinda hard to conceal this, come shower time," Alex said, pulling his shirt to the side and revealing his brand.

"Shit, white boy—why'd you go and do a thing like that?"

Crowley looked at the sun, stared a moment, refusing to blink. "My wife . . . was one of them."

Briggs looked away. "Sorry to hear that, man."

"Thanks."

"You're sure gonna love Lansing."

"Who's that?"

"Lansing? Oh, he's only the biggest bigot you ever met. You know, he was that guy always ranting on television."

"Oh, yeah," Crowley said. "Is he in here too?"

"Yep." Briggs nodded. "He's in our cell block, matter o' fact."

"What's he in for?"

"Manslaughter," Briggs replied. "But you ask me, it should've been murder."

A whistle blew. Inmates started filing back toward the building. "What's that mean?" Crowley asked.

"Means it's time to go to work."

18

CROWLEY estimated there were seven to eight cell blocks' worth of inmates gathered together in the work area. Workstations accommodated four inmates apiece. Each station had two sewing machines and several bins filled with black material.

"Do you sew, Alex?" Briggs asked.

At first, Crowley didn't believe this was a serious question. The look on Briggs's face convinced him. "No," he said.

"Fine," Briggs replied, taking the operator's seat at one of the machines. "I'll sew, you cut and glue."

Crowley sat, lifted a piece of the familiar-looking black material. "What exactly are we making?" he asked.

"Gloves. What else, man?" Briggs said. "Ever since the epidemic struck, the world can't get enough of gloves."

Of course, Crowley thought. He'd never guessed that gloves, one of America's largest exports, were manufactured by the penal system—though it made perfect sense. Movies, guns, and gloves. The three necessities.

He learned how to measure, fold, cut, and glue. Briggs was a patient teacher. While learning the machine itself, Crowley actually put the needle through his finger on more than one occasion. Each time, he required Briggs's assistance to free him from the machine.

"Damn," Briggs remarked when Alex got particularly tangled, the needle having pierced him twice and actually stitched him to a glove. "Don't that hurt like a bitch?"

"I'm good with pain," Crowley said.

At dinner, Crowley asked Briggs, "So where is this Nazi Lansing? If he's in our cell block, why doesn't he eat with us?"

Briggs was staring down at his plate, nudging vegetables he did not recognize. "What *is* this shit?" he said. "Lansing? Oh, he rarely comes out of his cell. Says he likes the comfort of bars. Keeps him at arm's length from the world, you know."

Crowley nodded. "Actually, I think I do remember his name in the news a while back."

"Yeah, he's a real celebrity, all right."

"He strangled some kid to death, didn't he?"

"Yeah," Briggs said. "A Depriver. He supposedly got sent by some radical group to blind Lansing."

"What for?" Crowley asked.

Briggs put his fork down, lowered his glasses on his nose. "Man, don't you ever read down past the headlines? Lansing wrote half those bills that got passed. The Articles of Deprivers' Rights Revocation. I even heard he's the man who started the Glove Act."

"And now he's making them. How ironic," Crowley smiled.

"Nah. He's still got too much juice to pull that kind of work."

"How's that?" Crowley asked. "If he's got so much pull, why isn't he being held in some fancy-schmancy prison? Why is he in here with us schleps?"

Briggs looked around, then moved close to Crowley's ear and whispered, "Man chose this place 'cause we've got a zero Dep population. He's fearing retaliation."

"Yeah," Crowley whispered back, "I bet he's freaked. But they can't get him in here. You get screened."

Briggs shrugged. "Guess that's how he sees it too."

"Hey, 845099!" a guard yelled out to Crowley.

"Yes, sir," Crowley said.

"It's time for you to see the shrink. Let's go!"

THE psychiatrist was a gaunt, elderly gentleman named Dr. Tevis, who walked with the assistance of a cane and, true to form, smoked a pipe as he worked. The room, uncharacteristic of the rest of the establishment, had an almost comfortable air to it. Crowley found the situation ridiculous, but the couch was quite comfortable.

"Tell me, Alex," Tevis asked, pulling his pipe, "have you ever been in therapy before?"

"Yes, Doctor," Alex said. "During my marriage. We were having some difficulty coping with some—I guess you'd say—interracial obstacles."

"And did you find it useful? Satisfying?"

Crowley nodded. "I still send my doctor Christmas cards."

"Maybe I'll look forward to one?"

"If you're half as good as she was—maybe."

"What are your hobbies, Alex?"

Crowley put his hands behind his head and stared up at the stucco ceiling. "Well, Doc, I guess I like to read.

Listen to rock 'n' roll. Play basketball. Foil assassination attempts."

"Yes. That's clever. Do you think the world is a fair place?"

Crowley thought on that. "No," he said. "Not when our government can mandate which people have full rights under the law and which do not."

"Yes, yes, and do you feel that you are one of the people without full rights now, Alex?" the doctor asked.

"No," Crowley replied. "I feel I'm free to act on my own accord. Although I may answer to superiors, I find I have enough freedom to act within my own moral code of ethics."

"Well spoken," the doctor said, nodding. "But do you feel that now, with your current incarceration, your freedom to act on those moral ethics has been limited?"

Crowley shook his head. "Doctor, my freedom, or lack of it, is truly ephemeral. I could be placed in solitary, set free tomorrow, or buried alive, for that matter. My free will to act is neither impaired nor enhanced by my surroundings. I still make choices according to my own gut instincts. My path is immutable. My soul's hidden intentions are ceaselessly working through my physical incarnation to dispense my karma."

"Ah, you're a Buddhist then?"

"Theosophist, actually, but I have studied all world religions. More and more I find myself leaning toward the Lakota Indian doctrines. I've been through several of their initiations."

"Fascinating." The doctor lay back against his divan. "I've always wanted to try an Indian sweat lodge. I hear it's very cleansing. You've tried that, then?"

Crowley sat up on the couch and stretched. "Oh, yes,

nothing like it. Opens you right up. Do you meditate, Dr. Tevis?"

"No, I'm embarrassed to say," Tevis replied. "I've never been able to get the knack of it. You?"

"Regularly," Crowley said. "Would you like me to teach you how? I can offer some simple techniques."

"I'd love it if you would."

"Wonderful," Crowley said, clapping his hands together. "Let's begin with your breathing."

A guard with no neck and a serious attitude problem escorted Crowley back to the cell block. Alex became aware of the latter characteristic when his whistling of "Three Blind Mice" was interrupted by a baton to the back of his head.

"I don't like whistlers," the guard said. Crowley rubbed his head with his hand as they navigated the catwalk. *Possible concussion,* he thought. *Careful about dozing.* Rounding the corner on the way to his cell, he finally caught sight of Lansing. His cell was located on the catwalk on the opposite side of the block, separated from his own row by a two-story drop. Using the knock on the head to feign slowness, Crowley checked Lansing. He appeared uninjured. He sat on a single bed, watching television. Talk about privileged. And was that a computer monitor in the far corner of the cell? Son of a bitch probably even has full Internet access.

When they reached Crowley's cell, Briggs sat up in his bunk. Crowley watched peripherally as the guard used his key to unlock the cell door: *Wrist turns clockwise, then presses forward.* The guard shoved him inside and ordered, "No whistling!" as he locked the door in a reverse of the previous motion, turned on his heel, and left.

"What's up with that?" Briggs asked.

"Harmonically challenged, I guess," Crowley said. He stripped off his shirt and jeans, and slid into the lower bunk. "Hey, Briggs, didn't you say that Lansing got blinded by that Depriver?"

"Yeah, so?"

"Isn't that a television in his cell? Not to mention a computer?"

"Yeah, he can see fine now."

"The deprivation wore off?"

"Oh, yeah," Briggs said. "The Dep who touched him had a short duration. Like half an hour, I've heard."

"So Lansing gets blinded by this kid, somehow gets ahold of him anyway, strangles him to death, then a half hour later he's not blind anymore—and he's got a dead kid on his terrace?"

"That's his story," Briggs said. "So they say."

"Sounds like the kid was sent as a warning," Crowley offered. "Teach one of the opposition firsthand that not all deprivations are permanent."

"Your guess is as good as mine," Briggs said. But Agent Crowley was pretty sure by that point that his guess was not as good as Briggs's. In fact, he was quite certain that Briggs was not guessing at all.

1 9

GLOVES. Gloves that fit men, women, children. And when they were finished, each pair was stamped: Do Not Remove Under Penalty of Law. *There's a life to be ruined with each and every pair,* thought Crowley the next afternoon as he folded and stitched. He considered himself lucky that his deprivation was one that had left him fully functional. In fact, it afforded him the luxury of knowing which hands were safe and which were not.

Crowley watched Briggs sewing intently and wondered how the man could endure the idea of fifteen more years in this place. Would he, himself, be able to handle prolonged imprisonment, Crowley wondered.

"Hey, 201814, report to the front of the workroom," the supervisor called. Briggs looked up, as aware of his call numbers as an old lady at a bingo table. Crowley glanced up from the glove he was working on.

"Wonder what that could be?" Briggs said.

Crowley shrugged. "Maybe you won the lottery?"

Crowley observed Briggs's cool stride as he moved to the supervisor's post. The supervisor pointed Briggs toward the door, and a guard opened it for him. Briggs left the workroom without so much as a backward glance toward Crowley.

Alex returned to his sewing. He decided it would be appropriate to say a small prayer over each pair of gloves as he worked. *"Mitakuye Oyasin,"* he softly hummed, his Lakota lamentation. He prayed that each owner could somehow find happiness, despite mandated solitude. *"Mitakuye Oyasin,"* he hoped that the Deprivers could find it in their hearts to forgive him for making their gloves—the second skin that offered so little sensation and separated them from the world. *"Mitakuye—"*

A tap on Crowley's shoulder brought him out of his meditation. He looked up. "You have a visitor," a guard said standing over him. "Come with me."

The guard led him out of the workstation along what Crowley determined to be at least a quarter mile of corridors. When they arrived at the visiting room, he was told that he had ten minutes. The guard let him in and closed the door behind him.

It was a small, sterile room with a full Plexiglas wall partition that separated the inmate from the visitor. He took a seat across from Agent Kelsoe, who sat with his feet up, tie undone, smiling and chewing a wad of gum.

"Hello, Alex," he said in his game-show-host voice. "I love your outfit."

"Thanks, Jack," he said, "it's good to see you."

"How's prison treating you?"

"Not as bad as I'd expected. Although there are a few people in here who'd like to bash my skull in."

"You always make friends fast. How's Lansing?"

"He's got himself confined to his cell. I don't see how

anyone's going to move on him. I'm planning on paying him a visit this afternoon."

"Any incidents?"

Crowley shook his head. "There's not a Depriver in this joint."

"It doesn't necessarily have to be a Depriver, you know. Your assumptions could be wrong."

Crowley stood up and paced a few feet before turning back. "No—they'll send in a Depriver. There'd be no justice in their eyes without a deprivation."

"Almost seems like you approve," he said.

"Come on, Jack," Crowley said, "you know I can sympathize with their motives while remaining detached."

"Your detachment is admirable," he said. "But I know that deep down inside, you'd like to see Lansing get what he deserves. His legislative actions have caused a lot of unnecessary suffering to countless Norms as well as Deps."

"Let's not forget that he strangled a kid to death," Crowley added.

"An assassin," he countered, then removed the gum from his mouth and stuck it to the bottom of his chair. "He almost got off on self-defense, you'll remember. And he may on appeal."

"You know full well that it was just a warning they sent."

Kelsoe nodded, tearing the wrapper on another stick of gum. "But Lansing couldn't have known that, could he? He was deprived—forever, for all he knew. You heard the testimony; he said the kid was getting ready to do him. So he struck back."

"I was at the crime scene, Jack. I saw what Lansing did. It wasn't just a flash of fear, believe me. What he did to that kid took hours."

"That's why the judge put him here."

Crowley shook his head in disgust. "They should've put that bastard in a Depriver facility. Let him feel the hand clamps he helped popularize. Let him walk in fear of every single contact."

"Alex, you need a serious debriefing after this." Kelsoe sighed.

"Yeah, well—the Ministry was nuts to put me in on this."

"The government requested Ministry aid. And crazy as it seems, you are the top-ranked spotter."

"And you think that's all there is to it? C'mon Jack—we both know they're testing me here—and I don't like it."

"I think you're testing yourself here, Alex," Kelsoe said. "I hope you pass."

A loud rap at the door signaled Crowley that his time was up.

"That's the guard," Crowley acknowledged. "I've got to go. Check the manifest for new prisoners about to be transferred to this facility, won't you? I'm sure a Depriver will be shipped in any day now, undetected. That'll be our man."

"I'll screen them myself."

"Thanks," he said, placing his palm to the glass. The guard opened the door and barked, "845099, your visitation allotment has concluded. Come with me."

As Agent Kelsoe left the prison through the main entrance, he narrowly missed a new guard coming on duty. He was clean-cut, medium height, and glowing blue.

20

CROWLEY swaggered as he walked out of the visitors' center. He whistled a few notes of Michael Jackson's "Thriller" and gave a few shoulder rolls. "You remember that one?" Crowley asked as he stopped and turned to the guard.

"No," the guard said, pushing Crowley forward. "Let's go."

"Come on, you know it. 'Thriller'?" He then launched into a manic pantomime of the ancient John Landis video with zombielike movements screeching, " 'This is *thriller! Thriller Night!* Ain't no one gonna save ya' from the beast about to strike! *Thriller!*' "

The guard pulled his baton and struck Crowley across the shoulder blades. Crowley went down to the floor.

"Hey, 845099," the guard said, "one more outburst like that, and you'll spend the next twenty-four hours in your cell."

Crowley stood up slowly, pretending to be in great pain. "Bullshit," he said, and then spat.

The guard grabbed Crowley by the arm and forced him down the corridor, past a checkpoint where he told the associate warden, "I'm locking this one away in his cell as a disciplinary action."

The associate warden nodded and opened the door. The guard dragged Crowley to his cell. "Is this good enough for you?" the guard asked him. "Or do you want solitary?"

Crowley turned his back to the man.

"I didn't think so," the guard replied. "Have a nice day."

He went back down the corridor, laughing, and Crowley quickly set to work.

First he scanned the corridors on both sides of the catwalk, his and Lansing's. No guards. *And why should there be with only two inmates locked snugly away in their cells?* Next, he sat down on his bunk, grabbed a wad of toilet paper, and went to work on his arm. It was there, like an itch he couldn't scratch, just below the skin. He dug his fingernail deep into the flesh on his left forearm, drawing blood from a quarter-inch gash. He then maneuvered the thin metal wire beneath the skin until the head pushed far enough out to grasp. He slid the gleaming pick out of his arm and set it down on the first wad of toilet paper. Applying pressure with his thumb to stop the bleeding, he listened again for footsteps. He cleaned up the blood, washed the pick in the toilet, and flushed. Then he went to work on the lock. Pressure down, clockwise turn, and the lock released. He looked, listened, and sniffed for the guards. Then he left the cell.

To cross from his catwalk to Lansing's, he needed the overhead pipes. He'd considered the route for over an hour the previous evening before allowing himself to sleep. He leapt up onto the railing and found his balance. He didn't look down at the hard concrete he knew lay some thirty feet below at the next block. He looked up, calculated, and sprang. He grabbed hold of the overhead pipe and swung his legs up after him. He pipe-crawled along his chosen route until he was in easy swinging distance of Lansing's catwalk. Down he went, landing with minimum clatter. Within seconds he was standing before Lansing's cell, staring through the bars. Lansing was lying on the lower bunk, facing the wall, and listening to music through a headset. The almighty official dressed in a stained cotton T-shirt and boxers, unshaven, hair disheveled. Crowley was surprised he wasn't giving daily anti-Depriver lectures in the cafeteria.

"Lansing," he whispered.

He didn't react. For someone who lived in fear of an assassination attempt, he wasn't too alert. Crowley reached in through the bars and tapped the steel bed frame.

Lansing sprang out of bed and landed on his knees on the floor. "Don't touch me!" he said, with an educated Southern drawl. There was terror in his eyes. "I didn't mean to kill that boy."

Crowley put a finger to his lips. "Quiet, Lansing. I'm here to protect you. I'm a Ministry agent."

Lansing sighed, cast the headset onto the bed, and stood up. He gripped the bars and said, "Then it's true? They're sending Deprivers in after me?"

"There's no conclusive evidence of that, sir, but it's conceivable that they'll try."

For a moment, Crowley was able to let go of his revulsion for the man. He felt compassion for his predicament. That sentiment was obliterated as Lansing added, "I'd like to strangle the life out of each and every one of those Dep bastards."

Crowley swallowed his anger and calmly replied, "Well, sir, I'm here to see that your direct participation will not be necessary."

"You're a spotter?" he said, scratching his chin.

"Yes, the name's Crowley," he said. "And my cell is right across from yours, there. That means I can get to you if I need to."

"Warden knows you're here, Crowley?"

Crowley nodded. "Now, they let you out for a walk in the yard at 7:45, when we're all at breakfast. You go with one of the guards, right?" Crowley asked.

"Yes," Lansing said, both perturbed and comforted by Crowley's knowledge.

"You'll be skipping that for the next few days," Crowley said.

"Sure, sure," Lansing said. "And while you're on work detail I take my shower. What about that?"

"You might want to request a bucket and soap for the duration."

"Fine, yeah."

Crowley stepped back and examined the wall outside Lansing's cell. "In case you need to tell me something. Do this. . . ." Crowley showed Lansing a spot on the wall that was within easy reach through the bars. "Draw me letters with your fingers, understand?"

"Yeah, I think so," he replied, nodding.

"Try writing *Help* now," Crowley said, stepping back against the rail.

Lansing reached through the bars to the clear spot, above the alarm box, and drew the letters out, one by one.

"Fine," Crowley said. "I'd better get back."

"Thank you, Agent Crowley. You're a credit to your service."

Crowley turned and climbed up on the railing. "Don't thank me yet, Lansing," he offered as he leapt from the bar.

Crowley managed to lock his cell only seconds before

the main corridor door was thrust open, and the inmates were herded into the cell block. As the din of conversation and footsteps grew closer, he stashed the pick by plunging it into his lumpy mattress. A guard arrived moments later, unlocking the cell. Briggs was with him. The guard pushed him in and relocked the door.

"Heard you're doing time for bad behavior," Briggs said.

Crowley nodded. "Bad behavior has an ever-changing definition here, it seems."

"Missed you at dinner," Briggs said. "Would have been nice to have you help me deduce the origin of the gray stuff they served us."

"Where'd you go this afternoon?" Crowley asked with nonchalance.

"Wife came to visit," he said.

"Oh, yeah? You get conjugal visits? 'Cause I'm not sure I want to be in here when you two—"

Briggs laughed. "No man, we get that once a month. And it's a private room. This was just a day visit. You play chess?"

Crowley sat on his bunk, with the board on his lap, in clear view of Lansing's cell, while Briggs sat on the toilet. Crowley threw the first two games for amusement. Briggs wasn't a bad player, but he was clearly unaware of the higher-level patterned attacks. Then something happened across the way, and Crowley paid strict peripheral attention.

Something was passed from an inmate two cells to the left of Lansing's to an inmate in the cell beside Lansing's, who flicked the object—Crowley guessed it was note paper—into Lansing's cell. Lansing immediately grasped it up and unfolded it. A look of distress came over his features as he read it. He moved to the bars and stared out at Crowley.

Crowley looked down at the chessboard, brought out his queen, and then looked back.

Lansing began spelling on the wall with quaking fingers. "T.H.E.S.C.R.E.A.M.O.F.T.H.E.B.U.T.T.E.R.F.L.Y," he wrote, then held out his arms in exasperation and Crowley lip-read his exclamation, "What the fuck?"

"You just left yourself open for attack on numerous fronts," Briggs said, indicating the board.

"I realize that," Crowley replied. "What do you know about butterflies?"

"Butterflies? Not a whole heck of a lot," Briggs said. "Why?"

Footsteps, and then a guard passed directly in front of their cell, smiling and swinging his baton. The unmistakable glow of a Depriver radiated off his face and hands.

"Checkmate," Briggs announced, clapping his hands together. "Man, this ain't your night!"

Crowley lifted the board and set it on the bed, pulling back the covers and reaching for the pick. He grasped it and pulled it free, rose, and moved to the cell gate.

"Hey man, what are you doing?" Briggs asked.

Crowley ignored him, jammed the pick in the lock. Down on the lower level he was horrified to see a second Depriver wearing a guard's uniform. That's when Briggs charged him. Crowley, expecting the attack, swung around and kicked Briggs hard in the solar plexus.

"I'm a Ministry agent," Crowley said. "And I know you, Samuel Briggs. I know you were sent in for subversive activities. You're not married, so I have to assume you've been involved in the planning of this. I warn you—don't interfere."

"Screw you," Briggs said, charging forward and smashing Crowley up against the bars. Crowley brought his elbows down hard against Briggs's back and felt the man wince. He scanned outside and now there was a third Depriver swinging his baton and descending a staircase to Lansing's floor.

Briggs delivered three blows to Crowley's kidneys and stepped away. Crowley caught his breath, centered himself, and then delivered a roundhouse kick, which caught Briggs square in the nose and dropped him with a spray of blood.

Crowley turned back to the gate and gasped. While Briggs had him up against the bars he must have dislodged the pick. *Where the hell is it?* He scanned desperately. There, hanging just on the edge of the catwalk. Briggs had tossed it over the edge, but it had caught on the mesh flooring.

Crowley looked out to Lansing. All three guards were converging on his cell. Lansing, who apparently now saw them, too, was trying to move his bunk in front of the bars, and he screamed, "Crowley!" out across the cell block.

"Hit the alarm!" Crowley yelled back.

Other prisoners were up against their bars now, trying to see what was going on. To their virgin eyes, this was merely an instance of guards rushing toward a wayward inmate.

Crowley flattened himself against the bars and reached out for the pick as the alarm began to sound. It was a good two inches out of reach.

Briggs slammed on top of him again. "You ain't saving that murdering bastard!" he said, gripping Alex's throat with both hands. Crowley slammed his forehead into Briggs's face and sent blood splattering everywhere. He rolled Briggs off of him and looked back. The guards had reached Lansing's cell, and one of them was unlocking it.

"No!" Crowley screamed. He got up, ran to his bed, and grabbed a pillow. He slid back against the bars and slung it out at the lock pick. For a second, it seemed to have caught the dangling wire. Crowley closed his eyes in prayer and then gently reeled the pillow back to him, his heart pounding in his ears like thunder.

The pick teetered . . . then plummeted over the edge, out of view.

Crowley released the pillow and gasped for air. He looked up. The guards had entered Lansing's cell. He closed his eyes again.

LANSING was crouched in the corner, behind the toilet, as the guards came upon him, beating him with their batons across his face, legs, and body until he lay relatively still.

"A message from Deveraux," one of them said, as he reached out and brushed Lansing's cheek. "And from every Depriver whose life your prejudice has touched. Now you'll be blind for the rest of your life!"

"No!" Lansing whispered, looking up in desperation.

The second Depriver stepped forward and touched him the same way. "Enjoy the pain, Lansing. In a few moments you'll never feel anything again."

"Please!" Lansing pleaded.

The third man stepped up and slapped Lansing hard across the face. "That's the last sound that you'll ever hear," he said. All three spat on him and quickly left the cell. Lansing sat there, shaking and drooling—his sight and his hearing and his sense of touch now dissolving away.

CROWLEY, his back to the wall in his cell, looked at the semiconscious Briggs, watching the blood pour from his nose as the alarms continued to blare. He heard the sounds of running feet and crashing doors. The perpetrators had little chance of escape, he knew. But what did it matter, really? They had struck a retaliatory blow to the government party who'd deprived them of their rights. In the end, the public would decide who was justified. Unsure whether to laugh or cry, Crowley looked to Briggs and said, "Once you touch a butterfly's wings, it can never fly again. You damage the essential powder. It's as good as dead."

"He could see," Briggs mumbled back, tinted spittle running down his chin.

"What?" Crowley asked.

"When he killed the boy—he could already see again. Not self-defense."

"How do you know this?" Crowley demanded.

"Phone records," Briggs answered. "They sent the kid in at eight-thirty. His orders were to wait until Lansing came out of it, then surrender to him. Since the blinding was temporary—"

"They knew he'd get off. Meanwhile, the story hits the news."

Briggs nodded weakly. "But Lansing didn't call the police until after midnight."

"Thanks for filling me in," Crowley said, looking out through the bars. "I'll do my best to corroborate that."

The warden arrived within minutes, and Crowley was released. He went directly to Lansing's cell. A doctor arrived and confirmed what he'd already surmised: Lansing was blind, deaf, and numb, reduced to a pitiful, quivering shadow of a human being.

Alex Crowley went home to his cat.

21

FIFTH-GRADE science class is not typically categorized as a catastrophic period in the life of your average kid. Not typically, but in this case, it certainly threatened to make short work of all of young Daniel Weisenbaum's opportunities for normalcy in a world gone touch-shy. Not that Daniel's teacher was in any way to blame for the chain of events that his alertness would trigger, like a match to a fuse, but he had made the phone call.

And the Ministry had been notified. And once the Ministry opened a file on you, regardless of age, nationality, or criminal intent, your life was bound for strange twists and turns on roads that were thankfully inaccessible to the common man. At least it hadn't been the Parent-Teacher Association Daniel's teacher had contacted. They'd have stormed the school, dragged the boy out of class, roped him to the flagpole, and set him on fire in front of the whole student body.

Agent Alex Crowley had Mr. Rubino meet him in the

school cafeteria during recess, while the children were out-side pummeling each other with dodgeballs from a good, safe distance. A teacher's aide was dispatched to find the Weisen-baum boy and bring him in to be interviewed.

"I'm feeling a little anxious about having reported this, Agent Crowley," Rubino said, index finger in his collar, "After all, I'm not *really* sure Daniel's the cause. It could be simply a remarkable coincidence."

Crowley sipped from his thermos-top cup of coffee and tried to quell the teacher's fears, though, in truth, things would be far from all right for the youngster from this point on if the reported deprivations were confirmed. "Relax, Mr. Rubino. I'm here to take the guesswork out of the equation. If one of your students is a Depriver, I'll know."

"You've got some sort of equipment that determines that sort of thing?" he asked, staring through the Plexiglas windows at the romping flocks of preadolescents.

Crowley followed the teacher's gaze out to the children, and recalled a childhood where he once played, uninhib-ited, on a recess playground—when teacher's aides were not required to make sure you kept your gloves on. An envi-ronment where a simple skirmish or the yanking of a pretty girl's ponytail wouldn't call for immediate expulsion. "Something like that," he said.

Crowley sipped at his coffee. So far, his scan of the chil-dren had detected no auras. Maybe this was a false alarm after all. "What sort of test was it that you administered, Mr. Rubino?"

"An American Optical. We were playing recessive-genotype games, Agent Crowley, not conducting tests. You know, how certain people cannot taste litmus paper, or roll their tongues, or smell certain smells?"

"Correct me if I'm wrong, sir," Crowley said, "but the American Optical? That's the test with the all the red and green dots on paper, correct?"

"Exactly," Rubino nodded. "Although it could be blue-yellow as well. Or light-dark. They place a hidden number in the opposing color within the dots, and if you're color-blind, you won't be able to see the hidden number."

"And how many of your students reported they could *not* see the hidden number?" Crowley continued. Outside, he noted through the window that the aide was returning, a student shuffling beside her with a downcast stare.

Rubino paled, took a quivering slurp from his cup. "All of them, Agent Crowley," he replied. "Every last student—except one."

As the aide pulled the door open to step inside, Crowley could see the child's face. A gangly, dark-haired youth with a worried look.

"Danny, this is Agent Crowley. Say hello," said Mr. Rubino.

Danny looked up at Agent Crowley with large, soulful eyes and gave the quick head bow that was the latest acceptable replacement for the forsaken handshake. "Hello," he said.

"Hello, Danny," Crowley replied warmly. "Would you mind taking a little walk with me? I have some questions to ask you."

"Sure," Danny said. "Are you a regular policeman, or are you FBI?"

"Neither one, exactly, but those are good guesses," Agent Crowley answered, bending down to see eye to eye with the boy. "I am here to help Mr. Rubino and your class, though, so it's okay to talk to me. Right, Mr. Rubino?"

"Right," Mr. Rubino said, looking to each of them in

turn. "It almost always starts at this time, at puberty. Isn't that right, Agent Crowley?" he asked quietly.

"There's a lot we still don't know," Crowley said. "But that seems generally to be the case."

Rubino excused himself, and Alex offered Daniel a stick of gum. The boy took it without question and had it in his mouth immediately.

"Mr. Rubino's the nervous type, isn't he, Danny?" Crowley asked.

"Yeah, he's pretty uptight," the boy said.

"Yeah," Crowley said. "Sorry to break up your dodgeball game like that."

"It's okay."

"You play basketball?"

"Sometimes."

"Me too. Wanna play now? With me?"

"Are you sure we can?"

"No problem. Anybody argues, I'll throw 'em in jail."

Danny laughed as he led Agent Crowley out of the cafeteria toward the gymnasium.

A short time later, Agent Crowley, *sans* jacket, tie, gun, and badge, was standing in the school gymnasium half lost in memory. Danny wriggled his hands into a pair of the school's mandatory sports gloves. Crowley easily dodged the boy, burst into a layup and slam-dunked the undersized basketball. "You're gonna need to grow a little taller, Danny—if you're gonna be able to take me on defense."

Danny, out of breath, replied, "Duh . . . you're a grown-up. You're supposed to be bigger and faster than me."

"That's right, Danny," Crowley said. "And as a responsible grown-up, it's also my job to look out for you. Tell me something, Danny. Do you know what a Depriver is?"

Danny nodded his head in the curious affirmative.

"Tell me," Crowley asked, keeping his tone casual.

"A bad person who takes away your eyes or ears or nose or stuff," said Danny, dribbling the ball.

Crowley sighed. "Well, Daniel, it's true that some Deprivers *are* bad people. But just like there can be bad people who aren't Deprivers, there can be Deprivers who aren't bad people at all. It's just that sometimes, people get frightened of Deprivers, and don't bother to find out if they're good or bad. Understand?"

Danny shrugged. "My dad reads about them every day in the paper. He tells about the bad ones, and that we should never touch strangers."

"Well, that's good advice in any case," Alex said, taking the ball from Danny and dribbling. "But I have to tell you, it's my job to spot Deprivers, and then to find out which ones are good—and which are bad."

"Really? How do you spot them?"

"I have a special way of seeing," Crowley said. "A *secret* way."

"Can I learn the secret way too?" Danny asked.

"Maybe," Crowley said. "It all depends."

Danny suddenly burst forward and swiped the ball from Crowley's hands. He stepped back, took the shot, and the ball bounded off the backboard.

"Nice move," Crowley said.

"Once you find them, how do you know which are good and which are bad?"

"That's harder to know, Danny, but I can usually figure it out if I watch them long enough."

"What happens when you know?"

Crowley considered his answer carefully. "When I know, I make sure the bad ones can't hurt anybody. And I help the good ones to learn to be careful."

"Careful how?"

"Oh, lots of ways. Careful not to accidentally deprive the ones they love. Their friends, parents, classmates. How to be safe."

"Safe from who?" Danny asked, the first trace of nervousness entering his voice.

"From people who don't understand that there are good Deprivers and bad ones."

Danny ran and retrieved the ball, then trotted back to Agent Crowley and handed it to him. "Am I a Depriver, Agent Crowley?"

22

AT the conclusion of the interview, Crowley met once more
with Rubino and the principal. He assured them that
the boy was not, in fact, a Depriver, but that the high incidence of color blindness at the school demanded further
investigation. He gave both men his cellular number and
requested the testing be repeated on the entire class every
day after recess for the next five days. "If the children are
indeed deprived, it's quite possibly a temporary affliction.
Certainly not life threatening," Crowley said. "Let's keep
this among ourselves until further notice."

Driving out of the school parking lot, Crowley still felt
unsure about the choice he'd just made. Oftentimes difficult
choices are required when lives are at stake. He simply could
not sound the alarm in this situation. The symptoms were
too mild to subject a human being to an entire lifetime of
alienation. It had been a tough call. He'd have to keep a
tight rein on the situation. With any luck, the deprivations

would prove to be of short duration, and the subject could be trained to . . .

Crowley was so engrossed in thought that he did not see a tractor-trailer approaching the upcoming intersection. He attempted to swerve at the last second but misjudged. The collision sent his Volvo scraping violently in a shower of sparks along the guardrail, which eventually gave way and threw him into a ditch.

When Crowley's head cleared, he was bent over at an impossible angle in the passenger seat, and the world was upside down. He looked for damage: blood on his forehead, matting his hair. His left shoulder, judging by the position of his hand, was either broken or dislocated. Of course, he felt no pain from the injury, so he slowly began disentangling himself from the wreckage.

Once free, he saw the tractor-trailer lying crosswise on its side. A man, the driver, he guessed, slowly limped toward him across the highway. Crowley knelt in the grass and tried to calm his breathing.

The truck driver, who was thankfully not carrying a jack handle, called down, "Ambulance is on the way. How're you doing?"

"I'm okay. You?"

"The leg hurts, but I think I'll be fine. Truck's not so good."

"Completely my fault, sir. Don't worry. You'll be fully compensated," Crowley said, knowing that the Ministry would not hesitate to offer the man a new, state-of-the-art vehicle and cash settlement in return for his silence.

Crowley sniffed the air, smelled the gas, and knew there was little time. "Please," Crowley asked. "If you can—there's a briefcase in the front seat of my car. Can you get it?"

The driver limped over and retrieved Crowley's case.

"Thanks," Crowley said, "Now can you help me across the road? My car is about to explode."

The man put an arm under Crowley's good shoulder, and the two of them limped their way across the highway and into a clearing of trees beyond the second embankment, at which point, as if on cue, Crowley's Volvo exploded. Moments later, the tanker truck followed suit. "Hadn't counted on that," Crowley said, his ears still ringing. "What were you hauling?"

"Pig shit," the man said.

"No wonder," Crowley said. "Would you mind opening my case and getting me my phone?"

The man opened Crowley's case and noticed the laptop with the Ministry logo emblazoned upon it, the 9 mm handgun, the files, the gloves, and the cell phone. Without question, he dialed the number Crowley requested.

Crowley called in his coordinates and asked that a new vehicle be sent to meet him at the nearest county hospital.

The ambulance arrived, and the medics did a preliminary exam on each man. The trucker had a mild fracture, they guessed, and set him up with a temporary splint. The medic who examined Crowley determined that his scalp wound was superficial, from contact with the windshield most likely. His shoulder was badly dislocated.

"Snap it back," Crowley said.

"Sir, I'm not actually a doctor yet, I'm not qualif—"

"Snap it back. I absolve you of any malpractice. Just do it."

The trucker and the other medic looked over to see what was going on. "All right," the medic said, taking a deep breath. "This is gonna hurt."

"I don't think so," Crowley said, thinking, *But one can always hope.*

The medic took the arm firmly, placed his shoulder against Crowley's chest, found the joint to Crowley's shoulder blade and made a quick wrenching movement. The second medic and the truck driver both flinched and looked away. Crowley appeared unfazed. When his shoulder was back in place, he tested his range of movement, found it satisfactory, and thanked the medic.

Riding to the hospital in the ambulance, Crowley typed up his report on his laptop and sent it in by modem. He didn't want a second spotter dispatched because of his accident.

The truck driver, whose name turned out to be Hank, was contemplative through most of the ride but eventually asked, "You're Ministry, huh?"

"Yes sir, that's correct."

"You a Dep catcher?"

"You might call it that," he said.

"One of 'em make you like that—so's you can't feel no pain?"

Crowley was impressed by the man's astuteness. Several Ministry personnel had never deduced his deprivation. Sure, they realized that he must have been deprived at some point to have gained the Depriver sight, but few had realized that his deprivation was permanent. "Yes," Crowley said, breaching security. He had, after all, nearly killed this man on the road. He felt he owed him an answer or two. "Can't feel pain, or warmth, or cold. My receptors have been permanently damaged."

The man thought a second and said, "Handy in a bar fight."

Crowley nodded. "Or a car accident."

At the hospital, Crowley's abrasions were tended to. Both his shoulder and scalp required stitches. He refused anesthetics during the procedure. Afterward, he checked on Hank, repeated his apologies, and signed himself out. All told, it had been a four-hour setback. His new Volvo was parked in the emergency room lot, the keys in a hidden compartment under the front seat. He checked the map in his briefcase and was soon on the way to his hotel.

Crowley pulled in to the Lamplighter Inn, parked, and ordered room service as soon as he checked in. He was ravenous. He stripped down and showered, alternating the temperature setting from scalding to freezing, his daily exam, inspecting his stitches and shampooing the gooped-up blood from his hair, all the while berating himself for the lack of concentration that allowed the accident to occur. He ran his fingers along the raised scar of the brand on his chest and closed his eyes. . . .

Julia was still alive, and they were very much in love. "Do you think it worked?" she asked, her nose inches away from his on the pillow.

"I don't know. I mean, I'm sure we did it right," he said.

"Yeah, well, we've had enough practice." She smiled. "Just think, Alex, if it does work, we'll have done something that no one has ever done before."

"Oh my God, Julia," he sat up in mock horror, "No one else has done this? Get up! Get dressed! We have to tell them—the pleasures of the flesh are not to be denied!"

"Shut up!" She was laughing. "You know what I mean."

"I know," he said, lying down next to her again. "I hope it worked too."

Crowley was jarred back to reality—the phone was ringing in the other room. He turned off the water and pulled a towel around himself, leaving wet footprints in the carpet as he crossed to the bedroom and picked up the phone. "Crowley here."

"Alex, it's Carl," came a friendly voice, one of the few Crowley knew. "I heard you were in an accident."

"News travels fast, huh?" he said. "I'm fine. A few stitches."

"Faster than you'd think," Carl said quickly. The tone he used told Crowley he had called for more than just chitchat. He paused and then reached into his case and brought out a scrambler device, locked it on to the jack in his phone.

"I'm secure now, what's up?" he asked.

"Command doesn't like what's between the lines of your report, Alex. They're questioning your motives," Carl said solemnly.

Damn, Crowley thought, *God damn them.* "What action are they taking?"

"They're sending down another spotter."

"Who? Donaldson? Perkins?"

"No, someone new," Carl said. "Agent Brin. A forensic. Former Russian covert field operative. She's probably already airborne."

"She?" Crowley asked.

"Yes, and I'm told she's a real stickler."

"I'll be careful."

"No, you'll be absent. You're off the case. Your orders are probably sitting and waiting for you in your in-box already."

"What a shame," Crowley said, perturbed now, "that my laptop was damaged in the accident."

"You already transmitted once, Alex. They know it's working."

"It was, but now it's not. Funny how things like that happen to field equipment."

"I understand. Good luck out there."

"Thanks. I owe you," Crowley said, hanging up. He left the scrambler attached to the phone and then got dressed. His day was growing worse by the hour.

23

AGENT Kendra Brin sat alone in the plush comfort of the Ministry Learjet and nibbled at the small meal the flight staff had prepared for her. She wore faded jeans and had her dark hair pulled tight in a ponytail. She had awoken less than an hour before when her vibro-pager suddenly went mad. Her driver had arrived minutes later. They took the back roads to Teterboro Airport, where the plane, fueled and ready, had taken off on priority clearance. She really had to hand it to them. They were much more efficient than Russian agencies.

She powered on her Ministry-issued laptop and read the file. They were sending her to upstate New York to investigate, of all things, an elementary school. An unregistered Depriver was almost certainly present and causing a threat to the population. Assignment originally posted to Agent Alex Crowley, senior Ministry operative, Deprivers Branch. Crowley had been recalled due to possible motives of cross-purpose.

Cross-purpose? she thought. *What the hell was that?* She had read several of Crowley's declassified case reports during her Ministry training. He was one of their top men, or so they had led her to believe. He'd been deprived by his wife, she recalled. Pain asymbolia. The wife was no longer alive. Well, they had a lot in common. Too bad he'd been recalled. It might have been interesting to meet him. She swiveled up her lipstick and began to apply it, watching herself in the tiny mirror of her compact.

By the time the plane touched down on the small airstrip in Binghamton, she was made up and dressed in a smart black Armani skirt and jacket. One of the flight crew carried her bag to a waiting limousine and gave her an appreciative wave as he left. She waved back.

The driver, a Ministry employee named Roger Naftel, had already been prepped on Kendra's condition. He tipped his cap to her as she got in the car, and then handed her a handwritten note that read, "Hi, I'm Roger. Where would you like me to take you first? The hotel or the school?" As she read it, he couldn't help grinning at her. She was much more attractive than he had heard. He couldn't keep his eyes from wandering up her legs.

"The school," she said aloud in her soft Russian accent. "And notes will not be necessary—just speak slowly and allow me to see your face."

They drove away from the airport, and the suburb dissolved into a quaint, sleepy little town with charming brick houses and fields that seemed to stretch forever. Hard to believe this was part of the same state as New York City.

The car slowed, and they made a sharp left off the highway through a grove of trees, then stopped. She looked out and saw the school, a single-story building with about an acre of fenced-in playground.

Roger thought he saw something behind the car in his rearview mirror. Then the rear door opened, and Crowley sat down beside Agent Brin. Roger drew his gun, swiveled his position, and aimed for Crowley's head. Agent Brin recognized the man almost instantly and smiled.

"I'm Ministry," Crowley told the driver. Then he turned to Agent Brin and said, "Nothing personal, but they are totally out of line assigning you to this case. I was acting in the very best interests of the members of this community, and I'll turn in my badge and weapon before I relinquish this post. So, before you waltz in there drawing suspicion and compromising young lives, why don't you just turn around and head straight back to the airport."

Crowley watched for her to back down, acquiesce, apologize for stepping on his toes, but she just sat there staring back at him. Roger was attempting to remove his seat belt while aiming his gun. "Do you hear me?" he asked finally, "Go home."

While Crowley waited again for an answer, she placed her ungloved hand against his. He never flinched. *Yes,* she thought, *he is who he appears to be.* Only someone who clearly saw that she was not a Depriver, without any trace of doubt, could be touched like that and not reflexively pull away.

Crowley, perplexed and frustrated, looked down as she took back her hand and up again when she signed, *"Don't waste your anger on me. I'm just following orders."*

Crowley fell back in his seat and covered his face with his hands. "Oh God, you're deaf—I'm sorry."

Brin nodded to Roger, and he put down his weapon. "Do you always accost women in the backseats of cars, Agent Crowley?" she asked.

Crowley could tell by the correctness of her speech that

she could not have been deprived of her hearing for more than a year or so. *"No,"* he signed back, *"I usually take them back to my room and accost them there."*

"You sign well," she said.

"Thanks," he said, offering his hand. "Let's start again. I'm Alex Crowley. Pleased to meet you."

She shook his hand and took him in fully, still impressed. "I am Agent Kendra Brin, and I am also pleased to meet you."

Then Roger said, "Would somebody please tell me what's going on?"

Crowley turned to him. "There's a diner about four miles up the road. I think we should head there for a cup of coffee."

"OKAY," Crowley began, sipping his coffee and then putting down the cup so that Agent Brin could read his lips clearly. "Here's my concern. This town has never, to my knowledge, had to deal with any significant Depriver incidence. Now we've got at least twenty-five children suffering deprivation. One child is the daughter of a city councilman, and another is the police chief's grandson."

"Wait," Brin said, "Your report denied that Daniel Weisenbaum was a Depriver. Are you officially rescinding that fact? Have you had further contact that has proven otherwise?"

"The boy is a Depriver," Crowley said, "but I could not determine the extent or duration of the deprivation. It's only color blindness, and it may turn out to be a relatively short duration."

"So, you're not going to report him?" she asked.

"No," he replied.

"Why? He needs training in any case. Protection."

Crowley nodded, trying to decide how far he could trust her. "Protection, Agent Brin, is often mistaken for ostracism or imprisonment. I'm used to tracking and spotting killers who use their deprivations as weapons. This is a ten-year-old with what amounts to a toy gun."

"If he's a Depriver, it's in his best interest to—"

"Bullshit," Crowley interrupted. "If his deprivation is two or three days, or a week, and we can teach him how to be careful, is ruining his life justified? Having everyone in this town, his teachers, his classmates, shunning and ridiculing him for the rest of his life? I don't think so."

Agent Brin was silent.

"And of course," Crowley said, "they may decide to institutionalize him."

"I don't wish this boy any harm. It's just my job to spot—"

"I know, but if you spot, you've got to take responsibility for the lives you affect. You can't just turn a blind eye on what comes after. Work with me. If the boy's effects are greater than my initial observation suggests, or if there are long-term effects, we can decide together on the proper course of action. Agreed?"

Agent Brin hesitated. She knew that Crowley's past involvement with various Deprivers, mostly on a personal level, must have had an effect on his politics. She now feared—as did many of her superiors, she suspected—that Crowley's motives could indeed undermine Ministry policy. Still, something in Crowley's pale gray eyes told her to trust him. "All right. I'll go along with you and suspend judgment until we know more."

"Thank you," he said. "I think you've made a good choice."

24

THE next morning Agent Crowley introduced Agent Brin to Mr. Rubino's science class, explaining to them that, although she was deaf, she could still read their lips if they spoke clearly enough—and that she could communicate with him and other deaf people through sign language.

"Does it hurt, being deaf?" asked one student.

Kendra smiled and said, "No, it doesn't hurt."

"Ms. Brin is just like everyone else," Crowley said, "she just can't hear voices, or alarms, or car horns, and she needs a little help communicating with hearing people sometimes. Any other questions?"

"How did she lose her hearing?" Daniel asked.

"That's a good question, Danny," Crowley answered, "Ms. Brin was deprived. How long ago, Kendra?"

"Just over a year ago."

"So you used to hear okay?" a student called out.

"Yes," Brin said, "I used to hear just like you do."

A girl in the back row raised her hand. "I know a deaf

girl who lives on my block. How come she can't talk?"

Crowley signed to Brin, who could not read the girl's lips from that distance. She turned back to the class and said, "Deaf people may not talk for many reasons. People who were deaf all of their lives may never learn to speak because it's hard to learn when you can't hear the sounds you're making. I speak pretty well because I can still remember what the words I want to say would sound like."

"Will she ever hear again?" Daniel asked timidly.

Crowley looked to Brin, and she shrugged sadly. "No one knows," he told the class, "but it is possible that her deprivation could wear off. There's still a lot we don't know about how deprivation works."

"Now—" Crowley clapped his hands together. "We have some fun tests that we're all going to do together."

They spent the rest of the afternoon entertaining the class with sign language lessons and testing the children with advanced visual exams that Agent Brin had requested from the New York lab. They took around twenty minutes per student to complete. The tests recorded various levels of perception, including positive and negative afterimage-detection ability, monocular comprehension, wavelength appreciation, retina integrity, and various frequency determinants.

While each student was engaged in testing, Mr. Rubino had the others drawing with crayons, which seemed to please the majority of the fifth-graders, who hadn't had a free day to spend coloring rather than studying in a long time. The principal kindly rotated the usual schedule to allow them to keep the class segregated for the entire day.

One of the students, named Timothy Stout, was summoned to the principal's office. Timmy left with the aide as Crowley signed, *"Police chief's kid,"* to Agent Brin.

Kendra nodded that she understood the implications.

After the children were dismissed for the day, the three sat discussing the test results.

Rubino spoke first. "Any conclusions?"

"I'll need time to review and collate the data," Agent Brin told him. "But I did notice that only twelve of the children are clinically color-blind. By that, I mean full monochromats."

Rubino looked perplexed, and Crowley explained, "A monochromat is an individual who is totally color-blind. Sees only black and white with corresponding shades of gray, but no color at all."

"Seven children are dichromats," Brin said.

"Dichromats," Crowley said, "can discriminate two-color schemes. Usually red and green, or sometimes blue and yellow, with an accompaniment of whichever colors can be derived from mixing the two."

"Which can they see? Red and green or blue and yellow?" Rubino asked.

"Some one and some the other," Brin said. "Which may be a good thing."

"Why?"

"Well," Crowley began, "take into account that there are five students who now appear fine, not including Daniel. Twelve are fully affected. Seven are partially affected. That suggests one of two trends. Either all of the students were deprived, and the deprivation is wearing off—or the deprivation is increasing and worsening by degree over time, the variables being duration of proximity and length of contact, or perhaps a higher tolerance in some children. Bear in mind that one or two students may have been color-blind from the start. If we assume that all of the children were originally affected, as you noted with your inital test, I'd say there's an excellent chance of full recovery."

"If you say it looks positive, I believe you," Rubino said.

"Excuse me a moment, won't you," Crowley said, "I need to use the rest room," and he left Rubino with Brin.

Rubino did not wish to disturb Agent Brin, who sat quietly typing on her laptop, so he took a seat at his desk and began riffling through the stack of the student's colored drawings. Their artwork was evidence enough of deprivation. There were pink suns, red skies, and gray faces. Only Daniel Weisenbaum's drawing seemed color-correct.

Agent Crowley was amused by the disparity of his adult body to the child-sized urinal in the bathroom. He needed to squat and almost lost his balance. When he was finished, he went over to the sink, reached for the faucet, and misjudged the distance. He struck his hand on the steel underside, scraping the skin off his knuckles, drawing blood. He inspected the cut, rinsed, dried off, and went back to the classroom.

"What happened?" Brin asked, seeing the blood on the back of his hand. "Did you get in a fight over lunch money?"

"No, it was stupid," Crowley said, "I accidentally hit it on the sink."

"Well, at least it doesn't hurt, right?" she asked, an unsure smirk on her face.

"Can you hear this?" he asked, holding his fist out with his middle finger extended downward. "Or should I turn it up?" As he rotated his wrist, they both laughed.

"I'm finished here," Brin said, packing her laptop into her bag and slinging it over her shoulder. "You ready?"

"See you first thing tomorrow," Agent Crowley told Rubino, as they left the classroom.

Rubino nodded and waved absentmindedly as he continued to review the students' crayon drawings. One picture disturbed him. It was by Scott Ryba, one of his weaker students, a shy child who rarely spoke up in class and was often absent. Agent Brin had classified Scott as one of the most heavily affected monochromats. The drawing was of a small boy, most likely himself, wearing swimming trunks. Standing behind the boy was a man. The man had his hands resting on the child's shoulders. Odd blue scribbles, like waves, came off the man's face and hands. Rubino guessed that was Scott's version of water. Still, it troubled him somehow.

2 5

ROGER pulled the car off the road at a conservative distance from the Weisenbaum residence, a quaint, two-story house with a cobblestone facade. Agent Brin took her kit from the trunk, and she and Crowley gloved up.

"Alex, I want you to be prepared for the consequences if this interview doesn't tell you what you want to hear," Brin said as they approached the house.

"What do you mean?" Crowley asked.

"I mean if Danny turns out to be a danger to others, I want you to be prepared to act accordingly. Because if you don't, I will," she said.

"Brin," Crowley smiled, "it's color blindness, and it's probably temporary. Keep your gun in your holster, okay?"

Daniel answered the door, and a younger boy stood behind him. Both Crowley and Brin were relieved to see that the second child had no aura.

"Hi," Daniel said.

"Hello, Danny. We're here to see your parents. Are they home?" Crowley asked.

"My mom is," he said, looking back over his shoulder.

Mrs. Weisenbaum came to the door, and they introduced themselves as Alex and Kendra, two new administrators from the school district who were evaluating Danny for a special program. She led them through the house and sat them at the kitchen table.

"The colors around the house seem reasonably well-matched," Brin signed.

"Has this got anything to do with Danny dropping out of swimming class?" Mrs. Weisenbaum asked as she poured them all coffee.

Crowley looked to Brin. "No, ma'am," Crowley said, "we weren't aware that Danny had been taking swimming classes."

"Oh, yes, well . . . he was, over at the recreation center after school, but he stopped."

"That's a shame," Crowley said. "Did he say why?"

"Not to me," she said. "I think Bob had a talk with him, though. He doesn't like the kids to be quitters."

"I know how he feels."

"Well then, how can I help you?" Mrs. Weisenbaum asked.

"As it turns out, Danny is actually quite special."

"Special in a good way or a bad way?" she asked.

"It depends on your point of view, Mrs. Weisenbaum. There are some who would say that *any* type of deviation from the norm at Danny's age, good or bad, can be difficult on a peer level. But Danny's a great kid. I've spent some time with him. He's going to be just fine." Brin tugged at Crowley's jacket under the table. "I know this is going to seem out of left field, but are either you or your husband color-blind, as far as you know?"

"No, I'm certainly not. I'm pretty sure . . . no, I know Bob's not. He goes on and on about that red Sportster he has out in the garage."

"Can you tell me what color my tie tack is?"

She squinted at the small rectangular pin. "Green and yellow," she said.

Crowley nodded; she was right. "So, Mrs. Weisenbaum, we think all Danny really needs at this point are a few extra hours of an after-school reading program."

"I knew it," she said, shaking her head, "Danny's always been lazy about his reading. Bob lets him watch too much television." She reached for the sugar bowl and inadvertently knocked over her coffee cup. Crowley reached out for the cup as it rolled, but was too late. It sailed over the edge of the checkerboard tablecloth and shattered on the floor.

"Darn it," Mrs. Weisenbaum said, "that's the third glass I've broken this week."

"Here, let me help," Agent Crowley said, reaching down.

"No, no, I've got it," the woman said, embarrassed.

"Mrs. Weisenbaum, please excuse us, we have another appointment we must attend to," Brin said as she stood up from the table.

Mrs. Weisenbaum reached up and patted Agent Brin on the shoulder. "You're so quiet," she said. "You should take a bigger part in the conversation. You hardly said a word. And you're so pretty."

Agent Brin smiled.

"We'll keep you up to date on Danny's progress, Mrs. Weisenbaum," Crowley said.

*   *   *

"VERY touchy-feely woman," Agent Brin said as they walked to the car. "Very clumsy also."

Crowley nodded, "What's your point?"

"Touchy like that. I can't understand how she could *not* be deprived by Danny."

"Okay," Crowley said. "So it's probably safe to assume that Danny's deprivation *is* only temporary."

"Alex, it's quite possible that a slow-onset deprivation that worsens with exposure and proximity could afflict a fifth-grader so gradually he'd take it for granted—but an adult would be acutely aware of the loss of color almost immediately. There's something we're not seeing here," she said, slipping into the backseat.

"Where to now?" Roger asked.

Crowley opened his side door and accidentally smacked his wounded shoulder in the process. "Damn," he said stepping back away. Brin got out of the car and came around to his side.

"Alex, are you all right?"

"Yeah, I'm just—"

"Deprived," she signed.

"What?" Crowley asked.

Brin signed at a furious pace. *"Mrs. Weisenbaum's clumsiness got me thinking. If she wasn't color-blind, and Daniel's a Depriver, what else could she be deprived of? You flipped your car. I've been watching you. Your manual dexterity is poor."*

"Okay, you may be right," Crowley said.

"Did you touch Daniel?"

"Maybe . . . we played basketball," he signed back, then aloud, "I think I may have just pulled my stitches open."

"Chort!" Brin cursed in her native tongue. "That's it, I'm going back in there."

Crowley caught her by the arm. "No," he said, forcefully,

then took a breath. "I mean—please don't. Kendra, I've seen too many families that were needlessly torn apart by this. A couple months ago I watched a mother held back and handcuffed to keep her from touching her four-month-old son. Please, not until we have to."

"Ultimately, I am responsible here, Alex. Like it or not, this is my assignment now. That family could be in danger if I am right. What you are asking is a lot," she said.

"I know," Crowley said, "but it is so important that we're sure, and right now we're not."

Agent Brin ground her teeth; then, without taking her eyes off Crowley, said, "You'd better take us back to the hotel, Roger."

26

SITTING on his bed, Crowley crumpled a piece of loose-leaf paper into a ball. He threw it at the waste bin in the corner—and missed. "Shit," he cursed under his breath.

"You're a mess," Brin said seriously.

"Tell me about it," Crowley replied.

Roger had gone to find takeout. Agent Brin removed her jacket and shoulder holster, threw them on the chair, and said, "Take off your shirt."

A thousand brash remarks went through Crowley's mind, but in light of the seriousness of the situation, he simply acquiesced. The removal of his shirt, like the stripping of camouflage, revealed many things to Agent Brin. She was immediately taken aback by the scar tissue that formed the mark on his chest. There were also several obvious bullet wounds, some which had healed well, some not so well. The coup de grâce was the deep wound on the shoulder he'd just reopened.

She dabbed and probed at his bleeding gash. "It's not

too bad," she said. "The stitches are pulled but not torn. I can tighten them and rebandage you, all right?"

Crowley nodded. She went to her bag and pulled out her field kit, removing alcohol, gauze, assorted bandages, and tweezers. "Don't worry, this isn't going to hurt at all."

He laughed.

She stepped in close. "I'd like to hear about the brand," she said, placing her ungloved hand against his shoulder blade, grabbing a stitch with the tweezers and applying pressure.

"Oh that," he said softly, seeming to forget that she was deaf as he lost himself in reflection. She watched his lips as she worked and he spoke. "I met her in college, my wife—Julia. I knew what she was capable of, but I didn't care. This was soon after the epidemic became public, and tensions were mixed. At the time, it was commonplace for every Depriver to take the *D* mark. They wouldn't allow me to take it though—I wasn't really one of them. She was killed at the first Tyrsdale rally in Washington. An assassin. A Depriver. Anyway, a close friend of ours named Sparrow, American Indian, told me that it was custom for his people to scar themselves—to remember the death of a loved one. They still didn't think it was right for me to get the tattoo, so, I designed this and asked Sparrow to brand me with it."

Agent Brin's eyes brimmed with tears, and as she pulled the last stitch tight she placed a kiss on Alex Crowley's forehead. He put a hand gently on the small of her back and closed his eyes. They were silent for a few moments while she finished bandaging him. "You should put your shirt back on now," she said when she was done.

Crowley dressed. "Judging from my symptoms, my guess is that it's my coordination that has been affected," he said. "Which means either Daniel Weisenbaum is the first Depriver with multideprivational abilities . . ."

"Or there's another Depriver in our midst," Brin said.

"Yes, another Depriver we haven't seen."

"Which means that if Daniel deprived you, he's probably not responsible for the outbreak of color blindness."

"And whoever is responsible would be someone with
direct access to the children." Crowley's cellular phone
rang, and he answered, "Hello, Mr. Rubino. Yes. I see. Yes.
No, that may very well be a valid discovery. Thank you. I'll
be in touch. Good-bye."

"What?" Brin asked.

"The Town Recreation Center," Crowley said.

THE center smelled of chlorine and was lit with fluorescent bulbs. Crowley and Brin went up to the registration
desk and spoke with an athletic-looking woman wearing
running clothes.

Crowley showed her his badge. "Would you please tell
us who your current swimming instructor is?" he asked
softly.

She was a bit shaken by the badge but soothed by the
tone. "We have two instructors," she said. "Mrs. Rosenblatt
and Mr. Stout."

"Stout?" Crowley asked. "Any relation to the chief of
police?"

"His brother," the woman said. "Is there some trouble?
Mr. Stout is a wonderful person and—"

Raising his hand to cut her off, Crowley said, "Of course
he is, which is why I know he'll help me out by answering
a few questions. Can you tell me where I might find him?"

"He's back in the pool area now, I think," she said.

"Thank you."

They found him in the pool, amid dozens of swimmers. He was unmistakable, standing there, holding the little girl afloat on her back, his aura casting softly against the water. The girl was Becky Schneider, one of the more optically damaged children they'd tested. Mr. Stout said something to Becky, and she laughed and squirmed in the water.

"There's your second Depriver," Brin said. Her vibropager went off in her jacket, but she ignored it.

Crowley was waiting for Mr. Stout as he came into the locker room.

Brin went to speak with Becky, who was happy to see her. She even remembered her signs for *"Hello, how are you?"*

Brin crouched down to the girl's eye level and placed her hands on the girl's shoulders, "Becky, this is a very important question. Has Mr. Stout ever touched you in any way that made you feel scared or uncomfortable? Take time to answer."

Becky cocked her head to one side, a little confused.

"Mr. Stout, are you aware of the fact that you're an SDS carrier?" Crowley asked.

Stout looked up at the man in the dark suit in disbelief, and just stood there, dripping.

TWO days later, Agent Brin found Agent Crowley dressed in shorts and sleeveless shirt, shooting hoops alone in the school gymnasium. His bruises and bandages caught her eye first, then the serious look on his face.

"Well?" he asked, tucking the ball in the crook of his arm.

"The test results are looking good," she said, smiling. "Three more of the kids have perfectly restored trichromat color vision. All of the monochromats have stepped up to dichromats. You were right, the deprivation was temporary and nondamaging."

"Yeah," he said, "but I had the wrong subject."

"I have a specialist meeting with each of the children to determine whether or not there has been any sexual abuse," Brin said.

"I don't think you'll find any," Crowley answered. "I think he's just a swimming instructor."

"I appreciate your optimism, Alex," she replied, "but I'm having him held under protective custody until that portion of my investigation is over. I also want to know who knew what and when. I think it's pretty obvious his brother knew that something was up when they pulled Timothy away from us the other day."

"That was a little fishy," Crowley said. "So, what about Danny?"

"That depends," she said. "How are you? That boy may have ruined one of our most valuable operatives."

Crowley answered by dribbling the ball between his legs and making a fast break layup. He stood back and grinned.

"All right, Superman," she said, "I'll make a deal with you and not register Daniel—for now. But I get to run more tests, and his parents will have to be informed. Someone in that family could have the same kind of accident you did and fail to walk away from it."

"Deal," he said.

"Still," she sighed, "I have to justify the expense of the demolished tractor-trailer somehow."

Crowley put his arm around Agent Brin's shoulders as they walked out of the gymnasium. "We'll tell them I was temporarily blinded—I couldn't see the light."

"Yeah," she said, "that ought to work."

27

ALEX Crowley was having another nightmare. One where strangers came and borrowed pieces of his anatomy—an eye for one, an ear for another—and left without issuing receipts. Eventually, a twist and a turn brought his head out from beneath the pillows, and that's when the red light pulled him out of sleep. The flash of an incoming message pulsed repeatedly across the screen of his laptop.

Crowley was up in a burst of movement, but his thoughts were still half lodged in his dream. He waited for his head to catch up to his body, hit the Receive button on the console, and scanned his room. Blue moonlight filtered softly through the curtains. He was alone, as usual, and all limbs and appendages were present and accounted for. He inserted the small earpiece.

"You have one encrypted message, which is password-protected," droned a digitized female voice. He typed in his password, the punch line to a tragic joke only he knew, then watched as the Ministry logo appeared and unfolded: the owl with a snake in its talons.

"Agent Crowley. Priority Alpha. Respond." *Shit, nowadays when wasn't it a Priority Alpha?*

He typed, "Crowley here."

A few moments later, the words, "Greetings Alex. Kelsoe here. Where are you?" scrolled across the screen.

"Saskatchewan. Mission accomplished," he typed.

"Excellent. Looking forward to your report. You're needed in New York ASAP. Prepare to download file. Agent Brin is available on standby if you find you need assistance. Luck to you, Crowley. Kelsoe out."

Crowley clicked the Download key and took the file. He brought it up and listened to it read aloud through the earset while he fished around for his clothes.

"At fourteen hundred hours a report was intercepted by Ministry ops that originated from the Eighteenth Police Precinct, Manhattan, Hell's Kitchen. The reporting officer was Lieutenant Frank Delafonte. His report did not, and will not, reach his superiors. He is in process, awaiting debrief at Ministry HQ, New York. Assignment is posted to Senior Ministry Field Officer Crowley, Deprivers Branch, Priority Alpha. Loading report . . ."

While the rest of the file loaded, Crowley searched the dark wooden floor for his socks and wondered what this poor luckless bastard could have stumbled on to that got him sequestered. The recording continued, now in the gruff Manhattanese of the man he guessed to be Lieutenant Delafonte.

"Responding to a code ten-twenty-four, I arrived at the Hell's Kitchen courts down off Tenth Avenue. An ambulance had already arrived, but the attendants held back.

Since code ten-twenty-four meant there was a high proba-
bility the situation involved a Dep, I gloved up and wore
my coat to avoid contact. The kids who had witnessed the
scene were really blown away. The victim, in his late teens,
was of African-American descent, and the kids called him
by the initials, T. C., short for Tyrone Charles Jackson. He
was wearing full pads, no face mask. When I got there he
was banging his head up and down against the pavement
and spitting up blood."

Luckless bastard, Crowley thought as the file continued.
None of this was atypical. He hoped they'd serve breakfast
on the plane.

A helicopter brought Crowley from the airport to the roof of
the Ministry offices just before noon. He was escorted immediately to reception by a silent, heavily armed Welcome
Wagon. He pulled his sunglasses off when he addressed
the receptionist.

"I'm Agent Crowley. I'm here to pick up a guest."

"Identification, please, Agent Crowley."

He handed her his badge. She paused, smiled, and
pointed to the counter. Embarrassed, he dropped it. She
picked it up and did something with it that confirmed he
was who he said he was.

"Thank you, sir," she said, placing the badge back on the
counter. "Your guest is in holding area one. Elevator to sub-
basement three. I'll tell them you're on your way down."

"Could you not do that, please?" Crowley asked politely.
"I don't want anyone readying the witness. I'd like to sit
with him for a while and maybe have a chat. Is there a
reception room set up down there?"

"Yes, sir," she said. "There is. Shall I send down some coffee and sandwiches?"

"That would be great," Crowley said. "I would really appreciate that."

Crowley was immediately recognized by the chief of security, a hard-faced, ex–field op from before the epidemic, as he entered holding area one. He sat conversing with a young woman who was perched on the edge of his desk. He waved Crowley over.

"Hey, Caldwell, how the hell are you?" Crowley asked.

"Agent Crowley, as I live and breathe. You here to interrogate the police dick?"

"Yes, I'm here to see Lieutenant Delafonte."

"I'll have him brought straight out—"

Crowley held his hand up. "Thanks, but I'd rather get him myself. Can you please unlock his door, and I'll take him his service weapon."

"Yeah, fine," Caldwell said. "Right down the hall. Janet will have you sign for the lieutenant's gun."

As soon as Crowley was out of earshot, Caldwell whispered, "That guy is into some weird shit. He's strictly Deprivers Branch. I think he might even *be* one of them."

The young woman stared down the hall. "Yeah," she said with a Brooklyn accent, "he's a hottie, but he gives me the creeps."

CROWLEY stepped into the holding room just as Lieutenant Delafonte laid the ace of spades across the two of diamonds. Standing in the doorway, Crowley silently reviewed the man's dossier. Joined the force at twenty-one. Made sergeant at twenty-five, lieutenant at thirty-one. Six years later, he was still waiting for the promotion to first-grade detective that would probably never come.

Delafonte looked up at Crowley with eyes that were weary and overwrought. His uniform was disheveled; he'd obviously slept in it. He was in need of a shave. He let the card snap down sharply and then drummed his fingers in a manner that pointedly displayed his frustration. It was unfortunate, Crowley thought, that sometimes injustices like Delafonte's incarceration were necessary to further the quest for knowledge.

"Hi," Crowley said, as he closed the door behind him. "I'm Agent Crowley. These belong to you. I apologize for the inconvenience."

He placed the lieutenant's service weapon and shield on the table, inwardly wincing at the demeaning inaccuracy of the word *inconvenience.* Still, the gesture of the returned weapon worked as Crowley had intended. Almost instantly, an air of confidence reinflated Delafonte's features.

"Thanks," the man said, retrieving his gun. "Has somebody phoned my wife to tell her I'm okay?"

"I'd imagine not," Crowley said. "But I can see to it. Lieutenant, I know this situation has probably been quite uncomfortable for you—"

"No," Delafonte broke in, "it has not been uncomfortable. It's been damned degrading. I'm out on the street doing my fucking job, and then suddenly I'm getting pulled in and questioned like some punk! Your Ministry is ass backward, Agent Crowley. Ya know that?"

"Yes I do, Lieutenant," Crowley said, "Sadly, you're not the first person who's pointed that out to me." When it was clear the lieutenant would make no further outbursts, Crowley continued. "I've had a conference room prepared, and ordered us some sandwiches and coffee."

* * *

ONCE he was cleaned up and fed, Delafonte turned out to be rather personable.

"Believe me, Agent Crowley," he began, "when they said code ten-twenty-four, I thought strongly about not responding to that call. I wish to hell I hadn't. I want nothing to do with those damned Deps. I had to hold a perp at gunpoint the other day—*at gunpoint*—to keep him from touching me. I had to throw him cuffs and have him cuff himself. It's gettin' crazy out there. You just don't know what they can do. You know?"

Crowley nodded. He did indeed know, though he wondered if Delafonte's level of deprivation paranoia would test above or below his unit's average. "Let's start with a description of the kids?"

"Sure thing." Delafonte sipped his coffee. "Tyrone Jackson is about six foot two and about two hundred thirty pounds, built like a rock."

"Tyrone is the name of the victim, correct? The deprived. African-American?"

Delafonte nodded, took a bite of a pastrami sandwich, continued. "Willie Carmen's a scab-kneed sixth-grader who's barely five feet tall and maybe a hundred pounds. Are you picturing this?"

"I take it that Willie's Hispanic?"

"Yeah, a barrio kid. I've had to talk to him before about his truancy. He's smart but really angry. Gets picked on a lot. Gets into a lot of scrapes. I made a report myself about three months back. Willie got thrown down a flight of stairs. One guess who he named as the kid who did the throwing?"

"Tyrone Jackson?"

Delafonte nodded. "So here's what the kids say happened.

They were playing ball. Suddenly Willie comes runnin' onto the courts screaming at Tyrone and then—"

"What was Willie screaming? Did the kids remember?"

"Yeah, yeah, he screamed something like, 'You goin' down now muthafucka! You goin' down hard. See what you like now!'"

"Thank you, Lieutenant, you've got that down pretty well," Crowley said. "So, Willie called Tyrone out."

"Right. And Tyrone's laughing at little Willie at this point, and threatening to give him a serious beating, and so on. The usual fight talk. I guess Tyrone took the initiative and hit first. Willie went down and was bleeding. Then he got back on his feet and yelled, 'You gonna be sorry now!' That's when Willie allegedly reached out and slapped Tyrone across the face. One hit only. A Latina girl who was behind the fence watching says she saw blue sparks flying off Willie's hand."

Crowley bit into his French dip.

"Tyrone lost his balance then and hit the pavement. The Depriver shit must've happened right away. Contact time's something we're supposed to remark on, right?"

Agent Crowley nodded, midswallow.

"The other kids hung back, and Willie started kicking the shit out of Tyrone. After about five minutes, he finally let up and turned on the others and yelled, 'Anybody else wanna mess with me?' Then he spat on Tyrone and left the courts. Tyrone started crying that he couldn't hear anything except a ringing in his ears, and the Latina girl ran off to call 911.

"When I got on the scene, Tyrone was so violently spastic it took three attendants to get him into the back of the ambulance.

"Willie's mother and sister have no idea of his whereabouts. He was last reported seen wearing a Knicks T-shirt, jeans, and black Chuck Taylors. He's also got a nice gash on his left cheek from the fight.

"That's just like how the report reads, Agent Crowley. I turned it in, and the next thing I know, it looks like I'm gonna be telling it over and over for the rest of my life."

2 8

"WHERE are we going?" Delafonte finally spoke up as the elevator began to slow.

"To check on Tyrone Jackson's condition," Crowley said, somewhat lost within the missing details of the lieutenant's story. "I need to see him. Don't worry about your unit chief, you've been reassigned to me."

"Agent Crowley," Delafonte said in a hard, flat tone, reaching out to grip the younger man's sleeve. The lieutenant was so pissed off, he didn't realize he was risking contact. "I don't think you understand me. I don't want to get deeper into this shit, I want out of it!"

Crowley did not flinch. In fact, he welcomed the indiscriminate touch. He replied in a monotone, "No, I don't think *you* understand. There is no 'out' of this shit. We fear the epidemic is about to take a turn for the worse, and if it does, human contact as we know it may cease to exist. Now, my instinct tells me that Willie Carmen can offer us a great deal of information. He knows you. Therefore, I need you.

So, are you a part of the problem, Lieutenant, or a part of the solution?"

The elevator chimed as they reached the med ward, and the doors slid open. The gravity of the situation seemed to sink in for Delafonte, and he followed Crowley out onto the floor. The corridor carried the odor of formaldehyde. They followed the directions of an orderly who'd been strolling toward the intensive care unit.

"Here are the parts of the story you don't know," Crowley began. "When the ambulance left you at the scene, the medics logged in that Tyrone had a complete loss of vision during first observation, but that during the ambulance ride he kept temporarily regaining his sight. Two hours later, ribs and skull bandaged in the emergency room, Tyrone lost all feeling in his outer extremities. Three hours later, the doctor on call was at a loss to explain why the boy had slipped into a coma. At first, they thought his injuries were caused by the physical trauma of the beating. Then, when your report hit the data banks, the Ministry made the correlation and had you picked up and Tyrone transferred here."

"So, let me get this straight," Delafonte interjected, "if I would of written a slipshod report, I'd be home right now eating Rosie's spaghetti?"

"Yep. Good work."

TYRONE Jackson had tubes and wires running in and out of him. Machines monitored his heart rate and other bodily functions, and printed out the data onto colored spreadsheets. His head was bandaged, and his eyes fluttered from time to time.

A distinguished-looking doctor in his late forties, dressed in hospital greens and bloodied surgical gloves, knocked on the window and motioned for them to come out to him.

"Sorry, I was on my way to scrub down," said the doctor. "Just delivered a baby."

The blood distressed Delafonte, and he wondered who would have their baby at the Ministry medical ward.

"Are you Alex Crowley?" the doctor asked, as they followed him to the scrub room.

"Yes, I am."

"Quite a privilege, sir," he said. "I'm Dr. Hauske. I've heard so much about you. Pain asymbolia, isn't it?"

"Warren Hauske?" Crowley asked, skipping over the mention of his affliction. "The neurovirologist?"

"At your service," the doctor said, his hands out of the gloves and in the sink.

"The privilege is mine, sir," Crowley said.

"Don't I recognize you from someplace?" Delafonte asked. "TV, maybe?"

"Yes," Hauske replied. "The broadcast from Amsterdam."

"Dr. Hauske has an electronic chip under development," Crowley explained, "that would be implanted in the brain to negate the effects of deprivation."

"If only we could determine the correct frequency modulation," Hauske said. "That's the trick."

"I had no idea you were working with the Ministry."

"It's a temporary arrangement," Hauske half whispered. "We're at odds on methodology just a little too often."

Crowley nodded knowingly. "We have some mutual acquaintances, I believe, Doctor."

"Yes," Hauske smiled. "How is Dr. Godfrey? Spoken to her recently?"

"She and Robert are both doing well."

"Good. Good. And the twins?" he asked, putting on fresh gloves and a clean smock.

"Nicholas and Cassandra," Crowley replied. "I hear they're doing okay."

"Fascinating case, those two," Hauske said to Delafonte. "Depriver twins. They have a form of natural immunity built up. Can't deprive each other."

Delafonte shrugged. This was all going over his head.

"I'd like to locate both of them," Hauske said. "I have some new tests I'd like to run."

"I'll see what I can do," Crowley said. "Nicholas and Claudette are expecting a child, you know, so I doubt they'd be up for anything for a while."

"Really?" Hauske asked, taken aback. "Agent Crowley, have you ever actually met Claudette Deveraux—in person?"

"No," Crowley said. "Why do you ask?"

"Just wondering. You see, I'm very interested in the third generation. There's a lot of promise there for my work," he said. "A lot of promise."

"What's the prognosis on the boy?" Crowley asked.

"Let's go and have a look," Hauske said, and they all returned to the room down the hall. The doctor switched into a more professional tone. "As I'm sure *you* can see, he's not a Depriver himself. I've been trying to formulate a theorem for why he keeps slipping in and out of a deprived state."

"I don't get it," Delafonte said. "Is he deprived, or isn't he?"

"That's just it," Hauske said. "One minute he is, the next he's reading all clear, and then another deprivation sets in. It's got me baffled."

"What deprivations has he been displaying?" asked Crowley.

"Blindness. Deafness. Loss of balance, paralysis, and coma."

"You're listing coma as a deprivation?"

"In this case, yes."

"What's your rationale for that classification?"

As if to answer Crowley's question, Tyrone groaned and began crying out. "Mom! I want my Moms! I can't see. Why the fuck can't I see? Moms! *Moms! Moms! Moms!*"

Hauske tried to keep Tyrone from ripping out his tubes and wires, yelling, "Nurse Pinchot, I need a sedative. Ten milligrams of Valium stat!" The nurse arrived moments later, half gloved, syringe in hand, and Hauske administered the injection himself.

The entire room seemed to settle down along with Tyrone.

"The reason I've termed it a deprivation, Agent Crowley—"

"Is because it keeps wearing off," Crowley finished for him.

"Exactly. That and the fact that he's experiencing revolving deprivations that seem to cycle. He was only touched by one Depriver, is that right?"

Crowley looked to Delafonte, and the policeman spoke quietly, startled by what he was hearing, "One Depriver, yes. Only one."

"So the single charge is leapfrogging from different parts of the brain. I've never seen anything like it. You?" Hauske asked Crowley.

Crowley shook his head.

"Well, you're the man to ask."

"I've seen more than my share since this all started, it's true," Crowley said. "Let me know if there's anything I can do to lend a hand with your chip research. I hear it's very promising."

"Listen Alex, it's a bit premature, but I'd be willing to show you the chip if you're interested. My lab's right down the hall."

"By all means," Crowley said.

Hauske led them out of the surgery, down the corridor, and through a security checkpoint that required his passkey swipe. The unoccupied room was a cold cement-gray, and the culmination of humming, bleeping, and flashing equipment gave Delafonte the impression of a machine shop rather than a laboratory.

"At the risk of sounding ignorant, what exactly does this chip you're making do?" the lieutenant asked.

Hauske looked to Crowley for the go-ahead to discuss his sensitive work in Delafonte's presence, and Crowley nodded. "Well, let me answer that by explaining a little how I reasoned it out."

Hauske stepped before a smooth, stainless steel console with an array of switches and inset panels that was dominated by a large, ceiling-mounted electron microscope. "Deprivation is basically a bioelectrical-induced virus that lives in the brain's control center, continuously delivering bits of misinformation that replicate and block synaptic transmission.

"So I started thinking about how the brain responds to electrical impulses, and this got me thinking about epileptics."

"Epileptics?" Delafonte asked, "You mean like people who have seizures?"

"Exactly," Hauske said. "Because what is a seizure but an electrical storm in the brain? A series of nerve cells firing sudden bursts of electrical energy at four times their normal rate—temporarily shutting down specific brain regions."

"Through overload," Crowley added.

"Correct," Hauske said. "Now, epileptics are usually treated with anticonvulsants, drugs that block the harmful misdirected brain impulses; however, the more extreme, nonresponsive cases required medical science to move in a new direction."

Crowley watched as Hauske punched a sequence of numbers into the console that resulted in the slow, mechanized elevation of a fist-sized velvet platform, on which were nestled several silver chips. "A device was created called the vagus nerve stimulator. It was the first antiepileptic therapy to use an implant—what we call a Neuro Cybernetic Prosthesis."

Delafonte laughed. "Sounds like something out of a movie."

"Maybe," Hauske said. "But I assure you it's been in service for over a decade. Now when those nerve cells fire their random electrical charges to the brain, the vagus stimulator counters and regulates the charge, halting the seizure. And these chips you see here, when implanted in the thalamus, will hopefully prevent the charge that delivers deprivation from affecting the particular sensory apparatus of a deprived patient. However, while we have isolated the various bioelectric strains that cause most deprivations, we've yet to isolate the proper charge to counter and cancel them."

"Amazing," Delafonte said, shaking his head.

"Thank you, Dr. Hauske, this has been very inspiring," Crowley said. "I'll check back with you periodically for reports on Tyrone Jackson's condition."

As Crowley and Delafonte turned to leave the ward, the doctor added, "I'd really like to get a readout on the Depriver who touched him, Agent Crowley."

Yeah, Crowley thought as they headed for the elevator, *so would I.* He flipped open his cellular phone as the elevator descended and began typing a text message. It read: *"Dep with multideprivation ability. Priority Alpha. Please assist."* He pressed the Send key as they reached the ground floor.

29

CROWLEY waited, deep in thought, while a temporary ID was created for Delafonte. He eyed the twelve-foot bronze plaque hanging over the main entrance, which read, "Sacrifice even your own liberation until all sentient beings are free from suffering." Good words, written by a Zen master named Narjuna over two thousand years ago—the Ministry credo in theory, rarely echoed in practice as far as he was concerned.

"Would you mind very much, Agent Crowley, if I called my wife to tell her that I'm okay?" Delafonte asked.

As they left the building a black sedan pulled up to the curb in front of them. The driver, an older gentleman with long white sideburns and soft, pale features, opened the door for them with a black-gloved hand.

"Forgive me, Lieutenant," Crowley said, stepping into the car. "Of course. Use the car phone. It's a scrambled line."

Delafonte, unaccustomed to riding in a chauffeured car, was slightly distracted as he picked up the phone. "Scrambled, huh? That's good. In case Rosie's trying to trace my whereabouts . . . Hi, honey. It's me. No, I'm safe. No, I'm not dead. They wouldn't, huh? No, I'm not deprived. No, really, Rosie, I'm perfectly safe. What? I dunno, hold on. Agent Crowley, will I be home for dinner?"

Crowley looked at his watch. "Sure thing, Lieutenant."

Delafonte then quite unexpectedly asked, "Would you care to join us, Agent Crowley?"

Surprised, Crowley missed a beat and then replied, "Yes, I'd like that a lot. Driver, please take us to two twenty-nine East Fourteenth Street."

"Rosie, I'm coming home now. We're having a guest for dinner. All right. Okay." Delafonte hung up the phone. "Agent Crowley, we'll need to stop off for some olive oil and bread."

ROSIE Delafonte was a little on the robust side, with jet-black hair hanging low and a smiling face that could charm just about anybody. Her antipasto was to die for.

"Would you care for a glass of wine?" she asked Crowley, "Or a beer?"

"No, ma'am," he politely refused. "I don't drink."

"Frank?"

"I'll have a beer, honey," Delafonte said, squeezing her hand.

They sat down to dinner, and Crowley's heart sank a little at the warmth of their home, the sheer normalcy of their lives.

"Tell me, Mr. Crowley, how long are you going to be keeping my Franklin out on these long night patrols?"

Delafonte twirled his spaghetti around his fork like he was spinning silk, enjoying Crowley's tension.

"Hopefully, ma'am, this case will be concluded within a few days."

"You think he might get a promotion outta this?" she asked bluntly.

Delafonte almost spewed his food, "Rosie!"

"You know, ma'am, it's quite possible that he could," Crowley said and smiled.

"Have another meatball," she offered, passing him the serving dish.

Rosie excused herself to wash up, and Crowley resumed his officious manner. "Lieutenant, I think—"

"Frank," Delafonte said. "In my house, you call me Frank."

"Okay, Frank," Crowley began again, "do you think you could take me over to the basketball courts after dinner?"

"Yeah," Delafonte said. "I'm up for a game."

THEY looked like two different people when the car let them off in Hell's Kitchen around sunset. Crowley looked a lot more natural in sweatpants and sneakers than Delafonte did, even though the clothes were borrowed.

When they got to the courts, a game was already in progress. Delafonte set his gym bag by a stone bench and started stretching. "None of our witnesses are here," he said.

Crowley nodded and continued to scan the participants as well as the observers. Basketball had changed so drastically since he was a kid. No more cut-off T-shirts and shorts. These kids were covered from neck to toe in brightly colored spandex. Synthetic gloves with special-grip fingertips made especially for ball handling—though Crowley supposed that nothing could surpass the sensitivity of bare fingers. The biggest difference to the game he remembered was, of course, the new foul system. Now that any direct hand touch was cause for a penalty, where was the soul of the game?

He watched the kids run back and forth, passing, shooting, blocking, avoiding collisions. So much of the energy was gone. It just wasn't basketball anymore.

When it came their turn to play, the two tall, dark, lean-muscled teenagers stood gawking at them as they walked on the courts. Delafonte pulled on his gloves and took the ball out first. He passed to Crowley, who went up for a shot. One of the kids darted into his path. Crowley knocked into him and someone on the sideline yelled, "Foul!"

"Nice going," Delafonte called over as the kid took his foul shots and scored both.

After the fourth time it happened, one of the kids yelled at Delafonte from across the court, "Yo, listen up, cop man. Your friend's gotta attitude problem."

"Gloves off," Crowley yelled back, sweat dripping from his face.

"What you say, crazy?" the other player said, snapping out of his foul shot posture, the ball clenched tight in his hands.

Crowley pulled his gloves off, pushed up his sleeves, and threw them down on the ground. "I'm not a Depriver. I *know* you three aren't Deprivers. Let's play a full contact game—strictly old school."

Delafonte was startled. How could a man of such high law enforcement status suddenly act so recklessly? These were just kids. He was endangering them. And he was setting a bad example for the other kids who were watching.

"Touch your friend there first," one of the players called out.

Before Delafonte could even flinch, Crowley had reached out and touched his face.

"Fuck," the policeman whispered beneath his breath.

"Now you touch *your* friend," Crowley called back.

Hesitantly, one kid walked up to the other. Their gloves came off and they high-fived each other up and down.

For a few moments, nobody said a word. Then two more sets of gloves hit the pavement, followed by the stripping off of jerseys. Some kid at the sideline yelled, "No shit— they playin' a skins game!"

"I hope you know what you're doing," Delafonte whispered.

"It's safe," Crowley said. "Believe me, I know. Play hard."

One of the kids went up for a shot, and Crowley slammed into him. That's how it started. Soon they were pushing back, then shoving, then slapping the ball from each other's grip. Whispers on the sidelines gathered into an audience.

"C'mon, old man, show me whatcha got," one of them dared Delafonte. He charged past the kid, faked left, and then took a shot. It bounded off the boards and felt damned good as it found its way back to his bare hands.

People began to cheer them, the crowd growing larger and larger. Kids hung off of the fences to get a look at the game. One player took a perfect pass and charged past Crowley, moving so deftly that Crowley ended up on his ass while the kid took the winning shot.

"Nothing but net!" he yelled as he strutted up and down the court before the howling onlookers, repeatedly slapping his teammate's hands.

From the ground, Crowley spotted a dazzling blue aura amid the crowd. A young boy wearing a Knicks T-shirt and ripped jeans. Crowley got to his feet, grabbed his jacket, and began easing his way past the kids who streamed onto the court.

Delafonte reluctantly shook both of the kids' hands, and they patted him on the back. He looked over his shoulder and saw Crowley leaving the courts. "Hey Crowley, don't be a bad sport!" he called. Then he caught sight of Willie Carmen's thin frame by the fence. He was staring into the court and cheering, his ungloved hands clinging to the mesh, oblivious to Crowley closing in on him.

Then, either Willie touched somebody crowding against him, or they touched Willie, because somebody in the crowd yelled, "Depriver!" and in seconds there were dozens of people tripping over each other to get away from the scene. Crowley was caught up in the surge of the crowd. Delafonte grabbed his bag, took out his gun, and shoved it into his waistband.

Willie Carmen touched at least three people as he ran across the street, apparent by the screams that followed him. Crowley saw a man crash to the pavement, convulsing and clutching his face.

The boy darted and weaved through the thick rush of the crowd, with no regard for who he touched as he went. Crowley zigged and zagged as though following a homing beacon, with Delafonte running close behind.

Willie stopped for a moment, looked back and saw Delafonte, then ran even harder. He had enough of a lead on Crowley to easily lose himself in the crowd, but crossing Forty-sixth Street, fate intervened.

CROWLEY passed the reception desk with Willie Carmen's limp body hanging loosely in his arms. Delafonte flashed his ID badge as they passed. Nevertheless, the receptionist depressed the silent alarm with her foot. When they got to the med ward, Hauske was already waiting.

As Crowley entered, Hauske directed him toward a private surgery with a prepped exam table. Crowley set the boy gently on top of it. Two gloved medics immediately moved in as Hauske called, "Straps!"

"What happened?" Hauske asked, ripping Willie's bloodied shirt off. His bare chest was bruised and bloody, mostly from a small tear near his left shoulder.

"Hit by a taxi," Crowley said. "Something you should know."

"Yes?"

"His aura is vacillating. One second he's blue, the next red."

"Red?" Hauske demanded. "You're telling me this Depriver is glowing red?"

"I have no idea what it means. It's something we've never encountered before. I've got a crazy feeling though. Save this kid, Doc."

"Believe me," Hauske said, "I'll do everything that I can."

Crowley left the surgery with a troubled look on his face, and Delafonte walked quietly beside him. They took the elevator down to the ground floor and left the Ministry building. As soon as they were out on the street, Delafonte turned to Crowley and asked, "Anything I can do?"

Crowley shook his head. "I've got a tough decision I need to make."

"Bet your whole life's full of those," Delafonte said.

"Yeah," Crowley said. "That's a bet you'd win."

Delafonte wondered what could possibly be causing the agent so much anxiety.

Crowley said, "Excuse me a moment, Frank," then stepped into a phone booth and closed the door behind him.

It bothered Delafonte that Crowley was using a public phone when he knew that the man was carrying a cell phone. He had no idea what that might suggest, but he trusted that Crowley had his reasons.

"Amsterdam," Delafonte heard him say. Then, "It's Alex. Are you in Jersey? Good, this is important. No, I need to see you. How fast can you get to the city? Right. Perfect. See you there."

Crowley hung the phone up and slid the door open. "Frank, there's something I need to take care of on my own. I'd like you to wait for me back upstairs. I should only be an hour or two. Will you call me if anything, I mean *anything,* happens with either Willie or Tyrone? Will you do that?"

Delafonte nodded, and Crowley handed over a card with his mobile phone number. "Thank you," he said, turning and walking down the street.

30

CROWLEY was there first, of course, and he took a booth in the back of the diner and ordered a cup of black coffee. Midway through his third cup, he was joined by a younger man he had not seen in several years. He'd cut his hair short, wore a button-down shirt—signs of impending fatherhood. No one in the restaurant, barring those with Dep sight, would ever guess he was a wanted man.

"You're looking good, Nicholas," Crowley said. "Thank you for coming."

"I'm trusting you, Alex," he said. "No Ministry bullshit. We talk, and then I walk out of here."

"Agreed," Crowley said. "Believe me, I wouldn't have risked calling you if it wasn't crucial."

Nicholas hung his jacket up and sat down. The waitress poured him a cup of coffee and returned to the counter. "You've got my attention," he said.

Crowley took a deep breath. "I've got a kid in custody with a red aura. He was normal, I mean . . . he was blue when

I picked him up, and then he changed. I've never seen anything like it. I'm wondering if you can tell me what it
means?"

Nicholas's eyes were cold and expressionless. "Red, huh?
Intriguing. What makes you think I'd know anything
about it?"

"If the Ministry doesn't know, who am I going to ask?"
Crowley said. "Look, I think it's important because he was
causing revolving deprivations."

Nicholas scratched at the back of his neck. "When he
was blue or red?" he asked.

"He hasn't touched anyone since he changed. He was hit
by a car running from me, and then I took him into custody."

"And you say there were multiple deprivations?" He
sipped his coffee.

"Yes," Crowley said.

"What's the cycle?"

"Blindness, deafness, loss of balance, paralysis, and
coma."

Nicholas seemed to be gauging the lesser of many evils.
"Where is he now?"

"Uptown in a Ministry facility. He's in surgery, under
the supervision of your old friend, Warren Hauske."

"I was afraid you'd say that." Nicholas got up and pulled
on his coat. "Listen, I can't help you as long as he's in Ministry custody. Especially if Hauske is involved."

Crowley stood, confused by Nicholas's sudden retreat. "I
thought Hauske was considered Dep-friendly, that his
work was—"

"Once upon a time," Nicholas said, removing gloves
from his pockets and slipping them on. "But times have
changed."

"Care to elaborate?"

"We worked very closely for a few months, Hauske and I," Nicholas said, "trying to determine the right charge for that damned chip of his. He's obsessed. For a while he got me obsessed."

"With finding the cure," Crowley said. "I can understand."

"No, it's not just about curing SDS for him," Nicholas said. "He wants to get inside it. He wants to control it. His methods are barbaric, Alex. At least Deveraux..." Nicholas paused midthought.

"What?" Crowley asked. "What about Deveraux?"

"It's not that I condone his actions, but he is truly concerned with our welfare. He is one of us, after all. Hauske couldn't care less about any of us. We're just lab rats. And now he's got the Ministry backing him. Can't you see what's around the corner?"

"I don't understand," Crowley said. "You're defending Deveraux? Is this about Claudette? His actions have caused major damage to your cause, Nicholas. He's all about hurting and exploiting Deprivers. I thought you realized that and—"

"Alex," Nicholas said quietly, "calm down, or this conversation is over right now."

The two men locked eyes for a time. Crowley composed himself and sat down. "Nick, I'm not the one running away," he said. "I just don't understand how you can defend Deveraux. Whatever you *think* his goal was when you and Claudette knew him, believe me, it's changed—he's gone over the edge. He's become nothing more than a murderous bigot. The Deprivers in his faction tolerate no Normals."

Nicholas sat back down at the table. "You've seen what goes on out there, more than most. Can you really blame them?"

"Bullshit thinking like that lost me my wife. I found her shooter. You know why he did it?" Crowley asked. "Because 'There is no such thing as a Dep-friendly Normal.' And Deveraux said the same thing to me the last time we spoke. Nicholas, whether he posted the job or not, he's behind Julia's death, and I will never forget that. Neither should you."

Nicholas rearranged packets of sugar thoughtfully. "I take your point. Just take my advice, Hauske is no better. If I were you, I'd get that kid away from him."

"So, you're not going to tell me anything more than that?"

"Shit, Alex," Nicholas said, "you work for the enemy. I will never understand that, but I believe you have reasons for your choices—reasons that you believe in, even if I don't. Regardless, it puts a lid on our friendship at a certain point."

Crowley had given up hope that anyone would ever really understand his position, caught between those who needed his help and didn't want it and those who had the power to help and wouldn't use it. "I'm the man on the inside, Nicholas. Isn't that obvious? I'm rooting for you, your sister, and the others. I like to think that my involvement has made a few intolerable lives a little easier. My badge lets me help where I can. Now, my gut instinct here is that all information regarding this boy needs to be shared by your people as well as mine. And my people have a way of making information suddenly disappear."

Nicholas dropped his head slightly at that. "So do we, Alex—so do we." And when he looked up, there was an old, familiar smile playing on his lips. "You don't understand that while I want to trust you, I can't risk that you might be manipulated into endangering us." And before

Crowley could protest he added, "Bring the boy to us, and maybe we can do some good. You know how to reach me."

Crowley was frustrated. "Why should I believe you know any more about this than Hauske does?"

Nicholas shrugged. "You shouldn't, I suppose," he answered. "But I'll offer you this—the boy's deprivation cycle—you've left something out. Something crucial. Think about it. I'll see you around."

Crowley made no move to pursue Nicholas out of the diner; it was pointless. He paid the bill and headed back uptown to the Ministry.

31

FOUR hours later, Willie was still undergoing surgery, and there was no word back from Hauske on his condition. Crowley and Delafonte sat in the med ward's waiting room, eating candy bars and drinking coffee, both very near to exhaustion. Neither had spoken in quite some time when Crowley asked, "Did you know that owls can't see the color red?"

Delafonte was taken aback at Crowley's randomness. "They can't see red? Why?"

"No one knows for sure," he said. "Their optics just don't tune to that particular wavelength."

"Well, if they can't see it, what do they see?"

"Something else, I guess."

"The way I got it figured," Delafonte offered in the tone of a strategist laying out his plot, "is that *you* got some kind of special sight. You can see who's a Dep and who's not. You said you *knew* I wasn't, and that those kids we played weren't. You picked Willie outta the crowd. Hauske and you were talking about auras, right? Deps give off a light or something?"

Crowley winked and sat up a little straighter. "Once you're deprived, you get the sight. Repeated exposure heightens it considerably."

"So you got touched by one of them once?"

"My wife was one of them."

"Oh, shit. I'm sorry, Alex. I've been bad-mouthing—"

"Nah, forget it. I've gotten used to it. Everyone experiences the same hysteria and prejudice initially. You're a good man, Frank."

"What was her name?"

"Julia. She died during that first riot, when Governor Tyrsdale was first trying to pass the Mandatory Registration Act."

"Oh, man." Delafonte exhaled. "I'm so sorry. I don't know what the hell I'd do if I lost Rosie."

"What would you do if she turned Depriver?"

Without hesitation he said, "Stand by her."

Crowley met his eyes and said, "I believe you."

After a long silence, Delafonte asked, "What did she, your wife, deprive you of? I mean, if you don't mind me asking?"

Crowley remembered the rally in Lafayette Park. Saw her smile over at him only moments before she was shot. He remembered how her gentle curls had fallen about her shoulders. How she smelled that day. How her mouth had tasted. Her hand in his, and then the gunshot. Five years later, he could still hear it echo there in the waiting room.

"No pain," Crowley whispered. "I don't feel any pain."

"Man. What do you do after something like that?"

Crowley let out a long sigh and then stated dryly, "You join the Ministry."

A gentle knock brought their attention to the striking, raven-haired woman who stood in the doorway adjusting the cuff of her Armani blazer. "Is this a private party?" she asked.

Crowley smiled. "Lieutenant Delafonte, meet Agent Brin. She's deaf, but she reads lips."

"Call me Frank," he said.

"Kendra," she replied. The three of them sat, and Kendra asked, "What have we got here?"

"Two kids," Crowley said and signed. "The deprived has rotating deprivations: blindness, deafness, loss of balance, paralysis, and coma. The Depriver who caused this has an aura that's vacillating; it was blue, now it's gone red."

"It's gone red?" she asked, arching an eyebrow. "You're telling me his aura is red?"

Crowley nodded, pouring her a cup of coffee.

She looked pensive. "This may be a newly developed complication of the syndrome," she said after a time. "Tell me more about the symptoms of the deprived."

"He comes out of one deprivation and goes into another," Crowley said. "We witnessed him slipping out of a coma into a state of blindness."

"The transition was instantaneous?" she asked with some urgency in her voice.

"Why?"

"Was there an asymptomatic lag between deprivations?" She asked. "A period where the deprived was reading—"

"All clear," Crowley broke in, flashing back to his conversation with Nicholas. *I'll offer you this—the boy's deprivation cycle—you've left something out. Something crucial.*

"What am I missing?" Delafonte asked, confused.

"Oh God, I'm an idiot," Crowley said. "I was so busy thinking that Tyrone is continuously deprived, that I'm missing the point. He keeps getting temporarily *cured* of each deprivation."

"So what does that mean?" Delafonte shrugged.

"I don't know, but it damned well could mean every-thing," he said. Then both Crowley and Delafonte were jarred by the sound of an alarm.

"There's an alarm," Crowley signed to Brin.

Crowley was first out of the waiting room, pulling his gloves on as he went.

They found Dr. Hauske alone, sprawled out beneath the empty surgical table, clutching the knob of the alarm switch and convulsing violently. Brin rushed to check his vital signs. Crowley had to shout above the alarm for Delafonte to hear. "He can't get off this floor without a pass. You go that way. Circle back!"

Delafonte drew his gun and whispered the Lord's Prayer as he moved quietly down the hall. He readied himself to discharge the weapon at every open doorway he passed, his back to the wall, step by step down the long corridor.

When he got to the very last room, the wall had become a smooth glass window. From inside, he heard the gentle, amused cry of a baby. He found himself standing in front of a nursery. *Strange that there'd be a nursery here,* he thought. He stepped inside, gun held low, and moved slowly between a row of pink- and blue-lined cribs, their tiny occupants staring up at him in delight as he passed. There must have been at least eight infants.

Willie sprang out from behind an incubator like a cornered animal and raked his naked fingernails against Delafonte's face, leaving a trail of blood.

Delafonte leveled the gun at Willie, and the shirtless boy cowered back against one of the cribs. The baby within cooed and tried grasping at one of Willie's bandages, which was hanging down just out of reach.

"No me touches!" Willie cried out, unable to back off any farther, eyes locked on the gun. "Don't shoot me!"

Just then, Crowley entered the room. "He scratched you?"

"Yeah," Delafonte said.

Agent Brin stepped into the room, her own gun drawn.

Crowley took a tentative step toward Willie, and in a soothing voice said, "Calm down. Nobody here wants to hurt you."

Instability wavered across Delafonte's face for a moment, then he stepped backward, off balance. He lowered the gun to his side, unsure of what was happening. He could see Crowley's lips moving, but he couldn't hear what he was saying. He looked at Willie, and there was a soft blue glow streaming out from his body. At first, Delafonte thought it was a trick of the light. He rubbed at his eyes with his free hand, but still the blue glow persisted. Crowley was a few steps closer when he understood what the glow was. *A Dep aura!* He was seeing what Crowley could see.

But wait, there was also a blue glow shining out from the crib behind Willie, he realized. Delafonte looked back over and saw that both Crowley and Brin were definitely not glowing. Then he looked around the room, and a twin sense of confusion and dread began to engulf him. Of the eight babies present, six gave off the soft, blue ephemeral glow.

Then something changed in Willie. His blue glow seemed to dampen somehow. It faded, dwindled, and, after a moment, stopped altogether.

Crowley froze in his tracks. He must be seeing this too, Delafonte realized. Then, as suddenly as it had stopped, Willie's glow came back on again, even brighter than before. But this time, it was red.

Agent Brin gasped.

Delafonte saw the blue glow surrounding the crib go out. He saw Crowley look around and followed his line of sight. Now that Willie was glowing red, none of the babies were glowing at all. Suddenly, Delafonte could hear the alarm sounding again.

"Easy Willie," Crowley said gently. "I know you're scared, but we can work this out."

Agent Brin put her free hand to her mouth. "My God, Alex—I can hear you. I can hear you!"

A look of wonder spread across Crowley's face. He reached out his hand to the frightened child and said, "Willie, listen carefully. I have the authority to forgive you for *everything* that you've done—and no one will hurt you, but you've got to give yourself up to me now."

32

CROWLEY needed time to think, and the Ministry complex, ablaze with alarms, was not the place. "Kendra, I need you to cover for me with Kelsoe."

"What—why?" Agent Brin stuttered, still unused to the sound of her own voice.

"Please," Crowley said. "See that Delafonte and Hauske are looked after. There'll be agents swarming up here in a few minutes. I'm leaving. I'm taking Willie with me."

Before she could respond, Crowley was already leading Willie out of the nursery, and she followed them wordlessly back to the surgery. Once there, he began searching drawers.

Brin looked down at the small, bare-chested boy, half bandaged and standing on edge with his hand clasped in Crowley's. His red aura confounding everything she knew regarding the syndrome's progression.

"Are these what you're looking for?" Brin asked, pointing to Willie's clothes.

"Get dressed," Crowley said. "And your gloves," he added.

"Alex, I can't let you do this," Brin demanded. "This is going to become a matter of national security."

Crowley exhaled roughly, stepping close to her. "Kendra, did you just see what I saw in that nursery? Those infants were glowing. I'll be damned before I'll hand over Willie to Hauske or whoever else is behind that shit."

"Damn it, Alex, there may be a reasonable explanation for those children, you don't know—"

"You're right, I don't know. Can you think of one?"

Agent Brin paused, searching for some rational response.

"Right," Crowley said, tearing Willie's chart from the board on the bed stand and then folding it into his pocket. "When your reasonable explanation comes, I plan on being someplace autonomous."

"Alex, if he's carrying the cure, then the Ministry—"

"Will act in its own best interest, as always. Screw that, Kendra."

Brin softened, backed into a corner by her own doubts. "Alex, where will you take him?"

"I don't know yet. I've got to think it through."

He reached out and embraced her, whispering, "If you can, confiscate all of Hauske's research and stash it." Then he let her go and led the boy toward the emergency exit.

Overwhelmed, Agent Brin stood still, unsure for a few moments, then whispered, "Thank you," and went to check on the downed men, snapping her fingers to her ears a few times as she went.

WHERE *do we go now?* Crowley asked himself as they made their way down a virtually empty Fifth Avenue. *Where do you go at one o'clock in the morning when you're holding the cure in the palm of your hand?*

Crowley ducked them into a subway entrance, and they descended amid the sounds of an oncoming train. He wanted to be safely away from Manhattan before the Ministry had a chance to take action. He reached into his coat and switched his cell phone off.

"How are you feeling?" he asked Willie.

The boy looked up at Crowley with scared, soulful eyes. "My shoulder hurts bad," he replied. "You said you gonna keep me outta trouble, right?"

Crowley nodded. "I promise," he said.

"Only you in trouble now too, right?"

"Yeah," Crowley answered, as they stepped into an empty train car and took seats. "But we're going to figure this out together. And I'm going to tell you the coolest story you've ever heard, and in the end, you're going to be the hero. I'm going to protect you from now on, okay?"

Willie nodded, sitting back in his seat and rubbing his shoulder as the train roared and bucked through the tunnels.

"Okay, partner," Crowley said, as they pulled into Penn Station. "This is where we get out, and when this is over, you and me are gonna get some front-row tickets to go see the Knicks upstairs at the Garden. How's that?"

"That's cool," Willie answered with a smile and a wince.

Moments later, they stood before the gigantic call-board. The majority of the shops were closed, and there were only a few scattered travelers asleep by their luggage, awaiting connections. One man in the ticket booth—though Crowley knew the entire station was under continuous video surveillance. Within the hour, they'd know he'd been here with the boy. Willie looked up at the board and began calling off random destinations. Newark Airport was accessible and led to any number of destinations ranging from Amsterdam and the protection that Gerrit *might* offer to Geneva and the World Health Organization; but flying was dangerous—they'd be easily tracked. Washington offered the FBI or CIA. Atlanta: headquarters to the Centers for Disease Control. Chicago: the center for Governor Tyrsdale's damned Deprivers Control. Maryland: the National Institutes of Health. Miami was Deveraux; not going to happen, though they'd surely be welcomed. New Jersey was Nicholas and Claudette; not the worst choice, but something there still didn't smell right. *Who can I trust? Where would Julia want me to take him?* They found an open shop and bought half a dozen donuts, coffee and juice, and a couple of comic books.

Less than an hour later, they deboarded in Stamford, Connecticut, and, by cover of night, Agent Alex Crowley taught Willie Carmen how to hot-wire a Dodge Caravan. Soon after, they were headed north on the freeway. Although Crowley was more than prepared for it, they had no difficulty in crossing the border.

33

CROWLEY curbed the tires and killed the engine at the end of a deserted street. He woke Willie.

"Where are we now?" the boy asked.

"We're going to see a friend," Crowley said. "Come on."

They stepped out of the car and zigzagged stealthily down a series of alleys. "There," Crowley said, indicating a doorway where a man sat guard on a stoop. As they approached him, the man rose to his full six feet, displaying a gun in his waistband, and said, "Sorry, this club is Deprivers Only."

"Believe me, we're welcome," Crowley said.

"You're not getting past me," the man assured Crowley, crossing his huge arms against his chest.

"Why is it always like this?" Willie asked.

"Change takes time," Crowley said. "Hey buddy, take a look at your hands. Notice anything different?"

The man looked down, and it took a moment before he registered the change. Crowley reached his ungloved hand out quickly and clasped his in a firm handshake. "Nice to meet you," he said, then proceeded inside, unhampered, with Willie trailing behind him.

The place was packed, techno music blaring. Several dozen Deprivers milled about, talking, drinking, their auras flashing in the dim light. Crowley scanned the place and quickly picked her out of the crowd, standing alone by the bar. Moving toward her, he was filled with controlled exhilaration.

She turned and saw them coming moments before Crowley was within reach, her blonde hair spilling across her face and her lips parted in astonishment. The way she looked at Willie spoke volumes to Crowley.

"It's been a long time," he said. "Willie, I'd like you to meet my friend Cassandra."

"Hey," the boy said.

"Hey yourself," she said. "Alex, my God, how are you?"

"Cassie, it's obvious to me from your body language that you can see his glow—which means you've seen this before?"

She chuckled nervously, looking back to the boy. "Not like this, Alex," she replied. "Not *hot* like this . . . oh my God, I can feel him all over me!"

She looked down at her own palms in wonder, then balled her hands tightly into fists. For a moment, he thought she would strike him, but instead she started to cry. "What the hell's happening to me, Alex?"

He reached out to put his arms around her, and she struggled against the contact. He could feel her body shivering, and a wrenching sob escaped her when he brought his bare hands up through her hair and held them against her face. Holding her there, nearly quaking, he motioned Willie toward the dance floor.

"Alex—" she whispered.

"I know," he whispered back, pressing even tighter against her. "I feel it too."

Willie stepped into the center of the gloved crowd and allowed himself to get lost in the pounding of the music. He began whirling and twirling around as he stared up into the flashing strobes. Crowley watched as his aura dazzled off like a shower of crimson light, dowsing every source of blue glow in the room.

The music stopped. One by one, the people began to realize what was happening. Crowley heard comments ranging from "I feel really strange," to "No fucking way," to "Oh my God, you've stopped glowing!"

A young girl stood staring down at herself in disbelief, then looked up and announced to the crowd, "I've gone Normal! My God, I've gone Normal. My light's out, and I feel it. Someone touch me—*please* touch me!"

A tense pause filled the room with static anticipation. Finally, one brave, towheaded young man stepped forward, pulled off his gloves, and touched her.

No blue sparks. No deprivation.

Alex Crowley stood with Cassandra in his arms, and they watched as the gloves came off throughout the room and people began to touch each other—tentatively at first, with caution and nervous excitement slowly building into a frenzy of caressing and hugging and crying and laughing and absolute shrills of delight.

"Is it permanent?" Cassandra asked through her surge of tears, still pressed hard against Crowley's chest.

"I don't know," he said.

"But will it still last when he's gone?" she whispered, pulling gently apart from him.

"Yes, but I don't know for how long," he said, in that

simple exchange deducing the key difference between the
effect of the boy and that of Claudette Deveraux. "My partner was deprived of hearing, a permanent deprivation. I
managed to contact her on my way here, and she can still
hear. But I've never seen anything like this before. I don't
know what will happen."

"My brother," she offered suddenly. "You've got to—"

"In time," he said. "But I'm not willing to surrender
him to Nicholas at this point any more than I'd hand him
over to the Ministry or the CDC. I'm opting for giving
those who need him most a chance. Exposing him to just as
many as I can. Seeing the results for myself."

She laughed that laugh of hers. "The freakin' Alex
Crowley traveling road show, huh?"

"Yeah, I guess," he said. "But here, you can give Nicholas
one of these."

Crowley reached into his coat pocket and produced a
small plastic canister from which he drew forth a tiny metallic chip, pinched between his fingers, and placed it in her
hand.

"What is it?"

"Something Hauske was working on. Nicholas will
understand."

She nodded. "Okay, sure, but tell me—how long will
you stay gone?"

"Until I'm satisfied," Crowley answered. "Then I'll
expose him visibly enough so that he can't be dismissed or
suddenly vanish—and I won't let him be exploited."

"You're playing God," she said.

"You think so?" he replied. "Feels like all the while
God's been playing me."

She leaned back against the bar and leered at him.
"Well, I suppose I can't make you do anything. You're

going to need some help, though. You can't cruise the underground without a map."

"I still know some people," he said, "but any tips would be appreciated."

"Tips?" she laughed. "You gotta be kidding me. You got yourself a navigator. I'll be damned if I'm not coming with you."

Crowley smiled. "I suppose I won't stop you from coming along," he said, "but we play by my rules. And I go where he goes. Got it?"

"I got it," she said, rolling her eyes. "Give me fifteen minutes to pack my stuff." Then she swiftly darted in and kissed Crowley. "That's from Julia," she whispered. "She'd be so goddamned proud of you!"

Willie came back to Crowley's side, joyful at the effect he was having on these people but sensing that they'd need to get going before the questions began, and people started out getting that possessive look in their eyes. But Agent Crowley wasn't paying attention to him. He was too caught up in watching the people as they were touching each other.

34

CROWLEY and the boy followed the throng of Deprivers turned Normals outside through the back entrance of the club. That's when they saw the fires spitting up from several oil drums. People were stopping to discard their gloves in them. So many that the parking lot reeked of burnt leather.

Willie trailed several feet behind Crowley as the agent walked over to the nearest of the flaming barrels.

From inside his pocket, Crowley pulled out a green pair of gloves that Willie had not seen before. They were cracked and creased with age.

Crowley looked down at the gloves, remembering the day she picked them up off the table outside the student center. He remembered the feel of them against his hands that glorious summer evening when she'd pulled back, after their first tender kiss, with a look of absolute wonder in her eyes. That he'd forgone all her warnings and kissed her anyway. A moment of unconditional acceptance, she'd called it—from foolish youth.

It's me, your fool, Crowley thought. *God, I miss you so much, Julia. I was such a better person with you, and I've done so many questionable things since you've been gone.*

Willie started getting nervous, and he looked around for Cassandra. He spotted her carrying a duffel bag, changed into jeans, headed their way.

I've got someone here I really wish you could've met, Crowley lamented, feeling the heat of the fire against his face and the rough, worn leather against his fingertips. *Helping him might help a lot of people stop being so afraid of each other, so afraid of making contact. I don't know, I just feel like I'm finally doing something good, and wherever you are—I wanted you to know about it. I love you.*

Agent Crowley dropped the pair of gloves into the oil drum and watched as they caught fire.

Just then, Willie reached his gloved hand into Alex's palm and squeezed hard as he could. "Ouch!" Crowley said, coming back to himself. "Okay—it's time to move on."